Praise for *Only the Dead*

"He's the real deal. I'm a fan."

—David Morrell, *New York Times* bestselling author of *First Blood*

"Carr presses emotional buttons that other writers wouldn't dare explore."

—*The Real Book Spy*

"Carr delivers a graduate level course in geopolitical politics while delivering the raucous good time that thriller fans have come to expect from the apex warlocks of combat storytelling. Don't miss the finest thriller of the summer."

—John Nantz, *Townhall*

"Superb action, Ludlum-like intrigue, and le Carré–like duplicity make this a seminal thriller and a brilliant entry in a great series."

—Jon Land

Praise for *In the Blood*

"Gripping . . . fast-paced . . . fans will get their money's worth."

—*Publishers Weekly*

"Quality plot, well-developed characters, and not too over-the-top. Add James Reece to your list that includes Harvath (Brad Thor), Reacher (Lee Child), Bob Lee Swagger (Stephen Hunter)."

—*Men Reading Books*

"Hands down, IN THE BLOOD is the best book I've read this year. I've said from the beginning that covering Carr is what I'd imagine it would have been like to discover Vince Flynn at the beginning of his career. . . . Carr deserves to be mentioned alongside all-time greats like Flynn, Thor, Clancy, and Silva . . ."

—*The Real Book Spy*

"IN THE BLOOD is Carr's best book to date and demonstrates a mastery of the genre—it rightly belongs in the constellation of Clancy, Thor, Morrell, and Flynn."

—*Townhall.com*

Praise for *The Devil's Hand*

"Take my word for it, James Reece is one rowdy motherf***er. Get ready!"

—Chris Pratt, all-around great guy and star
of the #1 Amazon Prime series *The Terminal List*

"Carr delivers engrossing back story, incorporates current events seamlessly, and never flinches from breathless depictions of violence."

—*Publishers Weekly*

"Carr continues to draw on his own experiences as a SEAL to give the story a level of realism that writers who've not actually served sometimes have a hard time achieving."

—*Booklist*

"THE TERMINAL LIST is widely regarded as one of the best debut thrillers of all-time, and rightfully so, but THE DEVIL'S HAND is even better, and should go down as one of the best books in the genre, period."

—*The Real Book Spy*

"An action thriller extraordinaire that is not to be missed."

—*Providence Journal*

Praise for *Savage Son*

"A great book . . . its f*cking riveting!"

—Joe Rogan

"A rare gut-punch writer, full of grit and insight, who we will be happily reading for years to come."

—Gregg Hurwitz, *New York Times* bestselling author of the Orphan X series

"Absolutely fantastic! SAVAGE SON is savagely good, and puts Jack Carr at the very top of the thriller genre."

—Marc Cameron, *New York Times* bestselling author of RED WINTER

"A badass, high-velocity round of reading! The three parts of this masterfully crafted experience says it all—THE TRAP, THE STALK, THE KILL."

—Clint Emerson, *New York Times* bestselling author of 100 DEADLY SKILL and ESCAPE THE WOLF

"Carr writes both from the gut and a seemingly infinite reservoir of knowledge in the methods of human combat. Loved it!"

—Chris Hauty, *LA Times* bestselling author of *New York Times* Editors' Choice DEEP STATE

"Jack Carr triples down with SAVAGE SON. From the book's gut-wrenching opening to its sleep-stealing conclusion, Jack's homage to THE MOST DANGEROUS GAME delivers the goods and then some."

—Don Bentley, *New York Times* bestselling author of HOSTILE INTENT

"A masterfully told, heart thumping tale of modern conflict."

—LtCol Oliver North, USMC (Ret.), *New York Times* bestselling author of THE RIFLEMAN and UNDER FIRE

"SAVAGE SON is amazing! This is the kind of book every author wished he could write . . . mind-blowingly good!"

—Simon Gervais, former RCMP counterterrorism officer and bestselling author of HUNT THEM DOWN

"Accurate, intense and raw, SAVAGE SON taps into our most primal of instincts. Jack Carr draws you into this predatory pursuit like no other because he's lived it!"

—John Barklow, Hunter, Navy Diver, Special Operations Cold Weather Survival Instructor, and Sitka Gear Big Game Product Manager

"Jack Carr is back and at the top of his game in SAVAGE SON, a heart-pounding, sleep-robbing, edge-of-your-seat thriller."

—Joshua Hood, 82nd Airborne veteran and author of Robert Ludlum's THE TREADSTONE RESURRECTION

"Whether you are a hunter of four-legged game or of man, SAVAGE SON will stoke the inner fire of your soul. Jack Carr's attention to detail and experience from the battlefield to the backcountry draw the reader into the field to experience the art of war through the eyes of a man who has lived it."

—Cole Kramer, Kodiak Island Brown Bear Guide and Outfitter

Praise for *True Believer*

"This is seriously good. I mean—seriously."

—Lee Child, #1 *New York Times* bestselling author of THE SENTINEL

"A powerful, thoughtful, realistic, at times terrifying thriller that I could not put down. A terrific addition to the genre, Jack Carr and his alter-ego protagonist, James Reece, continue to blow me away."

—Mark Greaney, #1 *New York Times* bestselling author of SIERRA SIX

"Jack Carr creates an incredibly vivid, emotional, action-packed tapestry of carnage and death."

—Justen Charters, Black Rifle Coffee Company, *Coffee or Die Magazine*

"Packs a punch. Carr's second effort is a well-crafted thriller with timely reflections on the increasingly complicated world of international terrorism."

—*Kirkus Reviews*

Praise for *The Terminal List*

"Double the trouble, twice the action, and quadruple the enjoyment. Careful while reading this one, it could leave a mark."

—Steve Berry, #1 *New York Times* bestselling author of THE OMEGA FACTORY

"Absolutely awesome! So powerful, so pulse-pounding, so well-written—rarely do you read a debut novel this damn good."

—Brad Thor, #1 *New York Times* bestselling author of DEAD FALL

"Told with a deft hand and a keen eye for detail, THE TERMINAL LIST . . . is explosive and riveting."

—Kevin Maurer, co-author of the #1 Bestselling NO EASY DAY and DAMN LUCKY

"Like a bullet from Jack Carr's custom built sniper rifle, the story arrives on target with devastating impact. Trust me, you won't be able to put this one down!"

—Mark Owen, *New York Times* bestselling author of NO EASY DAY and NO HERO

"Crackerjack plotting, vivid characters both in and out of uniform, and a relentless pace to a worthy finish. It's a great start!"

—Stephen Hunter, #1 *New York Times* bestselling author of THE BULLET GARDEN

"An extremely unique thriller! Absolutely intense!"

—Chuck Norris

"Bravo! Jack Carr is the real deal!"

—Sean Parnell, *New York Times* Bestselling author of ONE TRUE PATRIOT

"Not since Stephen Hunter have we seen an author who so accurately captures the essence of the gun—Jack Carr is a shooter."

—Clint Smith, Founder of Thunder Ranch Shooting School

"Jack Carr's THE TERMINAL LIST is a page turning thriller you won't be able to put down. The detail focused writing, personal characters and heart pounding plot line will keep you coming back for more. An absolute must read!"

—Katie Pavlich, *New York Times* Bestselling Author, Fox News Contributor

"Any fan of the novels by Brad Thor and the late Vince Flynn will realize that Jack Carr will soon be joining their ranks."

—*The Washington Times*

"The best debut thriller of 2018."

—*The Washington Times*

ALSO BY JACK CARR

Fiction

Red Sky Mourning

In the Blood

The Devil's Hand

Savage Son

True Believer

The Terminal List

Non-Fiction

Targeted: Beirut

ONLY THE DEAD

A THRILLER

JACK CARR

EMILY BESTLER BOOKS

ATRIA

NEW YORK LONDON TORONTO SYDNEY NEW DELHI

EMILY BESTLER BOOKS

ATRIA

An Imprint of Simon & Schuster, LLC
1230 Avenue of the Americas
New York, NY 10020

First Emily Bestler Books/Atria Paperback edition September 2024

EMILY BESTLER BOOKS/ATRIA PAPERBACK and colophon are trademarks of Simon & Schuster, LLC

Simon & Schuster: Celebrating 100 Years of Publishing in 2024

For information about special discounts for bulk purchases, please contact Simon & Schuster Special Sales at 1-866-506-1949 or business@simonandschuster.com.

The Simon & Schuster Speakers Bureau can bring authors to your live event. For more information or to book an event, contact the Simon & Schuster Speakers Bureau at 1-866-248-3049 or visit our website at www.simonspeakers.com.

Interior design by Dana Sloan

Manufactured in the United States of America

7 9 10 8

Library of Congress Cataloging-in-Publication Data is available.

ISBN 978-1-9821-8169-7
ISBN 978-1-9821-8171-0 (pbk)
ISBN 978-1-9821-8172-7 (ebook)

For Thomas M. Rice

14 August 1921–17 November 2022

101st Airborne Division

501st Parachute Infantry Regiment

First in his stick out of his C-47 over Normandy, France,

June 6, 1944

We have the watch,

and

For all those who stand vigilant in the shadows.

Only the dead have seen the end of war.

—GEORGE SANTAYANA, COMMONLY MISATTRIBUTED TO PLATO

I do solemnly swear that I will support and defend
the Constitution of the United States . . .
Against all enemies . . .
Foreign . . .
And domestic . . .

—OATH TAKEN BY MEMBERS OF THE UNITED STATES ARMED FORCES,
THE VICE PRESIDENT, AND EVERY MEMBER OF CONGRESS

"Against all enemies, foreign and domestic" is not included in the president's oath of office as specified by Article II, Section 1, Clause 8, of the Constitution of the United States.

PREFACE

"WE MAKE OUR DECISIONS. And then our decisions turn around and make us." Those wise words from F. W. Boreham are as true for each and every one of us as they are for James Reece, the protagonist in these pages.

Perhaps that is why Reece has resonated with readers of the series and with the audience that tuned in to watch Chris Pratt stack bodies as former Navy SEAL Sniper James Reece in the Amazon Prime Video series adaptation of *The Terminal List*.

Reece is on a journey, as are we all. That is something that brings us all together; it is something we all have in common—we are all on a journey. But our journeys are finite. Tomorrow is not guaranteed for James Reece, just as tomorrow is not guaranteed for any of us. If you have read my previous novels, you have noticed that time plays a central role. The essence of time is physically manifested through Reece's watch and theoretically manifested through lessons from Reece's father—*You are fast, James. I've seen you run, but even you can't outrun time.* None of us can outrun time.

James Reece is also evolving over the course of his journey. In this novel, he is not the same Reece as he was in *In the Blood*, just as that James Reece was not exactly the same as he was in *The Devil's Hand*. He is learning, evolving, becoming wiser, and he is applying the lessons of the past to his decisions in the present. Those decisions are "making him."

But we don't make decisions out of the blue. James Reece makes decisions based on a foundation that guides him. Decisions that come from solid foundations allow us to survive more experiences and hence gain additional wisdom. But Reece's goal is not just to survive. It is to prevail. He is a warrior, hunter, protector, and student. Always a student, he is constantly learning along his journey, arming himself with the tools he needs to prevail when the chips are down.

He is also human. The protagonist in these pages is not a superhero. If you are looking for highly sanitized depictions of combat, I suggest you look elsewhere. Through the medium of popular fiction, I explore the mind and heart of a warrior. I don't interview snipers who worked in Ramadi, Mosul, or Najaf, ask them what it was like to press the trigger in combat, and then try to describe it on the page. Nor do I talk with operators who were once trapped in an ambush in Baghdad in an attempt to pull from them how they felt and reacted in the moment. Rather, I remember. I remember what it was like to be a sniper in Ramadi, and I remember what I did on the receiving end of a night ambush in Baghdad. I then apply those feelings and emotions to a fictional narrative. The feelings and emotions in these pages are real. They come from my heart and soul and flow directly onto the page. If you are looking for a little more fiction and a little less emotion and truth, I recommend you put this book down now and pick up another. James Reece is not for everyone.

Each of my novels has a theme that guides the writing process. *The Terminal List* was a story of revenge without constraint. For my second novel, *True Believer*, I thought it would be disingenuous to just drop Reece right into his next adventure after the traumatic events of

The Terminal List. He needed to learn to live again. He needed to find purpose. He needed a mission, so I took readers along with Reece on a journey of violent redemption. *Savage Son* explored the dark side of man through the dynamic of hunter and hunted. In *The Devil's Hand* I looked at the United States through the eyes of an enemy that had twenty years to observe the American military on the field of battle and incorporate what they learned into their battle plans. *In the Blood* put Reece behind the scope for a sniper-centric novel of violent resolutions. The novel you hold in your hands is one of truth and consequences.

How much of what follows is fiction and how much is truth?

You will know when you turn the final page.

Enjoy the journey. Time is ticking.

Jack Carr
February 21, 2023
Park City, Utah

PROLOGUE

Newport, Rhode Island
1980

WALTER STOWE DEFTLY PILOTED the thirty-six-foot trawler through Vineyard Sound past Nashawena Island and into Rhode Island Sound. He kept Castle Hill Lighthouse to the boat's starboard side as he navigated a northeasterly course toward their destination. He had become quite adept at maneuvering small watercraft in dangerous waters, though the seas between Edgartown Yacht Club on Martha's Vineyard and Station 10, the New York Yacht Club's property in Newport, were not nearly as dangerous as the waters he had navigated ten years earlier, inserting and extracting Navy SEALs in the Mekong Delta. The route ahead clear, Walt turned from the helm to look at his wife. Martha sat behind him on the flybridge, her tan legs outstretched on the cushioned aft-facing bench seat, her face upturned to catch the fading rays of the late summer sun.

"Trawler" was a bit of a misnomer. It was a Grand Banks 36, and though it resembled the trawlers of Walt's youth, this vessel was built with comfort and touring in mind, not hauling in a catch in the hopes of making ends meet. A more than capable craft, bloody decks were foreign to her. This boat was built to impress the East Coast's prestigious yachting community.

The boat was hers, or, to be more precise, it belonged to her family—a family of means. A family with history.

Martha's grandfather had made his money investing in commodities. He had then used that fortune to purchase commercial real estate in New York City. It was rumored that he had run a profitable bootlegging business during Prohibition. That mythology naturally led to whispers of mob connections in Manhattan and Chicago. Her family had even been accused of delivering the Windy City vote in a presidential election for another high-profile Massachusetts family two decades earlier, when Martha was still in middle school. She had never witnessed her father or grandfather dispel those rumors. She suspected that a connection to the mob, real or imagined, didn't hurt in certain business dealings.

While blue blood ran strong through her stock, Martha had diluted the perceived nobility of the line when she married Walter.

The Stowes were seafarers. Walt and his brothers had grown up fishing and checking traps off the coast of Cape Cod. Most people associate lobsters with Maine, but as Walt and his brothers knew, wooden lath traps were first used in their Massachusetts home waters in 1810. The traps Walt would use over a century later operated in much the same fashion as their predecessors: A lobster would be lured through a funnel, unable to resist the temptation of the mackerel and herring bait. The smaller crustaceans could escape through vents, but the larger ones would remain imprisoned in their wood and metal cells until Walt and his brothers pulled them to the surface.

Wychmere Harbor in Harwich Port was their base of operations, and in a fickle industry with innumerable variables, Walt learned that in some years the catch was not enough to feed a young family. He had watched as his father took odd jobs around town to make ends meet, working as a handyman and bartender as finances and seasons dictated. The man never complained. From bullraking for littleneck clams to chasing striped bass to roofing, shingling, and a bit of carpentry, the elder Stowe put food on the table and a roof over the heads of his wife and sons.

All three Stowe boys believed their paths were preordained. The sea was calling. That was, until they started hearing about a country called Vietnam.

Because the United States never formally declared war on North Vietnam, Walt's older brother was one of the 2.2 million Americans conscripted for service in Southeast Asia under the peacetime draft established by the Selective Training and Service Act of 1940. The working-class Stowe family knew it was only a matter of time before Walt was drafted, so his father recommended his middle child enlist in the Navy. Rather than rolling the dice with the Army, the elder Stowe believed a ship off the coast would be a much safer way to ride out a tour in Vietnam. Neither Walt nor his father had ever heard of the Brown Water Navy.

Within the year, Walt found himself on a Mark II PBR in the Mekong Delta, learning the ropes from a weathered first-class petty officer—the boat's captain. Walt and the captain were augmented by a gunner's mate to run and maintain the twin .50-caliber machine guns and an engineman to keep the new Jacuzzi water jet propulsion system operational.

With the .50s in the bow and a .30-caliber M1919AH mounted to the stern, along with a hand-cranked Mk 18 40x46mm grenade launcher, the patrol boat and its crew of river rats operated throughout South Vietnam's extensive river systems, which cut through the country from the South China Sea all the way to Cambodia. With roads and rail lines still in rudimentary stages of development, it was the veins of rivers and canals that provided the lifeblood of Vietnam's economy via access to resources. Those who controlled the waterways controlled the country. It was upon returning from a patrol that he received a letter from his mother letting him know that his younger brother had been drafted by the country's first lottery. He wouldn't last three weeks in Vietnam.

Walt's commanding officer summoned Walt to his hooch in April 1970 to inform him of his brother's death. That same officer would summon him back a week later with news that Stowe was going home; his older brother was also dead, one of 1,448 service members to be killed on their last day "in country" and making the Stowe family one of thirty-one families to lose two brothers in the conflict.

Walt had a mission growing up in a family of lobstermen, and he had a mission in the Navy; the deaths of his siblings changed the course of his life and gave it new purpose. He returned from Vietnam and made use of the GI Bill, attending the State University of New York while working odd jobs in the city and earning his degree in three years. Walt could smoke dope and protest, or he could make changes from the inside. He chose to head into government. He thought his path to instigating change would be through the State Department, believing he could work his way up the ranks and help prevent another war that he viewed as a waste of blood and treasure, needless and avoidable, a permanent scar on the nation. He soon learned that rising to a position of influence would take longer than his patience would allow and that coveted ambassadorships were, for the most part, reserved for campaign donors and for people with recognizable last names. Ambassadors did not come from families who trolled and checked traps; they came from those who paid top dollar for the catch to be served at private dinner parties in second, third, and fourth homes from the Hamptons to Martha's Vineyard. He needed another avenue if he wanted to keep his government in check. He found it in politics.

The State Department had opened that door, as it was at a State Department function that he met Martha Stirling. Looking like she would rather have been anywhere else, her outward demeanor matched Walt's internal disposition. They hit it off immediately.

All of Martha's sisters had been married off to suitors approved of, and possibly arranged by, her father—suitors from other prominent, connected East Coast families of means, influence, and generational wealth. Martha was the problem child: Brown University, a Peace Corps mission to India, and antiwar protests across the nation formed the foundation of her rebellious tendencies. Men with what her parents and grandparents considered the "right pedigree" bored her to tears. Walt was the one. Plus, he was a lobsterman. Her parents would *hate* that. But, rather than being disavowed, Walt was accepted into the family. Martha suspected it was because her father thought he might end up being useful. It couldn't hurt to have a politician in the family, especially if you funded his campaign. *Favors.* Walt proposed under a tree she had climbed as a child on the Stirlings' estate on Martha's Vineyard, and they were married on the property the following spring. Walt knew fewer than a third of those in attendance, but he was well aware that he was marrying more than Martha. He was marrying into something bigger.

Martha tilted her head back, admiring her husband at the wheel. They had been married for just over six years and had two children to show for it. As a congressman from Massachusetts's 12th District, elected to the House just two years prior, Walter's star was on the rise. His background resonated with blue-collar workers, and his new affiliation with one of America's wealthiest and most connected families immersed him in the world of the political elite. He had already made waves as a staffer for Representative Otis Pike of New York, who led the United States House Permanent Select Committee on Intelligence. Better known as the Pike Committee, it was established to investigate overreach by certain agencies of the federal government, including the FBI, NSA, and CIA. The Pike Committee was the House's version of the Senate's Church Committee, a key difference being that while the findings of the committee chaired by Senator Frank Church were made public, the findings of the Pike Committee were suppressed for reasons of national security. It was as part of those investigations that Walt began to have recurring meetings that were not recorded on his official or personal calendars. At first, Martha thought he might be having an affair. That would not have been unusual for a man in his position. Martha's father was a well-known philanderer. Both of her sisters' husbands had strayed, but her sisters had, of course, looked the other way, as had their mother, following Jackie Kennedy's, now Jackie O's, example.

Secrets.

Martha despised secrets. She came from a family of secrets and swore she would not continue the tradition. She and her husband were partners. With Walt's reputation as a "man of the people," along with his political instincts and her family's fortune, they were a team. She was not about to be relegated to the backseat, as her mother and sisters had been.

As the former Navy man guided the boat around Fort Adams and into Brenton Cove, she thought back to the night she had begun to unravel the mysteries of his clandestine world. They had been staying in her family's Upper East Side building when he abruptly announced that he needed to meet with a potential donor late one evening. He had been having more of those recently. In her experience, meetings at odd hours meant a mistress. She was disappointed but not surprised. She hailed a cab, seconds behind his.

"Follow that cab."

"Are you serious?"

Her look told her driver that she was.

"Okay, lady." Walt's cab headed west through Central Park via the Seventy-Ninth Street Transverse and then took a right in the direction of the Upper West Side.

Where are you going?

A few blocks later, his cab pulled over. She watched her husband exit the yellow vehicle and run across the street, quickly ducking into another taxi. Thrusting a twenty-dollar bill at her driver, she asked him to make a U-turn.

"That's illegal," he said.

She shoved another twenty in his face; he cranked the wheel to a chorus of blaring horns.

Walt's new cab maneuvered through traffic toward the Hudson River, turning south onto State Route 9A. Fortunately for Martha, she was in the most common vehicle in New York; she was invisible.

Who is she?

Do I confront her? Him? Of course I do.

Bastard!

They continued south past Hell's Kitchen, Chelsea, and the Meatpacking District before making a U-turn on Clarkson Street and cutting right on Morton into Greenwich Village.

Walt's cab then took a left on Bedford Street and came to a stop in front of a lime-green building in the West Village sandwiched between two brownstones, marked only with the number 86.

"Keep driving," Martha ordered, turning in her seat as her husband exited his cab and stepped onto the curb.

"Pull over here," she said.

"Whatever you say."

She watched Walt approach a dark wooden door and disappear inside.

"Meter's running, lady."

"Keep it running."

Stay? Go inside? Leave? Turn a blind eye?

She glanced down at the gold Girard-Perregaux watch on her wrist.

Ten minutes.

She snatched two more twenties from her purse, handed them to her cabdriver, and pushed open the door.

Martha walked to the nondescript structure and closed her eyes to steady herself in preparation for what she was certain she was about to witness. Then she reached for the handle. What greeted her was not row upon row of doors to apartments, nor a foyer, as she had expected. Instead, she heard the hum of conversation, not between a man and a woman but the low, steady drone of a crowd.

She pushed the heavy red velvet curtain in front of her aside and stepped into a dark, smoke-filled room poorly illuminated by dim lights on the walls and ceiling. Two bartenders mixed drinks for patrons across a weathered wooden bar, and Martha noticed framed dust jackets of works from Fitzgerald, Hemingway, Salinger, Steinbeck, Cather, and Cummings adorning the walls. Tables lined the establishment, with drinkers who looked to be regulars deep in conversation. Very few were women. One man with a stack of legal pads next to him seemed to be writing.

What is this place?

She took in the scene, her eyes shifting from the bar to the tables until they settled on the corner booth. Walt's back was to her, but she recognized his jacket. She locked eyes with the man sitting across from him. The stranger wore a dark wool coat, its collar turned up, obscuring the lower part of his face. He zeroed in on the newcomer and then looked to Walt, who turned around. An expression of surprise was quickly replaced by resignation, and he waved her over. Stale air, thick with the smells of tobacco, sweat, and the damp, musty odor of whiskey barrels, parted way as she crossed the room.

Walt scooted to the side under a framed dust jacket of Theodore Dreiser's *An American Tragedy*.

"Martha," he said, as she slid into the booth. "Welcome to Chumley's."

"Hello, darling," she said. "Charming place. Old speakeasy? It's good to see your meeting is not with a woman ten years my junior."

She took stock of the man across the table. He wasn't smiling. The eyes weren't so much cold as they were perceptive and alert. *Penetrating.* She had not seen eyes like that before. "I'm Martha Stowe," she said, more of a pronouncement, reaching across the table. "And you are?"

The man's left hand was on the table attached to a coffee mug. His right was out of sight. A stainless-steel Rolex was on his wrist. When you grew up the way she did, you noticed things like that. The Rolex had become popular with Hollywood stars like Newman, Redford, and McQueen, ever since Connery had given it screen time in his early outings as Bond. The dive watches were even starting to adorn the wrists of New York City's financial class, but unlike the ones she had seen worn by Wall Street bankers, this crystal was worn and scratched.

Walt looked at his companion and raised an eyebrow. The man nodded.

"True name?" Walt asked.

The man's eyes had not left Martha's. He nodded again. "Martha, this is Tom Reece."

"Mr. Reece, I'm Martha Stowe. It's a pleasure to meet you. What, pray tell, are you and my husband discussing this evening?"

Tom hesitated, then reached his right hand across the table.

"Mrs. Stowe," he acknowledged, clearly less than pleased at the intrusion.

"Call me Martha, please. If you are working with my husband on what I think you are, you can use my first name."

"Martha," he said.

"May I call you Tom?"

"You may."

"Are you married?"

"Martha, *Jesus*," Walter said, shaking his head.

"Well, if you are meeting surreptitiously with someone who I can only assume is either a reporter or works for one of our government agencies, I'd like to know what he has to lose. He doesn't look like a reporter." She turned back to the man across the table.

His eyes took measure, evaluating, thoughtful. She caught a flicker of acceptance as he moved his left hand to his coat pocket and removed a pack of Marlboro Reds. He shook out a cigarette and placed the filtered end between his lips. He then tossed the pack on the table and pulled a worn silver Zippo lighter from his right pocket. As the flint wheel ignited the wick, she noted an insignia on its side—a red shield highlighted in yellow with what looked like a skull wearing a green beret. She couldn't quite make out the letters at its base, but the last three appeared to be *SOG*.

"Well?"

"Well?" Tom asked back before taking a long drag on his cigarette. "Am I married? Not yet."

She thought she caught the hint of a smile, as if a fond memory had risen from his subconscious.

"I see. So, you have nothing to lose."

"We *all* have something to lose."

"How right you are. I'll be direct. Anything you are doing, any trouble you may cause, doesn't just impact you. It impacts me. It impacts my children. It impacts my family. I just want us to be clear. Are we clear, Tom?"

"We are."

"Good. Now, what do I need to know?"

That had been five years ago. Tonight, Walt would give a speech at the New York Yacht Club's Newport clubhouse. He was young, but there was already talk of his future as a presidential hopeful, so campaigning outside of Massachusetts was good business. The comparisons to Camelot were not unfounded: an attractive political couple, a war veteran who happened to have served on the modern equivalent of a PT boat, and a family connected to bootlegging and the mob. If they played their cards right, there was the possibility of a run for the White House; the country missed Camelot. It was still two, possibly even four election cycles away, but in politics you had to play the long game.

After the speech and an hour of shaking hands, she planned to retire to their room while Walt would excuse himself and relocate to the

White Horse Tavern for a drink and a bite to eat. There he would meet with Tom Reece.

Walt did not share everything with his wife, but he shared enough. He thought it would alleviate her worries. In fact, it did the opposite.

The Church Committee's report and what had been leaked from the Pike Committee had exposed the dark underbelly of the intelligence community to the American public. She knew that it had also illuminated something more.

Martha understood that she did not have the full picture of what Walt was doing in his meetings with the man she now knew worked for the CIA, the very agency at the center of the investigations. Her husband had emerged as a strong and ardent voice for reform on the campaign trail for the passage of FISA—the Foreign Intelligence Surveillance Act. The threat was communism, and those in power at the highest levels of the country's intelligence apparatus would stop at nothing to curtail its advance; that included encroaching on the rights and privacy of U.S. citizens, politicians, reporters, and Supreme Court justices.

What else had Walt learned in the course of the House investigations? What was it that kept him awake? She had arisen in the middle of the night on multiple occasions to find him standing at the window, a bourbon in hand, staring into the night. Was it nightmares? The war? Work? What was it that scared him enough to go outside of official channels to meet with a renegade CIA officer? What was he doing with Tom Reece?

She knew they had met in Vietnam when Tom was a SEAL and had reconnected in the course of events surrounding the Pike Committee. She assumed that he was a source, but Walt kept the specifics of their dealings close. There were some matters he was not allowed to discuss with her, or so went the line. She could tell he was keeping things from her for her own protection. He promised he would tell her one day soon, that he just needed a little more time, an explanation she accepted as much as she disliked it.

Walt pulled back on the throttle and decreased speed, first to ten knots and then to five as they approached the long dock extending from the manicured grounds of the club. Martha stood and joined her husband at the helm.

"Want to dock her?" he asked.

"You know I do." She smiled.

With the children in the care of multiple nannies at her parents' estate on Martha's Vineyard, they were free—well, almost free. Campaigning was still work, but she knew it was in pursuit of the ideals she had shouted for in the antiwar rallies of the late 1960s. Rather than just be the recipient of the wealth that her family had accumulated and live a life parading from one social event to the next, she would have real influence. She could prevent conflicts like the war in Vietnam from happening again. She could fight to ensure that her children, and one day her grandchildren, would not die in an ill-conceived war, as had Walt's brothers.

Martha was confident behind the controls of the yacht and knew the waters in between the island and Newport the way most people know the roads of their hometowns.

Slipping the boat into neutral, she coasted toward the berth while Walt descended to the starboard-side deck, pushing rubber fenders over the side to prepare for docking. They were an hour early, which would allow them time to freshen up before the evening's event. She then moved the throttle into reverse and guided the craft alongside the pier. Walt leapt from the boat to the dock, pulling the bowline taut and expertly lashing it to a cleat. He did the same with the stern line, examining his work to be sure the boat was secure before reboarding the vessel.

"Great job," he called up to his wife on the flybridge.

"I know, dear."

Walt disappeared below deck to retrieve their overnight bags. Martha shut down the engines.

"Ready?" Walt called up as he emerged from the trawler's interior.

"Give me a minute," she said, rummaging through a storage compartment in search of her purse.

She heard the gate to the pier open and glanced up to see a man with a clipboard walking down the dock, the harbormaster coming to greet them.

"Hello," she heard her husband say. "Mind if I pass you these bags? Alan not working tonight?"

When Martha turned and looked back down at the dock, the harbormaster was no longer holding a clipboard. In his outstretched hand was a pistol with a long cylindrical attachment she knew as a silencer.

Walt slowly raised his hands and shook his head. "Don't."

The assassin fired. Due to the downward angle, the round entered near the top of Walter's head. It cut its way through the frontal, parietal, and occipital lobes, removing a large portion of the back of his skull on the way out, coating the lower portions of the side bridge windows with gray brain matter and bone fragments. Martha heard her husband's lifeless body drop straight to the deck.

Visions of her two young children overwhelmed her and locked her in place. Paralyzed and unable to react, she witnessed the assassin fire two additional suppressed rounds into her husband.

As the business end of the weapon swung upward, she gazed from the black pistol to her executioner's dead eyes. *Italian? Russian?* Martha was a good fifteen feet above the assassin. The setting sun was to her back. He held the pistol at her head and then dropped it to her upper chest and pressed the trigger.

It felt like she had been hit with a sledgehammer, her body contorting around the entrance wound.

The kids.

Walter.

Her parents.

As her body twisted, a swell rocked the boat and her knees buckled, which caused her to stumble backward and to the side. She felt another bullet impact her left arm and then had the brief sensation of falling. She collided with the safety rail that extended from the bulwark of the main deck before crashing into the waters of Brenton Cove.

As Martha sank into the darkness, she found herself thinking of someone else. A man she knew had experience with violence. A man her husband would have seen later that evening. A man with ties to the military and to the Central Intelligence Agency. A man named Thomas Reece.

PART ONE

EXILE

The important thing to know about an assassination is not who fired the shot, but who paid for the bullet.

—ERIC AMBLER, *A COFFIN FOR DIMITRIOS*

CHAPTER 1

United States Penitentiary

Florence Administrative Maximum Facility

Range 13

Special Housing Unit

Fremont County, Colorado

DARKNESS.

Suffering.

Prison.

Of the mind.

His soul in chains.

His body in solitary confinement.

Nothing but darkness.

All life is suffering, Reece remembered.

How long have I been in here? Days? Weeks? Certainly not a month.

It was hard to tell when you were living in darkness.

But he wasn't living in silence.

The voices were his companions.

What are you looking for?

"Salvation," Reece said.

What truth do you seek?

"I seek a reckoning."

You've found it.

"Have I?"

You are going to die in here, Reece. You deserve to die in here. In the dark. Alone. Your wife died alone.

"No, she didn't. She had Lucy."

And an unborn child. You failed them, Reece. You failed them all. Just as you failed your men in Afghanistan. Freddy died on that rooftop in Odessa because of you. You deserve what's coming.

"And what is that? The grave?"

Death would be too merciful for you. You killed them, Reece.

"No!"

You are beyond redemption. You killed your wife and daughter. Had you been home, had you hung up the gun years earlier, they would still be alive. It was an unwinnable war. You knew that from the start. You studied your history. Those who sent you neglected to study theirs.

"Imperial hubris," Reece whispered.

They failed you and those they sent to fight. For twenty years. They filled the coffers of their defense industry allies, enjoying dinners and drinks with lobbyists, none of whom had the balls to step into the breach. You knew it. You went anyway. And you didn't do it for God and country.

"Then who did I do it for?"

You did it for you.

"No."

Where is your faith?

"It's gone."

Gone or dormant?

"I don't know."

It never fully disappears.

"I feel forsaken."

You should. By surviving the ambush in Afghanistan, you sentenced your family to death. Had you died in the Hindu Kush, they would not have been killed in your home. You know it's true.

"I wanted to hold those responsible accountable."

But accountability wasn't enough, was it?

"There needed to be consequences."

Consequences?

"Yes. I believe in consequences. Judgment."

Darkness.

Pain.

Suffering.

Is vengeance yours? How does it feel?

"I did what was necessary."

Did you?

"Yes."

Or was it because that is all you know? Because that is what you do best? Because that is where you feel most alive?

"I wanted to die."

You needed to die. Death becomes you, Reece. War—it's in your blood. You became war.

"It was the only way."

And you are beyond redemption.

"I know."

You brought it home. You brought war home to those who sent a generation into combat. You put the fear of God into those growing fat off the dividends of death. You got what you wanted.

"I wanted justice."

No, you didn't.

"I wanted revenge."

You became vengeance.

"A reckoning."

Did you get it? And what of Katie?

Reece tensed.

If you stay with Katie, she will die.

"I'll protect her."

The way you protected your wife and daughter? The way you protected your troop? The way you covered Freddy on that rooftop?

"I need to get out of here."

You won't leave this cell. Its walls are already closing in. Soon, even you won't be able to survive.

"I will."

Are you a survivor, Reece?

"I'm a fighter."

Every fighter goes down.

"But they get back up."

Darkness. Welcome it. Become it. Get comfortable being uncomfortable. You are sealed in your tomb. Forever.

"Bullshit."

Life is pain. Life is suffering. Why didn't they just kill you? Why didn't you kill yourself? Save Katie. She deserves her life.

"There's a safe-deposit box I need to find."

What's inside is poison. And now Katie has the safe-deposit box key. A key to a box you will never find. You put her in danger again. If she dies, you are responsible.

"What's in it?"

Your father knew.

"What was his tie to Russian intelligence?"

What do you think?

"I don't know."

You will rot in this cell, Reece. You will die in darkness. You will never get answers.

"Where there is darkness, there is light."

Somewhere, but you will never see it again. Death is on the wind.

"No."

Yes.

"Then this is what I deserve."

It is what you deserve.

Suffering.

Darkness.

This room will drive you to madness.

"I know."

All you have is your mind. Your mind and one meal a day. Why do they want you locked up?

"Who is 'they'?"

Did Alice betray you?

"She warned me."

Maybe she did both. Is she friend or foe?

"Alice, where are you?"

All those who killed Lauren and Lucy are dead.

"I know."

You killed them. The man behind 9/11; you killed him, too.

"I did."

The man responsible for Freddy Strain's death.

"Dead."

The man responsible for your father's death?

"Dead."

Is he?

"They are all dead."

Then what of Russian intelligence? Why would Mikhail Gromyko take his own life? The head of the SVR, Russia's Foreign Intelligence Service, went to the grave with your father's list on his last breath. The list and Thomas Reece. What was Gromyko protecting? Who was he protecting? You will never know, Reece.

"I will."

You are not leaving this cell alive. Be it a day or decades, you will die here. Your brain will deteriorate, and you will spend whatever time you have descending into madness. You should smash your head against the wall until death comes. Force yourself to choke on what passes for food. Get creative. End it. Everyone will be better off without you.

"They will."

No one even knows where you are.

"Someone knows I am here."

You don't exist.

"The food coming in once a day tells me someone knows where I am. Existence is enough."

Is it?

"It has to be. There is still work to do."

You will never do it.

"Katie is looking for me. She will find me."

Then she will die.

"No."

Just like all those you have loved. Dead.

"No!"

You are granite, Reece. You will not change. But those who love you—Katie, the Hastings family—they will be battered to death against you, protecting you. Save them now.

"That's not true."

It doesn't matter. You are locked in this cell. A prisoner of your own mind.

"Freedom."

No.

"Hope."

No.

"To exist. That is enough."

Pain is life. Life is pain. Suffering and pain. That was your life out there. That is your life in here.

"Someone killed the president."

Someone killed him and framed you.

"Why?"

The answers are out there.

"I am in here."

You need to get out.

"I do."

You will never get out. That is your truth.

"What is truth?"

Give up.

"No."

Quit.

"No."

Fail.

"No."

Die.

"Not today."

Suffering.

Nothing but darkness.

Life is darkness.

All life is suffering.

"It must be enough to exist."

For now. But if you once again see the light of day, existence won't be enough.

Reece felt the cold concrete wall against his back.

"No. But it's enough for today. I'll get out and get my answers. And when I do, there will be a reckoning."

CHAPTER 2

The Residence at Cape Idokopas
Krasnodar Krai, Russia

PERCHED ON A CLIFF overlooking the Black Sea and sitting on 168 acres heavily forested with Turkish pines is a lavish estate protected by walls, sensors, and drones. The perimeter security and barricades along connecting roads are manned by enough armed uniformed guards to rival any military base in the world. Residents of the nearby resort village of Gelendzhik first suspected it could be a new hotel complex, then concluded it was to be a vacation home for one of the oligarchs, but as construction continued and rumors swirled, it became apparent that this property was for one man in particular, the president of the Russian Federation. Ownership of the estate is hidden through a myriad of corporations, shell companies, and offshore holding firms all put in place to give the actual owner plausible deniability, especially when its construction cost the Russian people the equivalent of $1.4 billion in U.S. dollars.

Protected by a natural reef near the base of the cliffs and prohibited special-use airspace above, more commonly referred to as a "no-fly zone," the structure draws inspiration from nineteenth-century Italianate architecture. The sprawling 191,000-square-foot residence boasts a host of amenities, including swimming pools, spas, saunas, a greenhouse, bars, a casino, an underground ice hockey rink, a shooting range, multiple wine cellars, a hookah bar, game rooms, theaters, a library with reading room, a 2,800-square-foot master bedroom, guest rooms to accommodate the entire Russian Security Council, and a strip club to keep them busy. The grounds contain multiple helipads, an airstrip, a chapel, a teahouse connected to the main structure via a bridge, an outdoor amphitheater, barracks, and administrative buildings. Bordering properties are owned either by Russian oligarchs or the FSB, Russia's internal security service. A marina at the base of the cliffs allows access to the surrounding waters by security boats of the Federal Protective Service (FSO). In addition to the impressive array of structures aboveground, an entrance dug into the hillside off the marina leads into an underground bunker complex designed to withstand a nuclear detonation. It was within one of those underground rooms that Pavel Dashkov and his longtime secretary Kira Borisova waited.

An electric rail system had transported them from just inside the entrance deeper into the bunker system to one of the conference rooms. Kira had taken a seat against the wall. She knew when to let her boss think and when she needed to intrude in order to keep him on schedule. Today was one of those rare times when he was on someone else's time.

The war in Ukraine was not going well from a tactical perspective. From a strategic perspective it had succeeded beyond their expectations. The Americans were drawn in, funding the corrupt Ukrainian government at levels unheard of even at the height of their follies in Iraq and Afghanistan. Unfortunately, the brinksmanship of the Cold War was back. Nuclear options were on the table, something that astounded even Dashkov. Until recently, he had been content to continue his tenure as the director of the FSB and a member of the Security Council. As long as he kept internal disruptions to a minimum, he could stay engrossed in premium vodka, gluttonous meals, and young hookers. It was not a bad life. If internal dissent grew too loud or threatened the Russian president in a way he perceived would weaken his hold on power or even degrade his authority in the eyes of the oligarchy, Dashkov knew he could find himself not just on the outs with the president but quite possibly in one of his own holding cells or, more likely, the unwitting recipient of an accidental fall from a Moscow high-rise or victim of a suspicious poisoning. Poisonings happened frequently to those who ran afoul of the president. Dashkov should know. It was he and his former counterpart in the SVR, Russia's external security apparatus, who issued the orders to eliminate threats to the motherland. It was not lost on Dashkov how quickly one could find themselves on the wrong side of the president.

Gromyko. Exactly why he ended up taking his own life with the cyanide cigarettes issued back when the KGB and GRU protected the nation remained a mystery. His body had been found unceremoniously dumped in the bushes in a particularly dark section of Gorky Park. Dashkov had met his counterpart there many times over the years; neutral ground. He had quite enjoyed their rivalry. What he did not enjoy was the mystery behind who had killed him. Officially Gromyko had died of the cancer that had slowly been eating away at him for years. *Natural causes.* Unofficially, the classified police report acknowledged that a black zip-tie had been secured around his neck. In his mouth were flakes of tobacco. The autopsy had confirmed that the cause of death was suffocation, not due to the zip-tie's restriction of blood to his brain and air to his lungs but due to cyanide poisoning. Gromyko had taken his life the way they had been taught as new recruits at the Elk Island training center outside of Moscow. *Why?* That was the question. And what did he give up before he died? Could his executioner have been James Reece?

In a closed-door session with the president, they had decided with high probability that Gromyko's murderer was the CIA assassin. Their previous attempts to put James Reece in the ground had failed, which meant the possibility remained, however slim, that he would eventually find the list and documents hidden by Thomas Reece before his death. The former SEAL was proving to be more of a thorn in their sides than had his father. *What was it with this Reece clan?* Thomas Reece first came to the attention of the KGB and GRU in Vietnam. He had stayed on the radar of Russian intelligence services up until the day he was killed. The son was continuing the family tradition. How fitting that he would meet the same fate at the hands of the very same organizations.

Russia had another problem. They needed to shift U.S. attention away from the war in Ukraine. As with the JFK assassination a generation prior, the Russian puppet masters would turn America's attention inward to a homegrown enemy. The Russians had given them James Reece.

Armed with information the SVR and FSB had extracted from a talkative Edward Snowden, now a full Russian citizen, and building on the expertise of the Spetssviaz bot farms and Russia's Internet Research Agency, they had created an electronic signature that put James Reece in the center of a conspiracy to assassinate the president of the United States. Of course, that plan, minus the James Reece patsy element, had been formulated by Gromyko a decade ago. Assassinations external to the state were the purview of the SVR, but, as one of the three ranking members of the Security Council, Dashkov had his part to play. Though he would never show the Russian president anything but unwavering confidence, in actuality he couldn't believe they had pulled it off.

It had worked beautifully. America had turned in on itself as social media erupted with conspiracy theories, all building on the internal division the Americans had proven so adept at creating among themselves: race riots, rampant inflation, a dependence on foreign energy sources, what amounted to an open border, even distrust in their own elections results—elections that had once been the model for emerging democratic republics the world over. They could agree upon nothing. They were eating their own, victims of their own success. What the

Americans were fond of calling their "Greatest Generation" had fought and built the United States into a beacon of democratic ideals. The current generation had inherited that greatness only to squander the sacrifices of generations past. It was good that Americans placed no value on history. Had they picked their heads up from their social media posts they might have had time to read about the fate that befell the Roman Empire and realize they were on the same path.

Had they learned nothing from the collapse of the Soviet Union? They kept spending money they didn't have, throwing gasoline on the coals of inflation, ostensibly increasing the gap between the rich and poor intentionally. They couldn't seem to find a war they didn't like. Politicians on both sides of the aisle, encouraged in no small part by the defense industry lobbyists who supported them, voted for massive spending bills in support of the corrupt regime in Ukraine. Billions of tax dollars. *Fools.* Their defense industry had reaped incredible profits over America's two-decade misadventure in Afghanistan and Iraq. Those profit and growth projections were on a trajectory that must not be allowed to wane. A war in Ukraine would help. New NATO countries were required to purchase NATO-compatible armaments; just the thing to keep the gravy train flowing. Their corporate media knew a good thing when they saw it. Even pundits who years earlier had been up in arms against the invasions of Afghanistan and Iraq now called for the United States to unconditionally support Ukraine. Anyone who asked uncomfortable questions about that support or the possibility of auditing exactly where U.S. tax dollars were going was immediately labeled a "Russian apologist" or "Russian agent" or was "doing Russia's bidding." A blue and yellow flag became almost mandatory in Americans' social media profile pictures, and #SupportUkraine littered the posts of Americans who just months prior couldn't find the former Soviet socialist republic on a map; virtue signaling was the flavor of the day. The Congressional Progressive Caucus even quietly rescinded a letter they had sent to the American president months earlier urging for a negotiated end to the war in Ukraine by working directly with Russia. That wouldn't help defense industry profits. The lobbyists had done their jobs. The war machine rumbled on. The lobbyists and lawyers were well worth the investment.

The U.S. response to Russian actions in Ukraine had been a miscalculation on the council's part. Chaired by the president, in conception, the Security Council of the Russian Federation was composed of the ranking members of the intelligence community and defense establishment, along with top state officials and representatives from the federal districts. In reality, the power rested with the director of the FSB, director of the SVR, and deputy chairman. Their counsel would inform the president's decision-making. The others were just for show. Inaction by the United States and North Atlantic Treaty Organization (NATO) following the 2008 Russian invasion of Georgia and the 2014 invasion of Crimea, along with the 2013 "red line" bluff in Syria, indicated that the U.S. and her European allies would follow suit with condemnation and sanctions. What the council had not considered was that in 2008, 2013, and 2014, the United States was bogged down in Central Asia and the Middle East. To give Russia free rein in Ukraine, America needed another war. The council had agreed on that. What they had yet to develop was a plan for how to make it happen.

The U.S. "sanctions" had the opposite purported effect, regardless of what politicians in Washington, D.C., continued to say on cable news. Russia's Central Bank posted an account surplus in the first half of the year of more than $110 billion. The ruble was now the strongest it had been in close to a decade, and the nation was posting a massive trade surplus, billions of dollars higher than before the special operation to retake Ukraine began. Russia's exports now exceeded its imports, creating an inflow of domestic currency; the exact opposite was happening in the United States. No wonder the entrenched Washington political elite wanted to distract the populace with the Russian menace, even if it was a world away in Ukraine. The Americans were fools. But were they foolish enough to push Russia into a nuclear confrontation? That remained to be seen.

Could NATO, not see that sanctions had inadvertently made the Russian president, and the oligarchy he protected, richer than they could have possibly imagined? Anyone with the most basic understanding of economics and geopolitics, not to mention common sense, would know that Russia was the world's largest gas exporter and second-largest oil exporter. Who is the primary customer for that gas and oil? The European Union, the same EU that was also sending money from their coffers to Ukraine without any ability to audit. Because of their dependence on Russian energy, the EU was transferring more cash to Russia to fund the special operation in Ukraine than they were sending to Ukraine to fight the Russian military. In the first hundred days of the war, the Russian Federation made $98 billion in U.S. dollars from energy exports and was currently bringing in over $1 billion every day.

Oligarchs, senior politicians, intelligence directors, military leaders, and other friends of the Russian president had all pre-positioned assets around the world a year before taking action in Ukraine. Some of that wealth was diversified through investments in U.S.-based tech companies. Though headquartered in the United States, they were in all actuality global corporations with no loyalty to the country that allowed for such prosperity. Would the American public even care that billions belonging to Russia's elite were invested in the same companies that poisoned their children and divided their nation? They hardly noticed when a former president received $500,000 for a 2010 speech at the Renaissance Capital Bank in Moscow when his wife was serving as secretary of state. She opposed sanctions on Russia back then, and her family made half a million dollars for a forty-five-minute speech for which Dashkov was in attendance. The speech was quite forgettable; something about global cooperation.

This massive increase in wealth among the elites had allowed the Russian president to consolidate his hold on power. It was true that the oligarchs had been inconvenienced; yachts and homes had been seized. That was the price they paid. Sudden and unexpected deaths had befallen more than a few dissenters, which had encouraged others upset about a missed vacation in Ibiza to get back in line. Strokes, heart attacks, poisonings, suicides, drownings, falls, and illnesses had struck down more than a few of those critical of the Russian president.

And what of America? She had once been a respected foe. Now the once-great nation teetered on the brink of a precipice, the weakest she had been since her rise in the dark days of the Great Patriotic War.

The American vice president had assumed the presidency soon after the assassination of President Christensen and had done her best to quell the voices of disruption and bring the country together, but President Gale Olsen was out of her depth. She was also an unknown entity without the baggage of decades navigating the political landscape. The previous president had chosen her to deliver her home state of Florida. The world knew it, as did the American people. She still needed to prove herself. What was she prepared to do? Dashkov was not sure.

America had ushered the world into a new age by dropping two atomic weapons on Japan. They remained the only nation on earth to have used offensive atomic weapons. The arms race that followed saw the creation and testing of nuclear weapons 6,600 times more powerful than those used on Hiroshima and Nagasaki in 1945. Russia had only recently declassified information on the Tsar Bomba, a 50-megaton test conducted over the Novaya Zemlya islands in the Arctic in 1961. Dashkov had read the classified reports from Lawrence Livermore National Laboratory and knew the United States had been in the early stages of developing a 10,000-megaton bomb, a weapon it was said would "contaminate the earth." It was a wonder anyone survived the U.S. and Soviet nuclear tests in the 1950s and 1960s. Though France, the United

Kingdom, India, Pakistan, Israel, Iran, North Korea, and China all had nuclear weapons at their disposal, it was only the arsenals of the U.S. and Russia that could destroy the world many times over.

The daisy-chained EFPs, explosively formed penetrators, that had been used to kill President Christensen bore the hallmarks of the improvised explosive devices (IEDs) so common in Iraq. Did that indicate that Islamist extremists were to blame? Or was it disenchanted veterans of the global war on terror? Or was it something else? That was the genius of the plan: confusion, division, "misinformation." For a day or two, American flags once again lined every Main Street in the country just as they had after the attacks of 9/11. But even quicker than Dashkov had predicted, fingers were pointed, wagons were circled, accusations were made, insults were hurled, and the nation was once again divided along party lines.

The cell was kept small by design. Even Dashkov didn't have all the details. The operation required his approval but, really, who would go against the Russian president? Patsies were identified via social channels, patsies who had already forecasted their distrust of the federal government online and at protests. The Americans were already focused inward. They seemed incapable of finding common political ground. The opposition needed to be destroyed. The free exchange in the marketplace of ideas, the very foundation that had made America such a formidable adversary during the Cold War, was a thing of the past. All it took was planted digital and physical evidence. The Russian assets took care of the rest.

What concerned Dashkov was that James Reece had not been publicly identified as a conspirator in the assassination. The best and brightest of the Spetssviaz—the Special Communications and Information Service—and the Russian Internet Research Agency had served him up on a silver platter, as the Americans were fond of saying. His past played right into the narrative: a deep distrust of the federal government, a government he blamed for the deaths of his SEAL Team in Afghanistan. He also had the training and experience to pull it off. He had the means. He had the motive. The Russians just needed to create and manufacture the opportunity.

The SVR reported that there had been a large law enforcement operation in northern Montana the night of the assassination—just hours after President Alex Christensen had been pronounced dead and the vice president had taken the oath of office. Then James Reece had disappeared. The psychological profile in his file indicated that he would go down fighting. Some on the council conjectured that he had been killed, but Dashkov knew better. And he had confirmed it hours earlier. What would the council do with the information that Reece had survived? Dashkov would relay that information shortly. He also wanted the newly appointed interim director of the SVR to know that although Dashkov headed the internal security apparatus of the Russian Federation, he had been at this game long enough to have sources abroad.

Rostya Levitsky had most recently served as the deputy director of the SVR under Michael Gromyko. Dashkov had an extensive file on the interim SVR director and deduced that Levitsky had risen through the ranks due to his loyalty to his superiors and, more importantly, to the Russian president rather than from operational successes or exploits in the field.

Dashkov heard the door open and looked up to see his counterpart in the SVR enter the room. Younger than Dashkov by a decade, Levitsky managed to walk the line between deference and arrogance with an unassuming half smile that crept up from the left side of his mouth. His crisply tailored suit and blood-red tie sat in stark contrast with Dashkov's wrinkled dark sport coat and white shirt that stretched over his robust midsection. It was rumored that he was up at 3:30 a.m. every morning and started the day with a brisk ten-kilometer run before thirty minutes of weight training, followed by sauna and cold bath immersions.

Dashkov unconsciously rubbed his perpetual five-o'clock shadow, noting that Levitsky appeared to have shaved just prior to the meeting.

Levitsky extended his hand and nodded in deference to the older FSB director, who remained seated.

"Good evening, comrade."

The ever-present smile might have been meant to disarm, but Dashkov reminded himself that, even though separated by years, they had received similar training. Dashkov would keep his guard up. They also shared lineage in the dark arts of espionage. Their ultimate goal was to subvert the West through active measures of sabotage, disinformation campaigns, assassinations, destabilization operations, and coups. They had just pulled off one of the most successful assassinations in history.

"Give us the room," Dashkov said without taking his eyes off his counterpart.

Levitsky nodded politely as Kira gathered her things and made her exit. He took a seat across from Dashkov, both of them wisely leaving the head of the table vacant.

"It is good to see you, comrade," Levitsky continued.

Whether that was true or not, Levitsky could very well move from interim director to director, depending on his relationship with the president. He appeared confident and spry for someone in his late fifties. His outward demeanor betrayed none of the stress most would feel in his position, something that put the older man on edge.

Though both agencies were born of the KGB, the SVR and FSB maintained cordial but at times adversarial relations. Dashkov knew that Levitsky had championed the twenty-first-century use of microwaves aimed at U.S. embassies and CIA annexes around the world, resulting in what the Americans had dubbed "Havana syndrome," to disrupt American intelligence-gathering operations and cause internal strife in U.S. intelligence and diplomatic circles. Truth be told, it was a weapon and a technology that had been in use throughout the Cold War under a variety of code names. Dashkov had read the top secret American files originating at the Defense Advanced Research Projects Agency on projects BIZARRE and PANDORA while still in training, courtesy of a highly placed deep-penetration asset, a spy who to this day had never been caught. What the American press neglected to report was that the CIA had been using that same technology against Soviet spies and diplomats since the 1960s.

"Any new information on the death of your predecessor?"

Dashkov could play the game as well.

Levitsky took a breath.

"I am afraid not, comrade. Cyanide 'L-pill' in his cigarette's filter. Suicide. Though the zip-tie around his neck indicates he was under duress. By whom and for what purpose is unknown. I know you have your theory, a theory we took extreme measures to act upon, though nothing officially ties James Reece to the murder. Gorky Park falls under your purview as FSB director, but my agency is at your disposal should you need additional resources."

Little shit.

"Since you bring him up, what have you learned about his current whereabouts and disposition? Foreign entanglements being the purview of the SVR."

"No chatter, no additional signals intelligence, and nothing from our sources in U.S. intelligence circles. Nothing since the arrest in Montana," Levitsky said.

"Remember, comrade, his arrest was not confirmed. He seems to have disappeared. Like a ghost."

"He is but a man, Director Dashkov. Men don't just disappear, unless *we* make them."

Dashkov had been on edge since the discovery of Gromyko's body in Gorky Park. They shared a long history together, and he had been given a dose of mortality tinged with paranoia, both newfound traits he intended to conceal from the rest of the council.

"Director Gromyko and I successfully ran the intelligence apparatus for years," Dashkov reminded the younger man. "I trust we will work together for the benefit of Mother Russia. Can I count on your cooperation, comrade? Regardless of how long you remain in your seat."

"You shall have it, and so shall Mother Russia."

"Good. Now, before we have an audience with the president, bring me up to speed on intelligence operations too sensitive for electronic communications."

CHAPTER 3

United States Penitentiary
Florence Administrative Maximum Facility
Range 13
Special Housing Unit
Fremont County, Colorado

COMPLETE DARKNESS.

Reece finished another set of twenty slow push-ups. He stood and began a set of squats. "One, two, three . . ."

He focused his mind on the pain of the lactic acid building up in his quads.

Burning.

Still alive.

All life is suffering.

He dropped back down into push-up position.

They must be watching.

Maybe not.

No, they're watching.

Don't give them a victory. Keep working. Work harder.

Blacked-out goggles had been put over his eyes upon leaving the Hastings family ranch, and Reece had been in darkness ever since.

Sounds and smells had indicated he was on an airfield less than an hour later. He was then shackled and led up a set of airstairs. He was strapped into a seat and a noise-canceling headset had been attached to his head. Not being able to see or hear, his other sensations were heightened. He had felt the plane taxi, gather speed, and take off, and he had felt the jolt of a landing hours later. He had been driven in what he suspected was a van to the facility in which he now resided before being stripped naked and marched to his holding cell.

Once in his cell he had been forced to kneel as the restraints were removed, as were his goggles and headset. He could sense the guards backing away and heard a door slide shut behind him. He made no quick movements. Instead he opened his eyes, expecting to see at least a slit of light, but there was only darkness.

He had deliberately moved his hands to the wall and up to his face, rubbing his eyes and temples.

Cold. Cold and dark.

Where the fuck am I?

Still naked, he turned himself around and pressed his back to the wall.

Cold.

Get it together, Reece.

Take a breath.

Okay.

Look around.

Can't look around. It's completely black, but I can explore.

Reece began to crawl.

He was in a box—a rectangular cell, to be more precise.

Walls, concrete.

Floor, concrete.

He continued to explore his new surroundings.

What's this? A narrow slit near the floor. For food?

He continued to crawl. His hands discovered a concrete pillar. He stood, still working his hands around it in an attempt to figure out what it was. Near the top he felt what could have been a nozzle for an old garden hose.

A shower? No way to turn it on. Is it on a timer?

Reece went back to his hands and knees and continued his exploration.

Are they watching me?

Most certainly.

A concrete block. *No, this was different. Stainless steel?*

Reece worked his way up. *What is this?*

A toilet.

Attached to the wall.

And this?

A small sink on the back of the toilet.

Is there a way to flush or turn this on?

As if the sink were reading his thoughts, it turned on. As it was more a drinking fountain than a sink, Reece bent his head toward the sound and ravenously drank the water until it abruptly stopped.

Breathe, Reece. Keep exploring.

Another concrete block. No, a rectangle. A concrete cot with a thin rubber top.

Are you back where you started?

Reece made two more slow explorations in the darkness and estimated his cell to be approximately seven by twelve feet.

Reece's world now consisted of walls, a shower, a toilet, a water fountain, a bed, and darkness. Concrete, steel. Dark. Cold.

Why are you in here?

"Just thirty-five minutes ago, shots were fired at President Alec Christensen by a member of the armed forces during a Veterans Day parade in the nation's capital."

"JAMES REECE. YOU ARE SURROUNDED BY FEDERAL AND LOCAL LAW ENFORCEMENT."

Reece visualized the rifle in his hands. It helped to think about every detail. Bravo Company carbine, Magpul magazine loaded with Black Hills 77-grain cartridges, Aimpoint Micro with magnifier, SureFire Scout Light, Viking Tactics sling, and an ATPIAL infrared aiming device.

"COME TO THE FRONT OF THE HOUSE, UNARMED. IF YOU SURRENDER PEACEFULLY, YOU WILL NOT BE HARMED."

"I love you, Katie."

"James . . ."

It was the last thing she had said to him.

He had put the rifle on the floor.

"Hold on to this for me."

The ring.

The key.

"OPEN THE DOOR—SLOWLY—AND SHOW US YOUR HANDS.

"KEEP YOUR HANDS HIGH, COMMANDER. SLOWLY TURN AROUND.

"WALK DOWN THE STEPS AND GO PRONE.

"CROSS YOUR LEGS, ARMS OUT TO YOUR SIDES. TURN YOUR HEAD."

He remembered the cool gravel of the driveway pressing into the side of his face as his hands were zip-tied behind his back.

"You are under arrest for conspiracy to assassinate the president of the United States."

He remembered hearing Katie's voice inside demanding to see a search warrant.

Katie.

Katie Buranek.

He had taken a knee to propose when the alarm had sounded, a warning from the deepest levels of the Internet. Did it come from his guardian angel or was it the ultimate betrayal? Alice, an artificial intelligence entity buried a thousand feet beneath the Sixteenth Air Force Cyberspace Center at Lackland Air Force Base in San Antonio, Texas, was known to only a select few at the highest levels of the United States government. She was also a sentient being. She had helped him in his mission to avenge Freddy. Had she then betrayed him and set him up as the fall guy for the assassination of the president? If not Alice, then who had that capability?

The president. Alec Christensen. A man whose life had been torn apart on 9/11. A man who, like Reece, took steps to avenge those killed that Tuesday morning. A man who thought strategically, doing what was necessary for two decades to reach the pinnacle of power in the United States. He had found Reece to be a kindred spirit, and together they had brought those responsible for 9/11 to justice. And now he was gone.

"Do you believe in the Deep State, Mr. Reece?"

"Sir?"

"The Deep State, or what people call the Deep State, anyway. Do you believe in it?"

"I believe we've found common ground, Mr. President."

"I thought we would, Commander. The Deep State is real, though it's not what's portrayed in the movies. I scare them. I wouldn't be surprised if I don't make it through my term. Does that surprise you?"

"Not much surprises me, sir."

Not much surprises me.

"I wouldn't be surprised if I don't make it through my term."

That had not meant anything to Reece at the time. He had chalked it up to the bourbon they were both sipping.

Reece replayed the news footage in his mind, the footage he had seen right before the black Suburbans descended upon his cabin in Montana.

"Our security analysts confirm that the president's motorcade was hit with what we are being told were chain-linked EFPs—explosively formed penetrators—improvised explosive devices that came to prominence during the war in Iraq. The president was rushed to George Washington University Hospital, where he was pronounced dead. The vice president has taken the oath of office and will address the nation at the top of the hour, some eight minutes from now."

He had pressed the safe-deposit box key into Katie's hand. Did the FBI have it? Did they arrest Katie? Search her? Was the key now entered into evidence?

Why would they frame me? And who are "they"?

Reece pushed himself back to his feet. Squats again.

He had tried sit-ups for the first few days but the hard concrete floor had rubbed his back raw. "Grinder Reminder" they had called it back in SEAL training. If he didn't want it to get infected he'd better not push his luck. Planks would have to do.

He knew he was losing weight. One meal a day would do that to you. There was no way to tell how much protein was in the stew they pushed into his cell each day. *Was it each day?* There was really no way to tell when living in complete darkness. He would first hear an outer door open, then a second small metal door opened into his cell and the food was pushed through. Was he being conditioned like Pavlov's dogs? They could be switching up the times just to further confuse and disorient him. A more reliable measure of time was the length of his hair and beard; his hair was now brushing his shoulders and he estimated his beard to have grown out about two inches. He knew the cell was kept cold by design. To keep him on the edge of hypothermia. To make him easier to break. But no one had yet asked him any questions.

Where was he? He estimated they had been airborne for about four hours, though the pilot could have had instructions to just keep them aloft to further confuse their prisoner.

Prisoner.

There was a time when he had contemplated eventually going to prison, when he had been crossing names off his terminal list, uncovering those who had a hand in killing his family.

~~Josh Holder~~

~~Marcus Boykin~~

~~Saul Agnon~~

~~Steve Horn~~

~~CJNG, Mexico~~

~~Admiral Gerald Pilsner~~

~~Mike Tedesco~~

~~J. D. Hartley~~

~~Lorraine Hartley~~

~~Leonard Howard~~

~~Hammadi Izmail Masood~~

~~Ben Edwards~~

But his reason for staying out of prison until he was ready had been to put each and every person responsible for the deaths of his SEAL Troop and his family in the ground. He just needed to stay alive and avoid capture long enough to finish the list to get to that final name: Ben Edwards.

Ben.

Reece had thought of himself as already dead back then. There were no societal norms, no laws that could stop him. There was nothing to live for—nothing but the list. He was free. He had become war. And he had won. And he had gone to die.

But he hadn't died.

For a moment, he had felt happiness, in the bush of Mozambique, adapting his skills and experience from the battlefield to protect the animals of Rich Hastings's concession from poachers. But the CIA had found him and knew just what to say to bring him back in. Freddy had tracked him down. Freddy knew where to look. And now Freddy was dead. Aside from Africa, the only true freedom Reece knew was when he was on the warpath. When he was hunting.

He did not know who was responsible for the president's assassination. He did not know who was responsible for framing him.

But now he had a reason to live.

Katie.

Reece finished the set.

Stay in your routine. Discipline. They want you to slip up, give up hope, give in to despair, give in to ruin. That's when they will come for you. When you are already on the edge of breaking. When you are on the verge of madness.

You can stay in here forever.

No, you can't.

Reece sat cross-legged and controlled his breathing. Even in darkness he closed his eyes so he could imagine the light.

The light.

Hope.

Katie.

Reece took a breath, held it briefly at the top of his inhalation, and then exhaled completely, forcing all the air from his lungs. He held his breath for ten seconds. Then he inhaled deeply, filling his diaphragm, and held his breath at the top for ten seconds. He repeated the process, adding ten seconds to each inhalation and exhalation hold. He was up to four minutes.

Four minutes and ten seconds today.

"You can do it."

Dad?

"You can do it, son."

They were next to the rocks of a small tidal pool in Kauai.

"*You got this, James. I'm timing you,*" Tom Reece had said, pointing to the Submariner on his wrist. "*You are almost up to a full minute.*"

Reece was eight, but his eyes were already set on the SEAL Teams. He was going to be a frogman just like his dad.

Reece forced the air from his lungs as his father had taught him, then took one big breath and pushed himself beneath the surface, counting, one one-thousand, two one-thousand, three one-thousand, as he held fast to the rocks of the small tidal pool.

Though James was too young by industry standards, he was scheduled for his first open-water dive the next day. It helped that his dad knew the dive shop owner, another SEAL finding refuge from the experience of Vietnam through laid-back Hawaiian island life.

James burst to the surface.

His dad swept the salt water off the dial of his timepiece with his thumb and nodded approvingly.

"One minute and two seconds. Not bad for a tadpole."

"I can go longer. I know I can."

"How do you feel?"

"I'm comfortable being uncomfortable, Dad. Just like you taught me."

"Good, son. Now it's time to push past uncomfortable."

"What do you mean?"

"It's time to transcend your line of control."

"I don't understand."

"You will. Someday you may need it. When you can push past just being uncomfortable, into a zone where you feel out of control, yet learn to control it—that is where true progress is made, son."

"How do I get back?"

"Most of the world will never move past being uncomfortable for a short time and returning quickly to their comfort zone. That's easy. If you can push past that, into a sphere that feels out of control, then return to control, and then back to simply being uncomfortable, well, then you've really accomplished something, my boy."

"I feel at home right now, Dad."

"Good. Let's go again. One minute and ten seconds for the record. Remember, we all come from the water. We will be free-diving for Uku, Ono, Kole, and Mahi off Lanai before you know it. You ready?"

James flashed a thumbs-up.

"Good. Three, two, one . . . fight!"

Reece closed his eyes and pushed himself back under the water.

CHAPTER 4

The Residence at Cape Idokopas
Krasnodar Krai, Russia

THE DOOR TO THE conference room swung open.

Expecting the president, both Dashkov and Levitsky stood out of respect and protocol. It was not lost on the FSB director that his new counterpart snapped to attention with much more enthusiasm.

Two security men took positions on either side of the door as a third held it open. Instead of the Russian president, the deputy chairman of the Security Council entered the room.

"Leave us," he said, waving his left hand as if he were brushing off a fly.

The deputy chairman's orders were best followed immediately.

Slightly older than Dashkov, Nikolai Kozak had at one time held the position of FSB director in the late 1990s. He was a contemporary of the Russian president, who had recruited him out of retirement from his riverfront dacha in Plyos and appointed him deputy chairman of the Security Council, a position that until just prior to the invasion of Ukraine did not exist.

More feared and respected in intelligence circles than even the president, Nikolai's name was synonymous with the old ways. His father was awarded the Hero of the Soviet Union and Order of Lenin for his actions as a sniper in the Battle of Stalingrad. It was with a similar Mosin Nagant M1891 that Nikolai learned to hunt with his father in the late 1950s and early 1960s. His father's rifle was proudly displayed in the battle museum on the west bank of the Volga in Volgograd (formerly Stalingrad), though rumor was that it had been replaced with a replica, and Nikolai was in possession of the original.

Most would have had a natural inferiority complex growing up in the shadow of the man whose name was synonymous with killing Nazis in battle, but young Nikolai had felt only admiration. His father had an enemy, an enemy that threatened to overrun their country, and he had stepped up to become a Hero of the Soviet Union. The Nazis were defeated. It was young Nikolai's duty to defeat their new enemy.

His father stressed the importance of having a trade, as one never knew when the fortunes of the Communist Party could turn. It was, perhaps, the ghosts of Stalingrad that drove the war hero to an early grave, the vodka doing what German tanks, artillery, and snipers never could. Nikolai dutifully followed his father's guidance, graduating from the Leningrad Shipbuilding Institute in 1975. He showed promise as an engineer following graduation, but Nikolai knew his path was not in design but in service. His background and intellect made him a prime candidate for the KGB. He cut his teeth in the Soviet Union's Committee for State Security alongside the Russian president, the late Mikhail Gromyko, and Pavel Dashkov. They were contemporaries whose enemies had not vanished with the end of the Cold War.

His hair had receded over the years, and what was left was a dark gray that reminded Dashkov of a foreboding evening cloud. His tie was straight and matched his suit in a way that complemented the shade of his hair and eyes. Those corresponding hues flowed directly into a walk that suggested the energy of someone decades younger. It was rumored that Nikolai Kozak had never touched a drop of alcohol.

Kozak approached as the door behind him shut with an audible click. Though they had known one another for decades, he still made Dashkov nervous.

"Chairman," Dashkov said, shaking hands with the taller man. "We were expecting the president, but it is always an honor."

"Pavel, it is good to see you, old friend." The words were warm, but the slate-gray eyes made Dashkov shiver. He felt a yearning to light the pipe in his suit coat pocket. The sweet flavor of tobacco in his mouth would soothe his nerves. That would have to wait until the meeting was over.

"Director Levitsky," Nikolai said, extending his hand.

"Chairman."

"Please, gentlemen, sit." Kozak gestured to the chairs from which they had just risen.

Instead of taking a seat at the far end of the long rectangular table as the president would have done, he sat at the head, closest to the two directors. Though a newly created position, the deputy chairman had the ear of the president. There were even those who believed he would be the next president of Russia.

"After conferring with the president," Kozak began, "we both agree that this meeting is best left to the three of us."

"Of course," Levitsky said.

Buried in the side of a mountain, only the three of them present, with no phones or electronic devices of any kind, they were about as secure as one could get in the modern world.

Kozak leaned forward and rested his elbows on the table. He interlaced his long fingers, sliding his index fingers and thumbs together, forming what reminded Dashkov of a pistol, which he then brought to his lips as if in meditation.

"Gentlemen," Chairman Kozak said. "The special operation in Ukraine is progressing, slower than expected, but progressing. Director

Levitsky, you are new to the council, but I trust you are aware of conditions, projections, and intent?"

"Intent, comrade?"

"*Da*, intent."

"Annex Ukraine and restore the historical boundaries of Russia."

"Ah yes, but there is more. Some you may have pieced together and parts you have not. I see Director Dashkov has not read you in on the more intricate aspects of the operation."

"I thought it best to wait until he was no longer an *interim* director," Dashkov said with an obvious emphasis on *interim.*

"A letter will be forthcoming," Kozak said. "The president has appointed you director of the SVR. Youngest in history."

Levitsky sat up even straighter in his chair.

"Congratulations, Director Levitsky," the chairman said.

"*Da*, congratulations," Dashkov said with slightly less enthusiasm.

"It is an honor and a privilege," Levitsky said. "I am but a humble servant."

"*Da*, a servant who now presides over the state's Foreign Intelligence Service. Because of the unique nature of Ukraine's position in the domestic and global arenas, both the Foreign Intelligence Service and Federal Security Service share intelligence responsibilities." Kozak stared at the president's appointed intelligence directors.

Dashkov forced himself not to squirm in his chair. He should have had a vodka before this meeting.

"The time has come to move into the next phase of the operation," Kozak continued. "What is the latest assessment of the United States' assistance to Ukraine?"

"The most current intelligence summary indicates they will continue to support Ukrainian forces with National Advanced Surface-to-Air Missile Systems, artillery and mortar munitions, Patriot missile batteries, counter-artillery radars, Bradley Fighting Vehicles, Javelin and

Stinger systems. They have even given them some of our old Mi-17 helicopters. We expect them to support with Abrams tanks within the year. They have supplied Phoenix Ghosts, Switchblades, and Puma unmanned aerial vehicles, but we have confirmed they have denied Ukraine's request for Gray Eagle or Reaper drones. They are worried we will acquire one and reverse-engineer them. U.S. troops remain on the ground in an advisory capacity, and the CIA has its paramilitary wing on the front lines. It is only a matter of time before we capture or kill one," Levitsky reported.

"Sanctions on Russia and military aid for Ukraine," Kozak said. "Status quo." He liked to use the American legal and military vernacular whenever possible. It helped to think like the enemy. "They exploit the compassion of their own people to enrich their friends in the defense industry." He shook his head. "They accuse us of consolidating power and wealth in the hands of an oligarchy when they have the very same system in the United States: politicians, defense, tech, pharmaceuticals. They have their oligarchy, too. They just refuse to acknowledge it."

"Their *Time* magazine just praised the Ukrainian president as their 'Man of the Year,'" Levitsky offered. "They honor a man who outlaws opposition parties, shuts down the Ukrainian Orthodox church, and uses American tax dollars to solidify his grip on power."

"All of that benefits us in the long run," Kozak said. "American supremacy is at an end. There are even large segments of their population who now take offense to the very word *American*. They believe it overtly promotes an American exceptionalism that disenfranchises others in the Americas. They have made this transfer of power to a new world order much easier than our predecessors could have imagined."

"Even so, comrade," Dashkov added, "they will not make the same mistakes they made in Iraq and Afghanistan with our special operation in Ukraine; they can't afford to."

"*Da*," Kozak pronounced. "I have cautioned the president that we must be prudent. Though weak, the Americans are still dangerous. We would be unwise to underestimate them. We must know what pieces to move and when to move them."

Dashkov had heard the deputy chairman opine many times and knew when to nod and when to interject. Now was time to nod.

"We telegraphed our moves in Ukraine well in advance, something we could do only when the United States gave up their energy independence. We have manipulated the relationship with Europe for decades, slowly making them more and more reliant on us for their energy, the very energy that allows their industries to function, to heat their homes in the winter. Their survival is tied to the deals they have with us. The Americans stepped right in line. Sometimes their moral vanity astounds even me."

"What of the sanctions?" Levitsky asked.

"Yes, it is inconvenient in the short term, especially for those who have made a habit of vacationing in the South of France, the Amalfi Coast, or mooring their yachts in Ibiza. But we all sacrifice for Mother Russia. The economic penalties the United States is so fond of touting have no discernible negative impact. In fact, they have the opposite of their intended effect."

"Excuse me, Chairman Kozak. Are you saying that the annexation of Ukraine was a bid to increase revenues?" Levitsky asked.

"An added benefit. More than that, it was a test."

"A test?"

"Pavel, explain," Nikolai said, leaning back in his chair, touching his two index fingers to his lips.

Dashkov cleared his throat.

"None of this is written down. It is not doctrine, which is why it was not in any turnover documents following Director Gromyko's murder."

"I understand," Levitsky said.

"I am not sure you do. Power in Russia is controlled by the council. The three of us, and the president. Now that you are no longer an interim director, you are among the few. That position means taking precautions."

"I have a robust security detail," Levitsky confirmed.

"I am not talking physical security. I am referring to financial security. I am talking about power. A group we sometimes refer to as 'the Collective' bought Brent Crude oil futures on the Intercontinental Exchange in February 2021, exactly one year prior to the beginning of hostilities in Ukraine and then supplemented those purchases during December 2021. We knew exactly what the United States and their European partners would do in response to our actions in Ukraine, which allowed us to prepare accordingly."

"You manipulated a global market?" Levitsky asked.

"The Collective did," Kozak corrected.

"The Collective?" Levitsky asked.

"The power of the council extends beyond the borders of Russia. There are relationships at play that were forged in the fires of the Great Patriotic War, relationships that cross borders and ideologies."

"I see," Levitsky said, nodding. "And these relationships, they are financial?"

"Out of necessity, comrade. To avert a nuclear Armageddon, a small council of Americans, Brits, and Soviets took an oath to a higher power."

"God?"

"Certainly not, though they did become saviors. Nuclear testing in the fifties and sixties, the Cuban Missile Crisis, and the events of Able Archer in 1983 proved that the Collective was necessary to safeguard the world from nuclear destruction. Up to this point, that is exactly what we have done."

"While at the same time amassing fortunes," Levitsky said.

"And power," Chairman Kozak interjected. "Power to save the world. And now, you are one of us."

Levitsky was well aware this was not an offer one could decline.

"Comrade," Kozak said, "we now control a large percentage of the world's oil supply. Europe is almost entirely dependent on us for their energy, as is the United States, though to a lesser extent. While they have outsourced energy to those they consider ideological enemies, they continue to spend billions of dollars they do not have buying energy from those very same adversaries. We use those billions to strengthen our economy and fund the war effort. Soon the world's economy will look to Asian stock markets. There is already a shift away from Europe and the United States. Their most astute economists are warning that the euro and the U.S. dollar will one day cease to be the world's dominant reserve currencies. We are going to help usher that shift along. The Bretton Woods system collapsed when Nixon suspended the dollar's convertibility into gold, but the Americans continued to provide security to all maritime trade the world over. That part of the deal is on borrowed time."

"And Ukraine?" Levitsky asked.

"Bringing Ukraine back into the federation gives us ownership over twenty-five percent of global wheat exports. We will then have control of a significant percentage of the world's energy and food supply. We can starve and freeze out the West. That strengthens our negotiating position. But we also need to take Ukraine to free our ethnic Russian peoples under Ukrainian rule. We misjudged how much the United States would be willing to invest. That has slowed progress."

"So, the United States needs a distraction?" Levitsky said, beginning to put the pieces together.

"That is correct," Kozak confirmed.

"What kind of a distraction?"

Kozak leaned forward and dropped his intertwined hands to the table.

"The battlespace is not physical. It's not Ukraine. It's the mind. It's always been the mind. The West is fickle. Their illogical support for the corrupt Ukrainian government is depleting their coffers, NATO militaries are massing on Ukraine's borders, and the CIA is operating with impunity inside the country. But they are falling into the same trap they set for the Soviet Union during the Cold War. It is time to hand them another defeat: Vietnam, Iraq, Afghanistan, and now Ukraine. As the president has said, 'The sower of the wind will reap the storm.'"

"What are you suggesting, comrade?" Dashkov asked.

"We are going to ratchet up the stakes."

A silence settled over the room.

Kozak clearly wanted to see if his intelligence directors had pieced together Russia's next move.

Dashkov took a moment to process what the chairman had said.

"We are going to use tactical nuclear weapons in Ukraine?" He paused. "Or perhaps a dirty bomb? Blame it on the Ukrainians? Prove that they detonated a dirty bomb on their own soil in an amateurish attempt to blame us and draw the U.S. and NATO into direct confrontation?"

"Would you have a problem with that?" Kozak asked.

"That would depend on how close I was to the blast, and which direction the wind was blowing."

"And you, Director Levitsky?"

"I would advise caution."

Kozak smiled.

"I am glad to see you both do not nod your heads like 'yes men.' Mother Russia will not lose Ukraine again. The nuclear option *is* on the table, but not in the way that you think."

Dashkov looked across the table at Levitsky. The new SVR director's ever-present half smirk was gone.

"As you both know," Kozak continued, "the president has had

multiple conversations with Xi Jinping of China. We delayed our re-annexation of Ukraine until after the Olympics. In exchange for China's support they received an extremely favorable no-limit deal of supplies of critically needed oil at just over production margin cost. In the past year the Americans have grown even weaker. The assassination of their president has thrown them into further turmoil, inflation is rampant, their military is coming off two embarrassing defeats in Iraq and Afghanistan and can't meet recruiting goals, they are dependent on Canada, OPEC, and Russia for the oil that runs their economy and their national defense, most of the products on their shelves come from China, and the precursor drugs for their antibiotics also come from China. Total dependence on their enemies only requires one additional step. Do you know what that is?"

"Microchips," Levitsky broke in. "Taiwan."

Dashkov was going to have to keep a close eye on this one.

"Correct," the chairman said. "Sixty-five percent of all microchips used in the U.S. come from Taiwan. Over ninety percent of their complex chips are imported from Taiwan. China has always claimed Taiwan as its own. They are ready to make it so in reality."

"There is a strong probability that the U.S. would come to Taiwan's defense," Dashkov interjected. "Losing the microchip manufacturing capability in Taiwan would cripple them. They will do everything they can to keep that from happening."

"Yes, China is hesitant. They will take Taiwan, but only if they are assured that the U.S. will not intervene. It is possible that the U.S. could support both Ukraine and Taiwan with intelligence and weaponry, prolonging both conflicts to the benefit of their defense industry." The chairman paused. "But not if they were actively engaged elsewhere."

"And where would that be?" Dashkov asked, desperately wanting to light his pipe.

"We took Georgia in 2008 and Crimea in 2014 without the U.S. making so much as a whimper. They were, of course, having a hard go of it against insurgents in the Middle East and Central Asia. We are going to redirect their focus back to the Middle East."

"And how are we going to do that?" Dashkov asked.

"We are going to serve them up a war they can't refuse."

CHAPTER 5

Afghanistan–Iran Border

MOHAMBAR RANJHA HAD MADE the trip into Iran many times. He couldn't remember how many, but it didn't really matter. There was no need to keep track. This is what he had always done and what he would always do. Why complicate things by trying to learn a new trade? He could drive just about any truck one could find in Afghanistan. Driving kept him out of the fields, and during the occupation, it had kept him off the battlefield.

The roads were much less dangerous than they had been when the Americans occupied the country. As a smuggler he had managed to stay clear of most of the fighting in Helmand. The Taliban knew that they needed to keep a cohort of drivers off the Americans' biometric databases and free from explosive residue that could be detected at American military checkpoints by explosive and explosive precursor detection devices. It was important to keep the money flowing.

Mohambar had made his first runs as a passenger in his father's Hanomag-Henschel F 163 K. It had rolled off the line in Germany sometime in the early 1970s when American and European college backpackers and tourists still made the pilgrimage to photograph the exotic gardens, architecture, and mountains in the "Heart of Asia." The road to Zaranj was dirt and rutted, which made travel slow going. That was before the Americans invaded.

As a member of the Barakzai tribe, the Ranjha clan had been warriors and farmers for as long as their oral histories recorded. Agriculture was the mainstay of Pashtun tribes in Helmand, and for Mohambar and his family, that meant poppies.

Opium was popular in Iran, and their neighbor just happened to be the world's largest producer. Iran's ports also provided a gateway into and out of landlocked Afghanistan for a host of products, including the precious poppy.

The Iranian border extended along Afghanistan's from Turkmenistan in the north to Pakistan in the south. Mohambar's experience was limited to Route 606 and the border crossing station at Zaranj. He had driven the road back in his teens when the journey took most of the day and roadside bombs meant for the Americans sometimes took out the wrong targets. India had invested millions to help build the motorway as a trade route to bypass Pakistan. Though construction began in 2005, the 218-kilometer road would take four years to build at the cost of over a hundred lives. Building roads in Afghanistan in the midst of a war was a dangerous business.

President Hamid Karzai opened the road in 2009 as a way to show the world that progress was being made in Afghanistan, and the new road had transformed what was formerly a twelve-hour journey into two. Now, with the Taliban once again in control of Kabul and warlords running the provinces, the drive was much safer. Gone were the roadside bombs and pressure-plate IEDs so common during the insurgency. Also gone were the divisions of American and European soldiers who rotated through every year and who, for a time, had made it their business to stomp out the opium trade. Mohambar always wondered why they focused so much energy on trying to force his tribe to seed their fields with wheat. The opium was bound for port cities in America and Europe.

Their mission to eradicate the opium crop had disastrous results for the Americans and for the citizens of Afghanistan. His older sister's family had been killed in a night bombing raid in 2017. His village chief had described the plane that dropped the bombs as a B-52 in something the Americans were calling "Operation Iron Tempest." *Badal*, the Pashtun tribal concept of revenge, required the Barakzai to step up their use of IEDs in Helmand. His sister, her husband, and their three small children had been avenged. The tribe had sent six Americans and two British soldiers home in coffins the following week.

The American poppy field eradication programs and their chemical herbicide spraying efforts had only turned more of the populace against them. Why were the Americans so intent on destroying a crop that produced something wanted and consumed in the West? The Americans were so easily manipulated by the warlords and local government officials who passed the soldiers information on their competition. It only exacerbated the war. Villages and families that owed the local warlords protection money for the opium crop now had to pay in other ways, which meant picking up an AK to fight rival warlords and the Americans. Mohambar thought the Americans had invaded his country to fight the Arabs. Then why did they open up a second front and decide to spend years at war with opium farmers? Didn't they see that only made the Taliban and al-Qaeda stronger? With all their technology and the satellites and aircraft that Mohambar had been told could watch him from space, the Americans remained blind to the ways of the Afghan.

The campaign for wheat harvesting to replace poppy cultivation as a mainstay of Afghan farming only succeeded in pushing poppy farming to other areas. Poppy seeds had now returned to the defunct wheat fields and production had flourished thanks to the American investment of wells and irrigation systems. How the Americans could build machines that rained death from the skies but fail so miserably in their efforts on the ground was a mystery to Mohambar. The British, Soviets, and Americans had all tried and failed to occupy and exploit Afghanistan. Whoever came next, they would fail, too. His village chief had told them that the Americans were looking for a Saudi who had helped Mohambar's parents and grandparents fight the Soviets. He had said that eventually the Americans would tire of losing their children to ambushes and roadside bombs. The elder had been right. The Americans had left. The night raids were a thing of the past. Order had been restored. Sharia law was reinstated, and justice was swift. The Taliban were back in charge, and as long as the village provided them with 20 percent of the opium profits there was nothing to fear.

Mohambar's journey began outside of Lashkar Gah, southwest of Kandahar, in a truck provided by his brother-in-law. He was afforded safe passage to Delaram in Farah province, where he took the Zaranj–Delaram Highway through Nimruz province on one of the most well-traveled roads in the country.

Some opium operation syndicates needed to avoid the Iranian border checkpoints. Iran was serious about opium headed to their cities. Punishments were harsh for users, dealers, and the smugglers who dealt in the illicit trade. Iran had a heroin addiction problem, and they were determined to stop it. But Mohambar did not have to worry about border guards or Iranian drug enforcement operations. His opium was headed elsewhere, with the full knowledge of the Iranian government and their enforcers in the Republican Guard. Mohambar's load was headed south, to the port of Chabahar on the Gulf of Oman. From there the opium would be transferred onto a ship, which would travel through the Arabian Sea, the Gulf of Aden, and into the Red Sea, where the Suez Canal led to the Mediterranean Sea and into the veins of the West. Iran was using Afghan poppies to poison America and her European NATO allies. Money paved the way. Mohambar had heard that the Republican Guard and Quds Force used revenue from the illicit movement of opium to fund their operations against Israel out of the Bekaa Valley. Allah truly worked in mysterious ways.

Mohambar crossed at Zaranj into Baluchestan province, Iran. The Iranian border guard examined his paperwork and waved him through. That a truck from the Republican Guard was waiting nearby, watching the interaction, ensured the process was smooth and efficient. As per his standard operating procedure, Mohambar pulled to the side of the road, allowing his new Iranian escort to lead him into Iran. Minutes later, a few miles south of Malik, the truck slowed and turned onto a dirt road. Mohambar followed, as was the custom, until they arrived at a dirt parking area well off the main thoroughfare. Mohambar swung wide in his Mercedes, then turned left and brought the truck to a halt next to a similar-sized Scania. He then shut down his rig, opened the door, and climbed down onto Iranian soil to stretch his legs.

Normally Mohambar would inspect the new truck and trailer, glance at the paperwork, confirm its destination, and be on his way. Today was different.

Instead of refined petroleum, wire, cereal, cork, or glass bottles that corresponded with the bill of lading, there were multiple documents stamped by the Islamic Emirate of Afghanistan.

Mohambar looked at the colonel who handed him the folder.

"Textiles. To Kandahar?"

"No, to Khoshab. Do you know it?"

"I have never been there."

"It is programmed into the GPS in the truck. Can you use one?"

"Yes, I am a driver."

"Good. Drive straight through. You are fully fueled. No stopping. Do not inspect the load."

"Of textiles?"

"Yes."

"Who is the receiver?"

"The Islamic Emirate of Afghanistan."

"I see."

Why did the colonel seem nervous? He was Republican Guard. There was no reason for him to be nervous.

"May I inspect the vehicle?"

"Of course."

Mohambar walked around the Scania. It was already running. He had driven them many times before. This one was about twenty years old but looked almost new. Someone had taken good care of her. The detachable semitrailer was hooked up to the tractor unit and also appeared to be in good shape.

"Locked?" he said, looking at the padlock that secured the doors of the trailer.

"Yes. That paperwork will get you through any inspections. The receiver does not expect you to have the key."

Mohambar nodded. What could he do? He was the driver, and although this was a little unusual, his job was to drive and deliver cargo.

"Follow that vehicle back to the border," the colonel said, pointing to one of his camouflaged trucks.

Mohambar nodded in deference and touched his hand to his heart. He made his way to the driver's-side door and pulled himself into the rig. The GPS was set and the route was active. The sooner he got to Khoshab, the sooner he would be back to his wife and baby girl. If it got too late, he could pull over and rest in the small sleeper compartment behind his seat after he dropped off the load. He would either get in late tonight or surprise them in the morning.

It was time to get going.

As he pulled out of the parking area and onto the dirt road that would connect him to A-71 to the border, he looked in the tall side-view mirrors. The truck he had delivered was being inspected by the driver who would take it the remainder of the way to Chabahar. The opium that had started as seeds nourished by the wells and irrigation ditches installed by the Americans would soon begin its voyage toward Europe and North America, contributing to the further decay of the West.

What was locked in the back of the trailer?

It didn't matter. He was a driver. Whatever it was belonged to the Islamic Emirate of Afghanistan. It would soon be delivered, and Mohambar would be on his way home.

He took one more glance in the mirror before turning out of the parking area. The colonel was standing there staring at him. He didn't stop until Mohambar had made the turn and disappeared in a cloud of dust.

CHAPTER 6

United States Penitentiary
Florence Administrative Maximum Facility
Range 13
Special Housing Unit
Fremont County, Colorado

MADNESS.

Darkness.

All life is suffering.

The letter.

Reece had read it so many times he had it memorized.

Where was it now?

Did Katie still have the key?

Where was the box?

Reece concentrated on his breathing and went back to the first time he had read the letter. A rainy night in a storage facility in Baltimore, Maryland. His father had left a key in an envelope with the address of the storage facility. Reece remembered inserting the key into the old Master Lock, feeling it pop open. He had inspected the roll-up door for IEDs and slowly pushed it upward. *Darkness.*

Reece had fished the small penlight from his pocket and pressed the tail cap switch to illuminate the inside of the storage unit, revealing empty shelving and a tarp-covered vehicle. Reece had taken it slow, looking for any signs of recent disturbance. The dust was helpful. When he pulled back the tarp his suspicions were confirmed, and he couldn't help but smile at the sight of his family's old 1985 Jeep Wagoneer. In its cargo area was a gun case containing a duckbill-modified Ithaca Model 37 shotgun, the weapon his father had carried as a point man in Vietnam, a safe-deposit box key, and a letter. He read it that first time via the LEDs of his tac light. He had read it many times since.

October 17, 2003

Dear James,

If you are reading this, then our time together was cut short.

They say you'll look back on your life and regret the things you didn't do. They are right. I regret I didn't spend more time with you and your mother. I thought we had all the time in the world. Should have known better, especially considering the path I chose. I knew those seconds were ticking by and that we would never get them back, but I always thought there would be more time in the future. Looks like I was wrong.

You grew up so fast, son. Too fast. I blinked and all of a sudden there you were, going off to war. Maybe it was like that for my dad, seeing me off for Vietnam. I wonder if he had regrets.

My days were numbered from the second I was born. All our days are numbered. Your days are numbered, too. Use them. Use them wisely.

Use the time you have, James. I've told you before, as fast as you are, even you can't outrun time. It has a nasty way of catching up with you. Trust me. I know. When you put down the gun, walk away. Don't live in the past. You've done your part. Love your wife. Raise your kids. And don't look back. Treasure each moment, because once it's gone, it's gone forever.

I tried to be present when I was home. I know I didn't always succeed. I hope you can forgive me. Writing this now, I am reflecting on our adventures diving in Hawaii, backpacking in the Sierras, hunting in Montana, and fishing in Colorado with your grandfather. Those memories warm my heart. If I could pass one thing on, be present with those you love. It's what they deserve. You can't save the world, but you can make sure your family knows you love them unconditionally and that they are your world. Concentrate on them.

I could not be prouder of the man you have become. And, though I might not act like it, I worry. Service was in your blood, but remember, being a SEAL is not who you are. It's a part of you, but you are more than that, son. When the time comes to put down the sword, don't look back. Look ahead. Move forward.

Watching you graduate from BUD/S was one of the proudest moments of my life. I also worry that those sending you into the conflict in which we are currently engaged don't know their ass from a hole in the ground. Too many similarities between the war on terror and my war. I pray Afghanistan and Iraq do not go the way of Vietnam. I pray those with the stars on their collars have studied their history.

Now to the point of this letter. Use your judgment, but if I ended up dying in a way you deem suspicious—suicide, drug overdose, car accident—it was to keep something quiet, something I have been investigating since the mid-'70s. This letter is also your "out." Details and evidence from my investigation are locked in a safe-deposit box. The accompanying key fits that box. The bank has your name and mine as the only two people who can access it. It's paid in full until 2030 through a trust set up by an attorney who specializes in such things. On January 1st, 2030, everything in that box will be destroyed.

The safe-deposit box will not be easy to find. Only one other person knows of its existence. In case it's not you reading this letter, said person is not named. You will need to find him, or he will need to find you.

I hate to put this on you, son. That's one of the reasons for this "out." It might be better for all if you don't find it. If you do, and you think the world is better off not knowing what's in there—burn it. Burn it all. And then live your life knowing you did the right thing. Never look back. But, depending on what has happened in these intervening years, when you go through the documents, when you see the list, do what you think is right.

I don't have the answer. I can't tell you what to do. Just know I support whatever decision you make. There is not a "right" one, believe me. I have been struggling with it for over two decades. Even when you open it, there is one piece that as of this writing remains missing. One link that remains elusive. I couldn't find it. And since you are reading this, that means I never did.

Powerful people and organizations will do anything to keep what's in that box from seeing the light of day.

Watch your back, son. Don't forget what I taught you. JDLR—if something "Just Doesn't Look Right," it's probably not.

And remember, trust no one.

By the time you find this, if you've found it, the time for mourning me has long since passed. Know that I am facing what's next with strength, humility, and grace, or as much grace as I can muster. I want you to think about something my father told me. If you recall, he wasn't much for words, which made what he said even more poignant. I think in his mind he was still living through the Pacific Campaign of World War II, fighting across the beaches and into the jungles, island by island, on his way to Japan. He told me shortly before he died that "death is not a destination—it's a doorway." He knew death was coming for him, and he wasn't afraid. Death is a doorway, son. I'll see you on the other side.

You will always have the faith that your mother and I instilled in you. Let it teach you hope and guide your future path.

I'll be watching over you. Godspeed. I love you.

Strength and Honor.

Always,
Thomas Reece

"I love you too, Dad."

I know, son.

"I am going to get out of here."

You will.

"I'll find that box."

A part of me prays you will not.

"I . . ."

A sound Reece had not heard before echoed off the walls of his cell.

"Prisoner B549. Lie facedown on the floor, cross your legs, and place your hands behind your back."

CHAPTER 7

The Residence at Cape Idokopas
Krasnodar Krai, Russia

A NUCLEAR DEVICE? HAD the chairman gone mad? Had the president?

Dashkov leaned back in his chair to contemplate what he had just been told.

"We are going to detonate an Iranian nuclear weapon in Israel and pull the Americans back into the Middle East."

There had always been a fine line between madness and genius.

"The Americans remain the only country on earth to use offensive nuclear weapons," Kozak said. "We came close to an exchange over Cuba in 1962, and the world has no idea how close to the brink we were in 1983. If not for this council and for our collective associates in the United States, the world would still be dealing with the aftereffects of a nuclear winter."

"Just to be clear, comrade," Dashkov began. "We plan to draw the United States into a hot war with Iran by detonating a nuclear device in Israel?"

Kozak nodded.

"And what of the Russian Jews in Israel?"

"Has all your good living made you soft, comrade?"

"It is only a question, Chairman Kozak."

"As with Stalingrad and Leningrad in the Great Patriotic War, sacrifices for Mother Russia are expected. The U.S. and Israel will destroy Iran. It will not be easy, but they will prevail and rid the world of the Iranian nuclear issue. But they are no longer strong enough to fight a two-front, and certainly not a three-front, war. They will shift all efforts to defeating Iran. When they do, we push through Ukraine and China will annex Taiwan."

"And our relationship with Iran plays directly into the narrative. Brilliant," Levitsky stated.

Had they all gone mad? Keep your cards close.

"The devil being in the details, how will we proceed?" Dashkov asked, careful not to betray his skepticism.

"Though not without risks, we are favorably positioned to instigate a shift in the established world order. We are conveniently dumped into an 'axis of evil' by the United States and NATO: Russia, China, North Korea, and Iran are almost preprogrammed into the Western parlance as ideological opposites—enemies of the West. U.S. talks with Iran to revive their 2015 nuclear deal are all but dead. The American politicians can lie to themselves and to their citizens all they want, but they are a nation in decline. All the signs are there. They have given up on national sovereignty, weaponized their justice system, politicized their military, and lost faith in their elections. As the president has stated publicly, we are on the cusp of a historic shift in the world order—a multipolar world order. Our political and military alliance with Iran only strengthens our position. We are using their drone technology in Ukraine with devastating results. They have drone pilots in Ukraine now just as we have advisors with the Republican Guard. They are one of our staunchest allies in the eyes of the West."

"In the eyes of the West," Dashkov echoed.

"You seem troubled, Comrade Dashkov."

"This seems to bear the hallmarks of what was dubbed a false-flag operation at the start of the Dagestan operation over twenty years ago."

"By your agency."

"When you ran it," Dashkov reminded him.

"Rogue elements, comrade. And admittedly incompetent. It is now time for bold adjustments."

"I understand the intent. A nuclear device detonated by Iran on Israeli soil, or even close to Israeli soil, triggers an attack by Israel on Iran."

"They will have no choice," Kozak offered.

"True," Dashkov continued, "the U.S. will probably come to their aid militarily."

"Not 'probably,' director. It is certain."

"Nothing is certain, chairman."

"In this case it is. The Collective has positioned someone to ensure this to be the outcome. They will be drawn into yet another war in the Middle East, though this one will not be limited in scope. The Middle East will erupt in conflict. Oil prices will skyrocket. Our gas and oil deals with China and Europe will make Russia the world's leading supplier of energy."

Dashkov wondered why the chairman was being so cryptic, but in the world of espionage, secrets were part of the game particularly when it came to the Collective.

"And the United States will not be able to sustain its military or financial support of Ukraine," Dashkov said, articulating the logical intent of the operation.

"Nor will they be able to repel a Chinese invasion of Taiwan," Kozak added. "They will lose their microchip and semiconductor trading partner as China positions itself as the world leader in the technology sector."

"And Russia and China become dominant superpowers in a new multipolar world," Levitsky finished. "I amend my previous statement; it's more than brilliant."

"And Iran?" Dashkov asked.

"There is no room for Iran in the new world order, at least not as a superpower. Iran is sacrificed to propel a Sino-Russian alliance to the top of the pecking order. Energy, pharmaceuticals, technology—the United States will be reliant upon us for their very survival."

"There is a flaw," Dashkov said.

"Oh?"

"All plutonium has a signature. It will be traced back to us. If the West proves that it was a Russian nuclear weapon that detonated in Israel, the United States may respond in kind against Mother Russia."

"With our nuclear arsenals, capability, and capacity, it is still mutually assured destruction," Kozak responded. "And, though I disagree with your assessment on the American response that if Russian plutonium were indeed discovered through nuclear forensics it could be countered with the convenient 'misinformation' moniker—the president brought up that very point."

"And?"

"And that is why the weapon will not be made using Russian plutonium. To successfully draw the United States into war, a nuclear forensic investigation must conclude the weapon was of Iranian origin deliberately targeting Israel."

"And just how are we going to do that?" Dashkov asked.

"We are going to build a bomb using Iranian plutonium."

"And where will we get this Iranian plutonium?"

"We are going to steal it."

CHAPTER 8

Khoshab Village
Kandahar Province, Afghanistan

SLAVIK DEYNEKIN WAITED IMPATIENTLY in the darkness. He looked down at the small tablet that showed a blue dot moving along Route A75. He watched as it pulled off the main road at Mandisar and began to work its way closer to Deynekin's position in an abandoned compound just west of Ahmad Shah Baba International Airport, more commonly referred to as Kandahar International Airport. The blue dot was a tracking device that had been secured to the outside of a truck that was inbound from Iran. Another tracking device was installed on the outside of a crate in the trailer section of the vehicle. What was inside the crate had the potential to change the world.

He tapped his wrist with his index finger.

"Ten minutes," he said to the men gathered around the Hilux trucks.

Ten minutes.

Deynekin kicked the dirt at his feet and watched the dust rise into a night illuminated by headlights. He couldn't recall ever seeing a darker sky. Without a moon, the stars were brilliant.

Fucking Afghanistan.

Afghanistan had not been his war. He was only two when his father was killed here. He wondered if the father he never knew had set foot on Kandahar airfield. Probably. Here or Bagram. He briefly wondered if his father had been flown home to Russia on a Black Tulip out of Kandahar. Not that it mattered. He had drawn his last breath here, his life stolen from him by the Islamist savages of the Hindu Kush. It warmed Deynekin's heart every time he put one in the dirt.

With a father dead in an unpopular war in a country with an economy in free fall, Deynekin's mother had worked from the predawn hours late into the day on her shift at Magnitogorsk Iron and Steel Works. Located at the southern edge of the Ural Mountains, Magnitogorsk was built around the Soviet concept of *Sotsgorod*, with housing built in proximity to work in order to increase steel production value for the state. It would be years until young Slavik realized that the "uncles" who knocked on the door to their state housing complex each evening were more than coworkers from the factory. Though he had often wondered about the odd sounds coming from his mother's room in their small two-bedroom flat, he had never heard her scream the way she did on a winter night not long after Slavik turned ten. When he opened the door that cold night, a man had turned toward him. To the young boy, in the ambient light from the hallway, it looked like the man's eyes were on fire. He had then twisted back and hit his mom again before pushing himself off the mattress. Deynekin could still see the perspiration on his face, his big hairy body bearing down on him, the sharp sting of the first slap, then the barrage of punches that forced Deynekin to the tile floor, the man's knee on his chest forcing the air from his lungs. His mother's scream sounded different now. Deynekin would hear screams like that again when he cut his teeth in the Second Chechen War a decade later with the 76th Guards Air Assault Division. They were screams of rage. Then the punching stopped and an eerie silence replaced the violent grunts that had exploded above him with each hit. When Deynekin eventually crawled out from under the heavy body, he was covered in blood. But it was the sight of his mother, battered and bruised, her stomach, breasts, and face also covered in blood, that stayed with him. Her eyes were empty. The knife remained in her hand even when Deynekin tried to help her sit on the bed. She still had it in her hand when the police arrived. They removed the kitchen blade from her grasp and handcuffed her without offering her clothes. Deynekin would never see her again. He became a ward of the state. An orphan. When he was twelve, he was summoned to an office at the orphanage. There a man told him that his mother was dead, that she had died of a disease she had caught from sleeping with all those men. At eighteen he enlisted in the military.

His first taste of combat had been seizing the Chechen town of Urus-Martan in December 1999. Deynekin and his fellow soldiers had been ordered to mop up anyone who had not fled the city, located on the outskirts of Grozny, the Chechen capital. All that were left were terrorists and insurgents. Their bodies filled mass graves dug into the frozen ground by Russian tractors. He remembered the elation of seizing the airport in Khankala to establish a base of operations from which to lay siege to the capital. The chaos, the cold, and the killing rekindled memories of the night his mother had saved his life. By the middle of February the Russians regained control of Grozny, but terrorist attacks persisted. It was during the hunt for the Islamist dogs who escaped the siege that Deynekin noticed units of men in black and green fatigues using weapons and equipment that seemed different from what Deynekin and his paratroopers were issued. He learned these units were special teams of the FSB's Spetsgruppa "A." They specialized in hunting down terrorists and collaborators in their homes, killing them in front of their families. The work was natural for Deynekin. Violence was hardwired into his system. It kept him warm.

Eight years later he would be tested once again, this time as a mid-level operator in the FSB's Alpha Group in the Russo-Georgian War. High command made no distinction between the terrorists and their families who harbored them. Deynekin was particularly adept at hunting. He knew families were the soft targets. They could be used to the advantage of Mother Russia. He had heard that the European Union Commission had called what he had done in South Ossetia "ethnic cleansing," which in no way bothered him. Those who harbored terrorists were just as guilty as the terrorists themselves. It had taken the International Criminal Court fourteen years to issue his arrest warrant. What did The Hague know of the brutality of combat? They too were the enemies of Russia. And to try him, they first had to catch him.

In 2014 his FSB Spetsgruppa "A" was charged with hunting down, questioning, and killing problem Crimean Tatars. His thirty-man Alpha Group unit was broken down into five-man hunter-killer teams, of which Deynekin's was the most adept. It was in the midst of the international outrage and condemnation of the war to defend Crimea that Deynekin's team was recruited by a new paramilitary organization with direct links to the president called the Wagner Group.

Syria, Libya, the Central African Republic, Sudan, and Mali followed, with Deynekin's star rising within the organization. *Alone you will kill the ferocious snake, on Gnitahade he lies, insatiable.* Deynekin now led Task Force Rusich, a special operations unit within Wagner. The unit was formed as the Diversionary Guerrilla Reconnaissance Group Rusich and trained to initiate false-flag operations in the Donbas region of Ukraine when Deynekin was still in Alpha Group. As with the operations for which they were trained, the Rusich moniker evoked multiple mythologies in a pedigree chart with links to a Norse medieval fortress, a video game whose hero was an eighth-century military leader who defended Russia from German and Swedish invaders, and the ROSICH 7th Russian Special Forces, from which the elite units of Wagner recruited. Though Western propaganda campaigns liked to associate Wagner and specifically Task Force Rusich with neo-Nazis and ultranationalists, to Deynekin it was a way to defend his country and protect the memory of his mother.

Regardless of the country, Russian prostitutes were never hard to find. Deynekin would always treat them with the utmost respect, overpaying for their services. A new Rusich recruit had bragged of almost choking a Russian prostitute to death in a hotel in Mali. Deynekin had beaten him to within an inch of his life and banned him from the organization. If one's fetishes included brutalizing Russian prostitutes, it was best to ensure Deynekin remained unaware. Ukrainian collaborators and hookers from Africa, the Middle East, or Eastern Europe, however, were fair game. Rape, torture, and executions were part of the Wagner Group's standard operating procedure. Deynekin's Task Force Rusich had built a reputation on a foundation of terror in and out of Russia. Posting mutilated dead bodies and burned corpses on social media helped solidify their standing. The ultranationalist leanings of their founders played well in the Western press but mattered little to Deynekin. Doing the work of the Kremlin for the advancement of Mother Russia, killing her enemies as had his mother, that was what Deynekin was born to do. A defender of the homeland by the most brutal of means.

"Adrik!" Deynekin yelled to summon the most junior member of the team.

"*Da*, comrade."

"Is the device ready?"

"It is."

"Good. Be alert," he reminded his lieutenant. Their security element from Taliban Bardi 313 Battalion was not to be trusted. They were standing next to their HMMWVs left behind by the Americans and were armed with suppressed M4s also abandoned by the Americans in their ill-conceived retreat from Afghanistan. It amused Deynekin to listen to Western pundits talk about the slow progress in Ukraine asserting that the Russian military was not nearly as strong as had been projected, when the U.S. military had had their asses handed to them by a bunch of barefoot, illiterate savages with AKs and IEDs for twenty years.

Deynekin had briefed his team on a contingency that required them to kill each and every one of their Taliban escorts. Half of his element was focused on the primary mission of securing the package. The other half had predetermined Taliban targets should things go south. *Fucking savages. Always have a plan to kill them all.*

Adrik nodded his head in respect and moved back behind the headlights.

Deynekin looked back at the tablet. It was almost time.

"Two minutes," he called.

He heard the rumble of the diesel engine at the same time headlights illuminated the open wooden gate of the compound.

Only Deynekin was aware of the contents of the crate. The other members of his unit just knew their mission was of the highest priority. Their orders were to take possession of the package and escort it back to Russia.

Soon this phase of the operation would be over and Deynekin would be flying out of the same airfield from which the body of his father had flown.

CHAPTER 9

MOHAMBAR RANJHA FOLLOWED THE GPS and turned off the dirt road and into the compound, shielding his eyes from the high beams emanating from a row of vehicles facing him in the middle of the large mud structure. He applied the brakes and brought the truck to a stop.

I'm in the right place.

He shut off his lights and rolled down his window.

"Hello?" he shouted over the rumbling of the diesel. "Shut down here?"

After a brief pause the reply came in Pashtu: "Turn around so your trailer is facing the lights."

"Sahee da." Okay.

Mohambar put the truck in reverse, rolled back a few meters, and then pulled forward to the left, expertly turning the vehicle around so the front end was facing the entrance that had now been closed behind him. He noted with growing concern the number of Toyota trucks and American-made HMMWVs that put his rig in the middle of an L.

He turned the key to shut down the engine, opened the door, and dropped down to the dirt of the abandoned compound.

Two members of the Afghan Armed Forces approached. Mohambar noted that they did not wear the uniforms he had observed on regular Islamic Emirate Armed Forces soldiers. These men wore the tiger-stripe pattern of the special forces. They were Bardi 313 Battalion. Their faces were covered by tan balaclavas under green helmets topped with night vision courtesy of the Americans, as were their M4 rifles and optics. What on earth was in his truck?

"*Maakhaam mo pa kheyr*," Mohambar said in greeting. *Good evening.*

"*Staa num tsa dhe?*" asked the taller soldier. *What is your name?*

"I am Mohambar Ranjha, from Lashkar Gah."

"Open the back."

"I was told you would have a key," Mohambar said in Pashtu as he began walking to the rear of the vehicle.

The smaller of the two men stepped forward and produced a set of bolt cutters from a pouch on his back. His partner raised the muzzle of his rifle and hit a light attached to its rail. The bolt cutters made short work of the steel shackle, removing what was left of it from the door and dropping it to the ground. The taller man turned back to the headlights that illuminated them from about twenty meters away.

Why are they standing so far back? Can't they see I am not a threat?

Mohambar saw another man standing by a Hilux swing his left hand upward.

"Open it," the soldier said.

"Yes, yes, of course," Mohambar replied, already pulling the narrow step-down from the bed. He pushed on the roll-up door and climbed into the trailer, shoving the door the remainder of the way up and peering deeper into the trailer.

A trunk? That's it?

"Just a crate!" Mohambar yelled back.

"Open it and show us what's inside," the soldier ordered.

"This is not a problem, my friend," Mohambar said, rubbing his sweating palms against his *perahan tunban*, the loose-fitting cotton dress beneath his wool vest.

Mohambar walked into the trailer.

"It's locked," he called back.

A silhouette appeared in the high beams and the man with the bolt cutters approached.

"Move," he said, taking a knee to gain better access to the second padlock.

Mohambar heard the snap of the steel shank separating.

"Open it," the soldier said.

The top of the crate swung open, exposing another box within.

The Afghan soldier indicated that Mohambar should continue.

The lid was much heavier than Mohambar expected.

Was this thing made of lead?

The soldier depressed the button on the back of his weapon's mounted light, exposing another box inside the first.

"Continue," he ordered.

Mohambar reached inside to open the second box. This lid was heavy, too. Why was he sweating so much?

The soldier raised his weapon to direct the light inside, revealing what Mohambar had smuggled in from Iran.

Three cylindrical rods that Mohambar guessed to be about twenty-five centimeters in length by seven or eight centimeters in width were set into a hard foam. In the light they appeared to be a slightly yellowing gray.

Though he didn't know why, Mohambar whispered a prayer to Allah.

"What's inside?" a soldier called from outside the vehicle.

"Three rods," the operator responded.

"Show us," came a reply from beyond the headlights.

Though his instinct was to shut the box and run, Mohambar knew he had no choice. He reached inside and removed a rod from its place and walked to the back of the vehicle, holding it up to the headlights. It was oddly warm, something that Mohambar attributed to being locked in the crate all day.

"Put it back in and close the box," came the order in Pashto.

Mohambar did as he was told and then walked to the open roll-up door at the rear of the truck with the soldier and climbed to the ground.

He stepped aside as a contingent of Afghan special forces soldiers clambered aboard and began moving the crate to the rear of the trailer.

Mohambar observed as they struggled to get it out of his truck and carry it to a waiting Hilux.

They returned with a smaller box, climbed back into the trailer, and secured it with a cargo strap to the floor.

"What do I do with that?" Mohambar asked.

"It will stay with the vehicle and eventually make its way back to Iran."

Mohambar nodded. He knew better than to ask further questions. He had heard rumors of the Bardi 313 Battalion, named for the 313 men of the Prophet Muhammad's fighters at the Battle of Badr. Mohambar wanted nothing more to do with them.

Only the soldiers' eyes were visible through the balaclava, and they suggested it was time for Mohambar to leave.

"*Makha de gulunah*," Mohambar said by way of good-bye.

As Mohambar shut the roll-up door and climbed back up to the cab of his truck, he forced himself to think of his wife and baby girl to take his mind off the fact that he couldn't stop sweating.

• • •

Deynekin watched the Afghans open the compound gates and heard the truck start up.

He looked back at the radiation detector in his hand. A wearable personal dosimeter, it had never registered over 0.1 gray, an international radiation measurement unit. This was well below the daily limit of whole-body radiation exposure. For the driver who had held the plutonium rod and the Afghan soldier who had opened the box, that was another story.

Plutonium 239. Iranian. A by-product from one of their nuclear reactors, it was quite stable and nontoxic if handled properly. It had not been handled properly by the smuggler. Even though Deynekin had been briefed that he and his men would be safe from the alpha particles the rods emitted, he was still skeptical. Russia had its own plutonium. Why were they surreptitiously taking it from the Iranians via Afghanistan? One thing that the mercenary knew for certain was that Pu-239 was used to make nuclear weapons.

With the package secured, it was time to exfil. Well, not quite.

"Adrik," Deynekin said to his subordinate. He slid the radiation detector back into his cargo pocket and held out his hand.

Adrik handed him the remote detonator, a small device that looked like a key fob.

Deynekin pressed the button.

A fireball erupted from the road outside the compound wall and rose skyward, the high-pressure gases climbing toward the heavens before being enveloped in a dark cloud of smoke.

"Load up. Let's get to the airfield and out of this shithole," Deynekin told his second-in-command. "But be ready: These savages will turn on us in a heartbeat."

Adrik went to get a head count and coordinate with their Afghan escorts. With any luck they wouldn't have to kill them all. Deynekin's crew still needed to get to the airport and out of Afghanistan. That path would be smoother if paved with bribes rather than with bodies, but the Wagner Group man was prepared for either contingency. Deynekin looked to the stars, cleared his throat, and then spat into the Afghan dirt.

It was time to get back to Russia.

CHAPTER 10

Longworth House Office Building
Washington, D.C.

CONGRESSMAN DOUGLAS LINDEN LEANED forward in the brown leather chair that was too big for his second-floor office in the Longworth House Office Building. He sat in one of the 251 offices housed in a structure that dated back to 1933 and continued to feign interest in what the pharmaceutical lobbyist across the desk was saying. Linden couldn't get rid of him too quickly, nor did he want to spend any more time with this smooth-talking weasel than was absolutely necessary. He had *actual* business to attend to that required his attention.

Linden had been in Congress long enough to know that it was all a game: the lying, the doublespeak, the favors, the insider trading. Family members of several high-profile politicians had recently been caught red-handed taking millions of dollars from foreign governments—governments hostile to the United States—as compensation for manufactured jobs for which they had no qualifications, and Congress had, for the most part, remained silent. As Linden knew, everyone was in on the hustle.

The congressman's mind was elsewhere, but an election was looming, and although he felt secure, one could not trust the polls these days.

That his constituency supported not having to show identification to vote favored his chances of retaining his seat, but one really never knew. Voting machines, mail-in ballots, ballot harvesting, no identification—who would have thought? Certainly not his father, an old OSS hand in the Second World War. Linden was not about to say what he thought was obvious. If you wanted to make elections more secure, you would get rid of the machines and require identification to vote. A government-issued ID was required to open a bank account, rent an apartment, apply for a job, buy a car, travel on a plane, purchase a firearm, or buy a six-pack. If someone in his position spoke the obvious truth, they would be destroyed by the Twitter mobs calling you a racist and a fascist. Linden could only smile. He was more than happy to take multiple votes from the same person; hell, he'd take votes from the deceased. What was it that Stalin had said about voting? *The people who cast the votes don't decide an election. What is extraordinarily important is this: who will count the votes, and how.* Something like that, anyway. The country was done for. How votes were counted, and which votes were counted, were more important than legal votes being counted. Negating your neighbor's vote was okay if they were voting for the wrong party. It was all about power. Luckily for Linden, his party seemed to be doing most of the counting.

One would think the downward spiral of his once-great country would concern the congressman, but it did not. It was inevitable, even necessary. The world had always been controlled by the few, the privileged, the bold. Allegiances to country, oaths, patriotic speeches—these were all for show. He still needed his congressional seat, though. At least for now. It added the illusion of legitimacy.

His father had died of COVID. Or was it *with* COVID? Regardless, Linden had leveraged it for political gain. It was before the vaccines had become readily available. The old man probably would have refused to take them anyway. *Tough old bastard.* He had been too busy working on his memoirs. On the old man's deathbed Linden had promised that he would publish them. The night he passed away, Linden had fed all 1,046 typed pages into the fire. He had already read them. The Philby years in D.C. had been particularly interesting.

The man across the table was exceedingly irritating, even for a lobbyist. The congressman had to be reminded of his name by his secretary just prior to the meeting. Karson Ash was an attorney, though Linden knew he had never practiced law. He received his degree from some second- or third-rate law school and found a home hustling lawmakers on Capitol Hill. He was currently employed by Pepperdine Pharmaceuticals, a company trying desperately to climb out of bankruptcy after being hit with civil and criminal investigations by the Justice Department for its role in the opioid epidemic. Linden seemed to recall he was from Arkansas, or was it Arizona? Didn't matter. He and parasites like him were accelerating the demise of America, a cancer destroying the country from within.

Ash's company, and the family that owned it, were responsible for almost half a million deaths over the past twenty years. Linden would still take their money, which is why he sat there pretending to listen. How did this guy manage to sleep at night? Linden could self-fund his campaign many times over, but that money, the dark money, the generational wealth, was hidden, as he knew it was for a handful of those in power. Those with allegiances to something greater than the country they served, regardless of what they muttered when they put their hand on the Bible, were quite astute at concealing assets.

Almost two decades younger than the congressman, Ash could have served his country after it was attacked on 9/11 but instead chose to let others do his fighting. His eyes seemed to be in a distracting permanent squint that only accentuated the broken blood vessels that betrayed a fondness for drink.

"Allowing just anyone to speak freely on Twitter has had a direct correlation to vaccine hesitancy, particularly for parents and their children. The numbers show that of those who got their kids the first shot, almost none have returned for boosters. That is impacting our bottom line and could negatively affect the budget for campaign contributions."

This spineless fuck and his ilk were swimming in profits, and it was the United States government that had become their de facto marketing department. COVID had been the lifeline Pepperdine Pharmaceuticals needed to pull themselves out from the depths of the legal repercussions of the opioid crisis they created. They might survive after all *if* protections remained in place to shield them from vaccine-related lawsuits. Profits became campaign donations, and the machine kept spinning.

"Do you know what Truman said about censorship?" Linden asked.

"Spare me, Congressman; this isn't about censorship, it's about *misinformation.*"

"Ah yes, misinformation. Well, for posterity's sake, he said, 'Once a government is committed to the principle of silencing the voice of opposition, it has only one way to go, and that is down the path of increasingly repressive measures, until it becomes a source of terror to all its citizens and creates a country where everyone lives in fear.' The benefits of going to Andover," Linden added.

"They didn't have the Internet in Truman's day, Congressman. My company, a company devoted to developing lifesaving vaccines, must be protected from lawsuits. You've seen what your party has done to the gun industry by pushing for lawsuits against the manufacturers of firearms used in shootings. Imagine holding Ford responsible for Chappaquiddick. They would be out of business."

"It was an Oldsmobile, and they are out of business."

"You get my point. If that happens to the pharmaceutical industry, the deaths associated with citizens *not* getting the shots they need and my company *not* being able to research and conduct testing would destroy the country and possibly the world as we know it."

"A touch melodramatic."

"I don't think so, Congressman. Just imagine—no insulin, no penicillin, no Viagra."

Even Linden had to laugh. If nothing else, this kid was smooth.

"The tactic is working. The gun industry is going bankrupt from lawsuits. That could happen to us, and if it does, the campaign donations will dry up."

"Your position is that the pharmaceutical industry is different than the gun industry and should be immune from lawsuits?"

"Of course we are different. We *save* lives. The gun industry takes them."

"Then why don't we allow lawsuits against kitchen knife companies or baseball bat companies? Those items are used in more murders than guns."

The lobbyist's eyes narrowed even further, making Linden uncomfortable.

How can he even see through those slits?

"The firearms industry makes weapons of war. Those weapons should only be allowed in the hands of authorized federal law enforcement agencies and the military."

"Certainly convenient for the government," Linden said, toying with the young lobbyist. "Especially if we need to enforce vaccine mandates."

"What happens when the next virus hits our shores, Congressman? And Pepperdine Pharmaceuticals is not there to create a vaccine? What then? The blood will be on your hands, Congressman."

"Ah yes, my constituents are clamoring for those boosters."

Ash sighed but pressed on. "As long as it remains an emergency-use drug, my company, all the companies working for the safety of the American people, are protected from unfounded lawsuits."

"You truly are our first line of defense," Linden said, the sarcasm evident in his tone.

"Thank you. And if we want to continue to fight this devastating virus, we must retain our immunity from litigation. That means, once the drug is approved, it must also be *recommended* for children."

"Or you are opened up to those *frivolous* lawsuits when the emergency use authorization expires."

"That's right."

"I was an attorney as well, Mr. Ash."

"I am well aware of your remarkable résumé, sir," Ash said, nodding at the congressman's "I Love Me" wall. "Thank you for your service."

"No, thank you for yours."

"I didn't serve, sir. Bad knee."

"Of course. I've forgotten. I hope it's not giving you too much trouble."

"What?"

"Your knee."

"Oh yes, it still acts up on me, but I'll manage."

"Of course you will. Your talents are much better spent fighting for the ability of all Americans to protect their most precious of gifts with your vaccines and boosters."

"Sir?"

"Their very lives."

"That's right, sir."

"As you know, I have no direct authority over vaccine recommendations," Linden said.

"Not officially."

"The Advisory Committee on Immunization Practices will make their recommendations to the CDC. The CDC will then recommend your drug for children."

"Which I am sure they will," Ash said in a way that indicated he already knew the recommendation was forthcoming.

With enough money, anything was possible. It was all a game, after all.

"We see good things on the horizon for you, Congressman," Ash continued.

Linden stood. He had wasted enough time toying with this idiot.

"Thank you for your visit today, Mr. Ash. Rest assured you will have my support. It is only right that we protect our nation's most valuable resource—our children."

"With the right votes, your re-campaign can count on the support of Pepperdine Pharmaceuticals."

"Good day, Mr. Ash."

"Good day, sir."

Keep filling the coffers.

Linden watched the door close and then slowly spun around in his chair to look at the diplomas and award citations that adorned the wall of his office. Cambridge like his father. Harvard Law school. Six years as a Marine Corps JAG officer that included two deployments with USSOCOM, where he had earned a Bronze Star. That the award hanging behind the glass frame was absent a V device meant it was an administrative award, but to most of the people who read his online bio or passed through his office, a Bronze Star was a Bronze Star. They didn't know the difference. Then it was private law practice and a run for Congress. Even Linden had to admit, it was an impressive résumé.

His father had told him long ago that the American experiment was dying. From Linden's position it looked to be on life support, and it was only a matter of time until it was taken off. A "Do not resuscitate" order was in place for the formerly great nation. More power was being consolidated among the few, and those few owed an allegiance not to the country but to the very power that sustained them.

He had fielded two calls on his KryptAll secure phone earlier that morning. The first was from Sidney Morgan at Morgan Holdings, a Wall Street firm that had handled his father's finances and now handled the congressman's. Morgan was recommending moving money reserves to gold held in Cyprus and buying futures in the energy sector in increments of $1 million from the cryptocurrency accounts in Switzerland. These types of calls were not so much for approval as for notification. Linden knew that more secure calls were going out across the globe and that moving this much money meant that there was a bold move on the horizon. Hardly a soul had noticed when $100 million was shorted on energy stocks and moved just prior to 9/11, resulting in a $1.4 trillion market loss. That there was no mention of it in the 9/11 Commission Report told Linden just how much power the people his father had referred to as the "Collective" really wielded. While conspiracy theorists were distracted by meetings of the Bilderberg Group, the course of world history was being determined from the shadows.

The second call was of more concern. A longtime associate had called inquiring about the current disposition of a former SEAL and CIA operative named James Reece. Linden was a member of the House Permanent Select Committee on Intelligence and had developed numerous personal and professional relationships in the secret world over the years. Linden had discovered that the SEAL commander was locked away pending the results of an investigation. Why hadn't his arrest been made public? Why wasn't his face plastered all over the news?

The President's Commission on the Assassination of President Christensen was still investigating the events of three months earlier. Both sides of the aisle were using the assassination to gain political points with their constituents, further dividing an already tense nation. It was clear that the Army private who had fired shots at the president had been radicalized online by yet-to-be uncovered sources. There were those who said it was ISIS, others who said it was the Quds Force of the Republican Guard, some were convinced it was a conspiracy involving the CIA, FBI, and military, and still others pointed fingers inward at anti-establishment forces within the United States.

Very few people knew who was actually behind the assassination of President Christensen. Linden was one of the few.

He had been ordered to hold off on leaking James Reece's name to the press, which meant that although the operation had been a success, they had misjudged the actions Reece would take when cornered by law enforcement. Linden did not know why killing Reece was of such high importance; all he knew was that it was. That was enough. His father would have known. One day Linden would know, too. He was positioning himself for a presidential run, which made him valuable to his associates among the Collective.

President Olsen had not yet announced if she would run in the next election. Linden had to admit that she was doing a much better job than he had anticipated. Even those in his own party who loved nothing more than to tout gender, race, and sexual orientation as job qualifications had dismissed her as window dressing for a ticket to deliver her home state. The past three months had proven them wrong. She was actually looking like a strong contender in the next election cycle. His turn would come, in this election or the next. When it did, his would be the most well-funded campaign in the history of American politics. That his allegiance lay not with the United States but with a collective of global elites made the power that much more enticing. With allies in media, tech, pharmaceuticals, and defense, Linden was on a path not just to lead America but to control the destiny of the world.

CHAPTER 11

United States Penitentiary
Florence Administrative Maximum Facility
Range 13
Special Housing Unit
Fremont County, Colorado

THE FIRST DOOR TO roll back was a bit more muffled than the second.

Outer door.

Inner door.

He heard the movement of boots across the cement floor. A different sound than the boots on the gravel of his driveway in Montana the night they had taken him.

How many? Too difficult to tell. At least six.

Handcuffs were tightened around Reece's wrists and shackles were secured around his ankles. A bag was placed over his head, and he was lifted to his feet. After all his time in the cold he could feel the warmth of the guard's hands through his gloves.

Human contact.

Don't blame them, Reece. They are just doing their jobs.

Where have I heard that before?

They turned Reece around in the direction of the cell's entrance and ushered him forward. Still naked, he stumbled, the chains attached to his legs allowing him only to shuffle.

BUD/S shuffle.

Unlike the hands that had pulled him to his feet in Montana, these hands were not nearly as rough.

Interesting.

Get ready for questioning, Reece.

Waterboard?

Worse?

If it was a black site, probably worse.

Where was he? Texas, Florida, North Carolina? Where did the Agency hide their black sites on U.S. soil? Was he overseas and about to get worked over by interrogators from a host nation's intelligence service?

They paused at what Reece pictured in his mind might have been the end of a hallway. He heard another door roll open, and then another.

They should have muffled my ears like they did when they brought me in. Why didn't they?

The floor beneath his feet changed. Not quite as cold. Linoleum?

More doors. These were not on rollers. Actual doors.

Another door, another change to the material under his feet. Colder again.

Heavy smell of disinfectant.

Two strong hands found his arms, and someone else undid his cuffs.

Now is not the time to fight.

His hands were placed on what felt like a table in front of him and the shackles binding his legs were unlocked and removed.

"Do not move," a voice said over loudspeakers that echoed throughout the space.

Reece heard his minders moving out of the room behind him.

He heard the door close.

"Remove your hood."

Reece stood up straight and pulled the bag from his head.

At first he could not see anything.

Blinding.

He closed his eyes as tight as he could, bringing up his right hand to help shield them as his left steadied him against what he thought was a desk.

Take it slow, Reece.

He concentrated on his breathing and let his eyes adjust through shut eyelids.

Cautiously, he peered through one and then the other.

The desk in front of him was actually a short four-foot wall behind which were four showerheads. He turned and saw a bench and a set of folded hospital scrubs.

Water began to flow from one of the showerheads. Reece looked around the room. Sterile. Whites and blues.

A bar of soap and toenail clippers were next to the scrubs.

I guess it's time to clean up.

He looked down at his hands and arms. Pale.

He reached down, picked up the bar of soap, and made his way to the spraying water, testing it with his hand. Lukewarm, but after the cold showers in solitary it felt like heaven.

He slipped under the stream and felt the water cascade down his back and shoulders.

Maybe they let you clean up before they execute you?

Small victories, they had taught him in SERE School. This was a small victory. His first real shower in a month? Two months? What was coming next? Didn't matter. Something had changed.

He started to scrub. Working the soap under the nails he'd been biting to keep in check, armpits, chest, down his legs to his feet. He leaned his head back and worked the lather into his greasy hair, parts of it so matted that only scissors would be able to untangle it.

He worked himself over twice before putting the soap down on the short wall separating the shower from the changing area. He then used the toenail clippers to trim both his fingernails and toenails before stepping back under the water to ensure that all the soap was washed away.

The water abruptly stopped.

"Put on the clothes and then lie down on the deck."

Deck. Whoever was speaking had been in the Navy or Marine Corps. Possibly the Coast Guard.

Reece moved to the bench and slid into the light blue pants and then pulled the shirt over his head.

"Lie down."

Fucking make me.

"Prisoner B549. Lie down."

Reece leaned against the small wall and looked at the door.

Would they tase him? Could his body take it in his current state? He needed food, he needed sunlight, and he needed answers. He was done with handcuffs.

After what felt like ten minutes the voice from the speakers again echoed across the room.

"Prisoner B549. Slowly open the door. No sudden movements."

Reece moved to the door.

Here goes.

He opened it and stepped into a hallway. At one end, dressed in green Nomex flight suits, helmets, and goggles and holding an assortment of lethal and less-than-lethal arms, including riot shields, was what looked like a prison SWAT team. They reminded Reece of the photo of Border Patrol agents raiding a house in Florida back in 2000 to seize Elián González to send the child back to Cuba. A Pulitzer Prize–winning photograph had captured the event and was plastered across television screens around the world.

We are from the federal government. We are here to help.

"Turn to your right," the voice instructed.

Reece did as he was told. He wasn't about to go head-to-head with a prison SWAT team.

"Walk to the end of the hall. No sudden moves," the voice reminded him.

Stay cool, Reece. You are in no position to fight.

"Open the door on your left."

Reece pushed down on the metal handle and stepped inside, letting the door close behind him. It locked shut with an audible click.

He found himself in a room that seemed enormous after his time in solitary confinement, though it was probably only four or five times as large as his cell. The walls were a light green, a color Reece knew was meant to calm prisoners and work on the subliminal elicitation of truth. Another closed door was visible across the room. There were no windows to the outside world and no obvious observation mirrors. A table and two chairs, none of which, Reece noted, were made of cement or attached to the floor, were positioned in the center of the room. One of the chairs was occupied.

Reece's eyes went to the man's hands as he had been trained as a child by his father.

Hands. Weapons. Threats.

The hands were empty.

Reece's eyes traveled from the hands up to the man's face.

It was someone he knew well.

"Welcome back, Reece."

CHAPTER 12

IT TOOK REECE A moment to register.

"Vic?"

Victor Rodriguez was a former 7th Group Special Forces soldier and a second-generation Agency officer. Though older than Reece by a decade, he had not let age or life behind a desk negatively impact his physical strength and stamina. When visiting his operatives at black sites in the United States or overseas, he always made time to hit the gym with the fittest among them, a habit that also allowed him to keep his fingers on the pulse of the organization he led. He was a rare intelligence executive who commanded respect from those above and below him in the Agency hierarchy. There were a few flecks of gray in his black hair, but not many. His dark features had allowed him freedom of movement in nonpermissive and hostile environments around the world as a Green Beret and as a clandestine service and ground branch operator with the CIA. The son of Cuban exiles, his father had gone over the beach at the Bay of Pigs in 1961. The Bahía de Cochinos and the implications it had for U.S. foreign policy guided his every action. He had risen through the ranks to first lead Ground Branch and now was the director of the CIA's Special Activities Center, responsible for the Special Operations Group and the Political Action Group, the two darkest organizations in the country's covert action apparatus.

If there was one person at the CIA that Reece trusted, it was Vic.

Trust no one.

Vic stood. For the first time that Reece could remember, Vic looked unsure of what to do. He stepped around the desk and approached the man he had recruited into the Agency's Clandestine Service.

He extended his hand.

Reece took it.

"Welcome back?" he asked. "From where? Where the hell am I? Katie and the Hastingses?"

"They are fine, Reece. You might want to take a seat for this."

The former SEAL hesitated, then accepted his position and moved to the table. He needed information.

"There are not many places where one can disappear in the U.S. prison system, Reece. This is one of those places."

"I'm in the U.S.?"

"Yes."

"A black site?"

"No. When you were taken into FBI custody, the options dwindled."

"Vic, where the *fuck* am I?"

"You are in Colorado. ADX Florence."

Reece leaned forward. His long hair was still wet from the shower and fell to either side of his face, framing his long beard.

"You stuck me in a supermax prison with Ramzi Yousef, Zacarias Moussaoui, and Robert Hanssen?"

"It was the safest place for you."

"Safest? Vic, you know I didn't kill the president."

"I know. And now *we* know, but there were those who wanted to hang you in the court of public opinion. We have a tendency to need a face in the aftermath of tragedy, a face and a person to blame. It makes people feel safe."

"Vic, tell me what the *fuck* happened and get me out of here."

"It was Alice."

"Alice put me in here?"

"No, she's getting you out."

"What?"

"Let me explain."

"How do you know about her?"

"There have been some changes since you've been in here, Reece. Janice Motley stepped down in the wake of the assassination. There is a new interim director, retired four-star, multiple stints at JSOC. You might remember him: General Marcus Howe."

"He's the guy they 'retired' early from CENTCOM after he issued a glowing rebuke in front of Congress on U.S. policies in Iraq and Afghanistan."

"That's right, Reece. From a career standpoint, he made the mistake of speaking truth to power."

"They don't like that, do they?"

"No, they certainly do not. But the new president does. She needed someone who is not afraid of stepping on toes. Someone who was not part of the Washington machine."

"He didn't take a board job at Northrop Grumman after retirement?"

"Get this: he went to teach high school history in Ohio. No résumé-building university provost jobs for General Howe, no leadership consulting company, no public speaking circuit, no tell-all book, no run for Congress, no board seats. I understand the president made an off-the-books trip to Ohio, sat down with him and his wife, and convinced him to come back to run the CIA."

"Says a lot about them both."

"The president didn't want a Warren Commission Report debacle with the country so divided."

"You mean they won't keep documents related to the assassination classified for the next sixty years?"

"We'll see, but I will tell you, Director Howe has seen all our documents and the report that Alice compiled and has supplied all of it to the President's Commission on the Assassination of President Christensen."

"Vic, how long have I been in here?"

Vic paused and took a deep breath.

"Three months."

"*Three months*," Reece whispered.

"I'm sorry, Reece, I worked as quickly as I could. We had to confirm everything we received in Alice's report."

"What report? When did you find out about Alice?"

"Part of those changes I mentioned. Director Howe wanted me read in so I would know exactly how we got the information that exonerated you."

Reece looked down at his hands.

God help whoever put me in here.

"Reece?"

"Just haven't been in the light for a long time."

"Solitary confinement was the safest place for you, Reece. I am so sorry."

Reece only nodded.

"It happened fast, Reece. They had planned it for a long time and only needed to implement it."

"Who is 'they'?"

"That's a bit of a mystery. I have my suspicions. So does Andy."

"Danreb? He's still with the Agency?"

"Not anymore. He resigned over this. Well, officially he retired."

"Why?"

"He had a theory on the Russian Security Council using 'rogue elements'—proxies, really—to plan and execute an operation to assassinate the president with the intent of turning the attention and resources of our intelligence agencies inward to find and eliminate threats to the republic. That would allow Russia greater freedom to maneuver in Ukraine. With Finland and Sweden joining NATO, he believed the defense industry would be satiated for the next few years. His theory was that Russia needed a patsy, and because of your media profile from a few years back, he thought you were the perfect candidate. He, and we, didn't know Russia had the capability they did in the cyber arena. We now think China may have helped them."

"Slow down, Vic. Russia? China?"

"He believes it's a partnership based on energy, cyber capabilities, and energy deals. He laid out his theory for the seventh floor, and when the Agency took too long to act, he resigned. He never even came back to clean out his desk. Just told a secretary on the way out that he quit. We had to send a team to his house to officially read him out of his special access programs."

"That sounds like Andy. What did they not act fast enough on?"

"On getting you out."

"He resigned over me?"

"Well, he had been threatening to leave for years, but, yes, he was disgusted with the slow pace of freeing you after he laid everything out. He brought up Stalin and Beria in his argument."

"I owe him a vodka."

"He was right, you know. He figured it out, and he didn't have Alice's help."

"What do you mean?"

"The night you were taken into custody, a report landed in the inbox of the Director of National Intelligence. He called an emergency meeting with the directors of the CIA and NSA and the National Security Advisor. Remember, the country was in chaos. The president had been assassinated. It had been over forty years since the attempt on Reagan's life, and almost sixty since the Kennedy assassination. Tips began flowing in immediately. A lot of it was conspiracy nonsense—neighbor versus neighbor and right versus left—but a very clear thread began to emerge early. The FBI pulled all his social media and emails and turned his home upside down. He was clearly troubled, probably wouldn't have been admitted into the military a decade ago, but recruiting numbers have fallen to record lows and standards have been lowered. He was radicalized online, antigovernment stuff, but when they began to unravel the facts, it was clear that the responsible entities were foreign. It was not a U.S.-based group. The search of his house revealed the same: books, materials, all antigovernment, all dead ends, except for email correspondence with someone in Montana."

"Me?"

"Yes, you. But it wasn't you."

"No shit."

"It all laid out too nicely, but you were already in the air. Already in custody."

"And the devices?"

"That's where it really gets interesting."

"Why?"

"Because Alice's report doesn't have data to back it up."

"Meaning?"

"Meaning whoever built the devices didn't communicate on text, or apps, or email."

"Professionals."

"Yes."

"Alice didn't have anything on them?"

"Oh, she did. She was able to get a partial via the IOT, the Internet of Things."

"I remember," Reece said, thinking back to his introduction to the quantum computer known as Alice. "And?"

"And the partial was from someone who used to work for the CIA."

"What?"

"In Iraq."

"Are you telling me that the CIA is responsible for training the person who killed the president?"

"There's more. We are still investigating. Let's get you to a SCIF at Langley so you can read Alice's report in full."

"The same one that went to the DNI?"

"Yes. I won't pretend to understand all the technical aspects of it, but Alice and the United States, our NATO allies, and Israel were all hit with a cyberattack from China and Russia—well, technically from proxy hacking organizations with links to the Russian and Chinese versions of the NSA. Banks, armed forces, intelligence, power grid, the works. Alice, as I would later learn, was diverted to defend against these attacks. At that same moment, the president was assassinated, and a trail of evidence was embedded into the system that implicated you as the mastermind of the attacks."

Reece's hands went to his temples. Another headache.

This whole thing started with headaches.

"You okay, Reece?"

"Not sure. I think the light is giving me a migraine. I've been in the dark for three months."

"Want some water?"

"No, I'm fine. Keep going. What happened next?"

"Alice's report comes in. The DNI diverts you from a federal prison in Virginia to Colorado to give us time to confirm everything in Alice's report."

"The old-school way."

"That's right. What if Alice had manipulated or manufactured data, even video, to exonerate you?"

Reece thought back to the journey deep beneath Lackland to meet Alice. The golden wires suspended from the center of the room, encased behind a Plexiglas shield, a prison cell. A voice that sounded like Lauren.

That voice.

"And it took three months?"

"It did."

"Why not tell me?"

"Any touch point ran the risk of exposure and a media firestorm. Containing it among the federal and local LE that planned the raid in Montana was difficult enough. They were sent a highly sanitized report the day after the raid detailing the high probability that you had been set up and that for reasons of national security they were issued gag orders."

"And Andy?"

"Andy didn't even know it was you at first. He put the pieces together without the benefit of Alice's report."

"He's old-school."

"That he is. And he is, or *was*, the Agency's foremost Russian expert. Unfortunately, the new generation is skeptical of dinosaurs. They only trust algorithms. And Andy did not have the benefit of being read in on Alice, and he does not know about your father's letter."

Vic opened a thick file on the desk and pulled out a letter. He handed it across the table to Reece.

The letter. His dad's letter.

"I assume you have read it," Reece stated.

"Many times."

"Why is it in there?"

"The FBI confiscated it in the search of your cabin. I think the president's assassination and your implication in it has something to do with this letter. What happened to the key?"

"Key?"

"The key mentioned in the letter."

Think, Reece. Did Katie not give it to them?

"I don't know," Reece lied. "There wasn't one. Just the letter. No key. No clues to the location of the safe-deposit box. It's a mystery."

Now it was Vic's turn to study the man in front of him.

"You can trust me, Reece."

"Can I? I've been locked in solitary for three months—something you say was for my own protection—no one let me know what was happening, and now suddenly I'm pulled out of the darkness and thrust into the light, and we are just supposed to pick up where we left off? It's going to take a lot more than that, Vic."

"I understand, Reece."

"And what did Alice do when you confirmed everything in her report?"

"We don't know."

"What do you mean?"

"Alice has gone dark."

CHAPTER 13

"GONE DARK? WHAT DOES that mean?"

"It's hard to tell, Reece. She now exists in a quantum cloud."

"What the hell is a quantum cloud?"

"I can only understand the CliffsNotes version myself," Vic said.

"Good. That's all I'll comprehend anyway. Explain it to me."

"From what I have been briefed, she is no longer contained in that vacuum of physical dangling wires you saw at Lackland Air Force Base."

"She's in a cloud?"

"Well, a virtual cloud created by a project at the Utah Data Center."

"And let me guess . . ." Reece conjectured. "You can't turn it off."

"That's right. At this stage there is no way to turn it, *her*, off."

"How fast is she now?"

"What would take a well-equipped computer millions of years to compute, Alice can do in real time."

"She's gotten faster," Reece said.

"She has. And she continues to learn and solve problems, but she is unreachable."

"*She's free*," Reece whispered.

"What's that?"

"I said, she's free."

"I still have a hard time wrapping my head around talking about a computer like she's a person."

"You get used to it," Reece said.

"I suppose. The question for the intel community is, whose side is she on?"

"Maybe she's on her own side."

"Maybe. In the meantime, Reece, now you are free."

Free.

Reece shut his eyes.

Find the light, Reece.

"Reece?"

He opened his eyes again.

"I might be out of solitary confinement, but I'm not free."

"Reece?"

"Someone put me in here. Someone killed the president. If this letter had something to do with it, I'm not free."

"I know. And you will have the full cooperation of the Agency to figure it out."

"No, we've got to keep this small. I need to talk to Andy."

"There is someone else you need to talk to."

"Who?"

"Reece, if Andy is right, the Russians want you out of the picture and were willing to risk a full-scale war to do that. As it stands, we can't directly connect the assassination to the Russian Security Council, though Andy makes a compelling case."

"Well, that's a start. Other than Andy, who else can help?"

Vic picked up a second file and handed it across the table to Reece.

"I think you know him."

Reece flipped open the first page and stared at a photo of a man he had not seen since he was in single digits.

"Poe?"

"That's right. William Andres Poe."

"He's still alive? I have not thought about him in years."

"You are more connected to the Agency than you know, Reece."

Reece looked up from the file.

"What do you mean?"

"Keep reading. William Poe—and the family your grandfather worked for after the war—had deep Agency connections."

"My grandfather took care of their property on the Taylor River. I learned to fly fish there. Got my first elk in the mountains behind the property with an old Winchester thirty-thirty. Iron sights. He helped me pack it out."

"You know your grandfather was Scouts and Raiders, right?"

"I do."

"Did you know he was also OSS and that he worked for the CIA in the fifties?"

"I knew he fought in the Pacific, but then I thought he came home and managed the Poe family ranch in Colorado. He never talked about the war. I found a box in the attic when I was a kid. Full of medals and maps. Don't know what happened to it."

"Let me fill in some gaps for you," Vic said. "Your grandfather worked for the Agency when he got home. The Philippines, Albania, Manchuria, China, Cuba. That's how he met the Poe family. William's dad was old-school OSS. Wild Bill Donovan time frame. Dulles, Wisner, Casey, Bissell, FitzGerald, Barnes, Colby, Lansdale. Then in the early sixties he took a job with the Poe family. Nothing in the file about why. William was already in the Agency at this point."

"That's like thirty years before I was born."

"As I said, you are more connected to the Agency than you know."

"My grandfather made it to ninety-four years old. Never whispered a word about the Pacific, the OSS, or the CIA."

"That generation died with a lot of secrets, and a lot of pain."

"They built the country into what it is today."

"That they did."

"My first memories of him are as a sort of majordomo on that ranch property. Horses, fishing, hunting, very private, a bunch of cabins, a main house, fairly rustic. I thought it belonged to someone at the World Bank."

"Your memory is spot-on, Reece. But Poe wasn't just an executive at the World Bank, although he certainly was that."

"Then what was he?"

"He never left the CIA."

"What?"

"Keep reading. Yale graduate like a lot of them were back then. Skull and Bones, played baseball, and rowed crew. Father was something of an industrialist, built oil tankers during World War Two as well as the East Coast refineries and pipelines that filled them. He was tied into the early days of the OSS. Funded a lot of operations and hosted a lot of dinner parties in Georgetown. Rubbed shoulders with Dulles and Donovan. William was enamored with the whole thing and joined the CIA. He missed Korea, but he was trained by the old guard, men who cut their teeth in World War Two and Korea, China, Albania, Iran, Cuba. William was early into Vietnam, ended up running the Phoenix Program."

"My dad was in the Phoenix Program."

"Their time overlaps in Phoenix, but Poe was in management, your dad was in operations."

"I see."

"Colorado was Poe's family property," Vic said.

"That industrialist money gives one some options."

"That it does. Poe Research Center, Poe Charitable Trusts. He was divorced in the seventies. One son who took his own life. Details are scarce. Remarried. Divorced again. No kids from the second marriage. Your grandfather ran the family ranch, though it was more than a place for Poe and World Bank executives to fish; it was a CIA holding area for defectors and spies."

Reece shook his head.

"Russian defectors were brought up from Mexico," Vic continued. "They were debriefed on the ranch in Colorado. There is a small airport nearby. Today it will accommodate a G550. Back then they were flown up in smaller single-engine aircraft."

"What does all this have to do with what's going on now?" Reece asked.

"I'm not certain, but I think there is a connection between Poe, your family, and the assassination of the president."

"How do you know?"

"Because Poe wants to see you."

CHAPTER 14

The Residence at Cape Idokopas
Krasnodar Krai, Russia

"STEAL IT? STEAL IRANIAN plutonium?" asked Levitsky.

"Yes, comrade, we are going to draw the Americans into a war they can't refuse. We are going to accelerate their demise," Kozak responded.

"Could the bomb destroy Israel's ability to respond?" Levitsky asked.

"Ah, they must respond, so the bomb will detonate in Israeli waters, not Israeli soil," Kozak said. "It will severely damage Tel Aviv, their economic hub, which just so happens to house the headquarters of the Mossad. We need to ensure they are galvanized against Iran. Israel will retaliate with a nuclear strike on Tehran. They will turn it to ashes. They will follow up with a conventional blitzkrieg not seen since the Nazis. The Americans will move their battle groups to support their ally. They will capitalize on the Iranian aggression and use it as an excuse to wipe Iran off the map."

"And the American defense industry will post record profits," Dashkov predicted.

"They will. Not only do they *want* a war with Iran, they *need* a war with Iran. America is in a recession. They might change the definition to manipulate their citizens, but they are in a recession, to be sure. Their people need a distraction."

"And what if Iran launches a full-scale attack before Israel and the U.S. can respond?" Dashkov probed.

"Israel is a small country, but it is united, especially against the threat from Iran. They have had required mandatory service since their inception. Every Israeli has invested in their country. They have ownership. They will fight, and they will respond immediately."

"And the Americans? What if they are slow to react?" Dashkov asked.

"Comrade, the Israeli lobby in D.C. is almost as strong as the defense and pharmaceutical lobbies. They *will* respond. They will have no choice."

"Brilliant, Chairman Kozak," Levitsky praised. "While the Americans are fighting over their pronouns, digital passports, and a social credit system, we will change the world order. For the first time since World War Two the Americans will know their place."

"Yes, and the Iranian plutonium ensures the blame is placed squarely at the feet of the mullahs in Tehran," said Kozak.

"I see you and the president have worked this through. What of second- and third-order effects to world markets?" asked Dashkov.

"The economic impact to the West will be devastating. They are not prepared, and ironically they have put themselves in this position unnecessarily. The UK economy will collapse. They will reluctantly provide support to the U.S., but it will be a symbolic gesture. Russia will in effect stay neutral by staying focused on Ukraine." Kozak smiled. "Oil prices will spike past levels ever experienced in recorded history, and we will make untold fortunes on our futures contracts and our enhanced dominance in the production market. Saudi Arabia will increase output in an attempt to capitalize on price increases, but on a percentage basis their cut of the market will be minimal. It will be the final blow to the West's poor economic position."

"The death of the West," Dashkov whispered.

"Yes. With the Americans fully committed to the Middle East, we release the military capability we have held in reserve for the past year and sweep through Ukraine up to the Polish border while China simultaneously retakes Taiwan."

"It's ambitious," Dashkov said.

"It's bold. The timing has never been better," Kozak said.

"Chairman, we have thus far, in coordination with our allies in America with the same goals, averted nuclear confrontation. You are proposing that we flip that model and use a nuclear weapon, something we have thus far successfully avoided."

"We use a nuclear device to *avert* a war with the West," Kozak corrected. "This course of action takes Iran off the board and propels us and our new Chinese allies to the top of the world order. America's days are numbered."

"The new American president, President Olsen, she is stronger than we initially assessed," Dashkov reminded his superior.

"Admittedly so, but she is not strong enough to hold her country together. There are too many forces pulling it apart from within."

"What are our next steps?" asked Levitsky.

"I will bring the recommendation of this council to the president. He will make the final determination. Barring any objections from you, we will proceed."

Dashkov began to do the math and calculate how far his dacha north of Moscow was from Tehran.

"The device," Dashkov said. "How powerful will it be?"

"Three plutonium rods—ten megatons. Five hundred times as powerful as Hiroshima but still small by current standards. We will build it to ensure it will work, but any evidence it was constructed in Russia will vaporize in the explosion, leaving no trace except the Iranian plutonium signature."

"And where *exactly* would we trigger the device?"

"Five kilometers offshore of Tel Aviv."

"What is the projected battle damage assessment?"

"The flash burn effect will carry to shore and send thousands of Israelis to the hospital with second- and third-degree burns. Infrastructure damage would be limited to coastal buildings that will collapse from the overpressure. Depending on prevailing winds, lethal radiation could result in tens of thousands of long-term cancer cases. The Israelis will naturally think it was a premature detonation and presume that Iran was attempting to bring the weapon closer to shore or into port. What we are truly doing is preserving Israel's integrity to respond."

"And what is the current status of the device?" Dashkov asked.

"The plutonium is on its way here now."

"Where is 'here'?"

"To the Rosatom nuclear weapon assembly facility in Zarechny, where it will be incorporated into the device before it is transferred to Cyprus. From there it will travel by sea to the coast of Israel."

"This is an international operation, normally under the purview of the SVR," Dashkov said, looking across the table. "Why is my new counterpart unaware of this mission?"

"Out of necessity," Chairman Kozak confirmed. "No disrespect, Director Levitsky. This was better handled off the books. By Wagner."

"Wagner?" Dashkov leaned forward again, the displeasure evident in his tone. "You trusted the most sensitive operation in the history of the federation to Wagner? Their ranks are filled with degenerates and prisoners."

"Their top-tier unit is highly capable. It is made up of former Alpha Group commandos. In this case, deniability is of the highest importance."

"And Wagner has a direct line to the president," Dashkov said, leaning back in his seat to process everything he had learned. "There is no turning back. You and the president acted unilaterally without the consent of the council."

"It was necessary to prepare the battle space, to put this option on the table. As you know, these operations take months, sometimes years, to plan. We will vote, but before we do, I want you to meet the man who killed President Christensen."

CHAPTER 15

NIKOLAI KOZAK PICKED UP a phone on the conference table. It was connected to a device at the guard station just outside the door.

"Enter."

The door opened.

"Comrades, I know you both know Lieutenant Colonel Sokoloff."

Neither Dashkov nor Levitsky stood to greet a man so junior, though his rank promotion had stopped when he left the GRU. His methods in the Caucasus region would only stand up to international scrutiny for so long. He was more valuable to Russia in the private sector.

"Please, Colonel, sit," Chairman Kozak said.

Though no longer a lieutenant colonel in the GRU, Dashkov noted that the chairman still referred to him by a rank he had abandoned a decade prior.

Andrei Sokoloff had a long-running relationship with both Nikolai Kozak and the Russian president. At sixty, his background in Russian Special Forces and the GRU lent credibility to his current role as CEO of the Wagner Group. Three times he had been awarded the Order of Courage by the Russian Federation and had received the title of Hero of the Russian Federation before leaving official government service. Along with his predecessor he had worked for the Slavonic Corps, a Hong Kong–registered private military company operating in Syria in 2013.

One of the founding members of the Wagner Group, he had returned to Syria in 2015 and 2016. It was there that he had lost his left eye.

As with his predecessor, he was an ardent Rodnover, a practitioner of a Slavic Native Faith grounded in *narodnichestvo*, a right-wing ethnic nationalism that also incorporated a fervent belief in reincarnation. His beliefs allowed Sokoloff to make decisions that were all the more bold and aggressive. After all, if he were killed in the execution of his mission, he would be reincarnated and get another chance at life. Whether this was a guise that he used to gain an advantage on the battlefield and in business, Dashkov was not sure.

He wore boots, cargo pants, and a dark polo shirt without markings. Thicker than Levitsky, he looked like he spent more time pushing iron than running on the treadmill. It was difficult to discern how much gray was in his hair, as it was cut short in a buzz. The black band of his eye patch cut into his scalp in a way that looked almost painful. His single piercing blue eye stood out in contrast to his dark features and imposing physique.

"Comrades," he said, nodding to both intelligence directors as he took his seat next to Levitsky.

"Anyone else joining us this evening?" Dashkov asked.

"No. This working group is small by design. The rest of the council will be aware of a nuclear device going off in Israeli waters only when they see it on the news."

Dashkov had given his blessing to the operation to assassinate the U.S. president, but as an international matter, the particulars fell to the late Mikhail Gromyko. Those events had been set in motion prior to his being found in the bushes of Gorky Park with a zip-tie around his neck and a cyanide cigarette in his mouth.

"Colonel Sokoloff," Chairman Kozak said, indicating that the former GRU man had the floor.

"Gentlemen, as you know, the operation to institute regime change in America was set up through the SVR under its previous leadership in a joint operation, if you will."

"Deniability," Dashkov said.

"Yes, deniability."

Sokoloff rubbed the red and black *kolovrat* tattooed on the inside of his left forearm before continuing. It looked like a wheel made of eight sickles, curved blades—a variant of the swastika.

"It started as an infiltration plan," he said. "In 2003, I did not know what we would eventually use them for or even if they would survive their testing by the CIA polygraphers, but it was too good an opportunity to pass up. Chaos always offers opportunities."

Dashkov moved his hand to his inside left coat pocket to feel his pipe.

Sokoloff's single eye narrowed. "Eventually the Americans were going to leave Iraq. It was only a matter of time. They were going to abandon their allies, those Iraqis who stood and worked with them as interpreters and soldiers. They did it in Vietnam, and they did it with the Kurds after Saddam invaded Kuwait in 1990. Why anyone trusts the Americans anymore is beyond me. I had an asset in Iraq's Ministry of the Interior. Low-level but with potential. He was already recruited when the Americans invaded. He went on the run, as did most everyone associated with Saddam's regime. He worked his way to Iran and made contact."

"You reinserted him. This time with a new mission," Dashkov said.

"I did. I discussed the matter with Director Gromyko. It was kept close hold."

"Understandably," Levitsky said.

"*Da.* He had started as a possible long-term plant with Saddam's regime. With the American invasion there was another opportunity. If handled correctly, he could pass us information not just on the new Iraqi government, specifically their Ministry of the Interior, but on the Americans."

"So you reinserted him into Iraq," Dashkov said.

"Yes, this time with a sizable financial incentive."

"He did it for the money?"

"At first. That placement put him on the front lines of America's covert action programs in Iraq. He passed back valuable tactical-level intelligence on U.S. capabilities: drones, manned experimental ISR platforms, IED countermeasures, troop size and strength. More importantly, he was able to recruit six other assets. When the Americans abandoned Iraq in 2011, we had a decision to make."

"Let me guess—leave him in place or get him to America?"

"That's correct, Director. Gromyko decided to leave half of our assets in Iraq. The others were tasked with leveraging their Agency connections, claiming asylum for what they had done for the United States. These were not like the thousands of other Iraqi soldiers and interpreters who were left behind. These were CIA."

"So they received preferential treatment."

"They did. They moved to the front of the line and were relocated to the U.S. in 2012."

"But they had been trained."

"Yes, they were trained. By the CIA."

"What made them want to leave their country?" Dashkov asked.

"We helped them with that decision." Sokoloff looked at Chairman Kozak, who nodded. "We had their families killed by al-Qaeda in Iraq, the group that would later become ISIS."

"You manipulated their motivations."

"Yes. Now it was not for money, it was for vengeance," Sokoloff continued. "The Americans had promised they would take care of them and their families. Mothers and sisters were raped and decapitated; brothers, sons, and fathers executed. We needed to give them a reason to want to exact that revenge. It was extremely successful."

The colonel spoke of ordering rapes and executions the way most people discuss dinner options. Dashkov would have to tread wisely.

"A powerful motivator," Dashkov confirmed.

"It was now a waiting game. All three of our assets were in the U.S.—one still in the employ of the CIA as a translator at their headquarters in Langley, Virginia. The two others worked menial jobs outside of Washington, D.C."

"Until you activated them."

"We only needed two; even the Americans aren't dumb enough not to connect the dots in a case like this," Sokoloff confirmed. "Two of them constructed the IEDs. Spetssviaz and the Internet Research Agency radicalized the young private who took shots at President Christensen. That put the Secret Service contingency plan in motion. President Christensen's motorcade had two choke points where we had the opportunity to hit him, and we did."

"And the patsies?" Dashkov asked.

"Spetssviaz and the Internet Research Agency coordinated efforts with the Third Department of the People's Liberation Army's General Staff Department, 3PLA, and mounted an attack against the West through proxy hackers just prior to the attack," Chairman Kozak interjected. "That drew the American cyberdefense apparatus into motion. The evidence against James Reece was planted at the same time."

"It seems complicated, comrade," Dashkov observed.

"It was complex, not complicated, Director Dashkov," Kozak corrected.

"And you have been running these agents through Wagner?" Dashkov asked.

"Yes. Deniability. Wagner is very convenient in that regard. And now the Americans are in the position of uncovering that CIA-trained assets were responsible for the assassination of their own president. The American public will not be able to make a distinction between these assets and the CIA. To their citizens, the CIA will have assassinated yet another U.S. president."

"'Yet another'?" asked Levitsky.

"They already think the CIA was involved in killing Kennedy," Chairman Kozak said. "The last two administrations have blocked the release of CIA files related to the Kennedy assassination, even though in 1992 their Congress mandated by law that the executive branch release them in 2017. Their release was blocked in 2017, 2021, and again in 2022. The CIA cited 'sources and methods,' as expected."

"They should have just destroyed them," offered Colonel Sokoloff.

"That they should have," said Kozak. "This presidential commission investigating the assassination of President Christensen will have to decide if they include the CIA connection to the IED makers in their report. If they do, the new president will have to decide if she will release that information to the public."

"Unless they arrest your three assets and offer them a better deal," Dashkov said.

"That is not possible," Kozak said.

"And why is that?"

"Because all three are dead," Colonel Sokoloff stated.

"Which just adds to the conspiracy," Kozak added. "Only two were involved, but all three had to die. The more mysterious, the better—just like all those mysterious deaths surrounding the Kennedy assassination. The U.S. will be thrown into further turmoil if that report is released exposing CIA ties to the bomb makers."

"How were they killed?" Dashkov asked.

"Fentanyl overdose for one; just one of seventy thousand Americans killed by a fentanyl-laced drug over the past year," Colonel Sokoloff said. "A mugging gone wrong for another; American cities are exceedingly dangerous these days. And a tragic suicide for the third. Hung himself in his bathroom."

"All arranged by Wagner on U.S. soil?" Dashkov asked.

"Through the Bratva. Deniability," Kozak said, quite pleased with himself. "A link that makes it even more believable is that James Reece was attached to the same CIA unit in Iraq as were the assassins."

Dashkov had to admit, as much as he disliked Colonel Sokoloff and the Wagner Group, they had pulled off one of the most impressive special operations in history.

"What did the American movie say about the JFK assassination?" Kozak asked, before answering his own question. "'A mystery wrapped in a riddle inside an enigma.' Though the writer did borrow the essence of that line from Winston Churchill's description of Russia as 'a riddle, wrapped in a mystery, inside an enigma.' Fast-forward sixty years. They haven't even figured out who paid for the bullets that destroyed Camelot. And that was back when they trusted their government. The Kennedy assassination was the turning point for America; November 22, 1963, was the day America lost her innocence. Khrushchev, even Brezhnev and Kosygin, couldn't see it. All they needed to do was wait. But they couldn't; they lacked the sniper's patience. It was all about the arms race: Vietnam, East Berlin, Czechoslovakia, our Afghanistan, 'Star Wars,' stealth technology, bioweapons, chemical munitions, ballistic missile submarines, mutually assured destruction. When really it's one man with a plan. One IED. One rifle. One man behind a scope can change the course of history."

Sokoloff was crazy.

"There is an issue, though," Dashkov interjected.

"Oh?" Sokoloff said.

"James Reece is alive."

The colonel stirred in his seat, uncomfortable for the first time since entering the room.

"He's discredited and either dead or rotting away at a CIA black site," the Wagner Group CEO said.

"What if I were to tell you he's not?"

"If, and I say *if*, he was not implicated in the assassination of President Christensen, then the Spetssviaz has much to answer for. Regardless, James Reece is off the board. If he's not dead, he's locked away—probably being tortured by the CIA right now."

"That is not good enough. My sources have confirmed he was being held at one of the Americans' supermax prisons," Dashkov said.

"What source?" Kozak asked.

"You know him, Chairman. He is one of us; a congressman on their intelligence committee," Dashkov responded.

"And you said James Reece *was* being held. Past tense?"

"He's being released."

"I see. We have underestimated the Reece family long enough." Chairman Kozak stood abruptly, much faster than normal for a man his age.

The two intelligence directors and the Wagner Group CEO followed suit.

"I have a meeting with the president. I will inform him of the council's vote to move forward with the Israel option. Continue to keep tabs on James Reece, and when he rears his head, I want you to take it off. Ensure the next breaths he draws are his last. Good evening, gentlemen."

The chairman buttoned the top button on his suit and left the room.

CHAPTER 16

United States Penitentiary
Florence Administrative Maximum Facility
Range 13
Special Housing Unit
Fremont County, Colorado

BECAUSE HE HAD NEVER been officially in-processed, there was not much in the way of out-processing. Vic had given Reece a small duffel with a set of clothes and given him a new phone, which Reece had proceeded to dump in the nearest trash can. They had offered him a shave and a haircut, but Reece wasn't letting anyone in prison near him with scissors and a razor.

He didn't even turn his head to look at the receptionist or the guards with M4s in the reception area. He needed air.

As he swung the door open, he encountered a bright, high-desert sun that was even more blinding than the lights of the room where he had met Vic. It brought on a sudden light-headedness, but Reece pushed through it and walked to the edge of a small forecourt that was separated from the parking area by cylindrical steel barricades. He supported himself by placing a hand on one of the barriers, letting his equilibrium stabilize. He then raised his head, shielding his eyes with the back of his other hand. His ride was waiting.

Reece stepped into the parking lot, the bag from Vic over his shoulder, and approached a tall, broad-shouldered man in jeans, Courteney boots, and a T-shirt who was leaning against the side of a mustard-colored FJ40 Land Cruiser. Wisps of dirty-blond hair protruded from beneath a camo Eberlestock baseball hat, his piercing green eyes standing in stark contrast to the light stubble on his face that disguised a menacing scar running from just below his left eye to his upper lip. Reece stopped about ten paces away to make sure he wasn't dreaming and about to wake up back in his cell.

"*Holy hell*, you look like shit, mate," boomed the voice shaded with the Rhodesian accent of Old Africa.

Reece cracked a smile at the sight of his dearest friend and Teammate, Raife Hastings.

"What happened to your Defender? Didn't start this morning?"

"Even your time in solitary confinement wasn't enough to bring you to your senses on off-road-capable vehicles. The Defender is running great, eh . . . but I wanted—"

"To ensure we wouldn't break down in the parking lot?" Reece said, finishing the sentence.

"I wanted you to be comfortable. It's good to see you, brother."

The two old friends exchanged a massive bear hug.

"Here, put these on," Raife said, handing Reece a pair of Gatorz sunglasses.

"You are a lifesaver, my friend."

"Just repaying the favor from a few years back," he responded, referencing the time Reece had carried his wounded friend up the side of a mountain on Medny Island, just south of Siberia.

"You have a ways to go."

"Hop in. I'd offer to help you with your bags in your weakened state, but . . ."

"Yeah, I can manage. It's empty," Reece said, gesturing to the bag. "I'm wearing what Vic brought down."

Raife nodded, the stoic former SEAL doing what he could to conceal his concern at the sight of his friend. Reece had taken some hits, but even pale and thin with sunken eyes, he still had an edge. The eyes were not vacant as Raife had anticipated. They were focused.

"I know you were never much for grooming standards, but this"—Raife motioned with his hand—"this is pushing it even for you."

"Don't like it?" Reece asked, as if becoming aware of his physical appearance for the first time.

"You'd fit right in tailgating at a nineties grunge band concert in Seattle. We can work with it."

Raife opened the door of the vintage Land Cruiser and then turned to look at the redbrick building rising out of the high desert. The front entrance looked like it could belong to any high school in the United States: red-hued boulders were arranged along the edge of the parking area interspersed with matching planter boxes containing native plants. A flagpole with the American flag was situated at the corner of a red gravel area, hanging lifeless in the late afternoon air. It was only when one looked up and noticed what resembled an air traffic control tower and looming light fixtures that it became evident this was not a school where two football teams would square off on Friday night. The lights were in place to illuminate every square inch of ground surrounded by multiple layers of high fencing and razor wire, and the tower was there to provide snipers clear lines of sight to any position in the facility. This was a maximum-security prison where the most dangerous inmates in federal custody were locked away from society. The modern equivalent of a dungeon.

Reece didn't look back. His eyes stayed zeroed on the horizon. The usually attentive former frogman was still in his cell.

Raife had seen it time and time again—operators who couldn't leave the war behind, who brought it home. Even when surrounded by friends and family thousands of miles from the battlefield, they were still fighting the war in the deepest recesses of their souls. Reece would need time.

Raife reached behind the seat and produced a ball cap.

"Stick Sniper Archery?"

"Yeah, Caleb Brewer's archery shop in Tucson. Figured you might want to hide that mane. I think there are still laws against vagrancy in Colorado."

"What would I do without you, Raife?" Reece said as he adjusted the hat and tucked his hair underneath to keep it out of the way.

"He sent up a new Hoyt for you. Origin tiger stripe. It's a nice setup. Feds took your other bows, so I figured it would be good to have one waiting for you. Help you get back in the groove."

"Thank you," Reece said. He knew Raife meant well, that archery had helped so many veterans of the wars in Iraq and Afghanistan deal with effects of post-traumatic stress and traumatic brain injury so prevalent after twenty years at war. But Reece's mind was not on bows or reintegrating into society. It was on a list.

Raife maneuvered the vehicle out of the parking lot and onto a main road.

"You drive this thing from the ranch?" Reece asked, referring to the Hastings property in the Flathead Valley of Montana.

"Hell no, mate. We had it hauled to the Broadmoor. I flew in last week just to wait on you. My mom and dad wanted to come, but we thought you might need more time after what you have been through. They're waiting at the ranch. Mom's been getting your cabin ready for you. The *bloody* FBI really did a number on it."

"I bet."

"They took everything except the Wagoneer, since even they couldn't get it to move," Raife said, in an attempt at humor.

Reece grunted.

"Where's Katie?"

"She flew in with me. She's at the Broadmoor. She's been a wreck, brother. I don't think she's slept since they arrested you. Liz managed to talk her into staying at the hotel until I got you out."

"Liz Riley is here too?"

"She flies for us and Thorn," Raife explained. "She still feels a debt to you for rescuing her in Iraq after her helo went down."

Tim Thornton was Raife's father-in-law, a Vietnam veteran, oil and gas magnate, and former senator. He still liked to fly his aircraft himself, but, concerned with his advancing age, Raife's father had convinced him to bring Liz along as his copilot on most of his adventures.

"She has more than repaid it," Reece replied, remembering his cross-country flight with Liz at the controls of a Pilatus PC-12 NG as he eliminated those who had a hand in killing his family.

"I don't think she will ever see it that way."

"Why did you bring your mom's Land Cruiser?"

"Why do you think?" Raife asked.

Reece scanned the instrument panel of the old vehicle.

"Nothing modern. Manual transmission. Carbureted. Cassette tape deck. No Bluetooth. No way to be targeted, surveilled, or listened in on."

"That's right. It's clean. And I don't have a cell phone on me."

"They gave me my wallet and my watch," Reece said, pointing to the watch that had once been worn by his father in the jungles of Vietnam.

"Well, that's something, eh?"

Raife pulled into a scenic overlook opposite the Arkansas River, put the car in neutral, and yanked the parking brake.

"What are we doing?"

"Remember when I told you that they took everything?"

"Yeah. It was like one minute ago."

"Well, they did. They cleaned out the house, including all your weapons."

"Figured as much."

"The cocksuckers brought in a couple semitrucks. I watched them through binos from a hide site on the hill. They couldn't believe the number of books."

"Yeah, well, I guess they aren't big readers over there at the FBI."

"Thought you might want this."

Raife opened the Tuffy console between the seats and handed Reece a holstered pistol.

Reece pulled it from its leather, ejected the magazine, and tucked it under his leg before pushing down a manual safety on the left side and racking the slide rearward. A round ejected, which Reece caught. He then locked the slide to the rear and confirmed the chamber was clear.

"Yours?" Reece asked.

"It is. SIG P210 customized by Bruce Gray."

"Where's the red dot sight on this thing?" Reece joked, twisting it in his hand as if searching for a modern reflex optic.

His friend ignored the comment.

"I know you can't handle the recoil of the .45 in my 1911s. Hence this nine-millimeter." Raife smiled. "And I know how much you enjoy rich-kid shit that someone else pays for."

"You do have me there."

"Bruce only built a few, so try not to lose it or break it or get it confiscated by the federal government."

"Don't you worry," Reece said. "Mind if I dry-fire it?"

"Be my guest."

Reece checked the chamber once more and rode the slide home out of respect for the gunsmith who had painstakingly customized the classic SIG pistol. He then rested his right thumb on the manual safety as he slowly pressed the trigger to the rear. *Click.*

"That's nice. I might have to get one of these with your dad's credit card. I don't think it's expired yet."

Raife smiled and shook his head.

Reece reinserted the magazine and racked the slide back once again, letting it slam forward to chamber a round. He then pushed up the manual safety, ejected the magazine, and pressed the round he had caught moments earlier back into the top of the stack before reinserting the magazine and pulling down on it to ensure it was seated properly.

"How many rounds in the mag?" Reece asked.

"Eight."

"*Eight?*" Reece asked, performing a quick press check as was his habit.

"I am well aware that you usually need more than eight rounds to hit your target, which is why that setup has eight in the mag and one in the chamber."

"Nine. Terrific."

"This will require that you actually use your sights," Raife said.

"I'll consider it."

"That pistol is AAF."

"AAF?"

"Accurate as fuck."

"I'll remember that when I need a tenth round."

"Here are two extra mags. Just in case."

"Thank you, brother," Reece said.

"And since I missed your birthday—"

"Do you even know when my birthday is?" Reece interrupted.

"—I thought you might appreciate this."

Raife reached back into the center console and removed a blade and sheath.

"Rafael Kayanan sent it. It's a RAT Sayoc designed by Harley Elmore at HeadHunter Blades."

"You were not wrong, my friend."

Reece had trained extensively in the Filipino martial arts in college with a local resident of Bozeman, Montana, who had emigrated from the Philippines. He had continued his training in the SEAL Teams with the Sayoc Tactical Group, and when he was deployed to Basilan Island in the southern Philippine archipelago targeting the Abu Sayyaf Group, Moro Islamic Liberation Front, Jemaah Islamiyah, and al-Qaeda–affiliated groups.

"*Ten thousand hands*," Reece said as he removed the knife from its sheath and admired it in the late afternoon sun.

"Pamana Tuhon Christopher Sayoc, Senior."

"That's right. 'When you draw your blade, ten thousand hands draw their blades with you,'" Reece said, quoting the Sayoc Kali master.

"Thought that would pair nicely with the SIG."

"Thank you," Reece said, clipping the sheath into the appendix carry position.

"And here's a new tourniquet, in case you cut yourself with that thing."

"Small," Reece observed.

"It's from Snakestaff Systems. Think of it as the equivalent of a subcompact pistol. Just carry it."

Reece pulled it out and made sure he was familiar with how to attach it one-handed to both arms and his legs before shoving it into his pocket.

"Take this, too," Raife said. "It's the new Dynamis Combat Flathead."

Reece pulled the toughest flathead screwdriver in existence from its Kydex sheath and examined the innovative coating on the latest generation of one of his favorite tools. He resheathed it and clipped it to the inside of his left front pocket.

"And lastly," Raife said, as he reached back into the console, "I think you are familiar with this." He handed Reece a Winkler-Sayoc tomahawk.

"This is your platoon gift," Reece said.

"It was, but I'll get another. I know a guy. I want you to have this one. Welcome back."

Reece hesitated, remembering the last time a former Teammate had given him a tomahawk. Freddy Strain had given his to Reece on the Agency plane en route to Ukraine. Hours later he had taken a bullet on a rooftop in Odessa. Reece and Raife had pounded their Tridents into his casket the following week.

Reece released the black bungee cord holding the sheath to the head of the ancient weapon, wrapped his hand around the wood handle in a punch grip just below the head, and ripped it from its sheath. He remembered separating Imam Hammadi Izmail Masood's head from his body with a similar hawk, dispatching a guard in the catacombs in Odessa, slaying a giant of a man in the snow and ice of Kamchatka Peninsula, Russia, on his quest to find Raife, fighting a team of Iranian mercenaries in Maryland, and finally burying it in the head of the sniper who had killed Freddy Strain.

Reece returned it to its sheath.

"Okay, now that that's done, let's get you cleaned up. Broadmoor is about forty-five minutes away, which is about two hours in this thing. Let's not keep Katie waiting."

Reece thought back to that night in Montana. The ring had been in his pocket while he and Katie discussed the future over dinner in the cabin. *Forgiveness.* Leaving the Agency. An archery shop, whiskey bar, café, and bookstore. *Abelards.* Then it had all been taken from him.

"Reece?"

"Huh?"

"I was just saying that Katie's waiting."

"Give me a minute."

Reece leaned his head back.

With his head back and eyes closed, Reece spent a few moments contemplating his newfound freedom, and his next move.

Free. No, not yet. Will you ever be free? Will Katie ever be safe? What's in that safe-deposit box?

"Raife?"

"Yeah?"

"What happened after they took me?"

"Well, they questioned each of us individually: me, my mom and dad, and Katie. We didn't say shit until our lawyers got there. They had warrants to search all the homes on the property. I think it took all my dad's strength not to start slotting them."

"I am so sorry."

"Hey, don't you be sorry, brother. This is nothing compared to what they went through in Rhodesia. They were just worried about you, as we all were. As we all *are*."

"Yeah."

"Vic flew in just two days after. He filled us in on what he could. That an investigation had produced overwhelming evidence that you had nothing to do with the president's assassination. He was vague about where it came from, but I'm guessing you know."

"I do."

"Well, he explained that it was going to take some time to sort it out. Unbelievably, nothing about you leaked to the press."

"Vic told me."

"It became a mission to get you released, but to keep your name out of the media spotlight we couldn't go public or request documents or information. We had to trust Vic."

"He got me out."

"Took his damn sweet time about it."

"They had to verify everything in the report."

"Did they?"

"Did they what?"

"Have to take three months. Let you rot in that hellhole? At the very least they could have picked up the pace a bit. *Fucking* CIA."

Raife was not one with an affinity for the federal government.

"Katie is dying to see you. You ready?"

Reece looked down at the stainless-steel watch on his wrist.

Time.

As fast as you are, even you can't outrun time.

Maybe I'm trying to outrun something else?

"Time," Reece whispered.

"Well, I'll tell you what, I'm on your time. Whatever you need."

Reece ran his thumb over the scratched crystal, thinking about where it had been and what it had seen on his father's wrist. It was getting late.

"Shall we?" Raife asked.

"Not yet. There is someone we need to see first."

"Before Katie?"

"Yes. Head west."

"West? Broadmoor is northeast."

"I know. There is something I need to do. Pull in at a truck stop. I'll grab a burner phone and call Katie."

"You sure?"

"I'm sure. I'll fill you in on the way."

Raife hesitated, studying his old friend. Then he released the emergency brake, put the Land Cruiser in gear, pulled back onto the road, and drove west.

CHAPTER 17

THE FJ40 PUSHED TOWARD the setting sun on U.S. Route 50 through southern Colorado, passing towns that time seemed to have forgotten: Buckskin Joe, Cotopaxi, Poncha Springs, Monarch, and White Pine.

Freedom.

Run, Reece. Run with Katie. Forget the list. Forget the key. Forget the safe-deposit box.

I can't. That's not freedom. If I do, they'll never stop.

Then stop them.

I intend to.

They had picked up a burner phone in Cañon City, which Reece used to make a call.

Katie had answered on the first ring.

When they were done, Reece dumped the phone in the gas station garbage can next to the pump where Raife had filled up the Land Cruiser.

"How'd it go?" Raife asked.

"The way you'd imagine."

Raife just nodded.

After catching Raife up on what Vic had told him at Florence, Reece took in the beauty of the landscape with new eyes, appreciating every detail. He had not seen a sunset in three months.

At Gunnison they turned north onto 135, keeping the Gunnison

River on their right until they veered onto the two-lane 742 toward Almont.

Reece had traveled this road many times with his father and grandfather. For a moment he was lost among the pines, firs, aspens, and cottonwoods on this western edge of the Rockies, revisiting their brilliance through the innocent eyes of his youth. Though he had not known it at the time, while he was exploring its trails, constructing forts, building traps, and fishing, something else had been happening on the sprawling property, something he had not recognized at the time.

"Pull over. This is it," Reece said.

Raife eased the vehicle to the side of the road, and the two former SEALs surveyed their surroundings. Corral fencing lined the property along the road for as far as one could see.

An iron gate was set between two massive wood columns offset with river rock around the base. A thick wooden beam stretched between the two supports. Most ranch entrances would have a clever name etched above the entrance, but a name on this beam was conspicuously missing.

"Not much in the way of security," Raife noted.

"Visible anyway," Reece agreed. "Let's check it out."

Raife glanced over his left shoulder to ensure it was safe to cross the road, then eased across and to the gate call box. Before he could roll down his window, the large wrought-iron gate began to open.

"Looks like they were expecting us."

"Vic let him know."

"Do you remember the way?"

"I remember," Reece confirmed.

Raife maneuvered through the gate and wound his way closer to the Taylor River. They heard it before they saw it in the dim twilight.

"I bet there are some big browns in there," Raife said.

"That's why they chose this place. Poe's father was a true fly fisherman. Traveled all over the world but kept being drawn back to the Taylor."

"And it just so happened to be close enough to Mexico to fly in spies and defectors under the radar in the Cold War," Raife said, echoing what Reece had told him on their drive.

"Certainly convenient for the CIA. Turn in here."

Raife veered off the gravel road, passing a long bunkhouse, and swung into a roundabout with a group of aspens in the middle. He parked behind a pearl-green Lexus LX SUV in front of a modest log-framed home. It had been tastefully updated over the years but retained its rustic charm.

"I prefer the high ground," Raife noted, looking across the river and into the towering mountains. "But, all in all, not a bad spot."

The outside light came to life, bathing the driveway and small porch in a yellow glow.

The screen door rattled open and two black Labrador retrievers bound down the steps and into the driveway, running circles around the new vehicle before chasing one another toward the tree line.

A man stepped onto the deck, holding the screen door open with his foot, and nodded at the new vehicle.

As expected, he had aged considerably in the decades since Reece had last seen him. He looked thin in the way of someone not afraid of a little hard work. His angular features reminded Reece of a hawk surveying his domain. He was clean-shaven and wore jeans, work boots, and a red and green Filson mackinaw to ward off the evening chill. He slapped a tan packer hat—a combination cowboy hat and fedora—against his left hand before placing it over his dark gray hair.

"That's him," Reece said.

"Looks more mid-sixties than early eighties," Raife observed.

"Must be the mountain air. I know it's not clean living," Reece said, opening the door and stepping onto grounds he had once considered home.

William Poe stepped down the stone entryway stairs that led to the driveway. He met Reece at the bottom, leather gloves in one hand and a silver whistle in the other.

"It's been a long time, lad."

"Yes, sir. It has."

Reece extended his hand in greeting.

"I don't think much has changed," Poe said, looking back at the house.

"It looks great. A lot of memories here," Reece said.

"For all of us," Poe responded. "And this must be Raife Hastings."

Raife approached from the driver's side.

"Yes, sir. Pleasure to meet you."

"Pleasure is all mine. I hear you make a mighty fine rifle, Mr. Hastings. I need to get my name on your waiting list."

"I'd be happy to move you to the top, sir."

"You apprenticed with D'Arcy Echols in Utah, if my sources are accurate."

"That's right, sir. Trying to keep the old ways alive."

"Yes, the old ways. Sometimes, even in today's world, they can still be effective."

"Been enjoying your articles as well. Written under 'S. Rainsford,' I believe."

"You have reliable sources," Raife confirmed, acknowledging the nom de plume he used to write articles in hunting and fishing journals.

"*Most Dangerous Game*, was it?"

"A nod to the old ways," Raife said.

"And you," Poe said, shifting his attention back to Reece. "You have been busy since I last saw you. When was that?"

"Eighty-six? Maybe '87? I remember coming here to visit my grandfather with my dad in the old Wagoneer, so it couldn't have been much past then."

"Ah yes, right before he passed away. My father and your grandfather, they were quite the pair on this ranch. They built a distillery in the bunkhouse one summer. Tasted like gasoline. I think they spent so much time here because they were the only two they could talk with about the war, and what they did afterwards."

"Vic filled me in on some of the history."

Poe peered out into the darkness. "There is a lot of history here, lad."

He raised the whistle to his lips and gave it a short, shrill blow.

"Castor! Pollux! Places!"

The two dogs tore from the woods to take their positions on either side of their master.

"Lads, this is Castor, and this is Pollux. My companions and confidants. Good thing they can't speak. Who knows what secrets they might divulge."

"May I?" Reece asked.

"Of course. They are friendly. *Free!*"

The dogs stepped to Reece and Raife, who both offered the backs of their hands to the dogs' noses before kneeling down to get acquainted.

"Hey, boys," Reece said, smiling as he scratched them both behind the ears.

"Beautiful dogs," Raife commented before standing back up.

"Thank you. Dogs like these will never let you down," Poe said. "As an administrative note, no cell service or Internet here."

"That's not going to bother us," Raife confirmed.

"You can actually think and breathe without interruption on this property. I have a landline in the main house, and you can make satellite calls from the field across the river. James, do you remember the bridge?"

"Yes, sir."

"It's a bit more robust now. The rains of '92 took the old one right out. The new one would probably survive a JDAM strike."

"Who takes care of the property now?" Reece asked.

"I've gone through a few caretakers over the years. Have a good one now. Former Marine NCO. Mike Bill. He lives with his family—his wife, Lara, two boys, and a girl—in the house at the end of the road," Poe said, gesturing downriver. "Keeps to himself for the most part. Cares for the horses, maintains the roads, keeps them plowed in the winter. Doubt you will see them during your stay. He's working on a book about Afghanistan down there. He let me read a few chapters. It's not bad."

"Finally, a book by someone other than a SEAL," Raife quipped.

"Get cleaned up in the guest cottage," the old man directed, pointing to the long rectangular structure a hundred yards west of the main house that they had passed on the way in. "There are towels and new toothbrushes in the bathroom. Jackets and blankets in the closet. I'll meet you on the back deck for cigars and whiskey in fifteen minutes. Smoked duck, wild rice, salad, and a fairly average Malbec for dinner."

"It's good to be back, sir."

"It's good to have you back, James."

Reece nodded.

"There is something else in the bunkhouse for you. An old trunk. It has some of your father's and grandfather's items in it. I've been slowly collecting them over the years and setting them aside. I think that's about everything. I knew one day you would find your way back. They are yours. Get settled, and I'll see you at dinner. *Castor. Pollux. Follow!*"

He looked at the Land Cruiser and then scanned the edge of the driveway before turning and walking back up the stairs, dogs on his heels, disappearing into the main house.

CHAPTER 18

"CASTOR AND POLLUX?" RAIFE asked, throwing his small pack on one of the six beds that lined the bunkhouse.

"He had black Labs even then. He thought they would blend in better in his duck blinds. I remember walking the field across the river with him when I was young. He was always training his dogs for the winter at his duck hunting lodge in Arkansas. Back then their names were Romulus and Remus."

"Romulus and Remus?"

"Yep."

"The founders of Rome," Raife noted.

"That's right. Poe is a student of history, of art, of warfare. But it is an interesting choice for dogs, considering Romulus kills Remus," Reece said.

"He strikes me as a man who doesn't do anything without a distinct purpose."

"Well, he certainly was familiar with you."

"He's an old spook," Raife said. "He was trained up by the generation that founded the OSS and then the CIA. You heard him—'the old ways.' He did his homework."

"And he wanted us to know it."

"He did."

Reece sat down on a bed. A weathered old OD green footlocker had been placed in front of it.

"This must be it," Reece said.

"Must be. You want to be alone?" Raife asked.

"No. I think I've spent enough time alone lately."

The brass locking clasps were tarnished, and the leather carrying handle had long since rotted and been torn away.

Reece reached forward, undid the clasps, and pushed the top open on its hinges.

In the dim light of the bunkhouse it was initially difficult to see what was inside, so Raife grabbed a reading lamp and held it closer to the trunk.

A stack of journals and books occupied the left-hand side. On the other, on top of what looked to be a green field jacket and a sweater, was something Reece and Raife both instantly recognized.

"Not many of those around. Especially in that condition," Raife observed.

Reece reached inside and removed the 9mm Smith & Wesson M39 from the chest. Better known in the SEAL Teams as the Mk 22 "Hush Puppy," it had earned a legendary reputation in the jungles of Vietnam for silently eliminating sentries and guard dogs. A black skeletonized stock was affixed to the back of the grip, allowing a shooter to shoulder it as one would a rifle. Reece ejected the thirteen-round magazine and confirmed it was empty before pulling back the slide and locking it to the rear. It was difficult to be sure the chamber was empty in the poor light, so Reece reached his pinky inside to be certain.

"Clear and safe," he said.

"I've only seen photos of those," Raife said.

"Yeah, I guess they weren't as strict with inventories back in the Vietnam days," Reece said.

"At least not in the SEAL Teams."

"Or maybe it's from his time at the Agency? Look at this—high-profile front and rear sights so you can use them with this suppressor," Reece said, tapping the five-inch-long "can" attached to the threaded barrel.

"And check that out," Raife said, pointing to the slide lock. "That makes it a single-shot pistol."

"Yep, no sound from the slide cycling to reload the next round."

"Is the holster in there?" Raife asked.

Reece dug his hand into the footlocker and pulled out a box of 9mm Super Vel subsonic ammunition.

Raife whistled.

"And the holster," Reece said, pulling out a long leather holster.

"Jeez, look at that thing. It's gigantic."

"I didn't think there was much we could add to the arsenal back in Montana, but this is one we don't yet have."

"Well, you, my friend, are starting your collection from scratch if we can't get your weapons back from the FBI or ATF or whoever has them now."

"This is a good start," Reece said.

"And you never know when you might need it."

"Isn't that the truth."

"Since you just got out of prison, I will do my best to ensure you get one good night of rest before you need to put it to use."

"Thanks. I'll keep that in mind."

"What else is in there?"

"Let's see," Reece said, pulling out an extremely worn set of blue jeans and a tiger stripe camouflage field shirt.

"The unofficial uniform of SEALs and SOG in Vietnam," Raife said.

"If this stuff could talk," Reece said.

"What's that?" Raife asked, pointing into the trunk.

Reece set down the jeans and shirt and reached back inside.

"Whoa!"

"Your dad's Randall?"

Reece removed a large knife in a worn leather sheath.

"I remember seeing this when I was a kid," Reece said.

Raife tipped the lamp closer to get a better look as Reece removed the blade from its sheath.

"Still in great shape," Raife noted as Reece examined the classic knife in the light.

The tan sheath had darkened over the years, the water of the Mekong Delta having mixed with sweat, blood, and the dirt of the jungle. A green verdigris was visible around the copper rivets, as was to be expected. A small sharpening stone was stored in a snapped compartment on the scabbard. Reece set the sheath down and tested the blade with his thumb.

"Still sharp," he said.

"Of course—Tom Reece put it away sharpened," Raife said.

"'Take care of your gear, and your gear will take care of you,'" Reece said, echoing the mantra bludgeoned into all SEALs during training.

The five-inch stainless-steel blade displayed the scuffs and scars of a hard-use knife carried into combat in Southeast Asia. Serrations ran along a portion of the spine, rising like aggressive sentinels ready to rip and tear their way through obstacles on mission. The original hollow hilt was wrapped in neoprene that had long since begun to deteriorate.

"What's in the hilt?" Raife asked.

Reece twisted the brass cap. It still had a strip of leather attached to a lanyard ring. It turned easily. Reece turned it toward his palm, expecting to find a P38 can opener, an emergency fishing kit, waterproof matches, and fire-starting material. Instead, what slid out was a golden lapel pin.

"What the hell is that?" asked Raife.

"Not sure," Reece replied, turning it over in his hand. "It's old, whatever it is. 'OSS.'"

"Whose was it?"

"I don't know," Reece said. "My grandfather's, maybe. I always knew he was Scouts and Raiders in World War Two and that they did operations at the behest of the OSS, but Vic just told me he did some work for the Agency in the early days."

Reece examined it more closely before sliding it back into the hilt and reattaching the end cap. "Something tells me Poe has answers."

"And I don't think he is someone who appreciates being kept waiting."

Reece set the pistol and the knife back in the case and closed the lid. "You would be right. Besides, I'm starving. Let's eat."

CHAPTER 19

"GENTLEMEN—ICE, CRYSTAL, AND AN assortment of whiskeys on the table. Nothing too fancy, I'm afraid," the old spymaster said, his breath visible in the cold night air.

The two former frogmen walked across a section of lawn separating the guest cottage from the main house and ascended the steps to the deck that overlooked the Taylor River.

"Thank you, sir. After the last three months I am more than ready!" Reece said.

"Haven't you eaten?"

"We stopped in Florence and got him two Husky Burgers and fries, but he suspected that one of the burgers had come within inches of mayonnaise so he wouldn't touch it," Raife said.

"So, I see you didn't outgrow your aversion to mayo."

"Disgusting," Reece said.

"Well, take a look at these," Poe said, lifting the lid on the old Weber charcoal grill, gray smoke wafting toward the heavens. "Greenheads and a few teal from Arkansas. I just love the way they taste on Kingsford briquettes. I know there are fancier ways to grill now, but I've always liked the taste of these birds on this old grill. I get a new one about every twenty years from the local hardware store in Almont when they rust out. I hope to make one more purchase before I pass over to the other side. Help yourselves. If you notice anything expensive over there, rest assured it was a gift."

"Can I get you anything?" Raife asked.

"Way ahead of you both," he said, holding up a cocktail. "Cheers, lads. Thank you for making the trip. I am aware that this might not be how you wanted to spend your first night out of federal custody, James. I understand you have a girlfriend who would very much like to see you."

The three men took sips and moved to the edge of the deck overlooking the river. A light breeze rustled the aspens as the dogs stood guard around the Weber.

"To tell you the truth, I think this is just what I needed," Reece said, looking out across the river to the field beyond.

"Your father used to come here. After a mission. He would sit on this deck with me and your grandfather. In the early days he'd have a cigarette. Your grandfather would have a cigar, and I'd have a pipe. Always liked that sweet tobacco. How has your fly fishing progressed?"

"I'm afraid it hasn't."

"Sorry to hear that. Tom spent a lot of time on that water out there," Poe said, tipping his drink toward the river.

"Did he come here to debrief?"

"A few times, but more often than not we'd talk about fishing, horses, the ranch. It became like a decompression stop for him, a place for him to recharge. He came once or twice after your grandfather died. I think there was a lot left unsaid between them. This deck, the mountains, the river, they offered him a connection to his father."

"How did my grandfather come to work here?" Reece asked. "I always thought he just found a job after the war, but Vic insinuated it might be something else."

"Oh, it's more, James. Hold on a minute, don't want to overcook the ducks," he said, moving to the Weber.

"*Castor. Pollux. Places!*" he said, pointing to two dog beds on the deck against the house.

"*Scoundrels!* They love duck. I cooked enough for them, too."

"Where did you get your dogs, Mr. Poe?" Raife asked.

"Rescues. I could have gotten dogs from a kennel or flown to Scotland with some of my waterfowl friends from Arkansas for the pick of the litter, but I prefer to get them from a shelter. Train them up. Give them a life. Truth is, they give me a life."

"Can we help with anything?" Reece asked.

"Salad and rice are done and already on the inside table. These ducks are almost there," he said, pressing on the top of the largest one with his thumb. "Oh yes, see, you want to put the briquettes on that side of the grill. Keep the ducks on this side, really smoke them. Hold that cutting board for me, will you, James?"

Reece picked up the cutting board and held it as Poe used the tongs to remove the ducks.

"These are ready," he said. "*Castor. Pollux. Beds!*"

They entered the main house through glass doors followed by the two Labs, who immediately went to their flannel-covered dog beds. A fire flickered behind the glass of a wood-burning stove in the corner opposite two overstuffed leather chairs. The dining room table was set for three, illuminated by an antler chandelier.

"Just set that there," Poe said, pointing to the table as he removed his hat and coat, hanging them on a rack against the wall. Reece placed the cutting board on the table and removed his hat and coat, as did Raife.

"I know, it could use a woman's touch," Poe said, motioning to the shelves filled with books and duck decoys.

"Looks just like I remember it," Reece said.

"Not much has changed: more books, additional decoys, less company. Please, sit," he said. "If you will allow me, before we begin."

He bowed his head in prayer. The two young men followed suit.

"Dear Heavenly Father, we thank you for these magnificent ducks you have provided us this evening and for the steady hand that brought them down. We think of those in service to this great nation around the globe tonight and ask that you watch over them and keep them safe. We also ask that you look out for their families while they are away and pray that they be reunited soon. We thank you for the safe return of James Reece, who has been away from this ranch for too long, and if we put on waders tomorrow morning, we ask for a good bite. In your hallowed name we pray. Amen."

"Amen," Reece and Raife echoed.

"Let's eat. Serve yourselves. Pass the wine. It's a 2017 Angelica Zapata Malbec."

Poe swirled the wine in his glass and brought it to his nose.

"Black fruit with hints of cocoa and oak; you don't have to spend a fortune for a nicely balanced medium-bodied red that pairs well with duck."

Reece sliced into the blood-red meat and tasted his first wild game since imprisonment. He closed his eyes, savoring the taste. Heavenly.

He opened his eyes to see Poe studying him.

"You know you had your first duck right here at this table?"

"I don't remember," Reece admitted.

"You were young. Maybe five years old. You couldn't get enough of it. That was two rusty Webers ago."

The old man smiled, pointing with his steak knife to an empty chair at the end of the table. "Your grandfather sat there. My father had just passed away, and I was recently divorced from my second wife. She got the house in Georgetown. Your grandfather told me that next time, instead of getting married, I should just find a woman I don't like and buy her a house."

Reece and Raife laughed.

"I didn't know my grandfather was that funny."

"Oh, he was. Not around kids. That generation believed that children were to be seen, not heard."

"That's how I remember him."

"He was a great man, your grandfather—complicated, but great nonetheless. I wish I had recorded some of the conversations between him and my dad. Now they are gone forever, may they rest in peace."

"What did they talk about?"

"The war. The OSS. The good old days. I know more about both of them from people I worked with at the Agency then I ever heard from either of them."

"Oh?"

"I was brought into the CIA by that generation. Their fight was with Nazi Germany and Imperial Japan. China, Burma, the Balkans, the Philippines, Albania, North Africa. They had been in the trenches and had to reposition for a new adversary in a new age."

"The nuclear age," Raife said.

"Yes. They saw storm clouds on the horizon well before the end of the war."

"My grandfather stayed on?" Reece asked.

"Well, as you know, the OSS was disbanded after the war. Your grandfather was there at the Riverside ice-skating rink in September 1945 when Donovan gave his final speech to the troops. Roosevelt was a supporter. Truman was not, though Donovan was ultimately vindicated when the CIA was created to oversee foreign intelligence collection in 1947."

"I've never heard that."

"There is a lot you haven't heard. Your grandfather wasn't just present for that occasion. He was one of the fourteen commandos that Donovan pinned medals on during the ceremony. His citation remains classified."

"Is that what Vic meant when he told me my connection to the Agency ran deeper than I knew?"

"Possibly, but I doubt Mr. Rodriguez knows that story. He certainly is not aware that everyone in that room—the ice was replaced with wooden floorboards to transform it into an office during the war—was given a certificate as a thank-you for their service."

"Not much has changed."

"They also had gold lapel pins with 'OSS' engraved on them for those who served during the war. The catch was, you had to pay for them. One dollar. Your grandfather refused."

"Now, that I believe," Reece said, looking to Raife.

"My father would hear nothing of it and purchased it for him. They joked about that pin for the rest of their lives. I think he gave it to your dad shortly before he passed away."

Mystery of the OSS pin solved.

"How did they know each other?" Reece asked.

"They met in the Pacific. Your grandfather was with the Scouts and Raiders, but they conducted operations in conjunction with the OSS, which is how he met and befriended my father. They both worked with Ed Lansdale in the Philippines."

"*The* Edward Lansdale?"

"The man himself. I didn't meet Landsdale until Vietnam. He had already started the Saigon Military Mission and had retired from the Air Force and the Agency, but he was back in a 'State Department' capacity while still very much in the employ of the CIA. I first met him with Daniel Ellsberg in Saigon."

"Daniel Ellsberg? Of the Pentagon Papers?" Raife asked.

"The very one. You have to remember, the CIA and U.S. military were not what they are today. Those with World War Two intelligence and early Cold War insurgency and counterinsurgency experience all knew each other, and they were recruiting the next generation of operatives."

"Of which you were a part," Reece stated.

"I was, and it was an honor. I had been born to privilege, but I was also raised by a man who had made his fortune in shipbuilding and then helped create the OSS—for God and country. I'm a workingman at heart, and intelligence was in my blood."

"I read about the Philippines and Vietnam in Lansdale's book," Reece said.

"Ah yes," Poe said, taking another sip of wine. "That book only covers his life up until 1956. It's the decade after when things get exceedingly interesting."

"He continued to work in Vietnam, didn't he?"

"Among other places," Poe confirmed. "Unfortunately, all of his personal papers were destroyed in a fire that broke out in his home library in 1972. Most of the written records from that time at the CIA have long since been destroyed."

"The CIA is good at that," Raife said.

"That they are," Poe confirmed. "Congress hauled him in front of the Church Committee in '75. I think he was the only person to appear without an attorney by his side. By that point he was done with the secret world."

"I can understand why," Reece said.

"You met Lansdale once," Poe said.

"I did?"

"Right here. He threw a football to you on the front lawn."

"What was he doing here?"

"Drinking, mostly. But he was here to talk with your dad at the behest of your grandfather and my father. He was long past caring about nondisclosures. I think he felt disenfranchised. He devoted his life to a country that thanked him for World War Two but then ignored him on Vietnam. The fire in his library did more than destroy his books and papers—the smoke inhalation led to his wife's death. He never got over it."

Reece shook his head. "Tragic."

"That it was, personally and professionally."

"Why did my dad want to meet with him here?"

"Have you heard of Operation Mongoose?"

"The CIA program to kill Castro?"

"Kill or delegitimize, dethrone, but yes. I talked with your father about it many times over the years."

"And why is that?"

Poe paused.

"He was looking for connections."

"Connections?"

"Remember, this is the late 1970s, early 1980s. Your dad was now at the CIA. A case officer. But he had an agenda."

"An agenda?"

"He was searching for answers."

"On what?"

"Vietnam. Connections between the CIA, Cuba, Vietnam, and the Soviet Union."

Trust no one, his father's letter had read.

"I don't understand."

"James, when your dad returned from Vietnam, his war wasn't over. He'd lost Teammates. Others were MIA. There were suspicions that POWs were flown to the Soviet Union and exploited for intelligence."

"I've heard that before. What do you think?" Reece asked.

"I think he was right. The Soviets had spies in place at the CIA, NSA, and FBI for strategic-level intelligence; we know that. Angleton was convinced of it, but it had been a while since they had someone with tactical-level intelligence in one of their interrogation facilities."

"Since Powers?" Reece asked.

"Yes. They had Gary Powers for almost two years after he was shot down in his U-2 in 1960. He was a pilot. They needed operators. Many of the Green Berets and SEALs rotating through tours in Vietnam also had served on teams to counter another threat."

"They had served in Berlin," Raife said.

"Yes. It wasn't all jungle ambushes for the men with green faces back in the sixties. Some had knowledge the Soviets desperately needed—namely, information on the ADM-4 and its successor, the SADM."

"Special Atomic Demolitions Munitions," Reece said. "Suitcase nukes."

"The Soviets were developing their own man-portable tactical nuclear weapons, but with the United States positioned in NATO countries with troops trained to deter and defend against a Soviet invasion through the Fulda Gap, they needed intelligence on our capabilities."

"And there was a group of men in Vietnam who could provide them with exactly that."

"Precisely. Some, designated 'Green Light' Teams, had been trained to parachute into Eastern Europe with SADMs; others were pre-positioned behind enemy lines. It was part of a limited nuclear war strategy popular in military and intelligence circles at the time. The intent was to slow the Soviet advance from East Germany and Czechoslovakia. The Soviets needed to know our capabilities and targets. Operators in Vietnam had that intel. And it wasn't just the Soviet threat. They had been trained to use what they called the 'backpack nuke' in Korea and Iran as well. They were a wealth of information, and their capture in Vietnam was an opportunity for the Soviets to exploit."

"And my dad thought some of his MACV SOG Teammates were among those POWs transferred to the Soviet Union?"

"He did. But that's not why he came to work for the CIA."

"I always thought it was a natural progression, from SEAL to CIA."

"It would seem that way, but there is more. His spotter was killed by a sniper in '67. That's why he kept going back. He was searching."

"Searching for what?"

"The man who killed his spotter."

"How could he possibly know, even if he did inadvertently come across him?"

"Because he called in an air strike after his spotter was killed. Decimated the hillside. He was ordered to retreat but went in to pass back his battle damage assessment. Do you know what he found?"

"What?"

"An SVD-63."

"A Dragunov?"

"Yes. And a tunnel complex. He was making entry with his 1911 when an NVA battalion emerged from over the hill, and he went on E-and-E. When he was finally recovered they went back to the hillside. The NVA were gone. But his partner wasn't."

Reece set down his wineglass.

"They had stripped him naked. The trees had been destroyed, so the NVA sharpened a branch and impaled him, from his anus to his lungs. And as if that wasn't enough, they cut off his genitals and stuffed them in his mouth. Left him there on the smoldering hillside with his dick and balls in his throat like a goddamn scarecrow."

"No wonder he never talked about it."

"The Dragunov had been mangled in the air strike. Totally inoperable. The enemy took the optic but they left the rifle hanging from the sling around his neck. And of course they booby-trapped it with a grenade, but that was disarmed before Tom and his teammates lowered him down. They had to remove that tree limb from their dead friend before they could zip him into a body bag. The NVA wanted to let the Americans know that there was a sniper in the jungle, a sniper with a Soviet SVD-63. As you well know, few combatants on the battlefield wield as much psychological terror as a lone man trained in the art of long-distance shooting."

"I'm aware."

"When he got home, he was lost. Happened with a lot of veterans back then."

"Happens with a lot of veterans today," Raife offered.

"Yes. It is a bill that comes due for every society that sends young men to war."

Reece's eyes narrowed.

"But you knew him. You had worked with him in the Phoenix Program."

"I had. He had a gift, your father. A gift I understand you inherited."

"You recruited him?"

"I did."

"You offered him a mission."

"I had a list. A list of Soviet GRU snipers 'advising' NVA elements in 1967."

"He was planning to track them down."

"Every one of them. I'd lost men, too. In the Phoenix Program, Project Delta, MACV SOG. Teams would leave the wire and disappear, operating off intelligence provided by the CIA. My intel."

"You suspected there was someone on the inside? A mole?"

"I did, or I should say, I do."

"Present tense?"

"There is just too much that has gone unexplained. The Soviets, now the Russians, think long term. Not as long as the Chinese, but longer than we do. We expect instant gratification. The Russians will wait decades; the Chinese, centuries."

"And you suspected that men who had worked for you and disappeared in Vietnam were taken to the Soviet Union?"

"As you know, intelligence is different from evidence in a criminal case. The men in government and at the highest levels of the Agency are lawyers and bankers. They act off evidence. Intelligence is a different animal altogether. They never understood that. I had—we as an Agency *had*—intelligence that there were American pilots and special forces soldiers from MACV SOG at camps scattered across the Soviet Union, kept in solitary confinement from Moscow to Siberia. Some remained in Laos and Cambodia, so when the Vietnamese government said there were no U.S. service members in Vietnam, they were technically telling the truth. We got close to launching a Delta mission to extract one of them in 1981. The intel was as solid as it comes."

"What happened?" Raife asked.

"It was called off at the last minute."

"Why?"

"A story about POWs in Vietnam broke in the *Washington Post*. Then another was published in *Parade* magazine. The powers that be used those articles as an excuse not to launch. It was only a year after Delta's failed hostage rescue mission in Iran. Senior-level Army officers, politicians, intelligence officials, and bureaucrats were not about to risk another black mark on their records. With the enemy now alerted through those articles, the chance of the prisoners' being moved was too high. It would have also been a perfect opportunity to draw Delta into an ambush. Those stories scuttled the mission. I thought we really had a chance."

"Who leaked to the *Post*?"

"Nobody knows. We could have still pulled it off."

"Who exactly canked the op?" Reece asked.

"They didn't tell us back then. It came from 'the highest levels.'"

"The White House?"

"Or the Agency's seventh floor. Someone didn't want to let the genie out of the bottle."

"But you still had a mission."

"I did. And it happened to overlap with your father's. Unlike Tom Reece, I understood the mechanisms of government. I wanted to work within that system. Tom wanted to burn it down."

"How could he hide all this? How did I never know?"

"He compartmentalized it. He wanted to be a father, a *present* father, to you. His dad was of a different generation, one that locked away what they did in the war and got to work. Raising kids was for the women. That's just how it was. Tom wanted to break the cycle, so he was one Tom Reece on the job and another Tom Reece to you. Do you know what they called him in Vietnam?"

Reece shook his head.

"Skinner."

"Skinner," Reece repeated.

"There was nobody as good in the woods as Tom Reece."

"And this has something to do with why Russian intelligence wants me dead?"

"I don't know, lad. I do know that he was putting together a file on everything he'd collected. Powerful people at the Agency and in Russia have a vested interest in making sure those files never see the light of day. There are still documents from the Kennedy assassination that remain classified sixty years after the fact, and have remained classified even after congressional mandates, laws, have ordered their release."

"The Kennedy assassination?"

"Tom was looking into any connections between the Soviet Union and Vietnam, and those in government service who may have hidden those connections or facilitated that relationship."

"Why would someone want to hide or downplay a relationship between the Soviet Union and Vietnam?" Reece asked.

"Because some of those connections could lead back to those in our intelligence agencies in the employ of the Soviets."

"That's an aggressive undertaking for one man," Reece observed.

"He wasn't alone. He had me, and he had an ally in Congress. He was building his case. For my own safety he never told me where he kept the evidence he collected. Did he ever give you a key to a safe-deposit box? I think that's where he was storing it."

"No," Reece lied again.

"He was convinced he had almost everything he needed, but he was always missing that one final piece."

"How were you involved?" Reece asked.

"I was what they used to call a 'rabbi'—someone who could look out for a more junior intelligence officer—a mentor. I played that role until Iran-Contra. That was my cue to get out and move on. I tendered my resignation the day Casey died. Then I assisted from the outside."

"How?"

"I took a position with the World Bank and then the International Monetary Fund. Money wasn't an issue for me; my father had made certain of that. I had connections, personal and professional, that were in demand. And I had 'institutional knowledge.'"

"What kind of institutional knowledge?"

"The kind that they get nervous about you testifying to under oath in front of Congress."

"Like the Church and Pike Committees?"

"Exactly. But your father had another reason for continuing his hunt."

"Which was?"

"He felt responsible for another death, and this one he thought he could do something about."

"Another death from Vietnam?"

"No. Closer to home. He was working with a congressman. Walter Stowe."

"He was gunned down on his boat in Rhode Island, wasn't he?"

"He was. He was also the man your father was working with in Congress to expose the Soviet program of transporting U.S. service members to the USSR. They both thought, as did I, that their off-the-books investigation had been compromised. Your father believed that is why Congressman Stowe was killed."

"Wasn't his wife shot as well?"

"She was. But there is something else. Something the newspapers left out about that day."

"What's that?"

"There was another man there. He was waiting for the congressman and his wife at the yacht club. He saw the assassin shoot Congressman Stowe, but it happened before he could do anything. He was bringing his pistol up when the congressman's wife, Martha, was hit. He took a hundred-yard pistol shot. Hit the assassin in the chest. He ran to the dock and put another one in his head before diving into the water to rescue Martha. Did an emergency tension pneumothorax decompression right there on the dock. Saved her life."

"Who was it?"

"Your dad, James. It was Tom Reece."

"I can't believe I didn't know any of this. What happened to Martha?"

"She made a full recovery, though she retreated from public life to raise her children out of the spotlight."

"Where is she now?"

"She still lives on her family's estate on Martha's Vineyard. Your dad worked with her to find her husband's killer for the rest of his life."

"I thought you said he killed the assassin on the dock."

"He did. But that was a low-level gun for hire. There were no digital footprints back then, no emails, no cell tower hits nor GPS embedded in mobile devices or in vehicles. The secrets died with the shooter."

"My father wanted to know who paid for the bullet," Reece stated.

"He did."

"And now, so do I."

CHAPTER 20

Interstate 70 West
Utah-Colorado Border

THE DRIVE FROM LOS Angeles to Las Vegas was uneventful. The paperwork in both the Tahoe and the Suburban was legit, and though the drivers were not the owners of the vehicles, the registration and tags were up-to-date. Aram had inspected both personally before they departed. Headlights, taillights, brake lights, turn signals—all were in working order. Maintaining the speed limit was the toughest part, but they had strict instructions. Use the cruise control to go three miles an hour over the posted limit so as not to stand out among the onslaught of vehicles hurtling up Interstate 15 toward Sin City. Any deviation from those instructions and Aram would be held accountable. The Armenian Mafia, better known as "Armenian 13," was not to be trifled with.

Aram Sivaslian had missed the North Hollywood gunfight that put the Armenian Mafia on the FBI's radar. He was too young. He'd been recruited in 2011, when a slew of federal indictments devastated its ranks. Aram had been instructed to join the military. Armenian Power, by then known as Armenian 13 due to links with the Mexican Mafia, wanted to build an army. The 2008 North Hollywood shoot-out, in which over fifty shots were fired, had resulted in only two fatalities. That event had taught them that to build an army, one needed training.

Aram spent his time in the Army attached to a Field Artillery Battalion of a Brigade Combat Team. Even though he didn't become a special forces soldier, Aram still qualified on his M4 carbine and Beretta M9 pistol. He did his time and managed to stay out of trouble as he had been ordered. He then returned to LA, to a life of crime. Eager to prove himself, he did a year for armed robbery in Chino. The DA had dropped the kidnapping charges. Since then, he had continued his rise up the ranks, working with *La eMe*, running drugs from San Diego to Los Angeles.

Two men in Aram's crew had fought in the Syrian Civil War. They had been sent there to gain experience. They had gained notoriety in Los Angeles organized crime circles when they were captured on video and recognized on a cable news broadcast. All nine had proven themselves to Armenian Power leadership.

A year ago, they had descended on the home of one of their members suspected of cooperating with the FBI. They made the snitch sit on his couch and watch as they smashed in the heads of his mother and aging grandparents with baseball bats. They then shot his father before turning their guns on the traitor.

Armenian Power was still small when compared to *La eMe*, MS-13, *La 18*, the Chicago Outfit, or the Bratva. They made most of their money through racketeering, prostitution, extortion, and protection within their own communities. Aram liked the money, the clothes, the cars, and the women, and as odd as it seemed, he liked the responsibility. He was seen as someone who could be trusted. His crew got the job done.

It was unusual that Armenian Power would stray so far from LA, but when he pulled into the warehouse on the outskirts of Vegas in the early afternoon, he understood why. This was a favor between the leaders of the Bratva and Armenian Power. The Russian mafia was tasking his crew with a mission. Whatever money or favors traded hands at the higher levels was lost on Aram. His crew would make a significant amount of money, which he correctly guessed was a small percentage of what was exchanged up the chain.

They had been told to dress in conservative attire and, if stopped, to say they were going to Vegas for their friend's bachelor party. They had traveled this far without weapons. That would not be the case for the remainder of the journey. All the more reason to use that cruise control.

The Bratva contacts gave them what they would need once they arrived in Colorado: two ARs, two shotguns, five suppressed Glocks, three push-to-talk radios, and four helmets fitted with night vision.

"These sighted in?" Aram had asked.

"I don't know. It doesn't matter. Get close. Use the Glocks. Make this look like a robbery gone wrong. Make it sloppy," the large Russian dictated.

They loaded everything into the backs of the SUVs and covered the equipment with camping gear also provided by the Bratva.

"What the fuck is all this?" one of Aram's crew had asked. "I'm not fucking camping."

"It's cover," Aram said. "We aren't *fucking* camping. We are going to go do the job and then get back to Vegas to party. Tomorrow night you will be spending your cut on hookers and blow in the Cosmo."

"Get to it. And don't bring any of this back," the Russian said.

Aram nodded, loaded his crew back into their vehicles, and continued toward their target.

CHAPTER 21

RAIFE SAT ON HIS bed, looking across the bunkhouse at his friend.

The bathroom light at the end of the structure was on, casting shadows across the floor.

The lights in the main house were off, the old man having long since retired upstairs to his bed.

Raife had placed a call to Liz from Poe's landline asking her to fly to Almont the next morning and file a flight plan from there to Martha's Vineyard. His parents had once owned a house there but sold it after the kids had grown. They were much more comfortable in the mountains of Montana.

Reece mumbled something in his sleep that Raife couldn't decipher.

Listen to that sixth sense.

It had kept his mother and father alive in Rhodesia, and it had done the same for Raife in Iraq and Afghanistan.

The man across from him had assembled a team of former SEALs and planned a rescue mission into Russia to save Raife's life. Reece had sent two arrows through the chest of the man who had killed Raife's sister. He had then carried his wounded friend up what amounted to a cliff and gotten him out of the country to medical care. It was a debt that Raife could never repay.

Reece had just spent three months in solitary confinement. Three months in the dark. Until Raife was certain his blood brother was on the mend, he was going to be his guardian angel. Reece needed rest. That meant "condition white" from Colonel Cooper's color code; completely situationally unaware.

Security was almost nonexistent on the ranch. It seemed like the old man had either resigned himself to his fate or believed the grudges of long ago had expired. Maybe he was ready for the grave. Raife was not. He was now a father, married to a woman he loved. His life would not be possible without Reece having risked everything to save him. And Reece, and Katie, would not be safe until they had figured out what was happening, why Reece had been set up, and what was in that safe-deposit box.

The shelves held books on hunting and fishing and the flora and fauna specific to the Rocky Mountain region. Copies of *Grey's Hunting Journal*, in which S. Rainsford had penned a few stories, were stacked on a coffee table in front of a small sofa. A desk with an old brass lamp was set against one of the windows that overlooked the river, and an old Orvis bamboo fly rod was mounted to the wall above. A wood-burning stove kept them warm, while an open window let in the fresh mountain air. The soothing noise of the river was peaceful. It could also mask the sounds of anyone approaching out of the night.

Sixth sense.

Raife stood. His blood brother was out cold. His first night out of confinement in three months. He seemed to be adjusting quickly; maybe too quickly. Raife walked to the bathroom and turned off the light. He then pulled on his Sitka jacket, moved to the door that led to the deck off the bunkhouse, and made his way to the back of the Land Cruiser. He unlatched a clasp on the bumper, swung the spare tire carrier to the side, and opened the ambulance-style doors. He unzipped a soft weapons case next to a small Eberlestock pack and removed a long black rifle. To the untrained eye it looked like an M4 on steroids. To the initiated, it was recognizable as a Knight's Armament SR-25 7.62x51mm sniper weapon system.

Raife was intimately familiar with the SR-25, having relied on it and its MK 11 MOD 0 variant both in Iraq and Afghanistan. Raife's father, Jonathan, had purchased the rifle in its SR-25 configuration twenty years earlier when Knight's sold the package used by SEALs on the open market as a commemorative edition. A suppressor was attached to the barrel, and a SureFire Scout light and PEQ-2A IR laser aiming device graced the rail. Raife rolled the rifle to the left and pulled back on the charging handle, confirming there was a round chambered by feeling it with his finger. He ensured the weapon was on "safe" and then reached into a pocket on the outside of the soft case, removing a UNS night-vision optic, also known as a PVS-22. He attached it in front of the Mark 4 LR/T 3.5–10x40 M3 Leupold scope, turned it on, and raised the rifle. The device turned the darkness into familiar shades of green.

He had scouted positions on the way in and knew exactly where he was going.

He would have preferred to put a protective detail on the man he considered a brother, but right now the number of people Raife trusted could be confined to one hand. There were too many unknowns in the puzzle he had just begun to put together. And until that puzzle was complete, Raife was going to mitigate what he could.

Both the main house and the bunkhouse were dark. No dogs barked to break the stillness of the night. The only sounds were the crickets and the calm lapping of the river cutting through the property as it made its way from various tributaries above the Taylor Park Reservoir to the Colorado River and eventually into the Gulf of California in northwestern Mexico.

Raife shouldered the light pack, closed the back of the Land Cruiser, and walked into the night.

CHAPTER 22

THEY CAME JUST AFTER 3:00 a.m. Someone in this crew had military experience, Raife thought.

The group patrolled along the edge of the road. Raife knew they felt safe on the road at this time of night. It allowed them to move faster and with less noise than had they approached through the bush. Headlights and the sound of an engine would alert them of an approaching vehicle and give them time to scatter into the tree line. They moved as though they knew exactly where they were going. They had either been here before, been briefed by someone familiar with the property, or studied Google Earth.

Steady, Raife. Make sure these aren't lost hikers or neighbors. Don't press this trigger out of paranoia.

He remembered what Tom Reece had once told them: *It's not paranoia if someone is really after you.*

A sleeping bag provided insulation from the elements to ward off hypothermia and provide some semblance of countermeasures from anyone who might be scanning the area with a thermal. The outside of the bag remained cold while the inside kept Raife warm and ready to fight.

Four men, single file. East side of the road.

No comms with Reece or Poe.

Can you drop them all?

Yes.

What if there are more?

Wait.

Do they have weapons?

Can't tell yet.

Hold.

You need to warn Reece.

How do you do that?

Raife reached forward and carefully removed the suppressor from the end of the barrel.

CHAPTER 23

ARAM LED HIS ELEMENT through the night.

His orders were to make it look like white-trash meth heads looking for a quick score. A robbery gone bad. That shouldn't be too hard to pull off. Most of the landowners in this part of the world with fancy ranches were back at their primary homes in California, Florida, or New York. Meth addicts would think they had an easy score on their hands. When they surprised the owners, they panicked and had to kill them. Bodies wouldn't be found for days, maybe weeks. The key was to not make it look too professional. Aram knew that wouldn't be a problem. His crew was not known for professionalism; they were feared for their brutality. If everyone on-site was found with two shots to the head, that would raise eyebrows, even with local law enforcement. The shotguns and ARs were reserved for backup. Even out here in the boonies someone might hear the echo and wonder what was happening in the middle of the night along the river. Aram and his crew would riddle their targets with 9mm rounds and then head for Vegas.

Three people were on the target list, and there were two structures on-site. They did not have confirmation as to which house their targeted individuals would be sleeping in, so they had decided to hit both buildings and kill everyone inside. They would then trash both, steal anything of value, and be gone before the sun came up.

When it came to hits, this one was on the lower end of the difficulty scale. Still, one could not be too careful, which was why he had a second element approaching from upriver. Splitting $150,000 between the nine of them wasn't bad for one night's work. Their marks had made the mistake of crossing the Bratva. A mistake that had left them with only a few more minutes of life. Maybe Aram and his crew would spend two nights in Vegas on the return trip to celebrate. In less than twenty minutes they would be able to afford it.

• • •

They knelt at the edge of the driveway.

These are not hikers or neighbors.

Wait until you see their hands.

From seventy-five yards away Raife could not make out what they were saying, but they appeared to be talking. Through the night-vision optic Raife saw something light up. On NODs the smallest light is amplified.

A push-to-talk.

Shit. There's another group. He's talking to someone.

Raife raised his head from the scope and looked toward the main house. A light went on and then off in the tree line just past Poe's residence.

Raife dropped his head back to the scope. The element he had been watching stood.

Pistols with suppressors.

Enemy.

Decision time.

Engage.

Raife's rifle was dialed in to his "hunter zero" of 250 yards, meaning at any distance from 50 to 300, he was going to connect with his intended target. He could cover the entire target area without adjusting for elevation.

Raife exhaled slowly as he flipped off the safety and exerted even pressure back on the trigger.

CHAPTER 24

REECE WAS ON A knee, looking up into Katie's deep blue eyes, ring in his hand, a future ahead with the woman he loved.

Katie, I'm done with the Agency. I'm done with the government. If you'll have me, I want to spend the rest of my life making you the happiest woman on earth.

She brushed a strand of blond hair behind her ear and opened her mouth.

Something was wrong. The hope and love that had emanated from her eyes a moment earlier was replaced by a frozen stare. Instead of words, a trickle of red blood oozed from her mouth as she fell forward onto Reece.

"Katie!"

He removed his hand from her back, wet with the blood of an entrance wound.

"Katie!"

He felt the jolt of another round entering her body, absorbing the impact.

Reece bolted upward in the darkness.

My cell. Prison. No, it's lighter than that. A bed with blankets. Windows, the sound of rushing water. A river.

The sound of the next gunshot brought him back to life.

The ranch.

Raife.

He looked to the empty bunk across from him and swung his legs to the floor, his hand finding the SIG P210 on the nightstand.

Raife was gone.

How many shots was that? Two? Three?

Get your bearings, Reece.

Who was shooting?

The dying embers of the fire gave Reece just enough light to see.

Reece quickly slid into his jeans, pulled the dark wool commando sweater from the trunk over his head, and stepped into the Salomon shoes at the foot of the bed.

Should I stay or go?

Take a breath, look around, make a call.

This is a known entity.

Too many windows.

If someone is targeting you here, it's a known entity to them as well.

Always improve your fighting position.

Move.

Reece grabbed his tomahawk and shoved the handle into his jeans behind the leather holster on his right side just behind his hip. He covered the distance to the door in less than a second, then paused. Another gunshot echoed up the valley.

Shooter to the south. Close.

If a sniper was after him, why didn't they shoot him when he arrived, or why didn't they wait until morning when they had a clear, unobstructed shot?

Because the sniper is not after you. The sniper is protecting you.

Reece changed levels. Dropping to a knee, he opened the door, low-crawled across the deck, and rolled onto the lower ground that fell away toward the river.

Get to the water.

The dirt, stones, and moss of the riverbank were cold and wet.

Just like my cell.

This is not your cell.

This is your childhood refuge.

And now it's a battleground.

Normally Reece would not maneuver to the low ground, but as he knew from his engagements downrange, the battlefield was a dynamic and ever-changing environment. It required constant adaptation, because your enemy was continually adapting to you. It was a deadly game where aggressive problem-solving won the day, and it was a game in which Reece had become quite adept.

Exploit all technical and tactical advantages.

Did the enemy have NODs?

Reece had to assume they did.

What can you work to your advantage?

The river.

Noise. Reece had always been comfortable in the darkness. Now, he felt as if it were home.

Use the dead space. If they have night vision, take that advantage away. They can't see through rocks, even if they have thermals.

He who flanks first wins.

Reece slid down the embankment into the side of the river, a place where he knew one could fish in waders without being swept away by the current. Five or six yards out toward the center was a different story.

The cold water soaked through his jeans up to his knees as he pushed himself upriver. He had played in these waters often as a child. He was on home turf. Whoever had come this evening was the visiting team, and they would not be going home.

Is this the life you want for Katie?

Not now. It's time to work.

With the nearby rapids masking the sound of his movement, Reece pushed north and angled around a boulder.

Darkness. But even without a moon, the stars provided just enough illumination to see movement. It wasn't the coordinated movement of a skilled element. It was confusion. Anyone who had seen combat could tell the difference.

A man in the rear shouted something into a handheld radio and looked to the north.

Reece froze.

There was someone else in the woods.

The thing about night vision is that it forces you to focus on only one of the five senses—the sense of sight. Reece could tell they were not wearing four-bangers—the NODs that give you peripheral vision. They were wearing PVS-15s or 31s, which meant they were looking through toilet paper tubes. For all practical purposes, their peripheral vision was nonexistent.

Reece heard the words first.

What was that? Russian?

The light of a small push-to-talk quickly illuminated his face and then went dark. Reece now had his position.

His new target thought he was alone in the forest.

He was wrong.

It was too quick to tell exactly what he was carrying. A rifle of some sort. Was this man overwatch? Command and control?

Didn't matter. He had come to kill Reece, Poe, Raife, or maybe all three, and he was about to pay.

Reece dropped back into the flowing water. The bank fluctuated from three feet to eight feet high, the river having cut its path through this section of country at the base of the Rockies for millennia.

Reece estimated the distance and pulled himself up the rocky berm.

The man's back was to Reece, his focus on his crew still confused by the shots that had broken the calm night and awakened Reece less than two minutes ago.

No suppressor on this pistol, Reece. If you shoot, the entire element will turn and send all their firepower your way. Keep the element of surprise.

Reece smoothly holstered the pistol. When his hands reemerged from his belt line he held the Winkler RnD tomahawk in a hammer grip in his right hand and the HeadHunter Blade in a reverse grip in his left.

The man turned as Reece closed the distance. Whether it was from the noise of Reece's approach or instinct, it didn't matter. It was too late.

The rise of the rifle was aborted as the man met the front spike and leading edge of Reece's tomahawk. It crashed into his right arm, just above the elbow, destroying his bicep tendon and ripping his hand from the rifle's pistol grip. His radio fell to the ground as he grasped desperately for the rifle's handguard. The violent attack spun him toward Reece, who thrust his Sayoc fixed blade at his opponent's midsection, hitting the rifle and using the position as a reference point in the dark, trapping the long gun to the front of his body. Reece flipped his wrist and changed the direction of the axe's head, swinging it down and across the man's neck, ripping through his throat from the side of his spine across his larynx. Following through, Reece's weapon ripped meat from his enemy's left shoulder and upper bicep, opening up a devastating wound channel and immobilizing his left arm. Reece slid his fixed blade up from the reference point on the man's rifle and pressure-cut through the sling at his right shoulder, causing the rifle to fall to the ground. He then sank the blade down past the collarbone and through the thoracic outlet, severing critical muscles, blood vessels, and nerves. Reece used his momentum to shift directions and swing the tomahawk down into the man's left clavicle, driving him to the dirt, and finished him with a devastating hit to the back of the head.

NODs on bump helmet. No body armor, Reece noted as he stepped on what was left of the man's head to pry the hawk from the skull fragments and brain matter that had arrested its direction of travel.

Reece shifted his attention back to the house, where four more intruders were stacked against the door, about to make entry.

Rather than lose time attempting to search for the rifle in the dark, Reece dropped his fixed blade and tomahawk and went prone on the forest floor. If they successfully entered the house, Poe was as good as dead.

As he sighted in on his enemy, the outside lights sparked to life. The man closest to the house carried an AR, the next two carried suppressed pistols, and rear security carried a shotgun. They were stacked on the back door. From forty yards away Reece could see one of them talking into a handheld radio, then looking at the man in front with the rifle and shrugging his shoulders.

Did they have sniper teams on the hillside across the river? A blocking force? A containment element? If they did, Reece would already be dead.

Four men. Reece had a pistol with eight rounds and two extra magazines.

Reece pushed down on the manual safety and let out his breath, slowing pressing the trigger to the rear.

The point man held on the door with his AR while the second man in the stack turned and mule-kicked it. It didn't open on the first kick, but it did on the second. But instead of turning to enter behind the point man, the unmistakable sound of a shotgun ripped through the night.

Reece watched as the breacher's body attempted to contort around the multiple wound channels that tore through his back.

Poe.

Reece sent a 9mm round into the upper chest of the point man with the AR. He followed it with three more in quick succession.

The confusion of moments ago turned to panic.

They were caught in one of the worst positions possible on the battlefield—the L ambush.

Another shotgun blast tore through the night from inside the house, removing the head of the man with the AR who had caught Reece's four rounds to the chest.

Two down.

Rather than assaulting through the attack coming from inside the house, the two remaining men in black ran.

Amateurs.

Even amateurs could kill you.

Especially when they were running at you with loaded weapons.

Only one man was in Reece's line of sight, as the second man was blocked by the first.

Reece pressed the trigger again—one, two, three, four to the chest, five to the face, tearing off his NODs and sending him to the deck not ten feet from Reece's position.

The empty pistol went to slide lock. The extra magazines were in his pocket.

No time to reload. Get to cover.

Reece rolled to his right and then pushed himself backward off the embankment and into the current.

CHAPTER 25

DON'T STAND TOO CLOSE to the edge, Reece had been admonished by his father and Poe many times in his youth. The river cuts its way south and eats away at the bank. The erosion creates an undercut, so it may look like you are standing on solid ground when you are in fact just standing on a few inches of soil about to fall into the ever-changing course of the river.

Reece used that knowledge to his advantage now.

As shotgun pellets impacted the water, Reece pushed himself under the bank, the noise of the rapids covering his movement as his left hand fished out a new magazine. He ejected the old and inserted the new, rolling his now cold hand over the top of the slide and sending it home, chambering a round. The frigid water was sapping his strength and affecting his fine motor skills.

He could feel the man continue to charge and shoot into the area where he had last seen Reece on the bank.

Now.

Reece rolled out from under the bank, his body covered in a foot of rushing water. From his back he brought his hands together, locking the pistol to his body with his elbows crushing into his sides. He saw the shadow looming over him looking out into the river, shotgun in his shoulder.

Reece pressed the trigger again and again, directing the rounds up into the thighs, groin, and upper chest of the man with the shotgun.

The rounds found their marks, and Reece felt his weapon go into slide lock.

New magazine. Last magazine.

Reece knew his shots were fatal, but he also knew that anything other than a shot to head meant that a dead man could still fight. Blood was still pumping. The brain was still working. Primal instincts were in command.

The attacker swung his shotgun down toward the man who had just filled him with lead as Reece's last magazine found the magwell of his pistol.

I'm not going to be fast enough.

The sound Reece thought would signify the end of his life broke through the night, but surprisingly Reece didn't feel the impact of the close-range blast of a 12-gauge.

Instead, the man's frontal cortex exploded outward from a shot to the back of his head, and he toppled off the embankment, directly onto Reece.

CHAPTER 26

"WHERE'D YOU GET THAT bloody pistol?" Raife asked from the bank above, where moments earlier the man with the shotgun had taken his last breaths. Raife was holding a sniper weapon system that Reece recognized instantly. "I think you need a handgun with a higher magazine capacity."

"Remind me to have some words with the guy who gave this to me," Reece said, holding up the black pistol. His slide lock reload had been interrupted by a two-hundred-pound body landing on top of him, so he replaced it with his last eight-round magazine and stowed the empty in his back pocket.

"At least it's accurate," Raife returned.

"Would have been nice to have another ten rounds," Reece said.

"I see your point. You should probably get a 365-XMACRO."

"Good tip. Mind helping me out of this river?"

"Pass me up that shotgun first."

Reece reached down and ensured the shotgun was on safe before handing it to his friend.

"I scanned the area on the night scope. Don't see anything else moving. That doesn't mean there aren't more out there."

"Poe?"

"He's fine. He made short work of two of these guys with his old bird gun."

"Sure looked like it."

"That guy got anything else on him?" Raife asked.

Reece grabbed the dead man by his jacket and shifted him so that his upper torso was on the bank, his legs still floating in the water.

"Wallet. Cell phone."

"Recognize him?" Raife asked.

"Not with his face gone."

"You're welcome."

"Let's check his buddy."

Raife reached down and helped haul his friend up the embankment.

Reece collected his tomahawk and fixed-blade knife. They disarmed the dead men as they checked them, the lights from the main house giving them enough light to see.

"Young," Raife observed.

"Yeah, and inexperienced," Reece said as they worked their way up the steps into the main house, where Poe had started a roaring fire. "Just one man back in the tree line as their overwatch, maybe their command and control. They had high ground across the river, which they didn't utilize."

"Lucky for us," Raife acknowledged.

"Lucky for us," Reece agreed. His adrenaline had warded off enough of the cold to keep him in the fight. His body now recognized that the threat had passed. He was chilled to the bone.

"Get out of those wet clothes, lad. There is a guest room with a shower just past the kitchen. I already put some clothes out that I think will fit," Poe said as his guests entered the room.

"We got this, Reece," Raife confirmed. "Get warm."

"My caretaker, Sergeant Bill, is on his way," Poe said.

"You're not calling the police?" Reece asked.

"Not yet, lad. The old ways."

Reece nodded and went to recharge his depleted body in a warm shower.

CHAPTER 27

REECE DROPPED HIS WET clothes in a heap on the floor. He stayed in the shower just long enough to warm his bones and bring life back into his extremities.

Dry clothes were laid out on the guest room bed when he emerged from the bathroom. It wasn't until he put on a pair of old jeans, thick socks, a white T-shirt, and gray pullover wool sweater that he noticed the photographs.

In the dull yellow light emanating from beneath a ceiling fan, he ran his eyes over the photos in frames of varying sizes on the dresser. Poe and his first wife. Poe with a young boy with rods on the side of a river. His son? This river? It was hard to tell. Someone Reece assumed to be Poe's father standing in front of a ship in drydock. Poe and his father kneeling in front of a slew of ducks, shotguns in hand. Poe on a boat with a woman. Older now. His second wife? Poe with Lansdale in Vietnam. Poe with Lansdale and Tom Reece on the deck of the house, a Weber smoking away against the railing. Lansdale held a glass of whiskey; Poe, a glass of wine; and Tom Reece, a Coors. There were other photos with people Reece did not recognize, but one stood out. He had seen it before. He picked it up and tilted it to minimize the reflection from the light above. It was a photo of men in World War II–era "duck hunter" camouflage carrying an assortment of weapons. Reece had seen the photo in

Vic Rodriguez's office at CIA headquarters. Reece knew the man holding the Johnson M1941 was Vic's father.

You are more connected to the Agency than you know.

Reece replaced the photo. He felt almost human again. Warm. Clothed. He could use another meal.

He stepped into the hallway between the kitchen and the main living area and looked through a window onto the driveway. An old Dodge Power Wagon from the late 1940s with a wood flatbed was parked behind Raife's Land Cruiser. He could hear voices from the front room. One, he didn't recognize.

When he stepped back into the main room, Mike Bill, the new majordomo of the Poe family ranch, had joined them. Short, with a barrel chest, and still sporting a haircut that left no question about his prior service as one of Uncle Sam's Misguided Children.

"Mike, this is James Donovan," Poe said, using Reece's Agency pseudonym.

"I'll buy that," Mike said, extending his hand. "Pleasure to meet you, sir."

"Sorry to wake you," Reece said.

"I don't sleep much anyway.

"As I was telling Mr. Poe and Mr. Hastings here," he said, nodding at Raife, "I scanned the property with NODs and thermals. Nothing's moving. I suspect I'll find a car or two a few miles north or south back off one of the logging roads. I'll put up a drone when it's light."

"Did you call Vic?" Reece asked Poe.

"Not yet. Take a seat. I put some hot cider on the stove. Can I get you a mug?"

"Yes, sir."

Poe moved to the kitchen, turned off the old electric stove, and poured the contents of a pot into a coffee mug.

"This should warm you up."

"Thank you," Reece said, taking a seat in one of the leather chairs by the fire.

"I'm going to hold off on calling Vic just now," Poe said.

"Why?"

"Because there were only a few people who knew you were coming here. That key and safe-deposit box your father mentioned in the letter—people will kill to keep you from finding it."

"And you think someone thought I had the key or knew where the box was?"

"Or that we might figure it out together.

"James, your father died before he could finish what we started. I'd like to finish it before I die."

Reece looked into the fire.

"I just want this to be done. They will keep coming, won't they? Until I put an end to it."

"I believe so, lad."

"Then I've got to find that key and that box."

"Other than me, there is only one person left alive who might be able to help."

"Martha Stowe."

"That's right, James. We have kept in touch over the years. I'll let her know you are coming."

"Any idea who these guys were?"

"I checked them all while you were in the shower," Mike Bill replied. "I've been trying to convince Mr. Poe to upgrade the security around here since my first day."

Poe waved his hand through the air dismissively.

"Maybe now he'll listen," Mike said, looking at his boss.

"With all that fancy security, you can get hacked, and it also tells people there is something here worth protecting. I saw it the world over with case officers and diplomats insisting on high-profile caravans of armored Suburbans when they would be much safer in a local taxi. It feeds the ego more than it satisfies a security concern. Besides, you've seen my liquor cabinet—very run-of-the-mill. Even the old shotgun wouldn't fetch much in a pawnshop. Though I do love that old A5 Browning."

"We have their wallets. California driver's licenses," Mike continued. "Armenian names. We also have their guns and cell phones. Gang affiliated, judging from the tats. LE should be able to ID all of them."

"Suppressors and NODs?" Reece asked.

"That part doesn't add up. The AR doesn't have an IR laser and isn't suppressed. And they had two shotguns in the mix. No containment force. I don't think this crew was tier one," Mike said.

"They were after me. I put you all in danger."

"Lad, we put ourselves in danger when we chose this life," Poe said. "Now it's time to solve the problem. This crew was following orders. From the names on their IDs, probably Armenian or Russian orders."

"There is a long list of reasons why Russians would want me dead."

"Then we start there."

"In the meantime, what do we do with these bodies?"

"Leave that to me," Poe said. "In the meantime, it's almost dawn. I'll get breakfast going so you can fuel up before you leave town. Mike can drop you off at the airport. Call me on a landline from Martha's Vineyard."

CHAPTER 28

The Residence at Cape Idokopas
Krasnodar Krai, Russia

DASHKOV WAS HAVING A hard time enjoying the touch of the naked young "dancer" who ran her oiled hands down his hairy back on the massage table she had set up twenty minutes earlier. His mind was on Armageddon.

Draw the United States into a war with Iran?

On one level it was genius. America had been yearning to wage war with Iran for decades. They had set the whole thing in motion with the 1953 coup. There were those who had tried to call it off. That was harder to do in those days. Kermit Roosevelt had pushed it forward. Dashkov wondered if he would regret it if he were alive today to see the repercussions of his actions.

Then came 1979. From that year forward, there was no turning back. The Shah was deposed, paving the way for Ayatollah Khomeini's rise to power, fueled by the fervor of Islamic fundamentalism. The "hot" portion of the Cold War was already being fought via proxies in conflicts around the globe—U.S.-backed guerrillas and dictators prevailing in some, Soviet-backed forces and regimes in others. Those hot wars were relegated to the back pages of the newspapers. The CIA and KGB were left to play their game out of the public eye. It was only when politicians committed forces to the battlefields that the people began to take notice. The Americans had their Vietnam and the Soviets had their Afghanistan. Both nations were forced to deal with the rise of Islamic extremism but had drawn extremely different lessons. Dashkov and his contemporaries had seen the success of Hezbollah and its affiliates in targeting Americans to reach a desired end state. They had introduced the Americans to the ways of terror, and the paper tiger had run. The West did not understand how to deal with terrorists. They only understood state-on-state warfare.

An Iranian nuclear device detonation in Israeli waters would give the United States exactly what it wanted—a war between nation-states in which they also had the opportunity to degrade or destroy the mullahs and Hezbollah proxies who were responsible for more American civilian deaths prior to 9/11 than any other terrorist group. The ties between America and Israel would ensure that response. And even if the American public balked, though Dashkov believed they would not—just look at their support for corrupt Ukraine—they were easily manipulated. Besides, the Israeli lobby in Washington was too strong. The war machine would keep turning, the lobbyists and bankers and defense industry board members would see profits, and the economy would get a temporary boost. Wars seemed to be the only things that garnered bipartisan support. The short-term gain would blind them to long-term strategic failure. Russia would sweep through Ukraine and China would take Taiwan, leading to the new Russo-Sino axis that would dominate the world as economic and technological powerhouses. There would again be two world superpowers, but this time they would be allied, and the United States would not be one of them.

Shifts in world power were inevitable: Egypt, the Ottoman Empire, Persia, the Han Dynasty, Rome, the Mongols, Spain, Britain, Germany, the United States. It was time for the next great shift. How could the

Americans have been so stupid at Bretton Woods? The end of World War II saw the United States poised to impose a Pax Americana on the rest of the world. Other than a few rather minor skirmishes, their home soil had been left unmolested by the ravages of the Axis powers, and they were just over a year away from unleashing the power of atomic weaponry on an unsuspecting Japan. The writing was on the wall. It was July 1944, and the United States was positioned geographically, politically, militarily, and economically to govern the world. A global American imperial system was on the horizon.

Dashkov could only imagine the surprise within the walls of the Kremlin when it was announced that the Americans had no intention of leveraging their newfound power and position to create the next great world empire. For what had they just sacrificed so much? Open markets with no conditions, all protected by the U.S. Navy? Did the American people even know they had signed on to essentially subsidize the world's economy with no direct benefit, even though they were the strongest they had ever been? Geography had protected them from the devastation of the Great Patriotic War, and they decided to throw that advantage away. Their decisions in New Hampshire that summer set them on the road to inevitable ruin. Dashkov was seeing it play out in real time.

As the 730 delegates from forty-four nations created the World Bank, the International Monetary Fund, and the International Bank for Reconstruction and Development that summer, war continued to rage in Europe and the Pacific. While young men fought and died, commanding officers wrote letters to widows, and parents received telegrams from the Department of War regretting to inform them that they would never see their children again, the ministers, economists, bankers, and government representatives decided America's future. They had been so shortsighted. That had always been their Achilles' heel. That agreement forecasted an end to the very international order they themselves created. Dashkov wondered how many Americans today even knew of the

Bretton Accords, the very agreement that had set them on their trajectory. In a sense, Russia was lucky the Americans were so stupid. It made them a much less formidable foe.

The Soviets had representatives at the Mount Washington Hotel in Bretton Woods, New Hampshire, in July 1944, watching, listening, reporting, and recruiting. They ultimately did not ratify what became known as the Bretton Woods Agreement. Instead, they decided to play the long game.

Dropping atomic bombs on Hiroshima and Nagasaki had been the de facto final signatures on the Bretton Accords. Would a nuclear device detonation with Iranian signatures in Israeli waters usher in the end of the world order shaped eighty years earlier? Dashkov knew that with the president, the deputy chairman, and his counterpart in the SVR in full support of the operation, Dashkov had very little choice. Maybe it was time for him to retire? Or perhaps it was time for him to take his place in the new world order just as his counterparts in America had at the end of the Great Patriotic War.

Dashkov grunted and turned over without warning, the small white towel that had covered him sliding to the floor.

The girl applied more oil and moved to his side, taking him in her small hands.

How could James Reece derail the plan? What was in that box his father had so carefully hidden? Could he have evidence that implicated the Collective? Their American contacts? What history remained under lock and key that could galvanize the American people against the Russian Federation?

Dashkov opened his eyes, watching the young girl work. He had seen her before, dancing on the pole in the hookah room. Had she pleasured him before? It was possible. The girls were kept at the Residence until they outlived their usefulness. They danced in the hookah bar, put on performances in the theater, and were available for "massage" at any time of the day or night.

Let her work, Dashkov thought. *Enjoy. Reality will rear its head soon enough.*

When he closed his eyes again, the phone rang.

Phones in the residence were all analog and connected via a switchboard on the property that was not connected to the outside world. If his phone was ringing here, it could be only a handful of callers, all of whom were also in the Residence.

"Stop," he commanded, throwing his legs over the side of the massage table.

The girl did as she was told, sliding into a thin bathrobe and moving to the door.

Dashkov took a moment and leaned against the table to support his considerable weight as blood rushed back into his larger head.

He waited until the girl had disappeared into the hallway and the door had clicked shut behind her before struggling into a thick terrycloth robe one size too small with matching slippers. He walked to the side table next to the enormous four-poster bed and picked up the phone.

"Da."

"I hope I am not interrupting you, comrade," Director Levitsky's voice echoed across the line.

Dashkov looked around the room. They were swept daily by the FSO, but he always wondered . . .

"Is he dead?" Dashkov asked the new director.

"The team failed to check in."

"I see."

"They were the best that could be done on short notice. This isn't an internal security matter where it is much easier to make a problem disappear," Levitsky said. "International operations oftentimes require a scalpel, not a hammer."

"So now the target knows we are moving against him?"

"That would be a fair assessment."

"Have our friends provided any additional information on his location or intent?"

Even though the line was internal analog, they kept the conversation lacking in specifics. They both knew exactly whom they were talking about.

"We have a flight plan. One that indicates he has put another piece of the puzzle together."

He is getting closer.

"We anticipated this contingency. We know where he is going, and we have professionals moving into position to intercept," Levitsky said. "Though it does now bring into question how much he has figured out and with whom he has shared that information."

"It does," Dashkov said.

"You and Director Gromyko failed to put an end to this problem. You had almost a quarter century, and you neglected to address it and bring it to a satisfactory conclusion."

"Take caution in your tone, Director Levitsky. It would be a pity to have such a short tenure as director. Those of us who have been at this game the longest did not remain here because we are afraid to exercise options."

"Is that a threat, Director?"

"It is fact. Another fact is that if you fail the chairman and the president again, you will not only be removed from your post, you will not be long for this earth. The cliffs at the Residence are known to be treacherous this time of year. Some of the menu options can also be disagreeable. Choose your next moves wisely. And the next time you call, the only acceptable words from your mouth will be that our target is no longer a threat. Anything else and I recommend you double your security on your morning runs. Good evening, Director."

Dashkov returned the phone to its cradle, feeling much better about his position in what was about to become the new world order.

PART TWO

FOUNDATIONS

If any question why we died,
Tell them, because our fathers lied.

—RUDYARD KIPLING

CHAPTER 29

Martha's Vineyard
Dukes County
Massachusetts

THE OLD STAIRS CREAKED under Reece's weight. He instinctively moved to the side to minimize the noise.

The house had been built where Planting Field Way became Planting Field Lane, among a collection of estates primarily owned by seasonal residents on the eastern end of Martha's Vineyard in the town of Edgartown. It faced north and looked out over Nantucket Sound toward South Cape Beach State Park on the mainland. The vines that snaked their way through the old wrought-iron gate permanently anchored it in the open position, giving the impression that the person or people beyond it were from a bygone era.

A pea gravel circular driveway led from the road to the front of the house, where an elderly caretaker, who looked like she needed a caretaker of her own, met Reece to let him know that Mrs. Stowe was expecting him.

Raife stayed in the rental vehicle. They had reservations at the Richard hotel, but Reece had insisted on going directly to Martha Stowe's residence. There was work to do.

"Mrs. Stowe?" Reece said, as he knocked on the partially opened door.

"Come in," a voice replied.

Reece stepped into the small room. Like the rest of the house, it appeared to have been frozen in a time capsule sometime in the mid-1960s. Floral wallpaper adorned the walls, and a small four-poster bed with pink sheets and a thick baby-blue comforter was centered against the wall between two small nightstands.

The top of a dresser was covered with framed photos of parents, grandparents, children, and grandchildren. An armoire was open opposite the bed, revealing a TV set that appeared only slightly more modern than the home's furniture.

Reece's eyes traveled to a cushioned glider rocker near glass doors that opened onto a small balcony. The doors were closed now to keep out the cold but still allowed the late afternoon light to brighten the room. A small side table was positioned next to the rocker. It held two books, reading glasses, a coffee mug, a remote control, and a set of binoculars.

"Please excuse me for not getting up, Mr. Reece. It takes most of my effort just to make it from the bed to this rocking chair these days." A blue wool blanket covered her legs.

"Not at all, Mrs. Stowe," Reece said. "Thank you for seeing me.

"And please excuse this," Reece added, indicating his beard and hair. "I'm usually a bit more put together."

"Please, sit," she said. "I apologize for having to meet upstairs. Inviting strange men to my bedroom is not something I am accustomed to at this stage of the game."

Reece smiled.

A chair had been moved from a writing desk against the wall.

"I don't get many visitors. For a while there I couldn't keep them away. That was a long time ago."

Reece took a seat across from the old woman. The wrinkles on her face disclosed that she had chosen to age gracefully, without cosmetic enhancements, and her hunched shoulders betrayed the fact that osteoporosis had taken hold. Her gray hair was cut short and arranged in an asymmetrical bob held in place with hairspray that Reece could still smell in the air. Though she was thin to the point of frailty, her eyes were anything but old. Bold and blue, they pierced through the late afternoon light.

"It is a pleasure to meet you, ma'am."

"You know, I was an associate editor for almost fifteen years after my husband died. Biographies, mostly. Gave me something to do. Have you read these?" she asked, pointing to the presidential memoir and a royal tell-all on her table. Though her body might be failing her, her mind remained sharp.

"I've been a little indisposed."

"Don't waste your time, dear. They are atrocious," she said, lingering on *atrocious*. "My former publisher gave him and his wife sixty-five million dollars for this one. Can you believe that? They bought a twelve-million-dollar estate just down the road. I shouldn't bad-mouth them—they are of my party, after all—but I refuse to be stifled in my old age."

"How's the other one?" Reece asked.

"Even worse. They gave the ungrateful royal twenty million for stabbing his family in the back. Instant bestseller, of course."

"The way of the world these days," Reece said.

"I suppose it is."

"Beautiful view," Reece observed, nodding to the glass doors.

"I once took it for granted, though no longer. I do love it here. It is filled with memories, pleasant and otherwise. At first it felt like a prison. But then I accepted it. Once I did that, I grew to appreciate it much more than when I was young. When my great-grandchildren visit, I can watch them through these binoculars playing on the grass and the pool and on the beach. When they are not, I can watch the boats sail or motor past.

Walter proposed to me under that tree right over there. I played tennis on that court there with friends until not that long ago, if you can imagine. It doesn't get much use now. Do you play?"

"Tennis?"

"Yes."

"I'm more of a rugby guy."

"Ah, just like your father."

"He introduced me to it. Wanted me to be able to play a sport the world over."

"He was a smart one, that Thomas Reece."

"He was."

"For a while there I feared we would never meet. I regretted not getting in touch with you earlier. I was torn, you see."

"Torn?"

"Yes; I am not sure your father would want you to find what's in his files. I, however, have a personal reason for wanting you to find them. What do you know about me?"

"Just what I learned from Mr. Poe."

"And what was that?" she asked.

"He told me that your husband was working on something with my father when he was killed."

"Did he tell you what your dad did for me?"

"He said he killed the assassin and dove into the water, pulled you out."

"Tom saved my life that day, though my tennis serve was never quite the same."

She smiled at an old memory.

"After that, I withdrew from the spotlight. I didn't want to see my children shot down for the sins of their father."

"I understand," Reece said, blocking out thoughts of his murdered young daughter.

"I'm sorry, James. A momentary lapse. It happens in these later years. Please accept my sincere condolences on the loss of your family. I followed the events closely and read the series of exposés by that journalist—what was her name? Katie something."

"That's right, Katie Buranek," Reece said.

"It was riveting. They should have given her the Pulitzer. I went back and read her book on the Benghazi fiasco. What was it called?"

"*The Benghazi Betrayal.*"

"Quite apt. She's a talent, that one. I should know. I still do my fair share of reading."

"Yes, ma'am."

"I am sad to say my own offspring did not amount to much."

"What do they do?" Reece asked.

"Other than wait around for me to die, they did a pretty good job of fucking up their early inheritance."

Reece's eyes widened.

"You weren't expecting an old woman to swear?"

"I guess not."

"Catches some people off guard. I find it tells me right away if I'm going to be friends with someone. I can tell we are going to be friends, James."

"Friends it is, Mrs. Stowe."

"Well, if it's friends, then I insist you call me Martha. Your father called me Martha."

"All right, Martha."

"After Walter was killed, I moved here full-time with my children. Raised them on these very grounds. Most of the people in our circles were seasonal—here for the summers and to get their Christmas card photo before returning to their lives in Manhattan or Greenwich. I was fine financially; we had money from timber and maybe a little bootlegging." She chuckled. "My children and grandchildren—some of them entered the political sphere. Some fared better than others. Some fared not at all. I am sure you have seen the gossip pages in grocery store checkout lines."

"Your family has endured more than its share of tragedy."

"As has yours, James."

"Mrs. Stowe—Martha," Reece corrected himself, "do you have a cell phone?"

"I do," she said. "I left it by the bed. I use it mostly to FaceTime my great-grandchildren. They are still young enough to want to talk with me out of the pure joy of seeing their gran, not like the others who pretend—the ones waiting for me to die. They think they are inheriting a windfall. They are going to be surprised." She laughed again. "What I would give to see their faces when they read the will. I have thought of faking my death just to have that experience."

Reece laughed along with her. The draw of her magnetic personality had not diminished with age.

"Do you mind if I put it in another room?" Reece asked. "You can't be too careful these days."

"You go right ahead, dear."

Reece picked up the iPhone next to the bed.

"Bathroom through here?" he asked.

"It is."

"Mind if I turn it off?"

"Go right ahead. No password."

He opened the door to the attached bathroom, powered down the phone, set it on the sink, and turned on the water before closing the door and returning to his chair opposite Martha Stowe.

"How well did you know my father?"

"I got to know him a lot better after Walter was killed. Before that I think he believed I was more of a nuisance, someone who couldn't leave well enough alone. I'm like that, you see."

"I can tell," Reece said.

"I went to all the prestigious schools, had the right pedigree, yet I never belonged to this world, never felt at home in it. I wanted to leave my mark, not just be someone's 'plus one' at a fundraiser. Sometimes I think it was that tenacity that led to Walter's death. Maybe it was something I did. I knew your father thought the same thing."

"So you teamed up in an attempt to find the person behind your husband's assassination."

"We did. Me, your father, and William."

"Mr. Poe?"

"Yes. I had the money, so did William, but he also had connections to the intelligence world. He was a dangerous man."

"How so?"

"James, what they now call the 'deep state' does not like it when people have nothing to lose, when they can't be controlled. William had wealth but showed no interest in flaunting it. He had connections to the OSS through his family and was an early recruit at the CIA. He knew people, knew their secrets, and he didn't need to work. He didn't have children who needed jobs or favors. His ex-wives were well taken care of in his divorces. He was beholden to no one."

"That made him dangerous."

"One of the most dangerous men in the Beltway. Also dangerous on the tennis court. We used to play down there," she said, pointing out her second-floor window. "He would play the occasional game of golf, but he hated it. He did it to study the people he played with. Did they cheat? Did they get frustrated? Did they love the game or do it to network? He kept track of all of it and kept extensive files on everyone he met."

"Sounds wise," Reece said.

"He was a man of honor. Never tried to sleep with me or take advantage of my grief, as did some others. He was on a mission, as was your father. When Walter died, he became a part of that puzzle, a puzzle that your father never stopped trying to solve. I think it got him killed."

"I don't think so, Martha. His death was linked to Vietnam. His SOG Team killed a Spetsnaz officer in Laos in an ambush. That man's son came after him all those years later."

Martha reached to her side table and lifted a mug to her lips.

"Tea," she said. "The woman who let you in makes it for me after breakfast each morning and again in the afternoon. Keeps me warm. She will be back later this evening to bring me dinner and lock up. She's a full-time resident from Tisbury. Been taking care of me for years."

"I met her out front. Seems very kind."

"James, it is possible that the man who orchestrated the assassination of my husband is still alive. I believe he was behind the death of your father. Yes, the Russians did it. William Poe was here last year and gave me a full update. That ended up being quite convenient."

"What do you mean?"

"Tom Reece kept me in the dark on his investigations. He said he did it for my own protection, the same thing I'd hear time and time again from my husband. I know there are things he kept from Walter, and William as well. Maybe he was right to keep me out of it, and that is why I am still alive. Remember, he was investigating off the books from *within* the CIA. That is something they do not take kindly. Just before my husband was shot, he told me that Tom was putting together a report."

"What kind of report?"

"That I am not sure. I assumed it was about a Soviet plan to infiltrate all aspects of American culture. They had limited success in infiltrating our military and intelligence agencies, though those were a primary focus. While they never stopped trying to penetrate or turn American citizens, they also had a parallel strategic deep-penetration plan. They recognized the power of American culture and sought to subvert that over time." She paused. "I see doubt in your eyes."

"It's not doubt. It's disillusionment."

"You mean, they died for nothing?"

"It seems like the country is on a path that negates all efforts to keep it free."

"I am not hopeful for the country. Yes, my 'side' won at the time; I believe a lot of it is because that report never saw the light of day. Today it would be erased at the touch of a keystroke."

"But back then it couldn't be."

"That's right. It was all on paper."

"And where is that paper?"

The old woman tilted her head to the side and studied him.

"Answer me a question, James."

"Yes, ma'am."

"Where do your allegiances lie?"

Reece took a deep breath and looked out the window. A fore-and-aft-rigged schooner cut through the whitecaps of Nantucket Sound in the distance.

"You mean, do they lie with my country?"

She raised an eyebrow.

"I don't know how to answer that question anymore. I want to find out why I was framed and thrown in prison, and I want to make sure those I love are not in the line of fire. Poe thinks it's connected to the investigation my father was running."

"And if you do find that report, whatever it may be, what do you intend to do with it?"

"I don't think I can answer that question honestly until I read it."

She looked into his eyes. She appeared to be weighing her options.

"James, I am an old woman. My sisters have passed on. My children are just cordial because, as I said, they think they are inheriting a windfall. I have no one; just a few cats that my caretaker feeds. I've been keeping track of you. Like your father, I wanted to protect you."

"What do you mean?"

"My husband wasn't killed by a lunatic, as was reported in the press. He was deliberately eliminated for what he knew—things not exposed in the Pike Committee and Church Committee hearings. But there was only so much he could do in Congress. He needed to be president. There were elements of the political and military establishment that could not let that happen."

"How did my father fit into it?"

"James, when Tom got back from Vietnam he was disillusioned, and the country was in turmoil; the Pentagon Papers confirmed that the Johnson administration had not only misled the American people and Congress but straight-out lied. Protests and riots had dominated the news for years, Watergate confirmed that both parties were power-hungry, corrupt political machines, *Six Days of the Condor* was a best-seller, and the Church Hearings exposed egregious legal violations by the most powerful agencies in the federal government. Trust in government was at an all-time low, and for good reason. Tom had lost men in Vietnam. Like many veterans of that war, and wars since, he wondered if the sacrifice was worth it. He saw that conflict for what it was—a battlefield of the Cold War played out in the jungles of Southeast Asia. The Cold War wasn't 'cold' for Tom Reece."

"That's why he joined the CIA."

"He didn't join, James. He was recruited. There's a difference."

"I see."

"The tragedy of Tom Reece is that he couldn't stop. The CIA knew that. They wanted to exploit it, and they did. What they didn't realize was that your father's loyalty wasn't to the seventh floor at Langley. I don't even think it was to his country. It was to those men who didn't make it home, rotting away in the jungle, wasting away in Vietnamese prison camps. He never verbalized it as such, but he didn't have to; call it a woman's intuition."

"So whatever is in the box has to do with American involvement in Vietnam?"

"I don't know. Nor do I know if what's in there will avert a war, or start one, but people are willing to go to extreme lengths to make sure it remains sealed. I think people on both sides of what was then the Iron Curtain were willing to kill to destroy it."

"And because they couldn't find it, they killed those who knew about it."

"I believe so, James. My husband, your father."

"Why not you and Poe?"

"I think they had intelligence indicating that we didn't know what was in those files and also didn't know where they were. Better to watch us in case we ever surfaced with them. Easier to do today now that everything is stored digitally, as I can see you appreciate," she said, nodding toward the bathroom, where Reece had left her phone.

"I've had some recent experience in the virtual world," Reece said.

"James, did your father leave you something? A safe-deposit box or storage locker key? Maybe both?"

Reece remained silent.

"Your father was a terrible liar, too. Dreadful poker player. I see you inherited that trait."

"I think I got some of the emotions from my mother's side."

"Ah yes; I never met your mother. Tom was exceptional at compartmentalizing the different aspects of his life. I think he wanted to protect you and your mother, as he wanted to protect me. I did manage to dredge up that her side of the family fought for the Confederacy. They came from gun-making stock if I remember correctly."

Reece nodded, remembering the letters his mother had shown him in his youth, memorializing his family history.

"Your father's side was Union, I believe. Enlisted. First Iron Brigade, he told me over chess one night."

"That's right. Second United States Sharpshooters. The soldier on my dad's side didn't make it. He was killed by a sniper, possibly by a gun my mother's family worked on."

"What rifle did they make? Your father thought it carried some sort of significance."

"They modified the Whitworth, from England."

"Officially neutral during the war, but private English companies supplied both sides."

"War has always been big business," Reece said.

"Yes, some things don't change, James, like the nature of man."

"Like the nature of man," Reece repeated.

"James, we have only just met but I feel an allegiance to you, to your family. Your father sacrificed so much for me, for those he served with in Vietnam. You are his legacy. I want to see you happy. Your father's life and fate do not have to be yours."

"I know that. I just want to do what needs to be done to end this so that those I care about don't have to live in fear."

"Those files might be the key to ending it, or they might be the start of something even more dangerous for you. We won't know until you find that box."

Reece made his decision.

"My father left me a letter."

"And a key, didn't he?"

"Yes. He said that only one other person knew the location of the box. Said that person was a 'he.'"

"Classic misdirection by Tom Reece. That other person is a 'she.'"

Reece leaned in and rested his elbows on his knees.

"I think it's time you found it, James. It's time for you to find peace."

"Where is it?"

"It's on the mainland."

"Where exactly?"

The old woman paused.

"Before I tell you, I want you to do something for me."

"What's that?"

"I want you to kill a man."

CHAPTER 30

REECE'S EYES NARROWED.

"Who?"

"The man who killed my husband. The man who gave the order. He stole a life from me, stole a father from my children, set Tom Reece on a mission that lasted until the day he died. I want you to find him, and I want you to kill him."

Reece ran his fingers through the beard that had grown so long and unruly during his confinement and contemplated what he had just heard.

"It's quite possible that it is the same person who threatens you and those you love," she added.

The shadows on the lawn below had grown longer, signifying the end to another day.

"Where is the box?" Reece asked.

"It's time you knew. It's in Boston, at an old bank that was once known for its discretion. Boston Safe Deposit and Trust Company."

"How do you know?"

"Your father told me. Made me swear to never tell a soul."

"Except me."

"Except you. He told me to trust no one."

"His letter said the same thing."

"There is a lawyer here in town," she said, taking a business card from under her stack of books and handing it across the table. "He is a trusted associate. He helped advise on how to set up the box, all without knowing specifics. In years past you could do things like that. He can help you if you run into any legal issues accessing the box, after all these years. All you should need are two forms of identification."

Reece looked at the card. Charles Ambler, Attorney-at-Law—with an address and phone number. He put it in his pocket.

"Martha, I am sorry for your losses, and I thank you for trusting me. I'll go see Mr. Ambler tonight."

"Not tonight, dear. I phoned him after I spoke with William to let him know he might have a visitor. He is expecting you at eleven a.m. tomorrow. It's a small office. He's a one-man operation."

"I'll be there."

"James, I am not sure what is in those files. For a long time I suspected it was a list of Soviet deep-penetration agents, but now I think that was just a distraction. Your father knew the Cold War was won even back then. This was about something more. I have to warn you, those threatened by what's in those files wield real power, dark power. I fear the odds may be stacked against you."

"That's okay, I never pay much attention to the odds."

Reece stood, retrieved Martha's phone from the bathroom, and handed it back to her.

"Can I help you with anything before I go?"

"I'll be fine, thank you. I am going to force myself to finish this biography and then go to bed. I'll be up before sunrise. If you need anything, you know where to find me."

"Good night, Martha," Reece said, reaching down to shake her cold, delicate hand.

"Good night, James," she replied, watching him walk toward her bedroom door.

"And, James?"

"Yes," he said, turning back to the old woman.

"Remember. Trust no one."

Reece nodded and shut the door quietly behind him.

CHAPTER 31

The Residence at Cape Idokopas
Krasnodar Krai, Russia

THE CALL CAME IN just before 5 a.m.

The analog phone woke Dashkov on the first ring. He blinked his eyes and swung his feet to the carpeted floor. Still feeling the effects of the vodka, he took a moment to collect himself. The bed was empty, the dancer having long since departed.

"*Da*," he said into the receiver.

"I hope I am not waking you, comrade," came the reply.

Levitsky.

Dashkov inadvertently glanced around the room.

"No, I've been up for hours."

"I didn't see you in the gym. Perhaps we just missed each other."

"Unlike you, I am working in support of the Motherland, not on my biceps. I trust you have good news."

"I do."

"Is he dead?"

"Even better."

"Better than dead. That sounds like failure."

"Death would be shortsighted. We are going to find and then destroy those documents that you and my predecessor were so concerned about."

"The files from the father?"

"*Da.* The very ones that have evaded you for decades."

"How?"

"Leave that to me, comrade. It clearly falls under the SVR's mandate, and we have just the man for the job."

Dashkov's pulse quickened.

"I will keep you informed. By the end of the day we will be in control of the files and our target will be dead."

"I pray you are right, Director Levitsky, for your sake. Because, if you fail, you will not only be remembered as the youngest SVR director in history but also the one with the shortest tenure."

Dashkov returned the phone to its cradle, swung his legs back into bed, and closed his eyes for another hour of sleep.

CHAPTER 32

Martha's Vineyard
Dukes County
Massachusetts

RAIFE HAD PARKED IN front of the quaint hotel between the Old Whaling Church and Vincent House Museum and gone to check them in. Located between Pent and Main Streets, just blocks from the ocean in the heart of Edgartown, the tree-lined boulevard appeared peaceful and serene. Raife returned quickly and handed Reece his room's access card.

"Liz is checked in. She's scoped it out and didn't notice anything unusual. She wants to see you but also wants to give you your space. I let her know to be on standby for tomorrow."

"Thanks, brother."

"Duffel is in the back with some clothes we had packed for you from the Broadmoor. You want to get some food?"

"I'll order up room service. I think I need to ease back into polite society."

"Okay. Let's get breakfast in the morning and then track down a barber before your meeting with the attorney."

"I was thinking of keeping it," Reece said.

"That's always an option. But if you want to avoid a run-in with William Teasle, you might want a bit of a trim."

"You make a solid point."

"Try to get some sleep," Raife said, handing Reece his key card.

"Hey, I'm fine."

"Yeah? That's what worries me, eh?" The Rhodesian was sneaking back into Raife's voice.

"Trust me, brother, I had a lot of time to think in there. Tomorrow, I need to find out what my dad left behind and then decide what to do about it."

"All right, I'm going to park this thing out back. I'll see you for breakfast."

"Sounds good. What time?"

"Whenever you wake up. Get some sleep."

"Roger that. And, Raife—*I'm fine*."

Raife did not look convinced as Reece grabbed his bag and exited the vehicle.

Reece glanced at his card. It was labeled "Lark Suite." Regardless of what he had said to Raife, he could feel the ghosts of his past close behind. He had lived with them in his cell for three months. There was no escaping them in the confines of prison, and they were not yet ready to let him go. Maybe a meal and sleep would help?

Reece passed through the small lobby. It was decorated in whites and soft blues with coastal touches. He noted a breakfast area and an outside garden with a rock fire pit. Avoiding the elevator, he took the stairs to the second floor, found his room, and slid his key card through the reader on the door. The light blinked to green, and he entered the suite.

The large windows were still letting in what little light was left in the sky, leaving the spacious room bathed in shades of gray. Reece dropped his duffel to the floor and reached for the light switch.

His peripheral vision caught the movement first.

I'm not alone.

Threat.

His hand went to the holster behind his right hip and found the grip on his SIG Sauer P210. He extracted it from its scabbard and brought it smoothly into a two-handed grip, pushing it outward until his elbows almost locked and his eye found the front sight, his finger going to the trigger.

"James, Jesus!"

He immediately removed his finger from the trigger and retracted the pistol back to the high ready position, not yet ready to believe his eyes.

"Katie?"

She stood not ten feet away. Her right hand over her heart. The fright in her eyes instantly softening as she took in the man she loved.

"Katie," Reece said again.

He holstered his weapon, his feet still locked in place.

If you'll have me, I want to spend the rest of my life making you the happiest woman on earth.

They moved to each other in the fading light, embracing. Katie buried her face in Reece's neck, their breaths coming faster, hearts pounding.

"Katie, I never want to let you go."

"Then don't," she said through tears.

I love you, Katie.

James . . .

Reece relaxed his embrace and took Katie's head in his hands, gazing into the deep blue eyes that had kept him alive in solitary confinement.

Beautiful.

"What's that?" she asked.

"I said, 'You are beautiful.' "

"You didn't forget about me?"

"You gave me hope in there."

He held her out and took her in—socks, jeans, and a white blouse, her blond hair falling just past her shoulders. She looked even more angelic than he remembered.

"*How?* What are you doing here?"

"Well, you didn't leave me much choice, Mr. Reece," she said, poking him in the chest. "Liz explained to me that you needed to do something before you saw me and that you were headed to the Vineyard. I managed to elicit where you were staying and, rather than argue, I had the hotel car service drive me to Denver. I caught the first flight east. Now here I am."

"It's not safe, Katie."

"James, it has *never* been safe with you. But I am in. You are not getting rid of me just because things are dangerous."

"How did you get in here?" Reece asked, looking around the room for the first time.

"The girl at the front desk is a fan. She wants to be a writer. I gave her some advice, gave her my card, and let her know she could reach out anytime. Told her I was surprising my fiancé."

Reece's eyes softened.

"We have a conversation to finish, don't we?"

"We do. But first, are you hungry?" she asked, taking his hand and guiding him to the kitchenette in the large suite. "I brought in some food and picked out a couple of bottles of wine."

She had already poured two glasses of Chardonnay. A bottle of Kistler was resting in an ice-filled stainless-steel wine bucket on the counter.

"Wine can wait," Reece said, reaching down to sweep Katie off her feet.

"Wine can wait," she whispered, pulling his head to hers.

Reece disconnected from their passionate kiss just long enough to carry her through the threshold to the bedroom.

CHAPTER 33

THEY BEGAN RIPPING CLOTHES from each other's bodies before they made it to the bed. Their lovemaking was frantic, breathless, fast, and hungry. The mounting arousal, exacerbated by anticipation from months apart, causing them to abandon all restraint until they exploded together atop the sheets.

When they recovered and caught their breath, Katie pulled the sheets and comforter over them, trapping the warmth still emanating from their passionate exertion. With their legs intertwined beneath the sheets, Katie rested her head on Reece's chest as the gray shadows of the day gave way to the darkness of night. Thin drapes let just the right amount of light into the bedroom, which was tastefully decorated in whites, grays, and blues to elicit the tranquility of a welcoming sea.

Katie's lips pressed into her lover's neck, her tender kisses growing more passionate. Moving to his ear, then his lips, she pulled herself atop him. This time their sex was slower, methodical, and patient, finding each other again, exploring, bringing each other to the brink and back down. There was no past, no future, only the now.

When their breathing returned to normal, Katie propped herself up on an elbow at Reece's side.

"What was it like?" she asked.

"You were magnificent," Reece responded.

"Oh hush," she said playfully. "You know what I mean. Are you okay?"

Reece took a deep breath.

"Well, as you can tell, I escaped without getting any prison tattoos."

She tapped him on his stomach. "You know that's not what I mean."

"I know. It was quiet. Dark. Cold. They kept me in a cell without a window the entire time. No human contact."

"They didn't ask you any questions?"

"No. Just kept me in my cell. Delivered food once or twice a day, I think. It was hard to gauge with no way to account for time. The shower would automatically turn on every two food deliveries. I think I need to hit the gym and eat about a hundred steaks."

"You are perfect," Katie said, turning his head with her hand so she could look into his eyes.

"I should probably clean up at some point," he said, pulling a long strand of hair out from the side of his head.

"You do whatever you need to do. I love you just like this."

"How did I get so lucky?" he asked.

"I ask myself the same thing," Katie said playfully.

Reece laughed.

"You want to take an intermission for halftime and have a bite to eat?" she asked.

"Halftime? That was just the first quarter."

"Don't you tease me, Mr. Reece," she said, smiling. "Do you want to clean up?" she asked, easing herself from beneath the sheets and standing next to the bed.

Without a word he let her take his hand, pull him from the bed, and guide him into the shower.

• • •

"Does the shower count as first quarter or halftime?" Katie asked, sliding the wineglass to Reece on the kitchen counter.

"Oh, first quarter for sure."

"I'm going to hold you to that, you know," she said, raising her glass to his.

"I'm counting on it."

"You know, I kind of feel like we've eloped and are on an illicit honeymoon," Katie said, her eyes gleaming conspiratorially. "Nobody knows I'm here."

"Raife and I passed about forty churches on the drive in," Reece said. "Maybe we should just do it."

"Make an honest woman of me?" she said with a wink.

"I can't believe you are back," she then said, her eyes filling with tears.

"I'm back, Katie. We are going to figure this out. I promise. But, before we do, what's for dinner?"

"Let me warm it up," she said. "I didn't know what you wanted so I picked up an assortment. It's from Alchemy Bistro, just down the street. Still open during most of the off-season."

Reece had a towel wrapped around his waist, and Katie was in a hotel bathrobe, their hair still wet from another round of sex in the shower.

"God, you look amazing," Reece said, looking past the food at Katie.

"Glad you think so, because you are stuck with me. Take your wine and sit down over there," Katie said, pointing to small alcove attached to the main room in a sitting area set up with a sofa and wicker-backed chair.

"That's an order I can follow," Reece said, taking a seat on the sofa.

"Well, don't get used to it. I do this for all my boyfriends on their first night out of prison."

Reece laughed.

"Here you are—appetizers: calamari and mussels," she said, putting the two dishes on the coffee table and returning to the kitchen. "And here is surf and turf, and local sea scallops, and the world-famous Alchemy Wagyu Burger. At least that's what they told me."

"This is incredible," Reece said. "Thank you."

"Eat up," Katie said. "You are going to need your energy later."

"Are you threatening me with a good time?"

"That I am."

As they worked their way through the meal, Katie refilled their wineglasses and opened a second bottle.

"I've been training, you know."

"Training?"

"Ox came in for a week while you were gone. Jonathan and Raife had him run the entire family through a team tactics training course: pistols, rifles, shotguns. They also had him evaluate the ranch's security measures. Someone hacked the sensors and camera systems the night the FBI raided. They now have their own servers on multiple power backups and more measures that are not technologically dependent."

"I can only imagine what those are."

"They monitor the roads and airports and have a HUMINT network set up in town through the former military community that's built up in and around Bozeman. Montana has attracted quite a few spec ops and Agency types. I think it's the space and freedom."

"And maybe a desire to get away from the government that sent them to war for twenty years without a coherent plan to win."

"There is probably a lot to that. Many of them are not fans of the federal government."

"Who can blame them?"

"You'd be proud; I've been carrying the P365-XMACRO, a fixed blade, and a tourniquet."

"Where is it?" Reece asked. "I didn't notice it as I was getting you out of your pants."

"Not that it would have distracted you from your mission, but it's illegal here in Massachusetts. They require you to get a Firearm Identification Card just to own one, to say nothing of carrying it. I looked it up before I left Colorado. That there," she said, pointing to the jeans on the floor of the bedroom, "has to be locked up. There is a ten-round magazine capacity law here, too, and no concealed-carry reciprocity with any other state. I think you are breaking like ten laws just having that pistol here."

"I might be good. It only has an eight-round magazine capacity."

"Okay, nine laws."

"Regardless, I guess we won't be moving to the Vineyard."

"Even my fixed blade is illegal here."

"Really?"

"Yep, it's double-edged."

"Okay, I'm back to breaking ten laws," Reece said.

"I still have my tourniquet," she said. "I left everything else in a bag locked up at the Broadmoor."

"That makes much more sense," Reece said sarcastically. "I can only imagine how many laws we are breaking with what's on the Hastings plane."

"I'm guessing hundreds."

"I am so sorry about all of this," Reece said between bites.

"Don't you be sorry. They arrested you and then instead of due process they threw you into what amounts to a modern-day dungeon."

"Well, the charges did disappear, and there wasn't a public hanging. That's something."

"It is, but it's not right. How many other people do they have locked up in these supermax prisons not adhering to due process in violation of the Fifth and Fourteenth Amendments?"

"I don't know, Katie. Maybe it's just me?"

"And maybe it's not. After they arrested you," she continued, "they ransacked the cabin. Took everything. Vic arrived two days later and let us know that a classified report, which he would not elaborate on, had exonerated you but that every part of it needed to be confirmed. I grilled him, but he wouldn't budge on where it came from and why it needed corroboration."

Reece took a sip of his wine.

"I think you know where it came from, though, don't you?"

"I do."

"Well?"

"I think the best way to describe it is as an extremely fast next-generation quantum computer. I met her as part of the operation to find Nizar."

"'Her'?"

"Yes, she's a computer, but more than that."

"You mean she's sentient."

"Maybe."

"I did some research after that call came in from 'Alice' the night of the raid in a place where we didn't have cell service or Wi-Fi. I had three months to put the pieces together."

"And?" Reece asked.

"*And*, if she's some top secret supercomputer—"

"Quantum computer."

"—quantum computer, why did they need to corroborate everything in her report?"

"I think to make sure she didn't fabricate any of it."

"In order to clear you?"

"Yes. Apparently she took a liking to me."

"She did, did she? Looks like I have some competition."

"Don't worry," Reece teased. "She's not nearly as good at warming up takeout as you are."

"I'll keep that in mind," Katie said with a laugh.

"Katie, I need to ask you something about that night."

Katie put down her fork and leaned back, her glass of wine in hand. "Shoot."

"The key I gave you. Did the FBI take it?"

Katie set her wineglass on the coffee table and stood up.

"Give me a moment."

She walked toward the king-size bed, picked up her jeans from the floor, and reached into the pocket.

"You mean this key?" she asked, returning to Reece and holding out a safe-deposit box key.

"That's the one," Reece said, turning it in his fingers and then setting it on the table.

"What does it open?" Katie asked, taking a seat next to him on the couch, pulling her right leg under her left, and leaning close to him.

"It just might unlock this entire mystery. Give me one second. I think this will explain it better."

He retrieved his bag, which still sat where he had dropped it by the door. He unzipped it and pulled out a letter.

"Vic brought it to me when they released me. It's a letter from my dad."

Katie carefully pulled it from its envelope and began to read as Reece polished off the Wagyu burger.

When she was finished, she carefully refolded it and returned it to its envelope, setting it next to the key.

"James, I don't know what to say. How long have you had that?"

"Since I returned from Russia."

"Two years?"

"It was in a storage facility."

"The one with the Wagoneer?"

"Yes. A weapons case was in the back with a shotgun and that letter—"

"And the key," Katie said, finishing his sentence.

"—and the key," Reece repeated, taking another sip of wine.

"It's a beautiful letter, James, but pretty vague."

"Yeah, by design. In case someone else found it."

"Do you know where the safe-deposit box is?"

"I do now. As of about three hours ago."

"What do you mean?"

Reece explained the backstory as Katie refilled their glasses, her eyes growing wider with each new twist in the story.

"So, tomorrow I'll meet with Martha's attorney and go to Boston to finally find out what's in that box."

"Whatever is in there, we can blow the lid off this scandal. Make it public. Then there is no reason for them to keep coming after us."

"I've thought about that."

"And?"

"And there is a reason my dad didn't do the same thing. I won't know why until I read the documents."

"I'll come with you. I can help."

"You can't, Katie."

"Why not?"

"I want to protect you."

"Yeah, I realize that. But remember, I owe Tom Reece, too. I wouldn't be here without him."

"I remember," Reece said, thinking of his father risking his life to smuggle Katie's father and his family out of what was then Czechoslovakia during the waning days of the Cold War. Reece was a child and Katie had not yet been born.

"I almost got shot the first time we had lunch, remember?"

"That seems like a lifetime ago, but it also seems like yesterday," Reece said, recalling their lunch at a restaurant in LA's Chinatown, learning of past connections between his family and hers. "I want to keep you safe forever, Katie. I feel like I'm nearing the end of a journey, like my dad's letter and what's in that box are connected to everything that's happened."

"Just know I am here for you, James. Forever."

He pulled her close, reaching down to untie her bathrobe.

"Before you get too frisky, mister, let me tidy up. You just relax."

He watched her dump the to-go cartons in the trash and quickly neaten up the kitchenette.

"Another bottle?" she asked.

"I think it's a three-bottle night," Reece said.

"I was hoping you'd say that. I found this Macauley Old Vine Zinfandel in a store about two blocks from here. Apparently, people on the Vineyard, where ironically there are no vineyards, like their wines."

She returned to him and set down her glass.

"Do you ever regret not sticking with your first major at UC Davis?" Reece asked. Katie had completed two years in the university's viticulture and enology undergraduate program before transferring to the University of California, Berkeley, for a degree in English. She then attained her master's from the Columbia School of Journalism.

"Never. But after all this excitement, I might apply for the sommelier job if you open that bar in Bozeman."

"Send me your résumé. I'll consider it," Reece joked.

"Maybe when this is over, we can escape to Napa. I can introduce you to some of my favorite wineries."

"Deal. Before we zip off to wine country, do you think you could do something about this?" Reece asked, messing up his tangled mop of hair.

"I thought you would never ask," Katie said, putting down her glass. "Wait here."

"I'm not going anywhere," Reece said as Katie retrieved her suitcase.

Reece watched as she knelt down, flipped it open, and removed a large purse.

"What's that?" Reece asked.

"Oh, just a few travel necessities I carry with me in case I have to do a live shot for an interview and have to do my own hair and makeup." She unzipped the bag and laid the contents out on the floor.

"That looks like something I've seen CIA interrogators use," Reece said.

"Tools of the trade. Here, sit," she said, pulling a chair from a small desk against the wall.

"Am I going to regret this?" Reece asked, taking a seat.

"It's possible. Take another sip and let me see what I can do. Though I am liking this look. Can I put it in a man-bun?"

"Man-bun? I played rugby, not soccer."

"Close your eyes," Katie said. "This is going to be the most sensual haircut of your life."

She straddled him in the chair and ran her hands through his hair, pressing herself against him in the loose-fitting robe.

Reece arched his back and settled into the soft chair, allowing himself to truly relax, completely surrendering to the hands of the woman he loved.

As Katie went to work with the small scissors, Reece remembered the words Martha had last spoken to him, words that also concluded his father's letter.

Trust no one.

CHAPTER 34

REECE STOOD NAKED AT the bathroom sink, staring into the mirror. Katie was asleep in the bed behind him, exhausted from their wine-fueled lovemaking. They had given each other all of themselves. Reece was again alone, looking into his own eyes. People had always told him he had his father's eyes. What else did he inherit from Thomas Reece?

Love your wife.

Raise your kids.

I need to keep her safe.

Best way to do that is to disappear.

No.

Yes. It's the only way.

I won't leave her.

Then she will die.

I won't let her die.

Is that what you said about Lauren? About Lucy?

Fuck you.

If you want to keep her safe, you find what's in that box, and then you disappear. Don't be the cause of her death. They are coming for you, James. They are coming for the ones you love. As long as Katie is near you, she's in danger.

Reece looked at his new haircut.

He ran his hand through his beard, still looking at the stranger in the mirror. His skin needed sunlight, and though his body was hard, he needed to eat, hit the weights, and put on some muscle.

He turned around and looked into the bedroom. A thin sheet partially covered Katie's naked body, the bathroom light cutting across her torso like the edge of a blade, her face peaceful and serene.

Beauty is truth, truth beauty.

Words from the closing stanza of John Keats's "Ode on a Grecian Urn" rose from his subconscious, evoked by the angelic figure he had left in bed. Why would those words come to him now? They were from one of his mother's favorite poems. She had passed it along to her son in one of the many long hours they had spent together reading in his father's absence. Reece swallowed. His mother had used the poem to teach him a lesson. He knew that the splendor of the words disguised a darker meaning: They were a warning to those who would go in search of remedies. Did it come to him now as an admonition to leave the safe-deposit box alone?

Beauty is truth, truth beauty.

Reece closed the bathroom door, raised the scissors to his beard, and started to cut.

CHAPTER 35

KATIE AWOKE BEFORE THE sun. She turned over expecting to feel the warmth of another body. She reached a bit farther. *Empty.*

"*James?*" she whispered.

Her hand confirmed that she was alone.

She slipped from beneath the covers and found her bathrobe on the floor, securing it with the tie around her waist.

Where is he?

The bathroom was empty.

She walked back across the bedroom and peered into the main room.

She smelled the coffee first. Half a pot sat warming in the coffeemaker. A towel was rolled up and pushed against the bottom of the door; another was spread out flat in the center of the floor. All the blackout curtains had been pulled except for one on a window overlooking the garden below. Reece leaned against a wall, coffee mug in hand. He was barefoot but dressed for the day in jeans and T-shirt.

"*Reece?*" she said quietly.

He took a sip from his mug and continued to stare out the window.

Katie edged closer. "Reece," she said, a little louder.

His head turned and he smiled. He pushed himself off the wall, stopping a few feet from her.

"I tried not to wake you. I made coffee," he offered.

Her head turned to the towel on the floor.

"Just got a quick workout in," Reece said.

"Did you sleep out here?"

Reece opened his mouth and decided that the truth was the only option.

"A little bit."

He answered her look of concern. "Don't worry, Katie. I'll come home. It's just going to take some time."

Time.

She went to him and wrapped him in her arms.

"Let's go home together. I'm here for you."

"In prison I slept on a thin rubber mat embedded in a concrete block," Reece told her. "Everything was cold. I did what exercises I could, along with the breath-holding exercises my dad taught me as a kid and some other ones they taught us in BUD/S."

Katie looked at the towel against the door.

"It was also dark in there. I think I got used to it."

Katie reached up and touched his clean-shaven face, the concern evident in her eyes.

"Oh yeah, I shaved. What do you think?"

"I think you are trying to change the subject, but in this case, I'll let you. You take all the time you need, James."

"Thank you, Katie. You want coffee?"

"Coffee? What time is it?"

"I think it's around five thirty," Reece said, turning his wrist to confirm. "Yep, five thirty-seven."

"That is about three hours too early. What time is your appointment with that attorney?"

"Eleven," Reece said. "I told Raife that I'd meet him and Liz for breakfast. Now I guess *we* will be meeting them for breakfast."

"Well, that gives us more than enough time."

"*Time?* Time for what?"

"Time for us."

Katie stepped back and let her bathrobe fall to the floor.

CHAPTER 36

Brighton Beach
Brooklyn, New York

STEPAN VASILIEV DIDN'T APPRECIATE being woken up in the middle of the night, but as a brigadier in the Bratva, the Russian mafia, when the *pakhan*, the boss, called personally, you picked up. He had two hours to assemble his crew to catch the first ferry from Woods Hole, on the near end of Cape Cod, to Martha's Vineyard.

Vasiliev didn't like having to scramble for an operation of this magnitude in only a few hours. This wasn't a hit on a mark within the Russian community in New York. They were stepping outside the family, just like they had when they were ordered to kill those three Iraqis in Northern Virginia. That meant complications. With half his crew still drunk or high from the night before, Vasiliev would have preferred to push the task a day to the right, but he was assured that this was of the highest priority.

They took two new Range Rovers. Driving the SUVs with New York plates in Martha's Vineyard, they might as well be invisible.

The key to this operation was *not* to kill someone, at least not right away. Killing was easy. This was more complex.

Vasiliev and his crew had gotten quite adept at moving people in and around the United States. The Department of Justice called it human trafficking. To Vasiliev and the Bratva, it was business. The sex trade, organ trafficking, and even the movement of babies for adoption were part of an international consortium of illicit networks that provided a necessary service. Where there was demand, someone would fill the supply. It was the most American of endeavors.

Today was different. Vasiliev and his crew were not dealing with traumatized and drugged underage girls. Today's target would fight back. As much as he hated the sport, Vasiliev always found it humorous when he saw "human trafficking" headlines in advance of the Super Bowl. It was all just for clicks and eyeballs. The Bratva usually avoided the larger events. What those articles didn't report was that moving these girls, and oftentimes young boys, into metropolitan areas was not the exclusive purview of the Super Bowl or other large sporting events. It was something his organization did almost daily. One of the perks of being on his crew was getting first dibs on new girls from Eastern Europe and Africa. Better to get in there early before they were run through by the next thousand customers.

Vasiliev had forced himself to think of them as property, especially the youngest ones, who he knew had the most valuable organs. He had read it was called *dehumanizing*. Whatever it was called, it was a part of the job. You didn't rise up the ranks of the Bratva by empathizing with your product. There was a market, and his organization helped keep that product flowing. Drugs, girls, boys: the appetite worldwide was insatiable. The Bratva was a business, a profitable one. They moved their illicit product, laundered the money in several investment vehicles, primarily real estate, and bribed or blackmailed law enforcement and public officials to mitigate the heat.

Usually, the business ran smoothly. When it did not, Vasiliev and his crew would eliminate the problem. Sometimes that elimination was messy and required cleanup. Other times that messy solution was meant to send a message to keep others in line.

Vasiliev did not like that they would be adding a new member to their crew for this operation. An unknown entity. A specialist. They were to meet him at the ferry. Vasiliev had been instructed to provide him with a clean, subcompact 9mm suppressed pistol. Vasiliev had selected a Glock 43 with a suppressor constructed by a source upstate. Suppressors were not hard to make if you had the right machines.

Vasiliev had been told that the specialist would leave his car in Woods Hole and travel with him and his crew onto the ferry. Reservations had already been made. Once at the dock, the specialist would relay the plan.

All Vasiliev knew was that it involved an abduction.

CHAPTER 37

Woods Hole
Falmouth, Massachusetts

MAX GENRICH ENJOYED LIVING in Germany. His business provided a "cover for action," allowing him to travel when and where he pleased. Though his family had strong ties to Russia, Genrich was now a generation removed from the red bear and had never visited. That added value in the eyes of his employer, the Russian Foreign Intelligence Service. Genrich was an assassin.

Germany had been a top destination for Russian immigration after the fall of the Soviet Union, and Genrich was born not long after his family arrived in Cologne. The Russian Intelligence Service saw that migration as an opportunity. His parents came of age in a time when one did not question the dictates of the Motherland. To protect the extended family they left behind, Genrich had begun meeting with an elderly gentleman before he had reached his teens. At first there were tests: language aptitude through conversation, problem-solving through chess, and agility through soccer, handball, and track and field. That testing evolved into training. Before he had graduated from college, Genrich was firmly in the grasp of the SVR.

Genrich knew that the KGB's program to infiltrate the West at the end of the Cold War had many tentacles, and his was but one. Though he didn't know how many, he knew there were others like him. German citizens traveled the world in greater numbers and frequency than Russians. Even though the U.S. had seen over 200,000 visitors from Russia every year before the pandemic, it was still safer to blend in as one of the two million annual German visitors to the U.S. That was why he had been assigned to eliminate James Reece.

He had not served in the Russian or German military or police force, so there were no records of him having a background in military, law enforcement, or intelligence circles or having developed skills in long-distance shooting, offensive driving, or close-quarters combat. He was one of many who had wrestled in his younger days and now practiced jiu-jitsu at a local school. Facial recognition technology would identify him as Max Genrich, a German citizen and business consultant with no criminal history or reports of government service. He was clean, just like the untraceable 9mm suppressed pistols he favored that came from local Bratva sources or contacts at a Russian embassy.

He was well compensated for what he did, his payments coming in the form of small percentages of investments in real estate, sports teams, restaurants, and stocks. He was financially free, though not in an extravagant way. His silver Audi RS 5 was fast but not flashy, and in the spring and summer he liked the freedom of riding his BMW café racer in the city and to surrounding towns. Officially he was a freelance business consultant with a profitable, but not too profitable, business in Cologne. His business website was extremely bland by design, and he had no social media presence either personally or professionally. At thirty-five he estimated he could continue to work for another decade, possibly two, until the years forced him into retirement.

Women found him attractive, and Cologne offered him enough culture and art to satisfy his intellect. He stayed in shape, enjoyed the city life, and could travel as he pleased—both the Bonn and Düsseldorf airports were close. He loved to travel Europe by train with female companionship. His longest relationship had lasted a year. He was very up-front with women that he was not the marrying type, though that just seemed to encourage the thirty-somethings he dated; they all thought they had the wiles to change him. Relationships were open from the beginning.

There were no alarm bells that rang on the occasions when he was called upon to travel for work. He operated his small business, paid his exorbitant taxes, took his girlfriends to nice dinners, and shook his head as he watched the news reports on German politicians continuing to outsource energy dependence to Russia.

That he was used sparingly and paid well told him that he was valuable. All his hits had been at close range with suppressed weapons that he would then dismantle and dispose of. He knew that patterns would get him killed, so he did what he could to avoid them. Using a 9mm pistol at close range violated that rule, but he used it because the round was so prevalent the world over. He wasn't told and didn't want to know the *why* behind his assignments—just the *who*. He would take care of the rest.

He preferred to operate in Europe, though he also took overseas assignments. He had killed a banker in Chicago, a tech company executive on vacation in Mexico, and a Russian double agent in Calgary.

For fifteen years the SVR had never mandated the timing of the hit, nor had they asked him to do anything but eliminate problems.

That was why this particular job made him nervous. For this one, he was being paid in investments worth five times as much as what he usually received. He should have said no. The compensation told him that the SVR was desperate. Desperate men made desperate moves. He also knew that one didn't say no to the SVR. His parents were still alive, and he had one sister working in England. That meant he could very easily be pressured into taking the job. Had he said no, his younger sister might be found dead of an "accidental overdose" in a London park, or the victim of the violent crime so prevalent in larger cities. No, it was best for all if he said yes, got it done, and then returned to Germany to take his new girlfriend, a recent graduate of the University of Cologne, to Switzerland for a weekend ski vacation.

It was also possible that an operation of this magnitude and complexity would mean he would have even more time between assignments.

Genrich did not approve of the rush job. An abduction, an errand, and an assassination. But the fact that all of it would go down over the course of a few hours made it more palatable. There would be no hostages, no negotiations to slow things down, and he had the Bratva to take the fall should anything get loud.

With any luck, he would be out of the country before the bodies cooled.

CHAPTER 38

Martha's Vineyard
Dukes County
Massachusetts

REECE WALKED IN THE direction of the harbor, enjoying his newfound freedom. It was the first time he had been alone since his release, and he relished the autonomy. The ocean winds had long since blown the leaves from the trees, and even in the late morning hours the streets were clear of the tourists and seasonal residents who would invade come June.

He was clean, freshly shaven with a new haircut, and dressed in his Salomons, Origin jeans, T-shirt, and a dark brown Triple Aught Design Talisman jacket that Katie had packed for him. Even his eyes felt better in the light, though he kept them shaded in sunglasses. The headaches brought on by the initial assault of the fluorescent lights when he had met with Vic were gone.

He sipped his to-go cup of coffee, holding it in his left hand, leaving his right free to go to the pistol holstered behind his right hip.

Better to be judged by twelve than carried by six, Reece thought. Though after his recent experience in solitary confinement, he wasn't so sure.

Raife and Liz were not completely surprised that Reece was not alone when he entered the small breakfast area at the hotel that morning. They knew Katie well.

As they caught up over a late breakfast, Raife was insistent on accompanying Reece to his meeting with the lawyer, but in the end, Reece was able to convince him to remain at the hotel with Liz and Katie. Raife was a protector, and he eventually relented. Truth be told, Reece wanted to be alone.

Reece smiled and nodded at an elderly couple on a morning walk with their Yorkshire terrier and caught himself wondering if he and Katie would one day take walks together like that in their golden years.

He took a right on South Water Street and passed the Edgartown Yacht Club. It was possible that the Beneteau Oceanis 48 that he had scuttled off Mozambique had started her journey that night in one of these slips.

Admiring the homes that lined the street, Reece continued his walk, the coffee cup emblazoned with THE RICHARD, telling anyone who noticed that he was just in for a night or two, enjoying the seaside town in the off-season. For a second he felt almost normal, walking through a small town on a bright winter morning. The fact that his coffee remained in his left hand, that his eyes continued to scan for threats, and that Katie was in the care of another hunter and killer of men back at the hotel reminded him he was not.

He turned right on High Street and walked until it crossed South Summer Street. Looking down at the card Martha had given him the evening before, he confirmed the address. It was a house that looked like it could soon be torn down and replaced with a Wall Street banker's summer home. CHARLES AMBLER, ATTORNEY-AT-LAW was printed on a white sign in light blue lettering that hung from the porch. It was obvious that this was a law office used by locals and had been there for a long time.

Reece looked both ways, noting a few cars parked on the street and a woman dressed in Lululemon, iPhone in hand, gossiping away through her earbuds as she power walked through the streets. This would have been a good time to have a phone so he could pretend to be texting or having a conversation. Standing there without a phone broke the rhythm of the day and looked out of place.

Five minutes early.

Reece crossed the street, opened the gate attached to the white picket fence, walked across the flat stones that cut across the tidy lawn, and ascended the steps to what was more a cottage than a home or an office. He knocked twice and heard a male voice say, "Come in."

Reece looked to his sides and then behind him. Still clear. He put his hand to the doorknob and opened the door.

The lead-filled leather sap connected with the side of Reece's skull and sent him to the floor. He felt strong hands grab him and drag him the remainder of the way inside. He heard the door shut and lock behind him.

His mind registered another body unceremoniously slumped on the floor across from him. He was dressed in a suit. One side of the man's head had collapsed, and blood trickled from his mouth.

A second hit with the sap sent Reece into darkness.

CHAPTER 39

REECE AWOKE IN A chair opposite a man sitting across a desk in the main office, just off the reception area of the front room. Reece's hands were zip-tied behind him, and his feet were zip-tied to the legs of the chair.

The headache was on the verge of crippling.

The throbbing.

The ringing.

The man across from him smiled. Black hair styled into position with some type of hair product, clean-shaven, wearing a sweater under a dark navy pea coat. He didn't look like a killer except for the Glock 43 with attached suppressor that was on the desk in front of him.

Reece blinked and shook his head. How long he had been out? Probably just long enough to get him zip-tied in place.

"Mr. Reece. James Reece," the man in black said.

There wasn't a discernible accent, but something about the man's voice was off. It was precise. Was there just a touch of England in his tone? Or was it something else?

"I have the benefit of knowing who you are and also the advantage of being in complete control. I apologize for the harsh treatment. I am sure you understand."

Reece looked around the room. Two men, each holding a Glock 19, stood against the wall to his left. He craned his neck and saw another manning the door. They wore suits and overcoats in a poor attempt to blend in. Even in suits they were not as well put together as the man at the desk. They looked like what they were—hired muscle.

"I am going to save us all a lot of time and trouble. I don't know why I was hired to kill you. That is of little importance. I just know there is something we must do together before I do."

"And what is that?" Reece asked, his mind running through options.

"My employer requests that we recover the contents of a certain safe-deposit box from a bank in Boston. Mr. Ambler was kind enough to phone ahead and smooth the way before we killed him. We promised to let his wife live if he complied. Their home is just on the other side of town. We have thus far kept our promise. We have an appointment with a Mr. Devine at the Boston Safe Deposit and Trust Company at four p.m. today. We are going to leave this house, lock up, get in our cars, and take the noon ferry to Woods Hole. We already have reservations. If, by chance, we miss that one, there is another leaving at one fifteen p.m. From there, it is approximately one and a half hours to Boston. You and one of my associates will enter the bank and meet with Mr. Devine. Only you will be allowed access to the safe-deposit box vault. You will go in, remove the contents of the box in their entirety, and then sign back out. My associate will then escort you back to the vehicles and we will go for a drive from which you will not return."

"That doesn't sound promising," Reece said, fighting off the urge to vomit from the acute pounding in his brain.

"For you it is anything but promising. For me it is lucrative, and for my employer it is necessary."

"Let's say I decide to tell you to fuck off?"

"Americans." The man shook his head.

So, he wasn't an American.

"If you decide to tell me to, as you put it, *fuck off*, your friends will not leave this island alive. Show him."

One of the men had an iPad in his hand. He walked to Reece and held it in front of his face.

"That is the Richard Hotel. Nice spot, from what I understand. I have four men, all armed, not with little pistols like these, no, but with fully automatic rifles, parked just outside."

"What's the deal?"

"The deal is this, Mr. Reece. You play nice like I know you can, your friends live. And you? Sadly, no. This ends poorly for you either way. You will not survive the day. But you do get to die a hero. Your cooperation and your death will save your friends. What do you say? You want your friends to live, you come with me."

I won't leave her.

Then she will die.

I won't let her die.

Isn't that what you said about Lauren? About Lucy?

Fuck you.

Katie.

"What was that, Mr. Reece? It sounded like you said, '*Katie.*'"

Reece looked back at the iPad screen, then at the man across the desk before speaking.

"We're wasting time."

CHAPTER 40

Boston Safe Deposit and Trust Company
Boston, Massachusetts

SAFE-DEPOSIT BOXES WERE BECOMING increasingly rare. Sophisticated home vaults contributed to the decline in demand, as did the fact that valuable documents could now be registered electronically and stored in the cloud. There were still those who preferred to keep papers, art, and valuables secured in an off-site facility guarded twenty-four hours a day. There was also an old-world status to having something hidden away at a bank that could not be replicated at home. And at home there was always the possibility that someone could force you to open your safe at gunpoint. There were also those who desired to keep certain valuables unknown to family members or business associates. For this exclusive clientele, certain institutions retained their physical safe-deposit boxes. Austria, the United Kingdom, Ireland, Switzerland, the Cayman Islands, Panama, Dubai, Hong Kong, Malaysia, Thailand, and Cyprus were all known for housing private financial institutions that still catered to those who preferred to safeguard their valuables and their secrets in off-site vaults.

Head throbbing, Reece had entered the Range Rover and sat between the two men in suits. It was the extended Autobiography edition, so there was plenty of legroom even for all three of them. Genrich sat in the front passenger seat while another one of the suits drove. Once across to the mainland, they were joined by two Escalades and two motorcycles, new black Ducati Monsters.

Katie will find me.

Then she will die.

No.

Just like all those you love. Dead.

"What was that, Mr. Reece?" Genrich asked. "You keep mumbling."

"Oh, nothing. Just want to get this over with so I can get along with the business of killing each and every one of you."

"At least you still retain a sense of humor. I empathize with your situation, and I apologize for putting you in it. We must accept that all our previous decisions led us both to this time and place."

"What are you going to do with the contents of the safe-deposit box?" Reece asked.

"Whatever I am told, Mr. Reece. Deliver it to my employers, or destroy it, I suspect."

"Are you curious why someone would go through all this trouble for whatever is inside?"

"I stopped being curious about those aspects of the job long ago. It does not help. In fact, it can be a detriment to accomplishing the assigned task."

The driver and the men to Reece's right and left remained silent.

"If it is any consolation to you, Mr. Reece, you do this, your friends will live, and I promise I will kill you quickly. No pain. Here one minute, gone in less than a second." He snapped his fingers.

"I appreciate the sentiment, and the consideration."

"A favor between professionals."

"I'll remember that when it comes time for me to put you in the ground," Reece said.

"I've heard that about you SEALs. Confidence? Or is it arrogance?"

"It's fact," Reece said, looking out the window.

"I was born to this life, Mr. Reece, as I suspect you were as well."

"I chose it," Reece said.

"Ah, well, then perhaps you are not quite as clever as your file indicates."

"My file?"

"Oh yes; I know quite a bit about you, Mr. Reece. It's how I am certain you will complete this one last mission. Katie Buranek, the journalist. So beautiful, so young. I know you would do anything to keep her alive and not be the cause of her meeting the same fate as your wife, daughter, and unborn son."

Reece's head snapped up.

"Oh yes—not many people know about your unborn son. He would be almost five now, wouldn't he? Surprised I know so much about you, I see. You must be a terrible *preferans* player, or what do you play here, poker? So emotional.

"Had you not come home from that last deployment, had you died with your men in Afghanistan, he would be in kindergarten, probably playing what you call soccer."

Definitely not American.

"Your wife, Lauren, that was her name, wasn't it? She would probably be remarried. She would certainly be fucking someone else. Your file had a photo of her. Quite attractive."

Reece's eyes were laser focused straight ahead, memorizing the license plate of the lead vehicle.

"Nothing to say? That's because you know I have only spoken the truth. I know you want to kill me, Mr. Reece. I'm sorry that you will never get the opportunity."

Genrich turned in his seat to look at Reece. For a moment he regretted engaging in conversation with the former SEAL. *Those eyes.*

He turned back in his seat.

"Pray that I die today," Reece said.

"Why? Because you will hunt me down and kill me? *Please*, Mr. Reece, both you and I know you are going to go into that bank, remove the contents of the box, and bring them back to me. Then I am going to take you outside the city and put a bullet in your head. I have given you my word: Your friends will live—Ms. Buranek will live. She will move on to a life without you just like Lauren would have. If anything does not go exactly as planned, she will not see the sunrise tomorrow. Trust me, Mr. Reece, this is what I do."

They had driven toward their destination on MA-3 North, passing Wompatuck State Park, then taking Interstate 93 North, first into South Boston and then downtown into the heart of the financial district, stopping across the street from One Boston Place.

"I will not be going in with you. Sasha here will accompany you inside," Genrich said, nodding at the large man to Reece's left. "Too many cameras for my liking. He has a phone and a radio. Two clicks of the transmit button and your friends will all be killed, so be on your best behavior."

The big man to Reece's left opened the car door and waved Reece out. Reece noticed that men had stepped out of the lead and trailing vehicles as well.

"Wait," Sasha said.

He unclipped a holster from his belt and passed it inside before closing the door.

"Let's go," he said.

They crossed the street.

Three fifty p.m. Right on time.

If anything does not go exactly as planned, she will not see the sunrise tomorrow.

They climbed the steps and passed under an American flag bracketed to the outside of the building.

Reece looked up at the white marble facade. Forty-one stories of imposing Renaissance-style architecture harked back to the days when bankers were kings. It was now home to both the Boston Safe Deposit and Trust Company and the Boston Stock Exchange. Security was tight.

They passed through the front entrance and approached a screening checkpoint. Reece dropped his wallet and key in the tray and placed it on the conveyor belt of an X-ray machine as one would at an airport before passing through the metal detector unmolested. Sasha put his phone, small radio, and wallet into the X-ray machine, walked through, and collected his belongings. Reece scanned the large lobby, noting the private security guards, cameras, the rows of flat screens with stock tickers, a coffee shop, and a bank of elevators.

A man in a dark blue suit rose from a chair in the lobby and approached.

"Mr. Reece?" he asked cautiously.

"Yes," Reece said, extending his hand.

"I am Ed Devine. I spoke with your attorney, Mr. Ambler, this morning."

A yellow pocket square peeked from the top of his left breast pocket and wire-rimmed glasses sat atop a hawklike nose. What was left of his hair was combed over a narrow head.

"Yes, thank you for meeting us. This is my secretary," Reece said, nodding at Sasha.

The large Russian scowled.

"I see. As I explained to Mr. Ambler this morning, we will go downstairs to my office, where we will take care of the necessary paperwork. Do you have two forms of identification?"

"Will my military ID and driver's license work?" Reece asked.

"That will be fine, as long as both are current. Regulations, you see."

"They are."

"And the key?"

"And the key," Reece repeated, removing it from his pocket.

"Wonderful."

"And your secretary, Mister . . . ?" he asked.

"Volkov," the large man responded.

"Mr. Volkov, we have a waiting area downstairs."

"Regulations," Reece said, looking at Sasha.

Devine used a key from a key ring to allow the elevator to access his floor. They took the elevator two floors down and exited into a small marble-floored lobby area. Two private security guards in light blue uniforms sat on either side of the elevator.

"Mr. Volkov, you may wait right in there," Mr. Devine said, indicating a small room with two chairs, a sofa, magazines, and a television.

"This way, Mr. Reece. My office is through here."

Reece took a seat in a comfortable leather chair as Devine parked himself in front of his desk and logged into his computer.

"There is less and less demand for safe-deposit boxes, Mr. Reece. We are one of the holdouts. Many of our long-standing clients still prefer to keep certain items with us."

"I understand," Reece said.

"I was not here when your father opened the account, but it looks like everything is in order. All payments are up-to-date. I'll need those two forms of ID."

"Of course," Reece said, reaching for his wallet and producing his retired military ID and Montana driver's license.

Devine examined them through his spectacles, made a notation in a ledger, and typed something into his computer.

"Mr. Reece, there is an addendum attached to this box."

"Meaning?"

"In addition to your identification and a key, there is also a required password."

Password? Reece's mind began to spin.

"It says here that only you and Thomas Reece know it."

Without that password his friends were dead.

"Ah yes," Reece said, stalling for time.

Password?

What could it be?

Think, Reece!

The letter.

And remember, trust no one.

"Of course, the password: 'trust no one.'"

"Thank you. Now, excuse me a moment while I make copies."

"No problem," Reece said.

Devine logged out of his computer and exited the windowless office.

Should he call Raife? Call the police? Sasha was just across the hall. Could Reece risk it?

Two clicks of the transmit button and your friends will all be killed.

Would Sasha's radio even transmit from this area?

No, Reece. Find out what's in that box.

Devine returned a moment later.

"We make physical and scanned copies of your identification," he said, handing them back.

"Of course."

"Please sign here," Devine said, passing a ledger across the desk.

Reece looked at the last signature. Thomas Reece. 11 November 1992.

"I see you and your father are the only signatories."

"That's right," Reece said.

"Mr. Ambler explained to me that your father passed on some years ago. Please accept my condolences."

"Thank you."

"Now, if you will follow me, we will retrieve the box and take it to an adjoining room where you will be able to access it. We close at five p.m. but I am happy to stay longer, so take all the time you need. Security is twenty-four/seven."

"I shouldn't be too long," Reece said, thinking of his friends on Martha's Vineyard.

"Very well, then."

They walked down a hallway. Devine produced a key from a key ring in his pocket and opened another door that led into a larger room where a large bank vault door had been opened. A secondary barred door prevented entry.

"Good evening, Karl," Devine said to a uniformed security guard sitting in a chair.

Karl pulled an earbud from his ear but didn't stand.

"Evening, Mr. Devine."

"What are you listening to?"

"The latest Rogan with Peter Zeihan. Fascinating."

"I'll have to give it a listen."

Reece noted the Beretta 92F on Karl's belt, which also had a stun gun, ASP baton, and handcuffs.

"Sign in here," Devine said, pointing to a logbook on a stand to the left of the vault.

Reece signed in with his printed name, date, time, safe-deposit box number, and signature.

Devine opened the gate and motioned for Reece to enter the vault.

The long, rectangular vault was lined floor to ceiling in locked boxes. Overhead fluorescent lights ran the length of the space, the sterile silver boxes gleaming under the iridescent glow.

"The vault is monitored with audio and video surveillance. After you retrieve your box, I will escort you to a room where you can open it in private."

Reece followed Devine deeper into the vault.

"Here it is," he said. "Two thirteen."

The box was the medium-sized option. Reece estimated it to measure twenty by four inches tall. He looked at his key.

What did you leave me, Dad?

Reece inserted and turned the key.

He then took hold of the small handle and pulled the case from its slot.

CHAPTER 41

"THIS WAY," DEVINE SAID.

The box wasn't excessively heavy, so Reece managed it easily.

They exited the vault, and Devine swung the gated door shut behind them.

"Through here," he said.

Reece followed him to the right and into a small conference room. An oak table was in the center of the room, surrounded by four leather swivel chairs.

"You may lock the door here if you wish," Devine said. "I'll be outside."

"Thank you," Reece said.

He walked to the table, set the box down, and returned to the door to lock the dead bolt. He then turned and approached the box, his heart beginning to race.

Calm down, Reece. Just get what you came for. Give whatever is in here to the man in black and accept your fate. Katie was destined to die if she stayed with you. Get it over with. Your death gives her life. Do it.

Reece circled the table and put his back to the far wall, giving the room a quick once-over. No obvious cameras, though there could easily be miniature cameras and audio recording devices hidden just about anywhere. He walked to the table and pushed a chair out of the way so he could remain standing.

It all comes down to this.

Powerful people and organizations will do anything to keep what's in that box from seeing the light of day.

Reece took a deep breath and opened the box.

CHAPTER 42

MAX GENRICH LOOKED AT the black PVD-coated Panerai on his wrist. It had been twenty minutes. How long did it take to access a safe-deposit box? He had estimated the process would take an hour and that comms with Sasha would possibly be cut off in the vault area. Still, he didn't like the exposure of being attached to the Bratva enforcers. It was not his style.

He was also concerned about James Reece. Genrich had killed a lot of men in his time, and none of them had been as calm about it as his current mark. Did this guy want to die? Was he searching for death? A death wish? Maybe. But perhaps it was something more.

Genrich looked down at his phone and texted the lead vehicle.

The front passenger door on the Escalade in front of him opened and Vasiliev approached.

Genrich exited his Range Rover to meet him.

"I'm going to circle the block, get some air," Genrich said. "Everything is going according to plan thus far. If he were going to alert authorities, he would have done so by now. Take my seat. It has a good view of the entrance. When he's back in the vehicle, pick me up just up at that intersection, State and Court Street."

Vasiliev nodded and climbed into the Range Rover. Genrich could tell he was not accustomed to taking orders, but also knew the head of the New York Bratva had instructed him to follow Genrich's every directive.

Genrich pulled up his collar and walked along the sidewalk, admiring the Old Statehouse on his right. He crossed the street a block down at the intersection of Washington and Court Streets and took up a position at the corner of a brick roundabout. Removing his phone from his pocket, he pretended to scroll, becoming all but invisible.

• • •

Reece stood looking down into the open box, a portal into his father's past, a past that had gotten him killed.

"I'll find that box."

A part of me prays you will not.

"I found it, Dad," Reece whispered, reaching in to remove a thick manila envelope that seemed at risk of bursting at the seams.

The envelope was not the only item in the box. Reece set it to the side and pulled out a dagger. The "pancake flipper" scabbard immediately gave it away as an OSS stiletto, a variation of the famed Fairbairn-Sykes fighting knife upon which it was based. Reece held the leather-wrapped center portion of the stamped steel sheath in his hands and pulled the double-edged six-and-a-half-inch blade from its sheath. Born of their experience with the Shanghai Municipal Police, William Fairbairn and Eric Sykes created a blade that became synonymous with World War II commandos on both sides on the Atlantic. The OSS modified the design of the Second Pattern F-S knife by shortening the blade by about half an inch and blackening the handle and blade.

Reece tested both sides of the blade with his finger. It was razor-sharp. A lot of people incorrectly believed the Fairbairn-Sykes fighting knife was designed only for stabbing. Reece knew better. He also knew that the OSS version of the venerable commando knife made during wartime by a home goods company in Connecticut was exceptionally brittle. In 1944, it was replaced by the M3 trench knife.

Reece looked down at what amounted to a museum piece in his hands.

I just need you to make it through the next ten minutes.

He set it aside and pulled out four passports: Malta, the United States, Portugal, and Argentina. They all had Tom Reece's face, with different names.

Putting the passports on the desk, Reece reached back into the box and removed four stacks of cash in rubber bands: multiple denominations of United States dollars, Argentinian pesos, Swiss francs, and Russian rubles.

Something else was in the box. Reece wrapped his hand around a handle of Tennessee hickory and brought his father's tomahawk into the light. Reece instantly recognized it as an original VTAC, designed by World War II Marine Corps veteran Peter LaGana. MACV-SOG teams favored the tool in the jungles of Vietnam. Some of those were designated Hatchet Force teams. They consisted of three to six Americans and a force of Montagnards specializing in cross-border operations into Laos, Cambodia, and North Vietnam. Those operations included searching for American POWs. Reece removed the tomahawk from its well-traveled oxblood-colored leather sheath and examined the unique wide upswept primary edge and the specially curved design at its base. He turned it and examined the V-shaped reverse spike on the back of the head. Sharp and ready.

Like father, like son.

Thank you, Dad.

Reece sheathed the tomahawk and set it aside. He then picked up the thick manila envelope and undid the red string and button closure that secured the seal flap to the back of the envelope. He carefully reached inside. Documents. Maps. Notes. Some in English but most in Vietnamese, French, and Russian.

Damn it!

Tom Reece had left one final encryption.

Reece needed to get these translated.

Would he get the chance?

It might be better for all if you don't find it. If you do, and you think the world is better off not knowing what's in there—burn it. Burn it all. And then live your life knowing you did the right thing. Never look back. But, depending on what has happened in these intervening years, when you go through the documents, when you see the list, do what you think is right.

There was one final envelope. Reece picked it up and read the outside.

JAMES REECE

It was secured with a red wax seal. A single rose was embedded in the wax.

Later, Reece. It's time to go to work.

He folded the letter addressed to him and put it in his inside jacket pocket. He stuffed the stack of U.S. currency into his front left pocket. He put the passports and other currency back in the box and closed the lid.

Time.

All our days are numbered. Your days are numbered, too. Use them. Use them wisely.

I will, Dad.

Reece reached for the tomahawk and removed the sheath, stashing it in his jacket. He then inverted it and placed it under his belt with the head secured in his back right pocket, the handle running up the right side of his spine under his jacket. He then took the sheathed dagger and placed it in the appendix position with the metal catch off. He tested it twice to ensure he could get to it quickly. He would need to.

Satisfied, Reece took the box and moved to the door. He unlocked it and swung it open.

Ed Devine was waiting patiently outside in a chair.

"All set," Reece said.

"Wonderful. We can return the box and sign out. I can have security escort you to your vehicle if you would like," Devine said, looking at the manila folder in Reece's left hand.

"That's okay," Reece responded. "I do have a favor to ask, though."

"Oh?"

"Where was that copy machine?"

CHAPTER 43

REECE AND SASHA TOOK the elevator up to the main floor with Devine.

"Thank you for trusting us with your business, Mr. Reece. Please see us again soon."

"Thank you, Mr. Devine. I appreciate the professional service. Is there a restroom on this floor?"

"There is, just around to the left on the other side of the elevators."

"Thank you. Take care."

The two men shook hands. Sasha only nodded, unsure what to do about the restroom question.

"I've got to go," Reece said, starting to walk toward the restroom.

"No, follow me," Sasha said. "And give me the folder."

Reece handed him the folder and kept walking.

"It's been hours; just a quick stop. You can come in with me," Reece said, pushing the door open.

Reece's scan revealed that the bathroom was empty aside from an elderly gentleman washing his hands at the sink who paid Reece and Sasha no attention.

Reece walked to the bank of urinals, partitioned with beige privacy dividers.

"I'll be quick," Reece said, picking a urinal at the far end of the bathroom.

Toilet stalls were to Reece's back, set up on the opposite side of the room from the urinals.

Reece took his time unzipping his pants. As he relieved himself, he heard the old man turn off the water and exit the restroom.

Sasha stood behind him and just off to his left, clearly uncomfortable with the situation.

Reece turned his head.

"Do you mind?"

Sasha looked from Reece to the door.

"Hurry up," he said.

Reece finished and made a production of getting himself arranged and zipping up his pants. He also removed the stiletto from its sheath at his appendix. The pommel was supported in the palm of his hand.

Make it quick, Reece.

Reece made a fist and hit the flush lever on the left side of the urinal, thinking the noise might muffle what was about to happen.

As the urinal sputtered with the sound of the flush, Reece turned around with his head down to allow him an extra moment to advance on his target. He judged the distance and exploded with a thrust that drove the six-and-a-half-inch OSS knife up under his minder's diaphragm, targeting the heart.

Sasha dropped the documents, his body convulsing in shock around the wound.

Reece's left hand shot to the back of his neck in a clench as his right hand ratcheted the blade back and forth, eviscerating his opponent's internal organs.

He's too big. Not hitting the heart.

Reece extracted the weapon from beneath his enemy's rib cage, blood spraying from the wound channel.

You can't walk out of here covered in blood, and you can't pull security or police into this, or Katie, Raife, and Liz are dead.

Reece grabbed the man's left triceps with his knife hand and spun him face-first into the urinal, trapping him between the two privacy partitions and smashing his face into the wall above the toilet's flush valve. He sent the blade into the man's right kidney, knowing a wound to the kidney would result in less external bleeding.

The Bratva enforcer cried out, arching his back as the deadly point penetrated his kidney's outer cortex and passed through the medulla to embed in the renal pelvis.

Reece's left hand slid from the back of the man's head around to the front, his little finger locking under his chin, palm covering the mouth, thumb and index finger pinching the nose to stifle any further noise.

He then sidestepped left, removing the blade from the Russian's body and driving it into his left kidney.

He's not going down fast enough.

Reece quickly retracted the double-edged weapon and shifted back to the man's right-side ribs, again ratcheting the blade in a violent attempt to send him to the afterlife.

Finish him, Reece.

Reece pulled the blade from between his ribs, removed his thumb from the ricasso just above the cross guard, and transitioned it into a reverse grip. Holding it like an ice pick, he drove the knife straight down behind the man's clavicle. In and down at a twenty-degree angle, Reece then rotated his wrist, severing the left atrium and pulmonary artery. He stepped slightly back to bring the man to the tiled floor.

Too much blood.

The man was dead. He just didn't know it yet. His reptilian brain was still fighting for survival. In one last-ditch effort to live, he pushed off the top of the urinal with his hands and managed to kick his right leg out, making contact with the wall and sending him and Reece across the narrow bathroom into the toilet stall behind them.

Hold on, Reece.

They crashed through the stall door and into the protruding toilet, which tripped them to the floor.

Wedged between the toilet and the partition, Reece wrapped his legs around the man's midsection, locking them in place. He retracted the knife from the side of the man's neck, dropping it toward his chest. He then moved his left hand around the man's body, placing it over the butt at the base of the knife. With the handle in the upward-facing palm of his right hand, Reece pulled the blade toward him, feeling it sink past the man's jacket, skin, muscle, and ribs, directing it into his heart. Reece felt the man go limp.

Move.

It took considerable effort to extract the blade, struggle out from under the big man, and stand up between the toilet and partition. Reece leaned against the side of the stall and caught his breath, the floor awash in blood.

That didn't work the way you had planned.

The human body could be extremely resilient.

You need to move.

Someone could walk in any second.

Reece wiped the blade on the man's pants and resheathed it. Walking quickly to the sink, he pushed his hands under the automatic soap dispenser.

Come on! The two seconds it took to release the cleansing foam seemed like an eternity.

Reece washed as much blood as possible from his hands and fingernails while examining his face in the mirror. Blood was evident on his left temple, cheek, and neck, which he hastily scrubbed away.

His clothes were dark enough that the blood would not betray him unless one looked closely.

Shoes.

Reece snatched paper towels from the dispenser and wiped the wet blood from his Salomons.

That should get me through the lobby.

Time.

Even you can't outrun time.

Reece walked back to the row of urinals, being careful to avoid the pools of blood, and picked up the manila envelope.

He then departed the restroom, grabbing and opening a yellow freestanding sign labeled DO NOT ENTER—RESTROOM CLOSED FOR CLEANING that was leaning against the wall. He set it in front of the door and walked to the exit.

CHAPTER 44

THE CONFUSION WAS EVIDENT as soon as Reece hit the street. Two of the Bratva enforcers stood by their vehicles expecting him to exit the building with Sasha. They certainly did not expect him to be alone.

Play it off, Reece.

Reece smiled and waved, jogging toward the three SUVs, looking both ways as he darted across the street.

Where are the motorcycles?

He moved toward the middle vehicle, the Land Rover in which he had been riding.

The driver was outside, his right hand out of sight.

"Don't worry," Reece called out as he approached. "He's just in the bathroom. Too much coffee."

The driver looked at his counterpart in the lead vehicle.

"He'll be right out," Reece called.

Reece opened the door and took a seat in the back left passenger seat. The driver remained outside, looking back at the bank.

The man in the front passenger seat turned.

It wasn't the man in black.

Don't get distracted, Reece.

Reece pulled himself into the middle position, next to the man in the right rear passenger seat, under the guise of leaving room for Sasha, and passed the manila folder up to the right front passenger as a distraction.

"Here you go," Reece said.

The manila folder had obscured Reece's left hand. In it was the OSS stiletto, prepped and ready to do the work for which it was designed.

As both Bratva enforcers' eyes went to the documents, Reece checked the rear passenger's left hand to his left leg with his free hand. The stiletto in his left hand, he punched it across his body and through the left side of the man's rib cage. The thin blade shot through connective tissue and cartilage to find the heart.

Hearing the commotion, the front passenger turned. He was too slow. Having pierced the heart of the man next to him, Reece had already extracted the knife and switched it to his right hand in a reverse grip. Reece jammed the point of the blade just behind the front passenger's left ear. Using the blade as a fulcrum, Reece pivoted himself forward, pinning the dying man next to him in his seat with his right leg extended in a side-kick position. He grabbed Vasiliev's head with his left hand and pushed him down toward the center console, folding him over to prevent him from drawing a knife or pistol. The vicious movement caused the stiletto to disengage from the man's head. Reece adjusted slightly and slammed the sharp blade just below the base of his skull, violently ratcheting it to sever his brain stem.

Reece released tension on Vasiliev in front to refocus his attention on the dying man to his right. He threw himself back into the rear bench seat and with the knife still in a reverse grip, sent a hook across the man's neck, slicing through the carotid artery and coating the back right window with blood. The enforcer's hands went to his neck, then fell to his sides as he slipped away to the afterlife.

Go for their guns.

Reece attempted to reach around the considerably thick body of the man next to him to find his pistol when the front door opened and the driver slid inside, unaware that death that awaited him.

Adapt.

As the door slammed shut, Reece transitioned the OSS stiletto into a forward grip position and shifted behind to the driver's side of the rear bench seat, reaching around to pull the man's head into the headrest while thrusting the long thin blade through the open gap between the seat and the headrest and into the back of his neck. The man's thrashing suggested he had not found his mark. Reece continued to pull back on his face, sinking his fingers into his eyes as he smashed his palm against the pommel, driving the blade deeper into the base of his enemy's neck.

The man reached up and pulled Reece's left hand from his face while twisting forward and to the center, trying to disengage from the blade.

He's going to get away.

No.

Reece let go of the blade, which was still partially embedded in the Russian's lower neck, and slid his right hand around the headrest, replacing his left hand with his right on his target's face. With his left hand he reached for the shoulder strap of the seat belt, pulling it out and forward, feeding it into his right hand and pulling it across the man's neck. Reece pulled it across his throat and yanked him back in the seat. Maintaining a grip on both sides of the seat belt, he pushed his left knee into the seatback to generate as much leverage and power as he possibly could to control the larger man in the driver's seat. The seat belt squeezed back on both carotid arteries, obstructing blood flow to the brain while at the same time crushing the windpipe. Reece felt him go limp.

Look around, Reece. You can only capitalize on surprise for so long.

As Reece pulled back harder on the seat belt, he looked through the front windshield. The Escalade's driver was still standing by his door looking at the front of the bank. In this brief tactical pause, Reece's eyes went to the rearview mirror to get a better angle on the trail vehicle. Initially, he didn't see anyone. Then he adjusted his angle and saw a man running toward his Range Rover.

Execute.

With the driver momentarily unconscious, Reece let go of the seat belt and pulled the stiletto from between the seat and headrest, removing it from the back of his adversary's neck. He reached around the seat, pinned the man's head back, and cut across his carotid, spraying the front window with blood and turning the inside of the vehicle into a cave.

Three down.

How many were there?

The rear left passenger door was thrown open.

Fight!

Unsure of what was happening, the Russian reached into the car, attempting to grab his prisoner, now slippery with blood. Reece pivoted and planted his feet on both sides of the door frame, pulling the larger man into the vehicle on top of him in a half-closed guard. Shocked by the car's interior awash in blood and bodies, the big Russian attempted to pull back, but Reece clenched the back of his neck with his left hand, trapping his head to his chest. With the knife still in a reverse grip, Reece thrust it first into the man's right kidney, then his left, and then unsuccessfully attempted to stab it through his back and into his heart. Reece slid the blade up to the base of the man's skull, grabbed it with both hands, and pulled it toward him. The man struggled in a futile attempt to escape, but Reece began to ratchet, cutting through bones, cartilage, and tendons. Meeting resistance, he pushed up with his hips, dislodging the knife from what had impeded its progress. He felt the man expire atop him as the blade severed the spinal cord and protruded through the front of his throat, coming to a rest against Reece's own chest.

More threats, Reece. Don't get sucked into the problem.

The encounter had caused them to slide off the leather seats slick with blood and onto the floor of the Range Rover, the heavy-bodied Russian pinning Reece to the floor of the SUV.

Reece frantically grasped at the belt line on the dead man's right side.

Where is his holster?

Nothing.

He could hear footsteps approaching.

This is it, Reece.

You failed.

You don't know how to fail, son. Fight!

No holster on the right.

He's left-handed.

Reece slid his hand down the man's left side, connected with a pistol, and yanked it from its holster. Glock 19. Bringing it up as the first man broke the plane of the door, he pressed the trigger, once, twice, three times, each bullet catching his target in the chest. A fourth bullet entered just below his nose and sent him to the pavement. In the close confines of the vehicle the report of the Glock was deafening.

Five down.

Where is the man in black?

Prioritize and execute, Reece.

Two more in the vehicles. Two motorcycles.

Reece hoped his math was on point, the intense ringing in his ears causing a moment of confusion.

Fight through it, Reece.

Reece squirmed out from beneath the big Russian and turned to see movement through the window at the right rear quarter panel. He pushed himself around to face the sidewalk side of the vehicle, noted the gun in the approaching Russian's hand, and began firing through the door, knowing the bullets would zip right through. Moving up, he continued to fire through the blood-coated glass. At least one of the bullets caught his assailant, dropping him to the ground.

Get out of this vehicle before it becomes a bullet sponge.

Still one more target in addition to the motorcycles. Plus the man in black.

Reece crawled across the dead man in the back right passenger seat, opened the door, and fell to the sidewalk. The Russian who had approached from the rear vehicle had both hands to his neck, blood pooling from both a neck wound and one to his leg that had hit the femoral artery. Reece put him out of his misery with a shot to the head, immediately rising to a knee to get his bearings, and then to a low crouch.

He was vaguely aware of screaming through the ringing in his ears.

Cops will be here any second.

The lead Escalade began moving.

Katie!

Reece rose and aimed at the SUV, estimating where the driver would be, and pressed the trigger, sending multiple rounds into the escaping vehicle, shattering windows as it veered to the right and crashed into a parked Subaru. Reece ran to the passenger-side window and saw the driver slumped over the wheel, struggling to get the car moving. He stepped to the side window, leveled the pistol, and pressed the trigger, sending a 9mm round into the driver's head.

The motorcycles.

Reece turned his head in time to see the two Ducatis speeding toward him.

They must have been circling.

How many rounds have you fired?

In the confusion of combat Reece couldn't be sure. Standard magazine? Extended magazine? One in the chamber from the magazine or did he add another after chambering a round to top it off? Fourteen? Fifteen? Seventeen? Eighteen?

The Ducatis showed no sign of stopping. If they escaped, Katie, Raife, and Liz were dead.

They might already be dead, Reece.

The man in black.

Control what you can.

As the motorcycles roared past, Reece stepped into the street and sighted in on the trail biker. His eyes found the front sight and he applied even pressure to the trigger.

You are responsible for this bullet, Reece. Be sure of your sight picture before you miss and hit a kid down the street.

You are a sniper.

Reece broke the shot.

He absorbed the recoil and reacquired the front sight.

Even through the ringing in his ears he could hear the bullet make impact with the helmet of his target.

He also felt the pistol lock to the rear.

Empty.

He could hear sirens that sounded like they were about a street over.

Go, Reece.

The financial district had become a war zone. Cars had stopped and blocked the road. Citizens cowered behind whatever cover they could find.

Reece dropped the empty pistol and ran to the front passenger-side door of the Range Rover. He threw it open and picked up the manila envelope from the dead man's lap. It was now splattered with blood. Reece quickly stuffed it into the inside pocket of his jacket, zipping it all the way up before sprinting to the downed bike.

Please work, Reece prayed.

He righted the bike, pulled in the clutch, hit start, and heard the engine thunder to life.

Slamming his foot down on the left foot peg to ensure it was in first gear, he then let off on the clutch as he twisted back on the throttle and took off in pursuit of his next target.

CHAPTER 45

MAX GENRICH WATCHED THE events taking place in front of the bank with a combination of horror and respect.

He had already decided that he would tell his handler at the SVR that the Bratva had fucked this up. That blame would not be hard to shift. This was why he preferred to work alone. In fact, it might even benefit him in the eyes of the SVR; no more assignments that relied on the Bratva to do anything other than procure him a weapon.

It was obvious that this was too complex an operation to pull off on such short notice.

What was in the documents that the SVR so desperately wanted him to recover? It didn't matter, and he would never know.

Genrich had captured the engagement on his phone. He stayed in the shadows as Reece roared by in pursuit of the lead biker. Only after the noise of the engines had been replaced by the scream of sirens in their wake did he optimize the two-minute-and-thirty-second video and send it to an email account with the subject line: U.S. Holiday.

He then walked to Congress Street, pausing to admire a statue of Samuel Adams next to the Freedom Trail, surreptitiously dropping his pistol and suppressor into separate trash cans.

Genrich decided he would only operate in Europe going forward. Much more civilized.

James Reece had killed seven armed men in the streets of the financial district in less time than it took most people to use an ATM. He must have somehow disposed of Sasha inside the bank. It was quite remarkable. Genrich did not hold out much hope for the remaining man on the motorcycle.

Reece could identify him visually, but other than that, there was nothing to connect them.

Genrich made his way to Clinton Street and hailed a cab.

"Airport," he said.

He would take the first flight out of the country. It did not matter where it was going. He would attempt to fly south. He was in need of a warmer climate. He would then take a circuitous route back to Germany that might take him a month.

He was clean. If the SVR wanted him to take another stab at James Reece, he now knew how he would do it. He had learned a lot from their brief encounter.

Genrich looked out the windows of the cab as they passed buildings now veiled in twilight and wondered if he would ever meet James Reece again.

CHAPTER 46

REECE GUNNED THE DUCATI and leaned left into the turn on State Street and then right into the turn on Cambridge Street. Weaving in and out of traffic, he increased speed, squinting his eyes as the wind threatened to freeze them in position.

Where are you?

There!

Reece caught sight of the bike about three hundred yards ahead.

You are mine.

Weaving in and out of vehicles, Reece closed the distance. He reached under and behind his jacket to extract the Vietnam-era tomahawk from his waistband and quickly transferred it to his left hand. He got back on the throttle, now relying on his right foot-brake pedal to slow him down. His quarry braked to avoid an opening door, allowing Reece to maneuver within a bike's length. The lead motorcycle took advantage of the reduction in speed to race into an alley on his right. Reece swerved left and then back to the right, gassing the throttle to pass the lead Ducati.

Now!

Reece spun the hawk and slammed the reverse spike into the man's back, violently ripping it downward. Reece passed as the man hit the ground with a backbreaking crack, his motorcycle careening into a dumpster. Reece almost went down but managed to control the bike, immediately applying the foot brake to bring his motorcycle to a stop. With the tomahawk still in his left hand, the bike sputtered and stalled. Pushing the kickstand into position, Reece dismounted the Ducati and sprinted back down the alley, passing dumpsters and trash cans positioned at the backs of businesses that faced the main street to the north. He transferred the tomahawk back into his primary hand.

Still in his helmet and gloves, the downed biker was struggling to get to his feet and reach for something in his waistband.

Reece's tomahawk connected with the side of his helmet, the rear spike penetrating the outer shell, sending the man back to the ground.

Solid helmet.

His next hit sliced through the man's carotid artery, spraying Reece and the street with blood. A third blow almost severed the man's head from his body.

Reece looked up and down the alley.

Had they escaped the confusion and chaos of the financial district?

Reece couldn't count on it. Time was of the essence.

He first reached into the man's waistband. Glock 19. Shitty holster. Reece removed it and performed a press check. One in the chamber. He then removed the magazine. Full. He reinserted it and slid it into the holster, which he then clipped to the back of his pants. They had taken his belt, so he would have to remember that if he drew the pistol, the holster would probably come with it, meaning he needed to discard it before getting to work.

He patted down the man's pockets. No extra magazines. He removed a wallet and stuffed it in his jacket. He then pulled out the dead man's cell phone.

Reece looked at it and took a breath.

What is Katie's number? Reece thought, going back in the memory banks.

He knew Raife would have a burner phone.

Password.

Reece knelt and struggled with the bloody strap that kept the helmet attached to the dead man's head. When he got it off, he put the phone in front of the corpse's face to unlock it.

He then typed in a number he prayed was Katie's.

"Hello?"

"Katie, it's me. Put Raife on."

"Reece, where are you?"

"Just put Raife on!"

The next voice was Raife's.

"Where the fuck are you, eh?"

"Listen, there is a team of Russian enforcers on you right now."

"How many?"

"Not sure. One car. Maybe two."

"Makes? Models?"

"Not sure. The men who took me were in SUVs."

"Roger. This a good number for you?"

Reece looked down at the partially decapitated body at his feet.

"I don't think so. I'll call you from a burner soon."

Not wanting to keep his friend from the task at hand, Reece disconnected the call. There were few people more qualified to attend to such problems than Raife Hastings.

Night was coming on quickly. Reece retrieved the downed Ducati and maneuvered it next to a dumpster. He then dragged the dead Russian to it and removed his leather jacket before dumping him inside and closing the lid.

A medium? Can't I find a biker with an XL? he thought, remembering his excursion through Italy almost a year prior.

Reece squeezed his extra-large frame into the tight jacket. Luckily it was cut a bit large, though it was still overly snug.

Get out of here, Reece.

One more call.

As Reece went to dial, the screen lit up.

Do I answer?

He hit "accept."

"Mr. Reece, do you recognize my voice?"

The man in black.

"I do."

"Good; then listen carefully. This is the last call I will make from this phone. As soon as we are done, I will dispose of it."

Reece remained silent.

"I want you to know that I pulled the men from your friends shortly after we left Martha's Vineyard. They took the next ferry back to the mainland."

"What?"

"I didn't need them, Mr. Reece. You were more than willing to sacrifice yourself with just the threat of the possibility that you might be responsible for their deaths. As I told you, your file is quite extensive. I was not exaggerating when I said your psychological profile indicated you would be a terrible poker player."

Psychological profile. That meant FIS—a foreign intelligence service. *Russia.*

"I am going to find you."

"Come now, Mr. Reece. There is no need for that kind of talk. We are professionals. I let your friends live. As you are on Lev's phone, I can assume he has met his end."

"You assume correctly."

"Let's come to an agreement."

"I'm listening."

"In exchange for my consideration of letting your friends live, you agree to not waste your life trying to track me down."

"If I refuse?"

"I would hate to have to pay you another visit, though I have enjoyed our conversations. Our next outing might not be as pleasant."

"I didn't catch your name."

"No, you didn't. And you won't."

"Don't you think your employer will have something to say about your failure?"

"They know where to place the blame: on those thugs you just killed. Most impressive, by the way. My compliments."

"You didn't leave me many options."

"I expect our paths to never cross again. If they do, you and those closest to you will meet the same fate as the men you just disposed of. Are we clear?"

Was this a ploy?

"Mr. Reece? Do we have a deal?"

Reece terminated the call and redialed Katie's number.

Raife picked up.

"Anything?" Reece asked.

"Nothing, my friend."

"Doesn't mean they still aren't out there. Stay alert and get ready to go."

"Where do I meet you?"

"I'll call you back in an hour. I need to get moving."

"Hey, Reece, please tell me that you are not in Boston."

"Why?"

"There's a TV behind the bar here. There's been some sort of shooting in the financial district."

"I'm okay."

"*Jesus*, Reece."

"Call you in an hour."

Reece picked up the dead man's helmet and ran to his bike, slipping the tomahawk back under his belt with the handle running along his spine.

He pulled back on the clutch, hit start, and shifted into neutral to let it idle while he punched one more memorized set of digits into his newly acquired phone.

"Yes?" came a distinctive voice on the other end of the line.

"Vic, it's me."

"I was wondering when you'd call."

"I need something."

"What?"

"Where does Andy Danreb live these days?"

CHAPTER 47

The Residence at Cape Idokopas
Krasnodar Krai, Russia

ROSTYA LEVITSKY RAN ALONG the groomed trail. The sun had yet to break the horizon. The prenautical twilight lit his path. He could hear the waves of the Black Sea crashing against the base of the cliffs below. They sounded angry.

The director had beefed up his personal security detail, but he also knew that if someone were to throw him from the cliffs, there was a strong possibility that it would be his very own protective team.

He would finish his run and then put in his customary thirty minutes of weight lifting before enjoying the benefits of the sauna and ice bath—all before his peers had opened their eyes.

He inadvertently pushed himself harder today. The video he had been sent from the Proton Mail account with the subject line "U.S. Holiday" played on a reel in his mind.

The video started when James Reece was halfway across the street. It was taken from a hundred meters down the road on full zoom, which made it slightly blurry, but not so blurry that he couldn't make out what was happening.

The man he knew was James Reece waved as he jogged across the road and opened the rear driver's-side door of a Range Rover parked at the curb. The Bratva enforcers stood outside their vehicles, waiting on someone still inside the bank. After a few moments, one of them started to run, throwing open the door to Reece's Range Rover. He disappeared inside. Then the men started dropping.

The phone's microphone was catching wind and traffic, so the screams and car crash were muffled. The video went to black after James Reece accelerated past on a motorcycle, but not before he reached inside the Range Rover and retrieved a large manila envelope.

Incompetent bastards.

Could what was in the envelope really derail the plan to draw the United States into another war in the Middle East? Something that would prevent the new alliance between Russia and China?

The plutonium rods had been successfully transported to Rosatom in Zarechny, a "closed city" southeast of Moscow where the most closely guarded secrets in Russia's nuclear arsenal were developed and stored. Once the device was fully constructed, it would begin its journey to warmer climes. Sokoloff and his Wagner Group Rusich unit would be with it the entire way.

The fall of the former Soviet Union had shifted power to the Americans, but as with the Bretton Woods Accords of 1944, they did not know what to do with it. With their treasury overflowing and military at the peak of its strength, what did they do? They squandered their treasury and downsized their military. The Americans were quick to adapt, but the generation that they were fond of calling the "Greatest" would soon be gone. Probably for the best. Russia would not make the same mistakes as had her adversary. That a few veterans of the Great Patriotic War would be alive to see the new Russia ascend to her role in the New World Order warmed his cold bones.

Would there be a shift in leadership after Russia pushed through Ukraine? Levitsky anticipated that the president would eventually hand over the reins to Chairman Kozak. That left Levitsky vulnerable. He needed to prove his loyalty and his worth. His agency needed a win. This recent failure in Boston would give Director Dashkov the ammunition he needed to undermine Levitsky's new position.

The files that had been so sought after were now in the hands of James Reece. Something was in them that made this Collective nervous. Bringing the SEAL down and retrieving the contents of the safe-deposit box was Levitsky's top priority.

Levitsky looked at the surf breaking on the rocks at the base of the cliff and imagined his body making contact with the sharp crags before becoming food for the crabs and creatures of the deep.

He turned away from the cliffs and picked up the pace.

PART THREE

REVELATIONS

New evils require new remedies.

—*THE TIMES* (LONDON) ON THE NUREMBERG TRIALS

CHAPTER 48

REECE STOOD IN THE hot shower, his head down, watching the blood rinse from his body, swirl around the drain, and disappear down the pipes.

He had been on the verge of hypothermia when he arrived at the safe house. The bike was hot, and he needed a clean ride. Vic had made him memorize the address and access code to the condo. It wasn't far. The CIA had properties scattered across the world that allowed an agent on the run to find temporary sanctuary. The United States was no different.

This safe house was the closest option to Reece's position, and it took him only ten minutes to arrive at the small second-floor condo with a one-car garage on Magnolia Street in Cambridge. Harvard and the CIA shared a long and involved history.

The blood on Reece's hands was already frozen by the time he accelerated onto the Longfellow Bridge and crossed the Charles River. He continued past the Massachusetts Institute of Technology, onto Broadway, and into the heart of Cambridge, a bastion of American academia.

The code opened the garage and Reece maneuvered the bike inside, leaving it wedged next to a dark maroon Jeep Grand Cherokee SUV. He then closed the door and sealed himself inside.

Reece didn't plan on spending much time at the condo; just a quick rest and refit. He made his way to the second floor using the stairs leading up from the garage and systematically cleared the space, which didn't take long. It wasn't huge. It consisted of two bedrooms with en suite bathrooms, a common living area, and a kitchen. A large, knitted Harvard University coat of arms was framed above the couch opposite a flat-screen television. On a shield of "Harvard Crimson" were three open books. VE–RI–TAS was printed across their covers.

Veritas. Truth, Reece thought, remembering the unofficial motto of the Central Intelligence Agency engraved on the wall at headquarters from John 8:32: "*And ye shall know the truth, and the truth shall make you free.*"

Maybe that truth will kill us all.

We will know soon enough.

Reece opened a cabinet, found a glass, and slugged down two large glasses of water from the sink.

He was cold and hungry, but there was something he needed to do before he raided the pantry.

Priorities.

He walked to the master bedroom and opened the two drawers in the nightstand on the left side of the bed.

Empty.

He moved to the right side with the same result.

Also empty.

Odd.

His eyes went to the alarm clock on the nightstand.

There it is.

Reece punched the garage code into the four-digit keypad on the top of the Vaultek Smart Station safe. The front of the clock slid forward to reveal a Browning Hi-Power, two extra thirteen-round mags, a fairly old leather holster, and a stack of cash.

Reece removed and examined the legendary pistol. He could tell this one had some history. In 1926, with 128 firearms patents to his name, Browning passed away of heart failure at his workbench at Fabrique Nationale de Herstal in Belgium while working on what would become his iconic 9mm handgun. Dieudonné Saive had continued to develop the pistol that the world would come to know as the Browning Hi-Power. It had been in continuous service since 1935 and had been a favorite of the CIA well past the time when most military, intelligence, and law enforcement agencies had moved on to striker-fired pistols with double-stack magazines.

Reece released the magazine and caught it in his left hand. Fully loaded. He then pushed down on the safety and racked the slide to the rear, ejecting and catching the round from the chamber.

He gave the pistol and magazines a quick inspection and then put the weapon back into condition one: round in the chamber, hammer to the rear with the safety lever up.

He closed the safe, transforming it back into an innocuous-looking standard alarm clock, and returned to the kitchen, setting the pistol and extra magazines on the counter.

Prioritize and execute.

Reece scanned the small pantry and removed two cans of Campbell's chicken noodle soup. He opened them with a can opener he found in a drawer and emptied the broth, noodles, and small chunks of chicken into a pot on the stove, quickly bringing the soup to a boil. He needed to get warm. He transferred the steaming contents into a large Pyrex container and brought it to his mouth, not bothering with a spoon. He ignored the burning on his tongue and the roof of his mouth as the hot liquid warmed his chilled body.

Under the sink he found a roll of large trash bags and pulled one out. Reece then marched to the master bathroom. He set the pistol and magazines next to the sink, closed the toilet seat, and took the thick manila envelope from the inside of his jacket, placing it on the seat. Next, he set his father's letter on top of the files. His wallet and the cash went on top of that, acting as a paperweight.

Reece turned on the water in the sink and removed the stiletto from its sheath at his appendix, using soap to clean the dried blood from the blade, handle, and pommel. He then wiped it dry on a hand towel, tested the blade—it needed sharpening—and set it aside. He then removed the tomahawk from his back pocket behind his belt, cleaning first the head and then the shaft. When he was done, he tested its edge. Still sharp. He set it aside, stripped down, and shoved his bloody clothes into the trash bag before stepping into the shower. He shut the glass door behind him and turned the water to an almost scalding temperature.

You can't wash away the past.

Nothing will wash away the past.

As the blood pooled and swirled, Reece checked himself for injuries.

Everything seemed to be in working order. All the blood was from other people.

Lauren, Lucy, Ben, Freddy . . . Katie.

If you stay with her, she's dead.

No.

You want to keep her safe, you disappear. You can't kill your way out of this.

Yes, I can.

Hollywood would have you believe that men who fought and killed were damaged, empty shells. The truth was dirtier. The truth was that killing was the most natural of human endeavors. Reece knew his ancestors had been good at hunting and killing. And it was not just Reece's ancestors: it was everyone's ancestors. For most of human history, if you could not put food on the table or protect the gift of life, you were not long for this earth. Some had repressed that call, the call to serve, the call to hunt, the call to fight, protect, and kill. To others, protectors like Reece, it was as natural as breathing.

You've killed enough.

I don't have a choice.

You have free will. You kill because you want to.

I kill because sometimes it is necessary.

You are a killer, a murderer.

I'm a fighter.

Reece was still under the shower head, when the water shifted from almost scalding to close to freezing. He remained motionless. Standing under the cold water, he was transported back to his cell in Colorado. Just days ago, an unseen hand or the emotionless setting on a computerized timer had shut the water off.

Control.

They exercised what control they could, when they could. But Reece was no longer in his cell. He was free. It was time to get answers, and then it would be time do what he did best.

Reece's hand went to the shower valve and turned it to the right. The cascade of water immediately ceased. He stepped out onto the bath mat, toweled himself dry, and then stuffed the wet towel in the trash bag.

Grabbing the Browning Hi-Power off the sink, he reentered the bedroom.

He was exhausted.

I need sleep.

You will get all the sleep you need when you are dead.

Reece set the pistol on a dresser and started going through drawers. Socks, underwear, T-shirts, and pants of various sizes awaited him. He picked out a few options, throwing them on the bed behind him before moving to the closet, where he began sifting through an assortment of shoes, shirts, jackets, belts, and hats.

He went for earth-tone pants and a flannel top. A thin black puffy jacket and a Harvard ball cap, Darn Tough socks, and a pair of Hoka running shoes finished off his new ensemble.

Next he selected a Fjällräven day pack from a collection of briefcases and messenger bags, returned to the bathroom, and placed the manila folder and letter inside. He collected the two extra magazines and put them in his left pocket with the rounds facing forward. His wallet and the cash went into the other.

Satisfied, he picked up the trash bag, and gave the room a once-over.

As he turned to leave, he paused. Setting the trash bag and backpack on the floor of the bedroom, he flipped off all the lights in the condo. He found a space on the floor between the bathroom door and the dresser and sat down. He removed the Browning from the holster on his belt and set it to his right. With his back flat against the wall, he closed his eyes. First he was back in his cell. Then he was in the tidal pool with his father in Hawaii.

Control limit zone.

Reece exhaled, forcing all the air from his lungs, inhaled deeply, held his breath, and started to count.

CHAPTER 49

Zarechny, Penza Oblast
Russia

SLAVIK DEYNEKIN HATED ZARECHNY. Four days in this hellhole felt like an eternity. That, and it reminded him of Magnitogorsk, where he had lived with his mother. Even his quarters in one of the "out-of-bounds" areas was eerily reminiscent of the housing complex of his youth.

Located seven hundred kilometers southeast of Moscow, Zarechny was once what was known as a secret city, and though it had begun to open up, it still retained the culture forced upon its 64,000 inhabitants during the Cold War, when it was identified in classified documents only as *Penza-19*. The Soviet Union had designated certain cities as "closed" and off-limits to all but a select few. Deynekin did not know how many of these secret cities had once existed. His government now acknowledged forty-four publicly, which meant there were probably closer to a hundred.

Built with slave labor from the Gulags following the Great Patriotic War, these secret cities were encircled by barbed-wire fences and "protected" by military guards. They did not appear on any maps, nor could one find buses or trains that serviced them from stations or depots in other parts of the country. Photography was banned, and no one could come or go without authorization. Residents did enjoy a higher standard of living than most of the country, with the best health care, schools, and day care that the Russian Soviet Federative Socialist Republic had to offer. Stores rarely ran low on goods, and the Soviet citizens who lived there were compensated with salaries that exceeded those for comparable positions on the outside. The people who lived within the cities' confines did not appear on the official census. It was as if they did not exist. Some lived their entire lives in their secret cities, never experiencing life beyond the walls. They were completely cut off from the outside world. News was strictly controlled. Informers were everywhere. They were socialist utopias.

Officially designated "closed administrative territorial entities," each closed city had a specific focus. There were "academic cities," "science cities," and "nuclear cities." Zarechny was the latter. Among the residents were an inordinate number of scientists and engineers supporting critical nuclear research-and-development projects for the Motherland.

In "public" areas, no one talked about Zarechny's sole employer—the Russian Federation's State Atomic Energy Corporation, better known as Rosatom. Headquartered in Moscow, Rosatom was responsible for all facets of the Russian nuclear production chain. From uranium mining to enrichment to nuclear fuel fabrication to mechanical engineering, Rosatom was Russia's one-stop nuclear shop. Zarechny was home to the Rosatom nuclear weapon assembly facility. The Sura River was conveniently close, providing a dumping ground for any radioactive waste.

Deynekin and his team of Wagner Group mercenaries had taken a chartered Kam Air flight from Kandahar to Kabul, where they boarded another chartered Kam flight to Tashkent, Uzbekistan. There were not an abundance of choices. Kam was Afghanistan's first private airline. Established in 2003, it served destinations domestically and internationally with its fleet of twelve aircraft. It even offered student discounts and advertised a frequent-flyer program.

Eager to avoid a repeat of the Airstan incident of 1995, in which seven Russian nationals had been held hostage for over a year at the hands of the Taliban before enacting a dramatic escape, Deynekin liberally handed out bribes to smooth their passage out of Afghanistan. The heavy box securing the three plutonium rods was labeled with biohazard plaques and accompanied by the proper corresponding paperwork with all the required signatures. No one was overly eager to open or inspect a box they thought contained highly hazardous biological material, especially after Deynekin handed them ten U.S. hundred-dollar bills to thank them for their cooperation.

The Russians were met at Islam Karimov Tashkent International Airport two hours after leaving Kabul by a military contingent from the Uzbek Air Force's 60th Separate Mixed Aviation Brigade for the short sixteen-kilometer transit to Karshi-Khanabad Air Base, known in military circles simply as K2.

Uzbek president Shavkat Mirziyoyev had favored a more pro-Russian agenda since assuming power in 2016 after the death of his predecessor, Islam Karimov, who had ruled the country since 1989. This renewed alliance led to joint military exercises and Russian military equipment purchases, which made it possible for a Russian Antonov An-124 Ruslan to land in Uzbek territory and pick up a box and eight passengers. Identified by its NATO designator Condor, the An-124 was the largest military transport aircraft in existence.

The high-priority flight and box labeled with biomedical plaques raised speculation that a senior-level Russian general must be in need of lifesaving organs, which was exactly the intent. The destination on the flight plan was listed as Moscow, but as soon as the An-124 entered Russian airspace it diverted to Vissarion Belinsky Airport in Penza. While his team slept soundly after safely leaving Afghan and Uzbek airspace, Deynekin stared at the aluminum flooring of the cargo aircraft. His men would soon figure out what they had transported out of Afghanistan.

The first half of the mission was almost complete. He knew to expect a re-tasking once on the ground, and though he didn't know the final destination or specifics, Deynekin had been in the game long enough to venture a few guesses. If any of his men showed the slightest bit of trepidation about the mission ahead, he would be required to execute them on the spot. Was he any less expendable?

Upon landing, the box was offloaded and transferred to Zarechny's Rosatom nuclear assembly facility. Deynekin's team boarded a bus and followed the armed five-vehicle military convoy past the gates to the secret city and then into an even more heavily secured facility where they were confined to quarters in a large gray concrete building that resembled a military barracks.

After dropping his bags, Deynekin was escorted into a conference room in an adjacent building. Andrei Sokoloff was waiting for him.

"Comrade," the former GRU man said in acknowledgment as Deynekin entered. "I understand your mission was a success."

The Wagner Group CEO wasn't in uniform, having long since left the GRU as a lieutenant colonel, but his military bearing was evident. His black eye patch matched his boots and cargo pants. He wore a green flight jacket with the sleeves pushed up. His thick forearms left no question that, even at his advanced age, he was not one with whom to trifle.

"Yes, Colonel," Deynekin replied.

"And your men?"

"They performed as expected, though, as you can appreciate, they are now wondering what was in the box and what we are doing in isolation at a secret nuclear facility. As am I."

"*Da*, it is imperative that this next phase of the mission be kept need-to-know. There is no higher-priority mission for the Motherland."

"Tell me," Deynekin said.

"The three plutonium rods you extracted from Afghanistan originated in Iran. They are being removed from their case as we speak."

"Why?"

"We are converting them into a more modern RA-115."

"A 'suitcase bomb,'" Deynekin said. "The Soviet answer to the American SADM."

"Yes, their Special Atomic Demolition Munition."

"Rumor has it that there are still RA-115s cached around the world."

"Those rumors might be true. I can tell you for certain there are multiple RA-115s here in this very facility. Right now the engineers are fitting one with the rods you delivered. The Iranian rods are of a different shape and slightly smaller than our older Soviet rods. They are being chemically decomposed and recast in the lab. They will then be reshaped and encased in a ceramic holder to fit the RA-115. The Semtex initiation charge, fuse, and timer were all prefabricated. The final device will fit into a large backpack."

"How long will it take them to complete the device?"

"Two days, plus another to test all the circuits."

"As I recall, the RA-115s were not built with an abort mechanism."

"The GRU didn't want an infiltrator to get cold feet, question his assignment, or think that arming the device would immediately result in detonation."

"Would it?"

"Yes, the act of arming would detonate it, but this one has been modified. To alleviate any reservations, the device will be armed in Cyprus. We certainly do not want to detonate a nuclear device there. And to give you further peace of mind, I will arm it there with you. Then you will see the mission through to its conclusion."

"And the men?"

"Tell the men that they are delivering it to Hezbollah—an at-sea transfer—at the behest of our new ally, Iran."

"But we are not."

"No, you are not."

"What's the mission, Colonel?"

"In five days, you will escort the weapon to Syria."

"Syria?"

"*Da*—a military transport flight to Khmeimim Air Base in Syria, which as you know is a Russian military base, so there will be no customs requirements. The device will be in one of many trunks meant to give the appearance of personal belongings going to one of our oligarchs with ties to the president. No one will question it."

"From there?"

"It will be concealed in a vintage Louis Vuitton trunk among a host of similar trunks with personal items. Transportation will be waiting, and you will escort the boxes to the port of Latakia."

"How far is the drive?"

"Twenty-five kilometers. You should arrive at the port in less than thirty minutes. There you will rendezvous with a vessel."

"Whose?"

"Ours, but not directly. It was purchased two weeks ago in Istanbul by one of our SVR agents, a former naval officer, through an LLC registered in Tunisia."

"What type of vessel?"

"A small yacht. Specifically, it's a twenty-four-meter trawler-class vessel built by Magnolia Yachts. Long-range cruiser. It's nice enough to blend in but not stand out; well below the ostentatious tastes of some of our oligarchs. The captain and first officer, also SVR, have been giving it a shakedown cruise and are now in Mersin, Turkey, awaiting instructions."

"And then?"

"You and your team will move with the vessel to Cyprus, where I will meet you. We will await final approval from the president, and, pending weather conditions, will activate the timer together. Then you sail for Israel."

"Israel?"

"Israeli waters."

"You are doing a poor job of selling what appears to be a suicide mission, Colonel."

"You will anchor in a predetermined position off the coast of Tel Aviv. Using a transponder, you will indicate your position to the *Yasen*-class attack submarine *Severodvinsk*. They will extract you."

"What is to keep us from thinking that you won't leave us floating out there to be incinerated by the blast?"

"Much too risky. Another boat might find you first. Return to Russia, receive your Order of Courage, and join me in running Wagner."

"Tempting. And the men?"

"They will receive their medals as well and continue to fight with Wagner in service to Mother Russia."

"Why Israel?"

"Why do you think, comrade?"

Deynekin thought for a moment.

"Iranian plutonium. It will leave an Iranian signature. Everything else will be vaporized. It pulls Israel and the United States into war with Iran."

"And draws their attention south."

"And allows us to take Ukraine without U.S. meddling."

"There is more to the plan that does not concern you," Sokoloff said.

"No need to know?"

"Nor do you want to know. Rest up. The next time we meet, you will be in Cyprus."

"Yes, Colonel."

Deynekin stood up to leave and began to walk toward the door. He stopped and turned.

"What's the name of the vessel?"

"Open Passages."

He nodded.

"And, comrade," Sokoloff added.

"Yes?"

"You will not fail."

• • •

Sleep did not come easy that night. As Deynekin tossed on the thin mattress in the single bed in the drab living quarters, his dreams were of a similar room. In his restless slumber, he could feel the weight of the man who attacked his mother atop him. He felt the punches raining down from above, only this time when the punches stopped it wasn't his bloody and bruised and naked mother standing over him with a knife in her hand. It was someone else: a man with an eye patch and a *kolovrat* tattoo on his left forearm. Instead of offering Deynekin a hand, he kicked the sweaty dead man to the side with a black boot, knelt by young Deynekin's side, and plunged the knife into his heart.

CHAPTER 50

Westport, Connecticut

IT WAS WELL PAST midnight when Reece crossed the Saugatuck River and pulled off Interstate 95. He turned onto Saugatuck Avenue and then onto Riverside Avenue and eased the Jeep Grand Cherokee to the side of the road in a quiet neighborhood on Connecticut's Gold Coast, searching the stone pillars that guarded the driveway for an address. He hit the brights and the address came into view.

This is it.

Reece turned off the street and drove slowly down the driveway. He parked next to an old 1972 Saab 96 on the side of the house in front of a lawn that sloped down to the Saugatuck River. The porch light was on, as were a few intermittent lights spread across the garden.

As Reece stepped from the vehicle his hand instinctively went to the grip of the pistol on his belt. He heard a door swing open, and a familiar deep voice, the Chicago upbringing still recognizable, boomed down from above.

"Vic told me you'd be stopping by."

Reece looked at the large silhouette in the door, recognizing the imposing figure immediately as Andy Danreb, the CIA's foremost Russian expert.

"Come inside before we both freeze to death," he ordered, stepping back inside and holding the door ajar for his guest.

Reece grabbed his backpack and walked across the stone path, maneuvering past a few overgrown hedges before making his way up the steps.

He stepped inside and extended his hand.

"Good to see you, Andy."

"And you," Danreb said, shutting the door behind them. "Looking thin, my boy. What can I fix you?"

"Whatever you have," Reece responded. "I'm not picky these days."

"Except for mayo."

"Except for mayo," Reece repeated.

Reece followed Danreb into the kitchen.

"Take a seat," his host said, gesturing to the bar seats by the kitchen counter.

Reece set his backpack at his feet and looked around. He peered into the adjoining living area, where soft yellow bulbs from reading lamps cast shadows over the couch and large leather reclining chair. Books not only filled every shelf but were stacked on coffee tables, end tables, the dining room table, seemingly everywhere there was space. Reading glasses were strategically located on top of certain stacks. Even the kitchen had not escaped the library's advance; Reece carefully moved a stack of books to the side as Danreb examined the fridge. The whole place looked exactly the way Reece remembered his office in the basement at Langley.

"I'd say excuse the mess, but it's always like this. What can I get you, other than this beer?" Danreb asked, sliding an Old Düsseldorf to his visitor.

"Anything warm."

"*Na zdorovie*," Danreb said in Russian, holding up his beer.

"What's that mean?"

"To your health."

"I'll take it," Reece said. "Cheers."

"Cheers."

Danreb and Reece both drained at least a quarter of their longnecks in the first pull.

"Perfect," Reece said.

"And for your main course, how about an omelet? I have some cheese, mushrooms, and bacon."

"I can't tell you how good that sounds."

"Midrats," Danreb said, referring to the Navy and Marine Corps slang for midnight rations—meals for those working through the night.

"Love the beer, but I was expecting vodka."

"Old dog, new tricks," Andy said as he ignited the gas stove and threw a lump of butter in a frying pan. "I decided to turn over a new leaf when I left the Agency. Less vodka. More beer. I think it's working," he said, tapping his midsection.

Andy wasn't fat. He was thick in a way that suggested an immense strength. Slightly taller than Reece, his ice-blue eyes and broad shoulders gave the impression that if you got into a confrontation with him, you'd better run; a single swat from one of his giant bear paw hands and it would be game over. His hair was cut short on the sides and was only slightly longer on top, in a style that suggested prior military service. It was hard to tell if any specks of black were left in all the gray.

"Vic told me why you left. I don't know what to say," Reece said.

"Don't say anything. I had already outlived my expiration date. It was well past my time to move on."

"How did you end up in Westport?"

"One of my daughters from my first marriage settled down here. Her husband is an architect. All the New York money fleeing Manhattan during COVID has kept him busy. He found this place. It started as a colonial farmhouse in 1792, but as you can tell it's been renovated here and added on to there over the years to reflect the tastes and needs of its generations of owners. I see myself as its guardian for the time being. The house next door was part of the deal. That one holds the majority of my books."

"You just might have more books than I do," Reece commented.

"I sold my house in McLean at a good time. I bought up here at not such a good time, but that's how it goes. I'd been frugal over my years at Langley; just ask any of my ex-wives." He laughed as he cracked four eggs into a bowl.

"How many do you have?" Reece asked.

"Just three, which I think is about average at the Company. That car outside, I got it used in Sweden with wife number one on our honeymoon. Never owned another."

"And now it's a classic," Reece said.

"So I'm told. The grandkids like it. I have two here in town; one's in seventh grade and the other's a sophomore in high school. Both of them row. I can watch them go by on the river in the mornings and afternoons," he said, turning from the stove to nod at the large window that overlooked the lawn and the river beyond. A Swarovski spotting scope was affixed to a wooden tripod in the corner.

"Great spot," Reece said.

"Better than Chicago," Danreb said, intentionally emphasizing the accent that he'd never quite gotten rid of even after all his years away from the Windy City, where he'd grown up. "But really, anyplace is better than Chicago these days."

Reece scanned the titles stacked on the kitchen counter. Biographies of statesmen, generals, and intelligence officials were intermixed with textbooks on Russia, Ukraine, and China. Reece's eyes traveled to a stack of novels, and he picked up the book on top.

"*A Perfect Spy*?" Reece said, reading the title. "You're a le Carré fan?"

"Only spy novelist worth a damn," Danreb replied, opinionated as ever. "Other than McCarry, of course. Charles McCarry is in a league of his own."

"The Paul Christopher series."

"You've read them? I've never met anyone younger than seventy who has read McCarry."

"I read a lot as kid."

"I knew I liked you."

Reece smiled.

"McCarry and le Carré are an escape from the serious stuff. One can only take so much," Danreb said.

"I understand."

"People who haven't read McCarry always point to *The Spy Who Came in from the Cold* as the greatest postwar spy novel ever written, but that one there," he said, pointing the spatula at the book in Reece's hands, "that one just might be the greatest spy novel *ever* written."

"I didn't peg you for a reader of fiction," Reece said.

"Even the best of us need a break," he said as he twisted a pepper mill over the eggs sizzling in the pan. "Ol' Cornwell was a craftsman of the highest order, and though I couldn't disagree more with his politics, I greatly admire his skill—the nuance of his work. Have you read him?"

"I read his early work when I was in high school and kept reading the newer ones up until 9/11. Then things got a bit busy."

"That they did. Le Carré worked for both MI5 and MI6. McCarry was a CIA man. I regret not tracking him down to shake his hand. I read that he wrote his memoirs not long after leaving the Agency, then burned them. He said he kept the 'atmosphere of secret life,' which set him free to write fiction. Fascinating. I did correspond with le Carré for a number of years, you know."

"You did?"

"I decided to write him on a whim after the Berlin Wall came down. I had no idea if he would ever receive it, much less take the time to read it. He had just written *The Secret Pilgrim*. My time as a Russian analyst was seemingly at an end, according to the *Times* and even some in the building at Langley. To my surprise he wrote back—handwritten. We corresponded for about a decade. I often thought he might use me for a character in one of his novels, though he never did."

"What did you talk about?"

"First it was the fate of the Soviet Union, then the Baltic and western republics, satellite states, coups, and the proliferation of WMDs. This wasn't a tremendous amount of communication, mind you, maybe a letter a year. After 9/11 the letters stopped. He was extremely critical of U.S. policies toward Afghanistan and Iraq in the early part of the twenty-first century. I saved the letters, though."

Andy slid the steaming omelet onto a plate with a fork and pushed it across the counter toward his guest.

"Water? Orange juice?"

"I'll take another beer," Reece said.

"I'll join you," Danreb replied, fetching two more beers from the fridge.

"That book there," he said, pointing to a thick book with a black-and-white photo of le Carré on the cover. "His son compiled a collection of his letters from 1945 onwards."

"*A Private Spy*," Reece said, reading the thick binding that faced him on the counter. "*The Letters of John le Carré*."

"I read it half hoping I'd find our letters recorded for posterity now that I'm out of the secret world, but alas, I was not nestled in among Sir Alec Guinness, Graham Greene, Sydney Pollack, Daniel Ellsberg, Ralph Fiennes, and Stephen Fry. He was a man of letters. Fascinating reading, even if they do seem to be written for posterity and with their eventual publication in mind. Sadly, his son passed away unexpectedly not two years after his father. He never even got to see the book's publication."

"Fathers and sons," Reece whispered.

"It did inspire me to write my own book," Danreb said.

"Oh?"

"Might as well put all this knowledge and experience to use," he said, sweeping his hand across the house. "Rather than write an academic book on Russia that no one will ever read, I'm giving a spy novel a shot. Nothing else to do, though I am in talks with the History Department at Yale—it's just up the road—to teach a course on Russian history from 1945 to 1992 as a visiting fellow. Not sure I have the patience for the spoiled students, or the entitled faculty for that matter. I wake up, watch my granddaughters row past as I enjoy a coffee. Then I write all day until it's time for their evening practice. I walk across the lawn with a drink in hand and stand right down there as they row past—give them a wave. It's not a bad life. I certainly don't deserve it."

"What's the book about?"

"Right now, it's set at the end of the Cold War."

"Let me guess," Reece said. "The Berlin Wall has just fallen."

"Am I that predictable? Hell, maybe I should write the textbook after all."

Reece smiled as he polished off the omelet.

"Want another?" Danreb asked.

"I think I'm okay for now."

"As the book starts, the Cold War is over. We'd won, you see. It was time to celebrate."

"You . . . your character, didn't celebrate, though, did he?"

"He did not. And neither did your father," Danreb said, switching back to the real world.

"How did you get to know him?" Reece asked.

"He just started coming down. They'd already moved me to the basement. We both had clearances. I was aware of your father by reputation. Everyone knew Tom Reece. Most were afraid of him. I don't think he let many people in."

"But he let you in."

"He did. First, he came down asking for reading recommendations."

"On what?"

"The Soviet Union."

"That makes sense. The Cold War was still in full swing."

"Yes, but it was more than that."

"What do you mean?"

"Hard to say; he didn't fully confide in me. I always felt like he was trying to protect me."

"What else did you guys talk about?"

"Other than the Soviets? Spies. Vietnam. Cuba. China. Even JFK and Able Archer."

"What's Able Archer?"

"It was a war game in 1983. We came closer to nuclear war than we ever did during the Cuban Missile Crisis. Andropov was convinced that Reagan was vying for a first-strike nuclear capability with 'Star Wars' and stealth technology. In 1981 the GRU green-lit Operation RYaN, one of the most extensive intelligence operations of the Cold War."

"How so?"

"Their goal was to surveil and assess and recruit those in the intel community and Reagan administration they believed would be responsible for a first-strike launch."

"They really thought we would launch first?"

"You have to remember, we were building up massive stockpiles of weapons. FleetEx in April had them on edge. Then the Soviets shot down Korean Air Lines Flight 007 in September, killing almost three hundred people, including a United States congressman. Tensions were at an all-time high. Able Archer was a NATO exercise in November that didn't look like an exercise to the Soviets. They thought it was cover for a real first strike. Think of it as the collision of Reagan's rhetoric and Soviet paranoia at the worst possible moment in history—when two rival nations had the capability to destroy not just each other but the entire world. Things came to a head when the Soviets mistakenly detected multiple ICBM missile launches from the continental United States."

"Jesus."

"Thanks to one sharp Soviet military officer on duty and one of ours, General Leonard Perroots, we averted nuclear war."

"Perroots? Didn't he go on to become director of the DIA?"

"He did. In '85. He worked closely with CIA director Bill Casey. But back in 1983 he was the assistant chief of staff for intelligence in Europe. When he retired in '89 he wrote a memo to capture the lessons learned from Able Archer. I've read it multiple times. Certainly interesting, though nothing I would deem as secret. Yet it remained classified until 2021 when it was released in a volume of something called *Foreign Relations of the United States*, which focused on U.S.-Soviet relations from January 1983 to March 1985. After it became public the CIA moved to reclassify it."

"Why?"

"That's a good question. The volume was subject to a four-year declassification review in which the CIA was involved. A judge ruled in favor of the Agency and the entire volume was scraped from the Internet. As you can imagine, I have a hard copy. Perroots's memo is critical of the CIA but is also incredibly insightful into the problems that plagued U.S.-Soviet relations in the 1980s, which just so happen to be the same issues that plague us today as we deal with Russia and Ukraine."

"Maybe that's why they reclassified it."

"Perhaps."

"What does Perroots say about it?"

"He passed away in 2017. I got to know him over the years. He went to work for Vector Microwave Research Corporation after retirement, which meant he was still working classified projects for both the military and the CIA."

"What did Vector Microwave Research do?"

"They were in what we used to call the 'foreign matériel acquisition' business."

"Sounds shady."

"It was. Businesses attached to the growing intelligence industry started popping up in the sixties and seventies. Some survived into the late nineties. They still exist, but they have had to adapt to a more transparent world. They would acquire hardware from the Soviets, China, and North Korea at the behest of the CIA and DIA. A lot of money was made and too many secrets were whispered in exchange for some of those deals."

"Sounds like they were a cog in the wheel of permanent Washington."

"That's exactly what they were. I can't do anything about it from my house here on Riverside Avenue, but maybe I'll write a fictional account of it one day. The bastards on Langley's Prepublication Classification Review Board will have aneurysms when they read it. Fuck 'em."

"Can't wait to read it."

"After Able Archer, things changed."

"How so?"

"There was a palpable shift in U.S.-Soviet relations. Andropov died in '84. His successor, Konstantin Chernenko, didn't last a year. He died in '85, which paved the way for Gorbachev. Then came reform: glasnost and perestroika, summits with Reagan, the Intermediate-Range Nuclear Forces Treaty, Soviet troop withdrawal from Afghanistan."

"That was all for the good, right?"

"So it would seem."

"You don't sound convinced."

"I connect dots, put the puzzles together, and fill in the missing pieces."

"Meaning?"

"Meaning, more than summits and treaties were at play. I believe your father thought the same thing, though, unlike me, he wanted to do more than peel back layers. He had a mission."

"What kind of mission?"

"I was hoping you could tell me."

Reece picked up his backpack and set it on the seat next to him.

"Answers might be in here. My dad left me a stack of documents. Most appear to be in Russian, Vietnamese, and French."

"You haven't gotten them translated? Has anyone else seen them?"

Trust.

"I just acquired them."

"Well, let's take a look."

Reece picked up the pack and followed Danreb into the main room. A large, dark red carpet covered most of the wood floor. A gas fireplace helped light the room. The furniture seemed to be arranged around books rather than the other way around. He opened the bag and handed the heavy envelope to the old Russia hand.

Danreb set a pair of readily available reading glasses just the right distance down his large nose and picked up the top document.

"Well? What's it say?" Reece asked.

"It's a financial document. Reece, I am going to need some time with these, and you look like you need some sleep."

"I'm fine."

"Reece, you're not. If your father were standing here, he'd tell you the same thing. I talked with Vic. He's on his way here now. It's a long drive from Northern Virginia, but he'll be here in the morning. And your friends are taking the first ferry over from Martha's Vineyard tomorrow. It's about a three-hour drive for them once they hit the mainland. Why don't you get some sleep, leave me with all this, and by the time you wake up I'll have a good idea of what Tom Reece left behind and perhaps answer the question we both have."

"What's that?"

"The most important question of all. The why."

Reece could feel himself getting anxious. He wanted to know now.

"Reece," Danreb said, reaching out to hold the younger man's arm. "Get some rest. I've got this."

Sensing Reece was unconvinced, he continued: "You have your specialties and I have mine. Give me some time. I'll be here when you wake up."

Reluctantly, Reece nodded his head. He knew he was exhausted and that his mind and body needed to recuperate.

"The guest room is right off the back here," Danreb said, escorting Reece toward a door at the back of the living area. "It's got its own bathroom, and I'll be right out here if you need anything."

"Andy, what do you have as far as security?" Reece asked as they approached the guest room.

"Probably not enough by your standards," the analyst said. "But I've got this."

Andy reached between two bookshelves and removed a lever-action rifle with an oversize lever loop.

"That's it?"

"It's all John Wayne needed."

Reece raised an eyebrow.

"Haven't you ever seen *True Grit*? How about Chuck Connors in *The Rifleman*?"

"Oh, I'm aware," Reece said, remembering watching the classic Westerns with his father. "Winchester Model 1892. It's a great rifle, but do you have anything, ah . . ."

"More modern?"

"Yes, more modern," Reece replied.

"There just might be an AR for you in there. I knew you were coming so I got it out of the safe. It's got a brace that the ATF saw fit to make illegal while you were in prison. But since it's illegal here in any configuration, I figured 'what the hell.' Fuck 'em if they can't take a joke."

"Thanks, Andy."

"Don't forget this," he said, handing Reece the smaller envelope with *James Reece* written on the front.

"Get some sleep, Reece. We'll figure this out in the morning."

Reece took the envelope, nodded, entered the guest room, and shut the door behind him.

• • •

Danreb spent a long time looking at the door to the guest room. His mind filtered through all he knew about Reece and his father, the CIA and the KGB. He recalled his numerous conversations with the man who had left his son documents to be found all these years after his death.

He then set the old rifle back in its place between the bookshelves and went through the house as was his custom, checking doors and windows before returning to the dining room table and pulling out a chair. Placing his glasses back in position, he carefully picked up the first document, intently reading in Russian as if it were his native language. He then moved on to the second.

When he finished, he looked at the stack.

What else do you have for me?

Andy set the two finished pages aside and went to the kitchen to start a pot of coffee. It was going to be a long night.

• • •

The AR was a SIG Sauer Rattler in .300 Blackout with an Aimpoint Micro red dot sight and folding front and rear iron sights. Reece extended the brace as far back as it would go, gave the weapon a press check, and ensured the red dot was illuminated. It was ready to rock.

He turned his eyes to the bed.

Not yet.

He set the SIG down and then stripped off the sheets and blankets, spreading them out on the floor. He then went to the bathroom and pulled a towel from the rack, pushing it up against the base of the door to block out what little light escaped from the main room.

He then removed his pistol, holster, belt, wallet, and cash from his pockets and arranged them next to the Rattler. He ran his finger over his name on the envelope. It was in blue ink, in his father's distinctive script. It looked like Tom Reece could have written it yesterday. That was the thing about letters, about signatures. They connect us to the past. Reece was not yet ready to read it. He gave it one last look before placing it next to the Hi-Power and lying down on the blankets. Pulling the comforter over himself, Reece was asleep in seconds.

CHAPTER 51

WHEN REECE OPENED HIS eyes, he wasn't sure if it was the sound of voices, the smell of coffee, or the fact that his body had taken advantage of the sleep afforded to it that roused him from his much-needed slumber.

Reece's hand immediately went to the Rattler as he pushed himself off the floor and moved to the door. He pressed his ear to the crack and recognized the voices. He then looked at his sheets and blankets on the floor.

There's work to do.

The former frogman gathered his makeshift sleeping pad and made the bed. He couldn't remember the last time he'd made a bed. *Maybe Officer Candidate School?* It just wasn't his thing. He had always felt like time could be better spent elsewhere. In Reece's case that meant training and preparing for war. Lauren would sometimes joke with him as she turned down the bed each night, asking if he had any idea how the bed got made each day. His small home office was just off the bedroom then. Reece would pick his head up from a book on Afghanistan or Iraq or a study on terrorism or counterinsurgency and reply, "Elves?" At which point Lauren would usually hurl a throw pillow in his direction.

He smiled at the memory.

Bed made, Reece removed the towel from the bottom of the door and returned it to the bathroom, splashing some cold water on his face to help jump-start the day.

He then dressed and holstered the Browning Hi-Power before leaning the Rattler in the corner of the small room. Satisfied that all was arranged properly, Reece opened the door.

Katie was standing at the dining room table. As the door opened, she dropped a paper she was holding and rushed into Reece's embrace.

"I'm okay, Katie" was all Reece could think to say.

Victor Rodriguez was sitting at the head of the table, adjacent to Danreb. He rose and approached his recruit.

"Reece, good to see you."

"You, too, Vic," Reece said as the men shook hands. "Where's Raife?"

"In here!" thundered a voice from the kitchen.

Raife appeared around the corner, cup of coffee in hand.

"Nice of you to join us," Raife joked. "Surprised you are up so early. It's not even noon yet."

"Then I'm going back to bed."

"Andy doesn't have your preferred light roast," he said, handing Reece a mug emblazoned with the iconic Eagle, Globe, and Anchor. Under the Marine Corps symbol were the letters *EOD*, for Explosive Ordnance Disposal.

"Only black coffee served here," Danreb acknowledged. "Remember, I was a Marine. It's a department of the Navy—the men's department. Sorry, Reece."

"At least it's not Folgers," Raife said. "Black Rifle Coffee Blackbeard's Delight. There wasn't any honey or cream, but I spiced it up with some milk and sugar."

"It's perfect," Reece said. "Liz here?"

"She's with the plane. She's flying it to New York so it's close in case we need it. Now, let Vic and Andy finish up while we feed you breakfast. New Joe's Special coming up."

It was obvious to Reece that his old friend and Teammate was still concerned about his health and welfare.

"Thanks, Raife," Reece said, as he and Katie made their way into the kitchen.

"New Joe's Special?" Katie asked, refreshing her cup of coffee.

"Eggs, spinach, ground beef, onions, mushrooms, a bit of garlic. I first had it with Reece and his dad back in college. Do you remember, Reece?"

"I do. We took a trip out to Salt Point in Northern California. Drove out from Montana in your Scrambler."

"Two-day drive just to get there," Raife said, as he mixed the concoction in a large frying pan. "When we pulled into the campsite, Tom Reece fired up the camp stove and made it to warm us up."

"What did you guys do there?" Katie asked.

"We dove for abalone," Reece replied. "Free diving. Breath holds. I'd been going up there with my dad since I was a kid."

"Isn't that a great white shark breeding ground?" she asked. And then to their inquisitive looks responded, "Hey, I watch *Shark Week* like everyone else."

"You are certainly part of the food chain out there," Reece replied.

"Abalone, lingcod, mussels," Raife remembered. "We ate like kings the next day."

"Good times," Reece said.

"That they were. Here you go," Raife said. "Eat up."

"Well, what have they found?" Reece asked between bites. "This is delicious, by the way. Thank you."

Raife and Katie exchanged glances.

"What?" Reece asked.

"I think it's better if we let Andy lay it out for you," Raife said.

"Is it that bad?" Reece asked.

"It's . . . what's the best way to say it?"

"Interesting," Katie broke in.

"Interesting, complicated, and there are still a few missing pieces."

"Well, I'm ready," Reece said, pushing his plate away.

"All right," Raife said. "Let's try and make some sense of this. But before we do, let me refill that mug."

CHAPTER 52

ANDY DANREB HAD PULLED a white magnetic board from somewhere and attached certain documents to it with magnets. Other pages were on the dining room table in front of him.

"Take a seat, Reece," he said.

Reece pulled out a chair and set the coffee mug in front of him. The others joined him.

"Okay," Danreb began. "I've been going through these documents all night. When Vic got here a few hours ago he helped put a few pieces together. Raife translated the French, and we used an iPad my granddaughters got me for Christmas to help translate the Vietnamese."

Reece's head snapped up at the mention of using an app.

"I know what you're thinking, and you're right. It's not the most secure way to translate, but we created all-new accounts to provide a bit of a barrier. I'd never even used the thing. As you can tell, I prefer a physical library."

"I noticed," Reece said. "What do we have?"

"It goes all the way back to the war."

"Vietnam?"

"Farther back, Reece. World War Two, from what I can tell."

"And what is 'it'?" Reece asked.

"I've been debating the best way to go about this. I think I'll give you the broad strokes first—a quick overview—and then spell it out in detail. You may want to take notes."

Reece pulled a yellow legal pad in front of him, indicating he was ready.

"Vic and I have been working this through all night, and I think we are close."

"Close to what?"

"Close to piecing together a collaborative effort between what can best be described as a very small number of elites in the United States, Russia, and to a lesser extent China to usher in a realignment of the world order, with Russia and China dominating world food, energy, tech, and pharmaceutical markets for the remainder of the twenty-first century and beyond."

"My dad died almost fifteen years ago. How could anything in these documents point to a plan today?"

"It's not the plan specifically. It's the players. From what we've read and what we know about Tom Reece, we think he came across this network of spies, for lack of a better term, when he was investigating something else."

"And what was that?"

"The betrayal of American POWs in Vietnam."

"Poe mentioned something about that, but he said my dad was looking for a GRU sniper even after that war—that the sniper was the reason he went to work for the CIA."

"Vic mentioned you had spent some time with Poe. I've had my run-ins with him over the years on Soviet and Russian analysis, but yes, in this case I believe Poe helped recruit Tom Reece into the CIA after Vietnam. The GRU sniper was the lure, but in that hunt he discovered something else."

"What?"

"Remember, your dad was a case officer, but because of his work with MACV-SOG in Vietnam, he had a foot in the paramilitary side of the Agency. He was one of the first to truly work both sides of the fence—not so uncommon today, but it was back then. He worked hand in hand with Poe, putting together intelligence on all the GRU advisors that operated in Vietnam. It was part of that investigation that led him to suspect there was an orchestrated attempt, a successful attempt, by the United States government at the behest of this group of elites to disprove that American POWs were left behind in Southeast Asia."

"Why would they do that?"

"Because some of those men the country abandoned were transported to the Soviet Union and to China for exploitation. Vic and I suspect that this group of collaborators were trying to avoid a war. At the height of the Cold War, proof that the Soviets had imprisoned and interrogated or tortured U.S. servicemen would have put both countries on the precipice of a nuclear exchange. Relations were tense."

"These collaborators were American and Soviet? Spies? Double agents?"

"They were more than that. It is apparent from these documents that your father did not know who could be trusted at the CIA."

"Weren't a lot of POWs returned to the U.S. in '73 as part of the Paris Peace Accords?" Raife asked.

"They were. Five hundred and ninety-one, to be exact. Operation Homecoming. Kissinger negotiated their release, but according to these records," Danreb said, pointing to a yellowing paper on the board, "he knew that there were more."

"And he left them?" Reece asked.

"Satellite photos and photos from our manned reconnaissance aircraft—U-2s, the OXCART, and SR-71—along with debriefs with POWs who were returned, indicated that, without a doubt, the list provided by the North Vietnamese delegation in Paris was incomplete. War reparations were tied to the POW issue."

"Meaning what?"

"Meaning that if the U.S. wanted its POWs back, they would have to pay."

"A ransom?"

"Essentially. It's a negotiation tactic as old as war itself. While I was still at my desk at the Agency, the National Archives released documents indicating that President Eisenhower was presented intelligence indicating that POWs from the Korean War had been relocated to camps in China and the USSR."

"How many?"

"The Agency had a source who passed along that at least eight hundred ended up in Siberia. The point is that Vietnam was paying attention to their communist brethren in the USSR, China, and North Korea. They had done the same thing with the French after Dien Bien Phu in '54. RAND Corporation issued a report in '65 on the Viet Minh holding French prisoners for years after the end of hostilities. Kissinger was well aware of all of this; in fact, he wrote a classified policy paper on it back in 1957.

"This paper right here," Danreb continued, picking up paper from the table. "This is a copy of the debrief from a defector in 1971, a Dr. Dang Tan, stating in no uncertain terms that at least five hundred POWs were not on the Paris delegation list."

"Just to play devil's advocate, how do we know he was telling the truth?"

"This document is from '79. Your dad was running an asset in Moscow who was present at a meeting of the Soviet Central Committee on September fifteenth, 1972, when NVA Lieutenant General Tran Van Quang briefed that over a thousand Americans were alive as prisoners of war in Vietnam, Laos, and Cambodia. Remember, antiwar pressure on the Nixon administration was at a fever pitch. The POWs were tied to bringing 'peace with honor.'"

"Wonder which PR officer came up with that one?" Raife said.

"Kissinger eventually agreed to a four-billion-dollar reparations package in exchange for American POWs from Vietnam, Laos, and Cambodia."

"So why didn't we get them back?" Reece asked.

"The deal fell through. Watergate dominated the headlines, and Nixon wanted to move on from the nightmare that was Vietnam. They declared that all U.S. servicemen being held in Southeast Asia had been repatriated with Operation Homecoming. Anyone MIA was now listed as 'Killed in Action.' Case closed."

"But it wasn't."

"No. Some of those five hundred ninety-one POWs returning home told a different story, as did the flood of refugees who fled Vietnam after the fall of Saigon in '75. In that stack there are the interviews with POWs and 'boat people' that fall into the 'highly credible' pile."

"Why didn't the CIA and Pentagon keep investigating?"

"Your father asked the same question. He also figured out why, and took his investigation underground."

"What do you mean?"

"The CIA and Pentagon, with a few exceptions, circled the wagons."

"No different than today with the withdrawal from Afghanistan," Raife noted.

"The official policy was that all living American POWs had been returned," Danreb said. "Congress looked into the matter under pressure from constituents and veterans' organizations, but their committees were set up to discredit rather than investigate. Most of the country was ready to put Vietnam in the rearview mirror."

"But not Tom Reece."

"Not Tom Reece," Danreb confirmed. "Operation Homecoming did have an unintended consequence, though."

"What was that?"

"Congress was unaware of Kissinger's and Nixon's four-billion-dollar promise of aid. They were also horrified by the condition of the POWs who did make it home—something which stalled out reparations and aid from the legislative branch. North Vietnam didn't distinguish between the branches of government. To them, four billion was promised but never delivered."

"Which meant U.S. POWs stayed in captivity."

"That's right. Nixon resigns. Ford steps in, followed by Carter. Deals are forgotten. The country moved on."

"So, what does Vietnam do with its American POWs in Laos and Cambodia?" Reece asked, already suspecting the answer.

"They send them to someone who will pay for them."

"The Soviet Union."

"These are photos of the target package your father helped put together back in '81 for a rescue mission into Laos. His asset in Moscow had passed him intelligence that the Soviets were going to buy the final batch of U.S. POWs. He knew that once they were in the Soviet Union there was no way to get them back. The Soviets would never admit to it, and the U.S. would not start a war with the Soviets over the failed conflict in Vietnam."

"That's single-source intel," Reece said. "He needed more."

"And he got it. A signals intercept corroborated that intel. The intercept specifically stated that twenty U.S. POWs were being moved into a prison camp in Gnommorath, Laos. The NSA tasked a satellite to photograph the village and the surrounding area. The imagery came back as inconclusive, so an SR-71 out of Kadena Air Base in Okinawa conducted an overflight. Those photos confirmed a prison with walls, guard towers, and irrigation ditches dug into the surrounding crops in the shape of a '52K'—escape-and-evasion code for fifty-two U.S. POWs."

"Fifty-two," Reece repeated, his voice low.

"The CIA and Delta wanted on-the-ground confirmation. This is only a year after Desert One, so Delta wants to make sure they succeed. After some bureaucratic infighting as to who should lead a reconnaissance mission into Laos, the CIA, against your dad's recommendation, was given the mission. And who did they send?"

"Tom Reece."

"He reestablished comms with Montagnards from his SOG days who had fled to Thailand. He recruited them and led them into Laos. They established an OP in a cave near the camp."

"What did they find?" Reece asked.

"According to these documents, they confirmed at least one American."

"Your father was the CIA liaison between the Agency and Delta. In April 1981, Delta was put on alert and began planning. By July they were ready to go."

"Poe told us that right before the operation was green-lit, a story broke in the *Post* about U.S. POWs in Vietnam and a mercenary force making preparations to rescue them," Reece said.

"Interesting timing, don't you think?" said Danreb. "They even pulled a retired Green Beret lieutenant colonel into the spotlight to help sink the mission. There was no way that mission was getting approved with the enemy on alert only a year after the disaster at Desert One."

"Who is 'they'?" asked Reece.

"There were certainly powerful political and intelligence entities in the U.S. that wanted only to prove that there were no U.S. servicemen still alive in Southeast Asia. The careers and reputations of extremely powerful and influential people would have been tarnished, possibly ruined, if the American public became aware that their own government knew that Americans were left behind in Vietnam and did nothing to get them out. They took this as an opportunity to both prove that no one was still imprisoned in Southeast Asia and to discredit anyone who might think otherwise."

"What happened to the POWs?"

Danreb and Vic exchanged a look.

"We don't know, Reece," Vic interjected. "These papers are inconclusive, but in one of Tom's last communications with his asset in Moscow, his source said that they had been executed. Moscow already had POWs that were transported to the Soviet Union during the Ford and Carter administrations. Now Reagan was in office. Instead of transporting more prisoners to the USSR or China, they were executed and their remains incinerated. You father's asset was found weeks later with his throat cut in his vehicle at his dacha outside of Moscow."

"What happened then?"

"Your father's notes end. Nothing on POWs from 1981 until 1992."

"What was he doing during that time?" Reece asked.

"He continued to rotate through case officer postings but shifted focus to the Middle East and the growing threat of terrorism," Vic said.

"The POW issue would surface from time to time over the years. The government took the official position that no POWs were left behind," Danreb explained. "Two servicemen involved in putting the target packages together for the scrubbed Delta mission went so far as to sue the government for the release of documents that would prove to the American people that the opposite was true. Of course, the judge sided with the government, which means he sided with the CIA citing 'sources and methods' and the high classification of the material."

"They knew we had live POWs in Southeast Asia and they left them to rot," Raife said. "Bloody cowards."

"These documents paint that picture. One of the last items was inserted in 1992. Your father had a conversation with Le Quang Khai, a member of the Vietnamese Foreign Ministry working on his graduate degree at Columbia. In his notes he writes that Khai stated that it was common knowledge in Vietnamese government circles that the U.S. had abandoned POWs after the war. Not long after that, Khai was deported."

"You said '*one*' of the last documents. There was another?" Reece asked.

"Yes. A satellite photo from 1992. Dug into the earth outside the Dong Mang prison in northern Vietnam, so that it was visible only from the air, was 'GX 2527.'"

Danreb handed Reece a photo. The resolution was much sharper than the photo from twelve years earlier.

"Authenticator code?"

"Yes, for Peter Richard Matthes. His C-130 was shot down in November 1969."

Reece set the photo on the table.

"Bastards."

Danreb pulled a document from the magnetic board and handed it to Reece.

"What's this?"

"Reece, your dad thought there was more to this than just Pentagon, intelligence officials, and politicians wanting to cover their asses and move past Vietnam in the name of political expediency. He thought that the evidence of U.S. servicemen being transported to the USSR was quelled by this small group of elites in our country . . ."

"And in the Soviet Union," Reece said, finishing the thought.

"It appears there are those in both countries who have allegiances to something other than their people." Vic held up a paper. "Tom Reece writes, 'In the wake of World War II at Tehran, Bretton Woods, and Yalta, certain intelligence officials met and formed a pact. They didn't trust their leaders, nor did they trust the people in any society, free or totalitarian. They vowed to avoid state-on-state conflict that could lead to a nuclear confrontation. To do so, they would trade secrets and manipulate markets to acquire the wealth necessary to wield the kind of power that can dictate the world order.'"

"An alliance?" asked Reece.

"Yes," Danreb said. "Tom references something called 'the Collective' in his notes."

"The Collective," Reece repeated.

"In our discussions in my basement office at Langley we once discussed the Soviet illegals program and their goal of having one of their own ascend to the office of the president. That was a distinct worry during the Cold War. Now, I believe Tom was thinking further ahead, past the end of the Cold War. His sights were already on the next ridgeline. He was focused on the Collective."

"Why is this group so interested in these documents now?" Reece asked.

"That's exactly what Vic and I have been discussing. We think it's because they are about to move a significant piece on the board."

"What piece?"

"That we don't know."

"In the letter he left me, my dad said there was one last bit of evidence he couldn't find."

"Whatever it was, I think he was close to finding it when he was killed," Vic said.

"Most of the people he lists in these files are dead," Danreb said. "But this was generational. Money still needs to be accounted for, moved, and hidden, whether it's cash, cryptocurrency, or tangible assets like gold, silver, platinum, jewels, art, or cars. Tom found the firm that handled their money, a small boutique firm called Morgan Holdings. I've studied them for years. They manage the money for many of the former KGB and current SVR officials and Bratva. There is one in particular who we made a deal with almost twenty years ago. We sold our soul on that one. The CIA, in conjunction with the FBI, agreed to a deal in which a former KGB man by the name of Luka Yevgenievich would be given U.S. citizenship and immunity in exchange for information on an asset, a Russian spy, working his way up the ranks at the CIA. He gave us the asset, and it was exactly what I feared. The SVR *wanted* him to burn their asset. He was a throwaway. In exchange they got immunity and citizenship for one of their own."

"Why didn't we scrap the agreement?"

"Couldn't prove it. And if it turned out that it was a lemon, senior-level officials at the Agency and the FBI would look ridiculous. They played it off as a success."

"What happened to Yevgenievich?"

"He runs the New York Bratva syndicate, protected by the power of the U.S. government. He's involved in prostitution, human trafficking, organ trafficking, drugs, money laundering, you name it. It's one of the worst deals we ever negotiated."

"How does he fit in?"

"His financial holdings increase at a rate disproportionate to those of other Bratva leaders across the United States and Europe."

"Maybe he's just better at his job," Raife said.

"Perhaps, but I think there is more to it," Danreb said. "I've been studying these guys since the early eighties. A few have stood out as—how do I put this?—*different*, connected in both America and Russia. It's not as easy as 'follow the money,' but that's not far off. I got more and more interested as time went on and took my suspicions up the chain at Langley. Of course, I was told to stand down. But I didn't. I couldn't. I kept investigating. I used the Agency's resources. It was easier to cover things back then. I mapped out his network to include the man at the firm who handles Yevgenievich's money. A man who also happens to handle money for those I suspect to be part of this group of elites both in the United States and Russia."

"How do we find him?"

"I just so happen to know a lot about him. But first, let's talk about something else."

"What's that?" Reece asked.

"Money."

CHAPTER 53

"MONEY?"

"Yes," Danreb said. "Oftentimes it comes back to money, or really to wealth, because that is where true power lies."

"All right, let's hear it," Reece said.

"There are three main ways to amass the type of wealth that one needs in order to wield true power. These are not people interested in a nice house with a white picket fence. They are interested in control—total control."

"Sounds familiar," Reece said.

"Option one is monopoly; controlling a sector or a commodity like shipping, groceries, alcohol, seafood, oil, gas, gold, silver, rare earth minerals, microchips, pharmaceuticals, sunglasses—you name it. Many of those sectors are controlled by a few closely held private corporations. Take the De Beers family, as an example. They have long controlled the world's flow of diamonds. They set the price and maintain scarcity to control the market. In actuality, diamonds are not that scarce or hard to find. De Beers holds millions of carats of diamonds in safes, purely to keep the price high. They control the supply side, and therefore establish and support the value of the global diamond market, artificially through their power in much the same way that OPEC has huge influence over oil prices through controlling the global supply. It is similar across the board."

"Give me an example in the U.S.," Reece said.

"When a small but growing company like Santa Monica Seafood begins to dominate a segment of the fresh fish market, putting pressure on big companies like Sysco or U.S. Foods, they simply step in and buy them out." Danreb snapped his fingers. "Poof! No more competition. If the smaller company won't sell, then the larger corporation, with more resources, squeezes them; usually by cutting off distribution and shipping. It's more coordinated and integrated than the Mafia, and most of it is even legal. Coca-Cola and PepsiCo do the same thing. They watch and monitor their sector, and when another drink company starts to get traction, they buy it or cut off its distribution. When was the last time you were in a restaurant or stadium or arena that served both Coke and Pepsi? Never happens. They split up the market. And chances are, any other available beverage that isn't owned by Coke or Pepsi is at least distributed by them, which is another means of control. The point is, if you start to be successful, you get crushed, unless you are in the club."

"You said there were multiple ways."

"The second way is through Private Capital, such as Hedge Funds, Private Equity, and Venture Capital, but most people can't afford to invest the amount of capital necessary to create monumental gains. These dark pools of private capital employ teams of analysts and forecasters, people on the spectrum, whose minds work through numbers in a way that even AI hasn't figured out. They put a million dollars into ten companies—eight of them fail, but the other two are the future Netflix, Amazon, Apple, Tesla, or any of the dozens of others that go up a thousandfold from the initial investment. It's an eight-million-dollar loss on the losers, but a billion-dollar gain on the couple winners. They can afford to invest in a way that the average citizen can't, and they continue to amass wealth and compound those billion-dollar gains. That allows them to continue to bet on ten and lose on eight. But again, it helps to be part of the club. That's how you get the best information and, more important, access to those two ultimate winners in the first place."

"I'd rather be doing almost anything else," Reece said.

"Numbers aren't really his thing," Raife commented with a smile.

"The third way is through Managed Speculation using market manipulation," Danreb continued.

"Explain that to me like I avoided all math and finance classes in college," Reece said.

"You speculate about the future by investing in futures, options or swaps, which are financial contracts, i.e., derivatives, whose value depends upon an underlying asset, which can be traded like a stock or bond. But here's the catch: the derivative's value is set to a predetermined amount on a future date—thus the 'speculation.' These financial securities are commonly used by legitimate companies to mitigate risk. A hedge, much like insurance. However, they can also be used to 'assume risk,' that is, to speculate with the expectation of significant reward if you predict the future properly, and here's where it gets interesting. By specifying the price of the trade and a future date, these derivatives safeguard the owners of the underlying assets against future fluctuations in the market. But, if you know what is going to happen in the future, you don't need the underlying asset and you can maximize your earnings and wipe out your enemies."

Reece shrugged and looked at Raife, who spent a few months on Wall Street after the military and before packing up and moving back to Montana.

"I think we need to go back to the part where I told you I didn't major in finance," Reece said.

"Let's try this," Danreb said. "You invest in futures, or options, which are derivatives of other asset types, like stocks or commodities—but you have influence, or control, over outcomes. Futures and options allow you to buy or sell a significant amount of stock or commodities at a specified price, at some specified future date—sometimes months or even a year into the future. Most investors use these instruments to hedge market fluctuations and volatility, essentially as insurance policies. But some investors use them to *speculate*, essentially making big bets on an outcome. And if you're willing to make bets that are 'way out of the money,' you can generate enormous profits, having put up relatively little money up front. Think of it this way: it's like going to the racetrack and putting $1,000 on the shitty horse with 200:1 odds. Nobody expects that horse to win, but if it does there's a huge payoff. Information and knowledge can be enormously valuable and even more valuable if you can actually control outcomes."

"We can't predict the weather," Reece said. "How do you essentially predict the future?"

"The idea isn't to predict the future, but to control the future," Danreb said. "Take Russian gas and oil exports."

"Didn't Russia lose out through sanctions when they invaded Ukraine?" Reece asked.

"It's a nice talking point, but, like most of what comes out of Washington, it's total bullshit. Think of it from their perspective. Russia had already built up vast stocks of oil *before* they invaded Ukraine, knowing full well that prices would rise, but that sanctions would likely follow, preventing Russia from selling and taking advantage of the price increase. In fact, Russia broadcast their intention to invade, and the U.S., in turn, showed their hand."

"Sanctions."

"That's right. Russian oil is cut off to Europe and prices skyrocket due to scarcity. Russian stockpiles go up immensely in value, but now they can't sell it."

"Okay, I get that part. But now someone has to buy them, right, and how can they with sanctions?"

"That's because they were already sold! Russia prearranged futures with China and India. Those countries bought up all they could to prevent having to purchase at an even higher price in the future. And there are always avenues to sell commodities with heavy demands, especially oil and gas, with sanctions in place."

"It's actually brilliant," Raife said. "The net effect of cutting off oil to the West was billions of dollars in sales to fund the war effort while making a small number of oligarchs even more wealthy."

"And therefore more powerful," Danreb added. "They also needed to generate cash to expand future oil production in Russia. After that sell-off, they had to rebuild their stocks. That takes money and time."

"Which is why they want to draw out the war in Ukraine," Raife said, finishing Danreb's thought. "They need time to rebuild their gas and oil inventory. They made money on the front end, but that severely depleted their stockpiles. Now they need to make money on the back side."

"Exactly," Danreb confirmed. "Lastly, there is the Black Swan. I assume you have heard the term."

"Yes. I read a few of Nassim Taleb's books," Reece said. "It's an unexpected, rare event, that changes the course of history."

"Correct," Danreb said. "He described it as an outlier with extreme impact. Reece, globalization of the world economy goes back to the Roman Empire, the Silk Road, but it saw an exponential leap forward at the turn of the twentieth century, which accelerated at the end of World War II. Today, blockchain communication and decentralized banking is fueling economic globalization."

"I'm not sure I follow."

"Insert a Black Swan event of global proportion, like a large-scale terrorist attack that disrupts global supply chains, which governments, and in this case a small group of elites manipulating these governments, use to acquire more power and control."

"Like the Patriot Act," Raife said.

"Exactly," Danreb said. "Today, the global derivatives markets are many times the size of the underlying assets they track and those instruments, derivatives such as swaps, options, and futures, can be used to buy and sell anything at any price at any time in the future."

"English, please," Reece said.

"Let me try," Raife said. "Rather than buying oil, you speculate with an oil future, which is an obligation to acquire oil at a set price, at a set time in the future. If, on that future date, the price of oil has gone up, then you pocket the difference; if it goes down, you lose your money. Further, when using derivatives as a trading tool, only a small fraction of the value—twenty percent, in the case of futures—needs to be put up to a brokerage company. Think of it as a down payment, but in this case it leverages or wildly amplifies your returns and losses. It's really fucking risky, but pays off big if you're right—like that race horse. And it's not risky if you're *controlling the outcome*. You just need to find a brokerage firm that can very quietly place the bets for you, without any peering eyes."

"Enter Morgan Holdings," Danreb said. "In the recent case with Russia, you need a large brokerage firm that can handle this scale of a deal on the international markets with money spread across multiple international corporations, all run with carefully selected crypto blockchain technology to be untraceable. Morgan Holdings has the connections and assets to handle deals of this size through multiple international accounts in a decentralized, virtually untraceable fashion."

"It's a coordinated move, but totally anonymous," Katie said.

"Anonymity is a major part of this equation," Danreb confirmed. "I assume you have all heard of buying low, selling high."

Everyone nodded.

"Well, this is where it gets a bit more complex, but also how you turn your money into generational wealth—speculating through futures and other derivatives contracts."

The nods of moments ago were now blank stares.

"You are buying pieces of paper—contracts. You are betting the value of that commodity on a certain day in the future. If the price goes up, you sell your contract, even before it expires. You never moved or owned actual oil, gold, wheat, or anything else. You bought and sold a contract. There is potential for billions in gains with a moderate initial investment."

"If you know the future," Reece said.

"And, if you know the future," Danreb echoed. "Then you write or sell contracts for the same commodity at the market high, in this case effectively selling an asset or commodity you don't actually own yet—selling high. This works only if you own the underlying asset in case you get 'called away,' or you know the outcome of the future. When the price of the commodity drops, your contract to sell at a higher price gets way more valuable, and you make the money all over again. How do you know what it's going to do? In this case you flood the market when sanctions are removed out of necessity after the Black Swan."

"Let me see if I have this right," Raife said, activating the finance side of his brain. "Turn one for Russia was our sanctions—they made money selling high-priced futures to China and India because Russia owned the oil, and the Russians knew the price would go up, but they wouldn't be able to sell it and take advantage of the price. But it didn't matter—since the oil was contracted, they effectively avoided the sanctions when China and India took delivery on their futures. Turn two was their speculation on futures contracts, because they controlled the outcome. They used the proceeds from their futures sales to China and India to buy more futures, knowing the price would go up, thus amplifying their return even further. Turn three, they wrote or sold futures contracts at the market high, knowing they planned to flood the market, betting that oil prices would decline and selling the right to buy oil at that price in the future. Since they control the oil and control hostilities, they can manipulate when sanctions will be lifted. They can flood the market, driving down the future price, making the contracts they sold worthless to those who bought them."

"But they keep all the proceeds," Reece said, processing all he had learned.

"That's essentially it. They sold or wrote futures contracts knowing they can force the price down by flooding the market with their oil reserves at any time of their choice," Danreb said. "When you buy or write a future, you are making an assumption about what is going to happen, but you can't really be sure, unless of course you control, or in this case, manipulate, the market. Russia has been controlling the game at every step. Buying long futures contracts as they built up their stockpiles, all the while knowing the war would make oil scarce. Just like De Beers, they are controlling the market, because they maneuver and determine what's going to happen. Instead of winning on two out of ten investments like we discussed, they are winning ten out of ten."

"I think I get it," Reece said. "If you truly invest in wheat futures, not knowing what the future holds, and the price goes down, maybe with favorable weather and a good farming year, you lose big-time. But if there is a bad year, a weather event decimates crops, or you launch a war into Europe's wheat belt, you turn millions into hundreds of millions, or billions into tens of billions. Is that right?"

"Quick learner," Danreb said. "Now, if you can create an event, a Black Swan, you can control your market. In the case of Ukraine, the world supply of wheat was cut by twenty percent. Have you been to a grocery store recently?"

"I've been having my food delivered for the past three months," Reece said.

"Sorry, Reece. But, yes, you've got it. In this case when Ukraine restricted shipping in the Black Sea, you just sell the contracts and make your billions. When shipping resumes, wheat prices fall, but you have already written contracts at a higher price. Your hundreds of billions become a trillion. World events can be controlled to make the wealthy even more so. Money is power. The more money . . . well, you get the point. It's world domination through economic control. That economic control then becomes political control and eventually becomes social control. The world has always been run by a very few at the top. I think—and these documents confirm—that Tom Reece thought so as well. He concludes that there is a tacit pact, an organization of officials, financiers, businessmen, politicians, and oligarchs in the U.S. and Russia who have been guiding world events since the end of World War Two."

"The Collective you mentioned earlier," Reece said.

"Yes."

"So why come after me now?"

"I think the next Black Swan is on the horizon, Reece," Danreb said.

"And now that they know we have these documents, they are going to push forward with the event," Reece stated.

"That is my assessment."

"How do we stop them?" Reece asked.

"Remember Morgan Holdings?"

"I do."

"During my time at the Agency I put a lot of time into Russian intelligence service funding mechanisms. Morgan Holdings has the key. The founder's grandson has taken the mantle as chairman and now handles the most sensitive clients."

"Like Luka Yevgenievich," Reece said.

"The very one."

"How do we find him?"

"As luck would have it, I've been tracking him for years."

CHAPTER 54

REECE AND KATIE SAT on the edge of the twin bed in Andy Danreb's small guest room. A nightstand, dresser with an attached mirror, and bookshelf packed with volumes adorned the space. A single wildlife print on the wall that looked like it had come with the home was the sole decoration.

Reece was ready to find out if the letter addressed to him from his father would shed any additional light on what Danreb had revealed. He wanted Katie to be with him when he opened it.

"Let's see if there is a final piece to this puzzle," Reece said.

He ran his thumb over the red seal; a rose was stamped into the wax. His name was written in cursive in his father's script on the other side.

"A rose," Katie observed.

"My mom had a rose garden at each of our houses. I remember she was never overly concerned with the actual house. She was interested in the garden. Every time we moved, my dad and I would check out the rooms and garage while my mom would be in the yard, looking at the angle of the sun and inspecting the dirt. We spent a lot of time in nurseries when my dad was away. They each had the same distinct smell: all those flowers, potting soil, fresh-cut wood planter's boxes, the moisture in the air. Every spring she would be in the garden, pruning away to make sure each rose had enough light and air, always watering them individually, twenty minutes at a time, careful to keep moisture off the petals."

"Do you think this rose was a tribute to your mother?"

"It's possible, but I've learned a lot about my father in the past few days. I'd venture that this rose has two meanings. Yes, it's a tribute to my mother's love of roses. But it's something more."

"Sub rosa?"

"Exactly," Reece said. "'Under the rose.' It comes from a story in which Cupid gives Harpocrates a rose to keep him quiet."

"About what?"

"Venus's indiscretions."

"Indiscretions . . ." Katie's voice trailed off.

"Maybe it's a sign?" Reece wondered aloud. "Something tells me there is nothing my dad did that was without meaning."

Reece's thumb broke the red seal and opened the envelope.

The papers inside had been folded to fit into the standard business-size envelope.

"Let's find out."

Reece began to read. As he finished a page he handed it to Katie, who read it as well. When Reece handed Katie the fifth and final page he leaned forward, setting his forearms on his thighs. He remained still and silent, staring at the floor as Katie finished reading. When she was done, she slowly refolded the pages and tucked them back into the envelope. She then put her arm around Reece's back and dropped her head to his shoulder.

"Do we tell them?" he asked.

"I don't know, James."

"He killed almost everyone he could find who had a hand in betraying our POWs."

"He did it for those POWs who couldn't fight for themselves."

"Katie, he spent over a decade figuring out who abandoned our POWs in Vietnam. He took his time. It was calculated. He made each one look like an accident."

"James, this is a confession."

"I know. But there was someone else. He must have put this in the safe-deposit box and never gone back, which means he could have figured it out and taken him—"

"Or *her*," Katie said.

"That's right, or her, out after he put this away."

"Then why not go back to the box and add that information to this confession?" Katie asked.

"Because they were onto him, or he suspected they were. And he wanted to protect everyone who they thought might know something: me, my mom, Martha Stowe, Poe."

"He lived like that for so long," Katie said, sympathy creeping into her voice.

"Poe mentioned there was someone else or some other piece of information my dad was looking for that remained elusive."

"Maybe it wasn't a person. Maybe it was this final plan. This Black Swan that Andy is talking about," Katie offered.

"It's possible. He detailed each one of the killings. Why would he do that?"

"He wanted you to know."

"He doesn't write about them like he feels guilty or wants their families to know. He wasn't interested in destroying their legacies. He was interested in something else," Reece said.

"Accountability?"

"Accountability and consequences."

"And the last part?" Katie asked. "If that last part is true, it means that every theory about the JFK assassination I've ever heard is wrong. It wasn't the CIA, the KGB, the Mafia, the military, or Castro. Not directly, anyway."

"But there aren't any facts or intelligence to back it up—just suspicion," Reece said. "A Cuban intelligence officer recruits Oswald at the behest of South Vietnam's President Ngo Dinh Diem and his brother Ngo Dinh Nhu as revenge for Kennedy's and the CIA's support of a coup that killed them."

"It makes sense if you think about it," Katie said. "If they suspected that Kennedy was going to betray them, why wouldn't they arrange for him to die in the event they were deposed and killed?"

"Revenge for the coup d'état, before it even happens," Reece said. "The KGB and maybe CIA, part of this group of elites, knew and did nothing to stop it."

"How would they know?"

"Because they had assets advising Diem at all levels. The U.S. was supporting the regime with military equipment and economic aid packages. We were also training their military and police forces. Saigon was crawling with case officers."

"And one or more of these Agency guys was part of this collective?" Katie asked.

"Or was being run by one. There are a few possibilities."

"And then, when the assassination is successful, they help cover it up. Convenient for everyone," Katie said.

"Oswald never even knew who he was killing for."

"James, if this gets out, it changes so much of what we understand about the country from 1963 onward."

"That one is just my dad's theory. The rest of this, the POW betrayal, is all backed up by intelligence in the files. There is nothing in them that points to the Kennedy assassination."

"Maybe he didn't want his suspicions to discredit that intelligence?"

"I don't know, Katie. Maybe. This started with him going to work for the CIA so he could track down the Soviet GRU advisors from Vietnam. That leads to the Soviet-Vietnam POW issue, which in turn leads to this connection between high-level officials in Washington and Moscow working to advance their own interests and not those of their countries."

"And don't forget, prevent a nuclear war," Katie said. "Which they seem to have done on at least two occasions."

"And along the way, as he investigates and fills in the missing pieces, he comes up with this theory on JFK. It was all connected."

"It's a lot," Katie said.

"It is."

"I've never been afraid to pursue a story. Benghazi, the Capstone Capital experimental drugs used on you and your men. None of those stories truly scared me. James, I'm afraid now. What are we involved with here?"

Reece turned and looked into Katie's eyes.

"Maybe we should drop this whole thing and go back to Montana," she said. "You can open that bookstore whiskey bar and the archery shop. We can leave this all behind."

Reece pushed a strand of long blond hair behind Katie's ear.

"They would keep coming, Katie. Especially now. I've put you in danger too many times, and now with this"—Reece shook his head—"you, me, Raife, Andy, Vic, Martha, Poe—everyone is in danger. It's my fault. I am so sorry, Katie."

Reece saw the realization seep in and the look in Katie's eyes change from fear to one of resolve.

"Well, then what's our next move?"

"I've got to get you someplace safe. You said the Hastingses have the ranch locked down?"

"Like Fort Knox."

"Good. I need you to go back. I can't operate if I'm worried about you. I love you with all my heart, Katie. If we are going to live without a constant worry that this group is going to send hit squads after us, I need to finish what my dad started."

"What are you going to do, James?"

"I'm going to finish his list."

CHAPTER 55

FSB Headquarters
Lubyanka
Moscow, Russia

KIRA BORISOVA HAD BEEN Pavel Dashkov's secretary for almost fifteen years. She wasn't sure whether to be flattered or offended that he had never tried to sleep with her. She was a fixture in many, but certainly not all, of his meetings. She held the highest security clearances and maintained the director's schedule. She arrived at Lubyanka promptly at 7:00 a.m. every morning, knowing she would have plenty of time to prepare for the day. Dashkov might arrive anytime between 8:00 a.m. and 10:00 a.m., though he was arriving closer and closer to the latter these days. He preferred to work late, which meant so did Kira. She arrived before her boss and left after, just as her mother had taught her.

Her mother had worked for the KGB, the FSK, and the FSB, all names for the agency responsible first for Soviet and then Russian internal state security. She had been in Red Square on December 25, 1991, to see the Soviet flag lowered. The red flag, with its distinctive hammer and sickle signifying workers and peasants, would never fly again. When she told Kira of that night she had smiled. Change was on the winds.

Kira's mother had been a devoted party member, even knowing

her family had been hit hard by Stalin's Great Purge of 1937. The Soviet Union was, if nothing else, a superpower. There was pride in that. She remained loyal until April 26, 1986, the day of the Chernobyl disaster. She had taken notes in meetings following the devastating accident and found herself wondering why orders to evacuate the Ukrainian city did not come until thirty-six hours after the Kremlin was notified that there had been a catastrophic meltdown in reactor four of the Vladimir Ilyich Lenin Atomic Power Station. She also became aware that the plant had a radiation leak in 1982 that was covered up by the KGB and that there were multiple nuclear incidents in 1984 that were never reported to the broader public. It was all kept under wraps by the state to maintain its position in the Cold War. After transcribing notes from a 1987 meeting detailing a successful KGB plan to switch out Chernobyl water and soil samples taken by a French journalist to keep the true magnitude and long-term impacts of the disaster secret, she made her decision. She contacted the Americans.

On her deathbed, she confessed her sins against her country to her only daughter. She stopped spying when FBI agent Robert Hanssen was arrested in February 2001. She feared she was under suspicion. Hanssen had intimate knowledge of FBI and CIA intelligence operations and was sentenced to five consecutive life sentences without the possibility of parole. March had come and gone, as did April, May, and June. She never conducted another dead drop or met with her case officer again. She had a daughter to raise. But before she passed over to the other side, she wanted that daughter to know what she had done. She passed along her secret. Not only that, she passed along the name of her case officer and the mechanisms by which to contact him. All these years after her passing, her mother's mission had fallen on her shoulders.

After work on Friday, Kira walked to the Biblioteka Imeni Lenina station of the Moscow metro and took the train south. Seven stops later she exited at Gagarina Square and strolled the fifteen minutes to

Neskuchny Garden. She found the bench her mother had taken her to thirteen years earlier and sat down to enjoy the rare late afternoon sun. As was normal for most young adults her age, she pulled her phone from her purse and scrolled through her social media accounts and a few news apps. She had arranged to meet a friend for drinks nearby, after which she would retreat to her flat in the Arbat District, an area known for its young bohemian flair. What was not so normal was to leave a small thumbtack pushed into the wood under the far right side of the bench.

She knew sleep would not come easily that night. Wondering if the FSB would kick in her door and drag her back to the Lubyanka for questioning in connection with crimes against the state was not conducive to a good night's rest. Kira had kept her mother's secret for over a decade and had not once visited the dead-drop location. Did the CIA still monitor the site? She would know soon enough.

Kira had struggled with what to do with her newfound knowledge, and, in the end, she had asked herself a simple question: What would Mom do? That was when she removed a small tack from her desk drawer while gathering her purse and coat. After all, it wasn't every day you had the responsibility of averting a nuclear war.

CHAPTER 56

Fairfield County Hunt Club
Westport, Connecticut

SIDNEY MORGAN CLIMBED THE steps into his Prevost Marathon motor home. Painted in stunning golds and blacks, it matched the Double D three-horse trailer with living quarters parked to his right. His driver had driven up the Prevost coach, and the two full-time horse trainers had hauled the stallions in the SportChassis Freightliner. They had arrived the day before, so everything was hooked up to power and water and ready for Sidney, his wife, Maggie, and their fifteen-year-old daughter, Amanda, when they arrived for the competition.

The club was less than a half hour from their home in Darien, so Sidney drove the Bentley that morning two hours after Maggie and Amanda left in the Mercedes G-Wagon. Even though they would sleep in their beds at home that night, Sidney still insisted that his driver move the extravagant motor home to each equestrian event. Regardless of how far they were from Darien, he would have a nice temperature-controlled environment in which to rest and conduct business and possibly even allow for a midday tryst with Maggie in the king-size bed at the back of the coach.

There would be no searching for a cell signal or looking for a quiet place in the shade to take a call, like many of the other parents. Sidney would have all the conveniences of home in an RV that tipped the scales at just north of $2 million. The linen-lined infinity ceiling light illuminated the entire forty-five-foot-long quad slide coach from front to rear. It boasted modern contemporary styling with a white leather sofa, a dinette and table, fireplace, two flat-screen TVs, and dual recliners. It also featured the "intelligence package," so Sidney could tell the coach to raise or lower the shades or change the lighting depending on conditions or his mood. Brushed aluminum fixtures, a carbon fiber cockpit, a large fridge-freezer combo with bottle storage, a half bath and full bath with a large shower, and custom tile work over heated floors completed Sidney's mobile sanctuary.

Amanda became horse crazy when she was twelve. Sidney had no time to learn the ins and outs of the equestrian world, so that responsibility had fallen to his wife. They purchased five horses from Europe specifically bred for dressage, a class of riding that tests horse and rider in a series of challenges with increasing levels of difficulty, in order to find the right three that Amanda would ride in competition. All of them came from the best bloodlines in the world and had been imported for $250,000 each when they were four. After the horse won a few regional and state competitions, the German Oldenburg stallion's sperm was now worth $50,000 a pop. The Dutch Warmblood stallion was used for jumping, and the Black Sterling Friesian along with the two that had not shown as much promise as the others had turned into extremely expensive pasture ornaments. After another $200,000 in custom saddles, tack, and show gear, along with hand-made Italian boots, vet bills, and private equestrian club memberships, the cost of his daughter's chosen sport dwarfed what it cost to have a kid on the local soccer team. At least Sidney didn't have to spend ninety minutes on the sidelines in the heat listening to soccer moms scream every time their kids got close to the ball.

Though Maggie didn't ride, she made sure her daughter had nothing but the best. She was right at home cheering Amanda on in her designer Callidae clothing next to the other trophy wives whose husbands provided the AmEx Black cards that paid for their lunches and spa visits. Sidney didn't think she was sleeping with either of the trainers, but one never really knew. Each passing year meant another trip to Los Angeles to see her plastic surgeon in Beverly Hills for Botox and lip injections, cheekbone fillers, facelifts, a Brazilian butt lift, and breast augmentation, of which Sidney was quite fond. Though he would never say it aloud, he thought she was starting to resemble a Kardashian.

It was only 11:00 a.m. but Sidney poured himself a shot of Bowmore 50 Year Old Single Malt Scotch Whisky and looked down at his stomach. *Maybe I should look into some liposuction*, he thought, before throwing it back. He poured another two fingers—this time to savor—set his glass down, and unlocked his laptop with his fingerprint before shutting himself into the half bath. Sidney avoided communal restrooms even in private clubs like the Fairfield. He planned to return emails before Amanda entered the arena. Maybe Maggie would join him while their daughter warmed up with her trainers. After all, he had paid for her new silicone bolt-ons, so he should at least be able to enjoy them.

He flushed the toilet, looked at himself in the mirror, and adjusted his Patagonia vest over his blue oxford button-up. His dark hair was visibly thinning with what seemed like each passing day, just like his father and grandfather before him. He was the third in his family line to run Morgan Holdings, and much like the horses he had imported from Europe, he'd been bred for it. Of his four siblings he had shown the most aptitude for the family financial business and navigating the complex web of relationships that went along with it, to include the secrecy required when dealing with people who acquired and grew their wealth through means in a gray zone the color of charcoal. It had become his normal, and, just as his father had, he moved money and made investments at the behest of a group that had an uncanny ability to forecast the future. He didn't ask how or why; he played his part, which kept his clients, and by default his wife, happy.

Sidney heard the front door to the motor home open.

"Maggie?" he called out. Maybe he was going to get lucky this morning.

He fumbled with the door latch and stepped into the narrow hallway.

Instead of his wife slipping out of her tight leggings as he had hoped, Sidney was met by a tall, broad-shouldered man in a baseball cap. His arm was extended, and in his hand was a black pistol.

Even though he had just relieved himself, Sidney felt his bladder loosen and a stream of warm liquid dampen the front of his slacks.

"What the *fuck*? Who are you?" Sidney said, his voice cracking to betray the fear that permeated his soul.

"Keep your voice down, Mr. Morgan. An associate is close to your wife and daughter right now. He will watch over them until we are done here."

"You *motherfucker*. If you know my name, you know who I am. One call from me and your world implodes."

"I highly doubt that, but I do need you to make a call."

"A call?" Sidney asked.

"Or send an email, or a text, depending on how you communicate."

"To whom?"

"Take a seat and let's talk about it."

Sidney slid behind the table in front of his computer.

"You are going to kill me, aren't you? I've seen your face."

"That all depends. Though if I decide to kill you, it certainly won't be because you've seen my face."

"I don't understand."

"I don't think you want to have to explain certain facets of your business to a slew of FBI and IRS agents."

"You're with the government?"

"Not today."

"Then what do you want?"

"I want to talk with one of your clients—Luka Yevgenievich."

Sidney swallowed and shook his head.

"I don't know who that is."

The big man paused. He looked oddly familiar, but Sidney couldn't place him.

"Sidney, I am going to be honest with you. Then you get to decide if you are going to live or die today. I think you just moved massive amounts of money into extremely risky investment vehicles, the kind of money you don't bet unless you are controlling the game."

"I don't know what you are talking about."

"You moved this money for very powerful people in the United States and Russia. Your father and grandfather did the same work for the same people and created quite a lucrative business that you've inherited. I know the type of people your clients are, and you are probably more scared of them than you are of me, perhaps rightly so, but that's not going to matter if I put a bullet in your head."

"I told you, I don't know what you're talking about."

"That's unfortunate," the man said, pulling a phone from his pocket and bringing it to his ear.

"Who are you calling?"

"My associate."

"Don't do this."

"It's you who's doing it, Sidney. All I need is an introduction."

"Please . . ."

"Yevgenievich won't kill you. You have too much of his money hidden around the world. He'll want to meet with me, I assure you."

"What do you want with him? Wait, never mind. I don't want to know. Let me get my phone and send a text."

"Good decision, Sidney. Slowly . . ."

Sidney reached into his pocket and removed his iPhone.

"He only meets in person. We never discuss business on the phone. How did you find me?"

"For someone who is so secretive about your clients, your family's social media is a wealth of information: your daughter's TikTok, your wife's Instagram, and this equestrian organization's Facebook. All those links and tags led me right to you. If you survive the day, you might want to visit those privacy settings and ask your family to hold off on posting about events until after they are over."

"Fuck."

"Live and learn."

"Who do I say wants to meet him?" Sidney asked, the phone vibrating in his shaky hand.

"James Reece. Let him know I have something his friends in Russia will want him to acquire. I'm willing to trade it."

"For what?"

"He'll know. Just tell him."

"I told you, he doesn't discuss business via text. We just use it to set up meetings."

"Then set it up."

"For when?"

"For now."

"Oh Jesus, come on, he's a busy man."

"He'll meet with me."

Sidney looked up from his phone and studied the man behind the gun standing over him.

Would this man be his executioner?

"Now I remember you. From the news a few years ago," Sidney said.

"Then you know you should do exactly as I ask."

"Christ, yes. Just hold on. I can see he's typing back."

"Time is of the essence."

"Okay, he said yes."

"See, that wasn't so hard. Where will he be?"

"At a spa in the city."

"What city?"

"Oh, for fuck's sake. Manhattan. *Fucking* New York."

"Why there?"

"Why New York or why the spa?"

"The spa."

"It's the only place we meet."

"Why?"

"He likes to be sure no one has any weapons on them."

"So, you meet him naked in a sauna?"

"I wear a towel. Plus, he owns it, so it's a controlled environment."

"What else?"

"He wants me to come, too. *Shit!*"

"Text your wife and tell her an emergency meeting came up and you have to run to the office."

"*Fuck, fuck, fuck,*" Sidney swore, as his thumbs worked the keypad.

"I'm going to need one more thing."

"Oh Christ, what?"

"Your client list, and before you open your mouth, you know the client list I mean. Your exclusive list."

"I give that to you and I'm a dead man."

"You don't and you're a dead man."

"I can't."

"Sidney, you said you recognized me. That means you remember why I was in the news. All those people who had a hand in killing my family and my Teammates in Afghanistan are dead. I told you I would be honest with you, so I will. Those I care about are threatened by some of the people on that client list of yours. Do you think there is anything I won't do to get that list?"

Sidney worked to swallow. His throat was dry, his hands sweaty. He looked up from his seat into the eyes of the most terrifying person he had ever encountered.

He nodded.

"Okay, Mr. Reece. But it's all shell corporations that my father and grandfather set up. In most cases I don't even know who the clients are."

"Just get me what you have. And, Sidney, don't hold back. I'm on my best behavior right now. You don't want me coming back in a bad mood."

As Morgan's hands worked the keyboard of his laptop, Reece moved to the side so he could observe.

Reece watched the finance man type twenty-six-letter passwords into multiple hidden folders until he arrived at a simple Excel spreadsheet.

"See, that wasn't so hard."

"I'm a fucking dead man."

"Count your blessings, Sidney. You're still breathing."

"These people, they will kill me. They will kill my family."

"Send it to this email address," Reece said, passing Morgan a slip of paper with a Proton Mail address belonging to Andy Danreb written on it.

"I hit send on this and my world changes."

"You don't and your world changes."

Sidney shook his head and sent the email.

"Well, you've fucking killed me. You happy?"

"Sidney, listen to me. Get me where I need to go today, and I'll do what I can for you."

"It won't be enough."

"Get me to Yevgenievich and then retire."

"I can't. You don't know these people."

"I'm going to get acquainted with them. Now, let's go to the spa."

CHAPTER 57

SVR Headquarters
Moscow, Russia

ROSTYA LEVITSKY SAT IN his imposing black leather chair, his back to the thick, bullet-resistant glass that allowed the director of the SVR to survey his domain.

Located in a heavily wooded section of the Yasenevo District past Moscow's Ring Road, SVR headquarters was referred to as *les*—"the forest"—by some and *kontora*—"the office"—by others who operated in the shadows. It had gone by different names over its century of existence, but its foundational principles remained in place. Its job was to protect the Motherland from threats from abroad.

The size of the SVR campus had more than doubled over the past two decades. In the early 1970s, when the SVR was still the First Main Directorate of the KGB, headquarters was in the famed Lubyanka building, in Lubyanka Square. Levitsky despised the place. That was Dashkov's territory, and he avoided it whenever possible.

Levitsky's office was on the twenty-first floor of a building at the apex of a Y-shaped office complex rising from the forest floor. It was far enough away from the capital's administrative hub to set it apart physically and psychologically from agencies that did not deal in the dark arts of espionage and assassination.

All of Levitsky's predecessor's personal effects had long since been removed, but the stench of Mikhail Gromyko's cigarettes still lingered. Even with a new desk and chair, the stale tobacco hovered in the office like a ghost.

Levitsky was a breath away from the presidency. Successfully bringing down James Reece and recovering the files his father had hidden away would elevate him above Dashkov as an heir apparent to Kozak, if in fact Kozak was next in the line of succession, as many suspected.

He had a meeting scheduled at the Kremlin with Chairman Kozak later in the afternoon. The plan to realign the world order was nearing its final stages, and any conversations pertaining to it would happen in person.

The phone on Levitsky's desk chirped, indicating his secretary had intercepted a call beyond the doors.

"Da."

"A call from New York, Director."

"Put it through."

The Special Communications and Information Service of the Federal Protective Service of the Russian Federation, the Spetssviaz, did what it could to secure communications in and out of the building. But in today's world it was safe to assume that all calls were being monitored on one end or the other, and at many points in between.

"This must be an issue of some importance," he said into the receiver.

"I would not call otherwise," the voice replied.

"Well?"

"That errand you asked me to run."

"The one that ended in failure?"

"The one that did not go as planned."

"Yes," Levitsky said.

"He's coming to me."

Levitsky sat up in his chair.

"He has managed to connect with a friend of ours—the banker," the voice continued. "They are on their way here now."

Levitsky felt his heart begin to pound. There was hope yet.

"Apparently he wants to trade the papers he acquired for something."

"Listen to me closely," the SVR director said. "Do what you must to gain possession of those papers."

"And then?"

"And then send them to me via the embassy."

"And the courier and banker?"

"The banker is still of use to us. The courier is not."

"Understood."

• • •

Luka Yevgenievich hung up the phone and tapped it with his index finger. A plate of traditional *goluptsi*—meat-stuffed cabbage—sat untouched in the chair next to him. This was where Yevgenievich conducted business—in the personal resting area of his private club.

A trade? With a man who just took out seven of my men in Boston?

That affront could not go unchallenged.

Politicians knew nothing of what it took to survive in the real world. They made their decisions from temperature-controlled offices behind gates in fortified compounds far from the streets where the battles were fought. Down here it was about fear and respect. Once you lost those, you had lost the war.

He made his decision.

"Misha," he said to the giant across the room, working on his second helping of *shashlik*—lamb kebabs.

The two men sat in chairs across the spacious chamber from each other, their backs to the walls, separated only by a shag carpet that smelled of chlorine. Freshly cut flowers were set in vases on end tables in each corner of the wood-paneled room. A muted flat screen on the wall played a DVD of Schwarzenegger in *Raw Deal.*

Misha Ustinov took another huge bite of his kebab and then set it aside, picking up a plate of herring.

"Who needs an adjustment?" Misha asked.

Following the death of Stepan Vasiliev, Misha had been promoted to brigadier. He knew that even though Yevgenievich didn't show it, the disaster in Boston had hurt the organization's standing in the underworld. To maintain position, retaliation would be swift and violent.

Misha had already hit the gym that morning. He liked to get a pump on early in the day so his tattooed arms and chest would look their best in the tight black tank top that made up part of his everyday uniform. He finished the herring. It was a small helping. He would have to order another. He set his thick forearms on his track suit–clad thighs and leaned forward, a heavy silver cross dangling from his neck like a lure.

"It is more than an adjustment, Misha."

"Give the order and I'll take care of it," he replied.

"A man is on his way to us. The man responsible for Boston. He will be accompanied by the banker, Morgan—you have escorted him to me in the past."

"I remember him."

"Leave him be."

"And the other?"

"Slice him into pieces and feed him to the fish."

CHAPTER 58

New York, New York

IN THE SHADOW OF the Brooklyn Bridge, just blocks from the New York Stock Exchange, is an innocuous-looking building nestled in among the restaurants, coffee shops, and bars. Its entrance is located between a tailor and a pizzeria, across from a vintage vinyl shop. It could have been any one of a number of anonymous businesses in Manhattan, but it wasn't. This one was owned by the Russian mafia.

Raife had tailed Reece and Morgan in the Agency Cherokee. They had taken an exit off I-95 and parked Sidney's Bentley in an office park before continuing into the city together in the SUV.

"For the record, I don't like this," Raife said as he pulled the vehicle to the side of the road just past a tower of scaffolding.

"It's okay; they want those files," Reece said from the backseat next to Morgan. "If I don't have them, they won't kill me. The goal here is to leave with Yevgenievich. He's the link to this collective. Sidney's client list might not cut it. It's specifically designed to conceal the identities of the real owners. Andy has it, but it might take some doing for him to figure it out."

"You think he's just going to walk out with you?"

"I don't think Moscow is going to let him do anything else."

"I'd feel better if you took your weapon," Raife said.

"They are going to frisk me and take it anyway. I'll leave everything here. Just hold tight. I'll be out shortly."

"We are both dead men," Sidney mumbled, shaking his head.

"Let's go," Reece said, opening the door and ushering Morgan outside onto the streets of New York.

Sidney led the way up the steps and pressed the buzzer next to a small brass plaque that read SPA 1917. The door clicked open, and the two men walked inside.

Unlike other Russian spas in the city, this one was private. A young girl who appeared to be in her teens stood behind a reception desk to the left. She nodded at a man in a blue track suit who stood holding a door open halfway down a long hallway.

"Guess we are going that way," Reece said.

"It leads to the private locker room," Sidney replied.

A narrow set of stairs flanked by damp stone walls led down beneath the streets, transporting the visitors back to Old Russia. One level down they entered a large dark room with a swimming pool in its center.

"Change in there," the track suit–clad man said. He posted up at the bottom of the stairs and pointed to a door on the right just off the pool's center.

Reece and Sidney entered the changing room. Stainless-steel partitions separated multiple showerheads affixed to the wall on the left. The floor was damp, and there was one large drain in the middle of the room. Hooks lined the opposite wall, and at the far end of the narrow space was a sink and counter flanked by a series of lockers.

"He won't see anyone unless they are in a towel," Sidney said, moving toward the lockers.

"I guess *Ivan* out there will take us to him when we change?"

"Probably. I am always escorted by at least one of his men."

"Terrific," Reece said as he removed his jacket and shirt, hanging them in the locker. Sidney did the same.

"I usually meet him in the stone-heated cedar sauna, but I've met him in the *shvitz* as well."

"What's that?"

"It's a sauna with ice buckets."

"Sounds delightful."

Reece kicked off his shoes and socks and removed his pants, shirt, and underwear, wrapping one of white towels stacked on a nearby sink around his waist. He positioned the split of the towel over his left leg, wrapped the right side in front of his waist, and then pulled the left side over it, adjusting it seam to seam and rolling it inward to lock it in place.

"Okay, ready."

Sidney, already winded from the exertion of removing his clothes, struggled to secure the towel around his pale, pudgy midsection.

"There is another side of the spa for members," Sidney said. "This side is just for Yevgenievich and his friends and business associates."

"What's that smell?"

"It's the oak leaves."

"Oak leaves?"

"Haven't you ever had a *platza* treatment?"

"No."

"The *platza* master scrubs you down with a broom of fresh oak leaves."

"Why?"

"It opens the pores, removes toxins, and exfoliates. I do it a couple times a month."

"You're a member here?"

"I am, though I only venture to this side when I need to talk with Mr. Yevgenievich."

"What else do you do here?" Reece asked.

"I don't partake in the girls, if that's what you mean. I'll do the cold plunge, get a massage, do the hot stone therapy," he said, pointing to a bucket of rounded basalt stones. "They soak them in oils and warm them up to apply to your muscles. You should try it."

"I'm not a big fan of other people's hands on me, especially large Russian men with connections to the Bratva."

"You seem to have trust issues."

"Just like your friend Yevgenievich."

Reece picked up one of the basalt stones. It was a little larger than a bar of soap. He then grabbed a towel from a stack on the sink, spread it out on the counter, put the stone at the top in the center, and rolled the towel over the stone to secure it in place. He then pulled both ends together to create a makeshift handle, turning the towel and stone into what his Kali instructor had called a *trapo*, Spanish for *rag*. Reece had assembled a flexible improvised weapon.

"What are you doing?"

"Trust issues," Reece replied, as the door to the changing area opened. The two men they had seen on the way in had been joined by two more. The man in the lead had jet-black slicked-back hair. His tight black tank top looked to be one or two sizes too small and was worn to ensure no one missed the tattoos that covered every inch of his chemically enhanced arms, chest, and neck. A large silver cross hung from a thick chain around his neck. Dark blue track suit pants with an Adidas symbol and expensive-looking dress shoes completed the ensemble.

Reece pretended to be drying his hands with another towel, which he dropped over the one concealing the stone.

"Mr. Yevgenievich is ready for you now," the largest of the four men said in a thick Russian accent.

Most people look at someone's face at first encounter. Not Reece. As always, Reece's eyes went first to the hands. That is how he saw the straight razor.

It was concealed in the man's right hand while his left beckoned Reece and Sidney to walk to them. The body language and hand positions of his associates indicated that they were armed as well.

"Where is Mr. Yevgenievich?" Reece asked to buy time.

"We will take you to him. Come."

"Sidney," Reece said in a low voice, turning to the Wall Street banker. "Thanks for getting me in here. I'd seriously consider that retirement we discussed."

Reece started to walk.

"You can leave the towels there. There are plenty where you are going," the Russian said.

Reece continued to pretend to dry his hands as he approached the four men.

Clothed, armed, and with their four-to-one ratio, they were overconfident and over-muscled. Reece would use that to his advantage.

"Let's go," Reece said as he approached, attempting to disarm them with a smile, his grip tightening on the towel handle in his grasp.

Four men, at least one with a straight razor, against a man in only a towel with nowhere to run would normally end poorly for their prey. Reece was not most men.

Once within striking distance, Reece saw the lead enforcer's body language change ever so slightly, blading his body to the side and shifting his weight to his rear foot. When his muscles tensed to lash out with the hand that had been at his side, the hand concealing the straight razor, Reece struck.

As he sent the top towel flying into the face of the man to his primary target's right, he smashed the improvised sap into the tattooed hand holding the straight razor, shattering the metacarpals and knocking the blade to the floor. Reece immediately snatched the *trapo* back and up, the stone connecting with the underside of the man's jaw, snapping his large head back. This gave Reece time to turn to his left and whip the stone into the second man's temple, sending him directly to the floor. Reece switched directions, slinging the towel-covered stone across the side of the first man's head.

Two down. Status unknown.

Two more.

The key to fighting multiple assailants is to use angles to "stack" them, to essentially fight one at a time. The narrow confines of the changing area had done that naturally, but now Reece had lost the element of surprise and was facing two opponents. At least one had a straight razor.

Reece lashed out with his improvised weapon, which extended his striking range by about a foot. The rock connected with the man's face and Reece flanked to the side, making him an obstacle to his partner.

Attack the weapon.

Using the *trapo*, Reece launched two circular strikes to the hand with the blade, but the enforcer held on, drawing it back, which gave Reece an opening to smash the rock into the bridge of his nose. Reece then braced off the towel rack on the wall to avoid slipping and followed up with a side kick to his sternum that sent him crashing into the man behind him. The trail man pushed his friend to the side to maintain his balance.

Another razor.

Get control of the weapon.

Reece threw the rock directly into the last man's face. It impacted just above his right eye. His hands coming up to block it exposed his blade.

Reece ripped off his own towel, leaving him completely naked. Initially holding it like a bullfighter with the tight seam of the towel extended between his hands, he twisted to the side and parried his opponent's first stab. He passed it to the side and attempted to foul the blade in the towel, but his opponent retracted it and attempted a backhanded slash, which Reece blocked and tried to wrap up in the towel again but without success.

Fight one at a time, but remember, there are four of them.

Reece let go of the towel with his left hand and fired an uppercut into his adversary's ribs, and immediately followed it with a hook to the side of his head, causing him to step back.

Two men still on their feet. Two on the floor.

The man he'd kicked earlier made another assault, leading with a jab, which Reece parried. The gangster followed with a right cross. Stepping to the inside of the blow, Reece extended the towel and used the center to strike the man's face and wrap his head up in the white cloth. With the man's vision obscured, Reece sent two elbows into the side of his head and threw him to the side, smashing his head into the tile wall before firing another elbow to his temple, knocking him to the floor.

Still another on his feet.

Reece turned and squared off with a man in a track suit. He used the time and space to quickly twist his towel into a roll to give it additional weight. As the Russian closed the distance Reece caught and wrapped his knife hand in the rolled towel, twisting it and ripping it down and toward him, stripping the blade from his enemy's grip and bringing the man to the ground. Reece fired a knee into his face, knocking him back and onto the floor. He turned to grab the blade but felt the impact of a body tackling him to the floor. Reece immediately turned and caught the larger opponent in his guard. Now fighting from his back on the tile floor, Reece used the towel in his hands to parry two punches aimed at his face from the man above. Pulling himself up, he wrapped the towel around his enemy's neck from the front, reaching behind the head in an improvised cross-collar choke. He then swept his opponent around, putting him into the mount position. Maintaining the trapped arm, Reece put the man to sleep. Sensing movement, Reece reached for the razor on the floor. He grabbed it, positioning the handle in his palm and pinching the flat sides between his thumb and index finger, bracing it at the joint to secure it in the open position. Reece turned in time to see the huge man in the tank top scrambling toward him. He slashed his razor across his attacker's wrist, then turned his own wrist and cut across the side of his tattooed neck. As the man's eyes opened wide in the primal surprise of impending death, Reece took the rear mount with his knee on the man's back and grabbed a handful of his greasy hair, pulling it back. Reece inserted the corner of the straight razor behind his left ear and cut all the way across the top of his throat to the other ear, spraying the changing room floor with bright red blood.

Reece heard footsteps on the tile, and from his position atop the muscle-bound corpse he pivoted in time to see a roundhouse kick coming at his head. Bringing his left hand up to absorb some of the blow, his right brought the razor across to slice through the femoral artery of the kicker. Even as the blood began to flow like a garden hose, the man did not yet know that he was dead. He planted his leg on the floor and moved to throw a knee to Reece's head, which left his groin open. Reece sliced up. He felt the razor cut through soft tissue between the man's legs. As the man's mouth opened to emit a primal scream, Reece launched himself to his feet, continuing to cut up and through the man's light track suit, opening his stomach until the blade hit the sternum. Reece continued to carve upward, feeling the straight razor bump each of the ribs protecting the man's chest cavity until it sank back into the soft flesh of the neck. Pushing him against the wall, he changed angles with the blade and sliced through the carotid artery, feeling the warm blood cover his face and upper body. The man went limp and sank to the floor.

Reece spun to survey the narrow space. Sidney was at the far end by the sinks, sitting on the ground, knees pulled to his chest, wearing a look of frozen shock. The two remaining gangsters were pushing themselves to their feet, looking at their dead friends, at each other, and at the naked savage covered in blood who had moved into position between them and the door, blocking their only escape. The predators had become the prey.

Reece turned and locked the dead bolt on the door. He then reached down and picked up the improvised *trapo*, adding it back to his arsenal. With the towel-covered rock in his left hand, the straight razor in his right, naked and dripping with fresh blood, he resembled the Koschei demon they had been warned about in fables from their youth.

The environment had changed. It was two on one. The floor was slick with blood, and the men Reece faced had each taken hits. Both were unsteady on their feet. One held a razor.

"Was your plan to kill me?" Reece asked.

"That is still our plan. *Schas po ebalu poluchish, cyka, blyad!*"

The lead man charged. From eight feet away he covered the distance quickly. Reece timed the charge and pivoted to his left, swinging out with the *trapo*, which caught the Russian in the side of the head. As his attacker tried to switch directions, his feet slipped on the blood-covered tile floor. Gravity caught hold and pulled him to earth. His head cracking on the hard tile floor sounded like a gunshot in the confined space. The last man saw his friend go down and tried to stop, but it was too late. Reece's towel-covered stone caught him in the teeth and then circled back and hit him in the back of the head, knocking him unconscious. Reece bent at the knees and finished them with four brutal hits to their skulls with the basalt stone.

Reece straightened his back and stood up straight, checking his body for wounds. All the blood was Russian.

Have to move quickly.

Careful on the slick floor, Reece walked to the sinks, set down the *trapo* and razor, and attempted to wipe away some of the blood with the clean towels.

"Sidney. Sidney!"

The Wall Street man looked up from his position on the floor.

"Where is Yevgenievich?"

"I . . . I don't know," he stammered.

"Okay," Reece said, wrapping a new towel around his waist. "What direction do I go outside that door if I want to find the sauna where you usually meet him?"

"Ugh . . ."

"Focus, Sidney."

"You went through them like they weren't even there," Sidney said, in stunned disbelief.

Reece knelt so he was eye to eye with the banker.

"Sidney, I need you to think. When I go out that door, which way to the sauna?"

"Take a right. Keep the pool on your left. If you keep going you will run right into it. There is a cold-plunge room and a resting area down there as well."

"Stay here and wait for the police."

"What do I tell them?"

"Whatever you want."

Reece took a step in the direction of the lockers when he heard a fist pounding on the changing room door.

Default aggressive.

Reece grabbed his weapons and sprinted to the opposite side of the changing area. He chose his foot placement carefully, stepping on only the brown tiles not coated in blood.

Don't wait. Go.

Reece unlocked the dead bolt and threw open the door.

CHAPTER 59

A NAKED MAN COATED head to toe in drying blood is not what most people expect to see in the course of their daily travels, even if that person is an enforcer for the Russian mafia.

Reece clocked the Beretta 92F first, then the black jeans, white T-shirt, and black leather jacket. The pause at Reece's bloody appearance was all the former SEAL needed to step into grappling range and encircle the man's right arm with his left, the hand that held the towel and stone. Reece spun the man off balance and threw him into the wall to the side of the door, his peripheral vision confirming that they were alone in the pool room. The bloodied razor still had work to do.

The blade had been slightly dulled by the job it had done in the changing room, and it caught in the thick leather collar of the man's jacket.

Adapt!

Keeping the man's gun arm trapped, Reece turned the blade and shot the base of the handle into the man's left eye socket but was deflected by his opponent's left hand, which flew up in defense, causing Reece to drop the blade. The former SEAL pressed his attack, driving his right thumb into the corner of the Russian's eye closest to the nose to avoid the stronger muscles protecting it. Reece felt his thumb sink deep into the man's left eye socket, past the cornea and retina to hit the optic nerve.

A guttural roar emerged from the man's throat. Reece pulled his thumb from his eye socket and grabbed the back of his neck, yanking down while at the same time launching the top of his head into the man's nose. The intrusion of Reece's thumb and the blunt impact of the headbutt caused the man to loosen his grip on the pistol. Reece stepped slightly back, dropped his *trapo*, and ripped the Beretta from the Bratva man's grasp. He quickly locked it back at a position of retention, ensured the safety lever was up with his thumb, and pressed the trigger. The bullet ripped upward through the thoracic cavity, piercing both lungs. Parts of the mechanism were fouled by the target's clothing, which prevented Reece from taking a quick follow-up shot without running a malfunction drill. Reece wanted to avoid shooting again, even if he was one floor underground. One loud bang could be explained in a lot of people's minds among the commotion and constant construction of a big, loud city. Multiple gunshots were another story.

As the man opened his mouth in an attempt to breathe through collapsing lungs, Reece smashed his head backward with an open-hand strike under the chin and then followed it with the fouled Beretta, the muzzle striking him in the teeth. Reece then closed his hand around his throat, spun him to the left, and launched him into the pool.

Solve the problem, Reece.

Reece removed the magazine from the Beretta and racked the slide to the rear three times to clear the stoppage. Reinserting the magazine, he racked the slide again to chamber a round. He then performed a press check, pushed down the de-cocking lever with his thumb, and then flipped it back up, taking it off "safe." Kneeling, he picked up the razor, folded it, tucked it in his towel, and moved toward the sauna.

CHAPTER 60

REECE PUSHED HIMSELF ALONG the bathhouse wall, the Beretta leading the way.

As he approached the corner of the underground room, he read the signage on the doors ahead of him: SAUNA, *SHVITZ*, and COLD-PLUNGE POOL.

Don't kill Yevgenievich by accident. He's the key.

Reece advanced on the cold-plunge room and looked through the small glass window in the thick wooden door.

Is that him?

An older man sat semisubmerged in the water. He had short, buzzed gray hair and was covered in tattoos.

Could be.

Move, Reece.

Reece's left hand went to the doorknob and he entered the space, pistol at the ready.

Clear your corners.

The baseball bat connected high on Reece's right arm, sending a shock through his entire system. His pistol dropped to the floor.

His body recognized that his right hand was immobilized.

Temporarily? Or is it broken?

Doesn't matter.

New threat.

Fight!

Reece turned in time to see the bat coming toward his head. It was held by a large man resembling a grizzly. A towel was wrapped around his waist, and he was covered in tattoos.

Do not let him get ahold of you.

Too late.

Reece stepped in to avoid the full force of the blow, blocking the hit with his left forearm lower down on the bat.

One direct hit with this bat and you are done.

The new threat unexpectedly dropped his weapon and grabbed Reece in a bear hug, pinning his arms to his sides and throwing him up against the wall. Reece felt the air being crushed from his body. The large Russian reared his head back and smashed his forehead into the bridge of Reece's nose.

He then let Reece go, grabbing him by the neck and hitting him in the side of the head with a closed fist that almost put Reece out.

Fight it.

Yevgenievich is the key to putting an end to this; to ensuring Katie can live in peace.

This guy is untrained. He is used to relying on his size to intimidate. Use that to your advantage.

Reece's hands came up and slammed into the ears on both side of his aggressor's head, giving him the second he needed to drop to the slick, wet floor. The Russian shifted positions and squatted down to stabilize Reece with his left hand, drawing his massive right paw back and slamming it down. Reece defended with his legs and one arm while he did a quick function check on his hand that had taken the blow from the baseball bat. Life had returned to the appendage; it wasn't broken. Reece used his right hand to grab his opponent's ankle, allowing him to spin on his back to get his head out of the direct line of fire. Scrambling to his feet, Reece sent a side kick into the man's ribs and succeeded in knocking him back slightly, his towel falling to the floor.

Where's that Beretta?

Reece's eyes frantically searched the floor.

Unfazed by Reece's kick, the man threw a sloppy jab, followed by a rear uppercut and a lead uppercut. The blows were ineffective but did allow the monster to close the distance and grab Reece by the head, putting him into a guillotine choke. With Reece's head locked in the crook of his arm, the beast cranked upward, cutting off the air in Reece's windpipe.

You don't need the pistol. You've got something else.

The bloody razor had not yet claimed its last life.

Reece's hand went to the seam of the towel still snugly attached to his waist. Steadying himself with his left hand on the man's arm attached to his throat, Reece found the straight razor at his appendix, flipped it open with one hand, and cut the inside of the man's high femoral on each side. In the cold space with adrenaline pumping through his system, the man didn't feel the cuts that took his life. He kept applying pressure to Reece's neck. On the verge of blacking out, Reece reached through the man's legs, felt the crease of his right leg and butt cheek, twisted his wrist, and sliced deep into his upper thigh from behind, severing his sciatic nerve.

Reece felt the man let go of his neck, a guttural howl emerging from his lungs as he dropped to the deck, having lost all function in his right leg. Reece stepped around the dying creature, grabbed him under his chin, and cut his throat.

Reece turned back to the man in the cold bath, who had taken the opportunity to emerge from the tub and run to the door. Reece grabbed him by the back of the neck, turned the naked man around, and slammed him up against the door.

"You're not Yevgenievich. Where is he?"

"Fuck you, *cyka*," he responded, spitting in Reece's face.

"One last time. Where is he?"

"You are a *fucking* dead man. You better kill me now, because after this there is nowhere on earth you can hide. I'll kill your parents, your kids, your friends. And they won't just die. They will suffer. You got a wife, *cyka*? We will take extra care of her. We'll turn her into a little drug-addicted *blyad*—a *fucking* junkie whore. She'll be begging for more smack and more dick in this very building. All your doing, *cyka*. No one *fucks* with us."

Reece stared into his dark eyes. About sixty, he was thin compared to the monsters Reece had just put in the grave. Stars were tattooed across his chest, and his shoulders were decorated with epaulettes that reminded Reece of portraits he'd seen of Napoleon. Spiders crept out of the ornate shoulder pieces and were crawling up his neck. A woman with large breasts encircled with flowers was inked on his chest. She was surrounded by spires rising from a large cathedral piece on his stomach.

"We'll kill you last. You'll experience all their pain knowing you caused it. Go to hell, *cyka* bitch!"

"You first," Reece said, without a hint of emotion.

Reece yanked the smaller man from the wall and dragged him by the throat to the cold tub, heaving him up and into the freezing water. The gangster lost his breath as he was violently plunged into the icy liquid. Reece pushed his head down, pinning him underwater by his neck against the side of the tub, legs and arms thrashing, the frigid water splashing onto the floors and onto Reece's bloody body. Even after the gangster went limp, Reece kept him submerged, the vison of all those he loved being tortured and executed by the Russian mafia playing in his mind.

When Reece was sure the man was well past dead, he stood up and adjusted his towel. He retrieved the Beretta from the floor, ensuring it was still operational. Then he tucked the bloody blade in at his waist and exited back into the main room.

CHAPTER 61

REECE SURVEYED THE CAVERNOUS chamber. Most of the light came from the underground pool, a pool that now had a dead body floating in it, giving the space a ghostly blue iridescent glow. With its brick arches, tiles, and stone, it resembled a dungeon. Reece knew that in other parts of the building, young girls lived, barely surviving, in actual dungeons, drugged in rooms or cells not unlike his in solitary confinement.

Stay alert, Reece. Find Yevgenievich.

Reece turned to his right and continued down the dark wall to the sauna. A sign on the wall read SAUNAS OF LIFE. Without a window there was no way for Reece to know what awaited inside. He slowly opened the door, stepping to the side to clear it using the angles afforded him. It led into a small space with another door that Reece assumed was there to help contain heat. He stepped inside, already sweating profusely.

His hand went to the next door, and he swung it open, ready to go to work with the Beretta.

Instead of being met by a slew of bodyguards, the room was empty save for one man in a towel, sitting on a bench, leaning against a cedar wall. The walls on either side of him were stone. Bright yellow lights in the corners lit the space. It reminded Reece of a primal decompression chamber, which is exactly what it was.

Reece shut the door behind him and raised the pistol.

"Luka Yevgenievich," Reece stated.

The man opened his eyes, quickly masking his look of confusion with one of stern authority.

"Mr. Reece. Still alive? Perhaps I should hire you. You've taken out more of my men in the past two days than any rivals or government entities have in decades. Even so, we'll make an example of you."

"Something tells me you are not going to get the chance," Reece replied.

"My men were supposed to cut you into small pieces and feed you into the Atlantic. We will do that to your friends and family instead. Maybe make you watch. If you leave now, I'll make sure I kill you first. That's the best deal you'll get."

"Today is going to turn out differently than you'd planned," Reece replied.

"You are aware you can't touch me. I have an immunity deal with your government. And I am a U.S. citizen, if you can believe that."

"I know all about your deal, and unfortunately for you, I don't give a *fuck*."

Reece stepped forward and smashed the Beretta into the side of the mob boss's head, knocking him unconscious.

Reece bent down and positioned his left shoulder under Yevgenievich's chest, wrapping his left arm around his upper back. He then jerked up and rolled him onto his shoulder in a fireman's carry.

With the Beretta in his right hand, still clad only in a towel, and covered in the blood of the Bratva, Reece exited the sauna and made his way along the pool and up the stairs toward the light.

It was time to get his answers.

CHAPTER 62

IT HAD ONLY BEEN ten minutes, but it felt like an eternity for Raife to be sitting in the Jeep Cherokee, waiting for his friend. Luckily, cops in New York had more to worry about than a guy in an SUV parked outside a pizza place, probably waiting on a pie.

His head was on a constant swivel, scanning up and down the street and back up the steps to the Russian spa. He expected to see Reece emerge and walk down to the vehicle with Luka Yevgenievich, possibly with Sidney Morgan in tow. What he did not expect was to see the door burst open and a half-naked Reece, covered in blood, with a man in a towel slung over his shoulder, descend the steps and rush toward the vehicle.

"Bloody hell."

Raife hit the door-unlock button to ensure the rear door would open. His hand went to his Heirloom Precision 1911 under a shirt in the seat next to him, his eyes looking for any threats that might be behind his blood brother.

He could see Reece cradling a pistol as one would a football, fingers careful not to cover the muzzle, to obscure it from pedestrians on the sidewalk.

"Heart attack," Raife heard Reece say to a startled man in a blue suit as he passed him and reached for the door handle.

Raife lunged between the seats and opened the rear right passenger-side door, pushing it wide.

Reece tossed his package on the floor of the SUV and jumped in after him, pulling his legs inside so the door would shut.

"Go! Go! Go!" he shouted as Raife's foot pressed down on the accelerator and jettisoned them away from the curb.

Raife maneuvered through traffic and scanned the roadway ahead as Reece looked back. No one followed him out of the spa. For the moment it looked like they were clear.

"Reece, what the fuck, brother? Are you bleeding?"

"I don't think so. This is all other people's blood."

"Well, lie down back there so I don't get pulled over for transporting a zombie."

"Roger that," Reece replied, leaning onto his side and pressing Yevgenievich's head to the floor, ready to smash his skull with the Beretta if need be.

Raife pulled onto FDR Drive, keeping the East River on his right as he drove up the eastern side of Manhattan. Taking the George Washington Bridge into New Jersey, he then headed north back into New York State and merged onto Interstate 87 toward their destination.

When they were well out of the city, Raife exited at Monroe and parked at the far end of a Home Depot parking lot. Leaving Reece and the Russian in the Jeep, he entered the home improvement retailer with his shopping list. Fifteen minutes later he returned with zip-ties, a zip-tie gun, duct tape, a medical kit, a moving blanket, wet wipes, garbage bags, and an assortment of Carhartt pants and jackets.

While Raife stood guard, pretending to be on his cell phone, Reece zip-tied their prisoner and covered the ties with duct tape, which he also wrapped around his eyes and mouth. Only his nose allowed him to breathe. He attached a final zip-tie around Yevgenievich's neck and let him know that if he made any aggressive moves, Reece would simply pull on the plastic tie and take his life. It was a technique Reece knew worked well. He then covered the Bratva man with the moving blanket and cleaned himself as best he could with heavy-duty cleaning wipes before struggling into pants, a long-sleeve T-shirt, sweatshirt, socks, work boots, and a beanie. He deposited the bloody wet wipes and his towel in a large black trash bag and put it behind him in the cargo area. He then shoved the Beretta under the flannel-lined Carhartt jacket in the seat next to him and knocked on the window to let Raife know he was finished. He watched as Raife pulled the battery from his Alcatel burner phone and threw it and the phone into the bushes.

With Raife back behind the wheel, they continued their journey north.

"I let our friends know we have the package," Raife said, referring to Vic and Danreb.

"Good copy."

"Do they know where we're going?"

"No. Until we figure out who we can trust, that's staying between us."

"And K?"

"She's in the air on the way home," Raife said, keeping things cryptic in case the old man on the floor could hear with Reece's boot on his head.

"Good."

"That guy still breathing?" Raife asked.

Reece lifted his boot and pulled back the blanket.

"He's breathing," Reece responded, throwing the blanket back in place and placing his foot back on the side of his head.

CHAPTER 63

TWO HOURS NORTH OF New York City, just west of the Hudson River and north of the Ashokan Reservoir on the edge of the Indian Head Wilderness, lies one of the oldest organized clubs in America. Founded in the wake of the Civil War by two German businessmen who owned an exclusive sporting goods store in Manhattan, the club began as a place for like-minded men to escape the confines of the city and become familiar with rifles from Holland & Holland, Rigby, Westley Richards, Parker, and Purdey before embarking on hunting safaris to Africa. Christened "The Jäger Club," membership included presidents, generals, authors, and even the founders of the Boy Scouts of America. Unlike other exclusive clubs popping up on the East Coast, this one was not cost prohibitive. Dues were relatively inexpensive. But it was also a club that would not open its doors just because one could stroke a large check; one could not make a "donation" and buy their way in. This was a club for sportsmen. It was exclusive in that all those invited to join were hunters of big game. Anglers were added later on, as the property offered some of the best fishing in the Catskills. The membership roster remained classified and was kept in the same thick ledger that included the name of every member since 1872. No women would be found in the club's membership records, nor more recently was there a website or any presence on social media, or even any mentions in the hunting magazines. The club stayed out of the spotlight and therefore did not have to deal with the negative publicity as did their Bohemian Grove counterparts in California. It did not matter if you were a carpenter or the CEO of Goldman Sachs: hunting, fishing, conservation, and a genuine love of the outdoors were what drew people to the club. It was by invitation only.

The grounds included a rifle and pistol range; trap, skeet, and sporting clays; a lake; a communal clubhouse; and a few small cabins owned by individual members. There was water and electricity in the clubhouse and in the caretaker's home, but, per the club bylaws, cabins were limited to 1927 technology. A few members had installed water tanks and generators over the years, but for the most part the small cabins remained as they were up until the early twentieth century. Any additions had to maintain the look and feel of the original. As such, the doorways were low and the insides dark and musty. All of them had stone fireplaces to ward off the cold.

The clubhouse sported a full bar, and for weekend events a chef and bartender were brought in from Manhattan to keep members fed and happy. Cigars, pipes, and cigarettes were smoked without guilt, and the whiskey flowed freely. Talking business or networking was prohibited. Politics, however, was fair game, though most members fell on the capitalist, libertarian, and/or conserative side of the spectrum. Now, as then, the grounds were a peaceful place to enjoy nature, easily accessible from the city, where men could eat, drink, smoke, fish, and shoot without the threat of intrusion by wives or girlfriends.

On the classified list of current members was the name Jonathan Hastings, Raife's father.

The two SEALs had not been to the club since college, when Jonathan had invited the two boys and Reece's dad to the annual Outing, a father-son competition in the woods of upstate New York. Tom had impressed everyone and walked away with the top scores in canoeing, bait and fly casting, pistol, rifle, and shotgun events, and even a woodsman fire-making contest. Tom and Jonathan became fast friends, a friendship that lasted up until Tom's death.

Former United States senator Tim Thornton, a close friend of the Hastings family, was a member as well—a member with a cabin.

Jonathan had made the arrangements and alerted the caretaker that Reece and Raife would be arriving that evening and staying in Thorn's cabin. He got the new gate combination and passed it to his only son. No one else would be on the property, and "the boys," as the caretaker called them, would have the run of the place.

It was after dark when Raife pulled off the thruway and took the winding back roads to the club's entrance. Reece stayed in the car with their package as Raife dialed in the code, popped open the shackle on the brass Master Lock, and swung open the gate. He then returned to the vehicle and drove onto the property, stopping to close and lock the gate behind them before continuing past the caretaker's house and weaving up the dirt lanes until they arrived at the cabin where they had stayed back in college.

Raife turned off the engine, putting them in almost pitch blackness.

"You ready?" he asked.

"Let's do it," Reece replied.

"I'll go check it out. Stay here."

Raife exited the vehicle and approached the small log cabin. Reece watched him rummage in a woodpile next to the door for the key and go inside. A few minutes later Reece saw the windows light up with the warm blaze of kerosene lamps.

Reece opened the rear passenger door and yanked Yevgenievich out by his zip-tied feet. Raife emerged from the cabin and helped carry the bound and gagged Russian gangster inside. They set him in an old leather recliner positioned next to a two-person sofa across from the fireplace. They cut his zip-ties and strapped him to the recliner with duct tape around his chest, arms, and legs. He was completely immobilized.

Vintage hunting books, boxes of ammunition, fishing rods, and taxidermy filled the space. A black bear rug was draped over the back of the couch, its head and teeth positioned in a vicious snarl only a foot from their prisoner's.

Even with multiple kerosene lamps blazing, the two small rooms were cast in shadows.

"I'll get a fire going," Raife said. "It will help light this place up."

"While you do that, toss me another burner phone. I need to make a call."

Reece stepped outside with the phone and placed a call to Andy Danreb.

"Yes?"

"It's me. We have him."

"Are you sure you want to do this?"

"I don't think there's a choice. I need to know a little more about this guy, and I need you to talk me through an interrogation technique I read about the Soviets using in Gulags."

CHAPTER 64

WHEN REECE HIT "END" on the call, he looked down at the phone. Then he removed the battery and tossed it back in the car before reentering the cabin.

"Still alive?" Reece asked.

"I can see him breathing," Raife responded.

"I know he can hear me," Reece said. "I'm going to try 'good cop' first. Then, if he doesn't cooperate, I'm going to get answers. You don't have to be here for it. You can wait outside."

"We are in it together now, brother. Let's get those answers and put an end to this."

Reece looked at his friend. He knew that Raife would do anything to protect his family. Reece also knew that he and Katie fell into that category.

"All right, then. I'll take lead. Can you see if there is another first aid or trauma kit in here? I'm going to need a tourniquet or two and as many ACE bandages as you can find. A kitchen knife, flashlight, some rope, and wire cutters if you can find them."

As Raife rummaged through cabinets, Reece pulled an old wicker-backed chair in front of his detainee. He then moved an oak coffee table from in front of the fire next to him and laid out the tools he might need to extract information from a hardened Bratva leader. He arranged the zip-ties and zip-tie gun on the table so Yevgenievich would be able to see them when they pulled off the duct tape.

Raife returned and placed his Snakestaff Systems tourniquet and three North American Rescue Combat Application Tourniquets from the medical kits next to the zip-ties, along with a long Maglite, wire cutters, a kitchen knife, a bundle of 550 cord, and four ACE bandages.

Even with the flickering light from the fireplace to Reece's back and the glow of the lamps, it was still difficult to see. He would have to make do.

He nodded to Raife, who went to work removing the duct tape from the Russian's head, revealing first his eyes and then pulling it from his mouth as Reece undid his towel and threw it in a corner. Yevgenievich was left naked and secured to the chair. Reece watched as he looked around the room through narrow eyes, taking in the moose, mountain lion, mule deer, whitetail, and elk that were occupying every inch of the space. He came eye to eye with the bear on the sofa back to his left.

"Where am I?"

"As I am sure you can appreciate, you are not really in a position to ask questions," Reece responded.

Raife stood behind the prisoner so his presence could be felt but he could not be seen or heard.

"You are still a dead man, as are all those you care about," the Russian said.

"We seem to have a misunderstanding," Reece said. "I know a lot about you, as I am sure you know a lot about me. I am going to break one of the cardinal rules of interrogation and start by asking you a question I don't know the answer to: Why try to kill me in the spa? Did your handlers in Moscow not want the files I have? I'm sure they told you about those."

"*Moscow*," Yevgenievich said with disdain. "They do not *handle* me. You know my arrangement with your government. You are breaking that contract. I am valuable to them. Our deal still stands. Let me go now and I'll kill you before I kill your family, to save you the pain."

"Luka, I understand you have a young girlfriend. How old is she? Nineteen? Twenty?" Reece said, using the information from his phone call with Danreb.

Yevgenievich's face hardened.

Reece picked up the zip-tie gun and set it to the "firm" setting. He pulled the trigger so that the Russian could see what he was doing. The gun clicked with each pull of the trigger, creating what looked like a ring. It then cut the zip-tie. Reece held the small ring in front of his prisoner.

"I am going to explain how this works. You might be familiar with this interview technique, as it originated in your home country. You may have even used it. The Soviets were the masters of reversible torture," Reece explained. "I'm not telling you anything you don't already know. The Chinese were good, but you guys took it to an entirely new level."

Reece reached down and pulled one of Yevgenievich's fingers straight. His hand was still secured in place by the duct tape, but his fingers were free. Reece placed the zip-tie over the Russian's left index finger and pulled the trigger until the plastic band was tight around his finger like a ring.

"That's one finger, Luka. In about fifteen minutes it's going to be excruciatingly painful. In an hour it will be about a twenty on a one-to-ten scale, and there will be no saving it."

Reece pulled out the index finger on the prisoner's right hand and applied another zip-tie. He could already tell Yevgenievich was getting uncomfortable contemplating life without both index fingers. He was playing on the Russian male fear of being dependent.

"You think any of your girlfriends are going to want to wipe your ass and feed you applesauce for the rest of your life?" Reece continued, moving the zip-tie gun to his left thumb. "Opposable thumbs, Luka. I'm sure you know how important those are. If you had any question, you are about to find out," Reece said, securing the zip-tie in place. "Now, my next question is, how crippled do you want to be?"

Reece could see the sweat building on the Russian's temples as he contemplated his situation.

"Don't think too long; these thumbs are not going to save themselves," Reece said, cinching down a zip-tie on the other thumb. "The only thing that is going to keep them attached to your body is you telling me what I want to know. Did Moscow order you to kill me?"

"Whether I live or die, it doesn't matter. You are a dead man, as is every single person you care about. *Fuck you!*"

Reece leaned forward and used the zip-tie gun to apply plastic cables to Yevgenievich's middle fingers.

"Luka, as you can tell, I don't have time to build rapport and draw this out, so I am going to get to the point. Did you ever notice all the amputees in pictures from the Gulag days? They are disproportionate to the number of accidents associated with the mining and industrial projects you forced upon them as enemies of the state. In reality, they came from situations just like this. Purges. Political prisoners disloyal to Stalin would find themselves missing arms and legs after interrogation."

"Spare me the history lesson."

"History is important, Luka. It provides context," Reece continued, leaning down to cinch zip-ties to both of his prisoner's big toes. "In this case it provides lessons. If you want to remain out of twenty-four/seven care for the rest of your life, you will consider that context. You still have your deal with the U.S. government. Talk with me and you just might walk out of here. Choose to fuck around, you are going to get wheeled out. By the way, without your big toes, balancing becomes quite difficult. You are on the clock."

Yevgenievich's eyes darted around the room, searching.

"I don't have the answers you want."

"Then you are in for a long night."

"Did Moscow order me to kill you? No. And you calling it 'Moscow' tells me all I need to know. You don't know shit, *cyka*. It's bigger than you. It's bigger than me. You are about to get squashed. You are nothing more than a bug to these people."

"Who are 'these people'?"

"You've got as much as you are going to get. You might as well kill me now."

Reece studied the man before him. Even a Russian mob boss would rather die than talk about the Collective.

"Suit yourself," Reece said, picking up an ACE bandage and the knife from the table beside him.

Reece sliced through the duct tape securing Yevgenievich's right leg to the recliner, set it on his shoulder, and stood up like he was executing a squat.

The Russian attempted to struggle but Reece locked his leg in place straight up. He then began to wrap the leg as tightly as he could with the ACE bandage.

"You've escalated things to the next level, Ivan," Reece said, intentionally using the wrong first name. "While you think about life without your fingers and toes, let me tell you about what's happening now. I am forcing most of the blood from your leg. It's draining into the rest of your body."

Reece reached down and threw the 550 cord to Raife, who looped it around Yevgenievich's foot and pulled back to keep his leg in the vertical position. Reece then applied a tourniquet to the Russian's upper thigh, twisting the windlass down as tight as he could.

"Usually we use these things to save lives," Reece explained. "We are doing the opposite in your case. You have about forty-five minutes until you lose your digits. Your leg will take about two hours, but you will start begging me to kill you way before then. Now, tell me about these people who want to squash me like a bug."

Yevgenievich shook his head in an attempt to cement his resolve.

"The NKVD, Stalin's secret police, would sometimes put pads under the tourniquets," Reece continued. "That way there would be no marks. As you can tell, I'm not concerned with that. I'm more concerned with pain. About forty-five minutes is the record, from what I understand."

"What do you mean?" the Russian asked.

"To get someone to talk. The pain was so acute, by forty-five minutes the NKVD would have gotten what they wanted—usually names of collaborators and others who were disloyal to Stalin. Then they would arrest a new batch of traitors and do the same to them. All to protect the party. I am not protecting the party. I am protecting those I love, the very people you keep threatening. Don't think for a moment we won't break records tonight."

Reece reached down and cut the duct tape securing Yevgenievich's left leg to the chair and applied another ACE bandage and tourniquet in the same way he had with the right leg.

"In the interest of time, I'm going to do the same to your arms," Reece said.

He cut the tape, first on the left arm and then on the right, holding each arm up to drain the blood and then force it all the way out with the application of ACE bandages. He then applied the final two tourniquets six inches above each elbow. Raife threw a strand of 550 cord over the rafter to keep the arms extended over Yevgenievich's head.

"You look pathetic," Reece said, stepping back to assess his prisoner, once again digging into the Russian's psyche. "You are naked, alone, and about to be in more pain than you have ever imagined. And that's before you lose your arms and legs. I doubt you will be of much use to the Bratva or this so-called Collective after that. I almost feel bad for you. But then I think about the young girls you have locked up around the country, the abuse, the prostitution, the organ harvesting. When I think about that, I don't feel so bad."

Yevgenievich's face had begun to show real fear. He was no longer the defiant gangster of the sauna room. He was realizing his greatest fears at the hands of the American.

"There is one part of you I haven't taken yet," Reece said, nodding to the area between the Russian's legs. "Now, tell me about the Collective."

Sinking into the most vulnerable of states, the Russian's pain receptors had already begun firing to a degree he had not known was possible.

"The Collective," Yevgenievich stammered. "It's only whispered about. Even in Bratva circles."

"Who are they?"

"That's just it. No one knows. Is it me? Is it our president? Is it your president? That is their power. No one knows. Some say I am a part of them, and I may be, though it's only a small part. I know I've gone as high as I can go in our organization, but I am also useful to both our governments."

"You keep talking in riddles and I'm going to use that zip-tie gun to attach a cable to your cock and balls. Now, why would you try to kill me if you were ordered not to?"

"Why do you think? You killed my men in the streets of Boston. That's not good for business. You had to be dealt with. Sometimes men like Levitsky don't understand that."

"Who's Levitsky?"

"The new head of the SVR."

Reece nodded, thinking of when Levitsky dumped the body of his predecessor in the bushes of Gorky Park.

"Is he a part of this collective?"

"I don't know. Sometimes high-level intelligence officers are brought into the fold. Other times not. It depends on their level of usefulness."

Sweat was flowing down the man's face, dripping onto his chest. The woman tattooed to his chest appeared to be crying.

"What did Levitsky ask of you?"

"He wanted me to get a file or files from you. He told me to do whatever it took. *Fuck* Levitsky. No one kills my men without retribution."

"And the man in black?"

"Who?"

"The other man who was with me in Boston."

"Ah, he lives?"

"He does. He left your men to die."

"I don't know. They say he is German. An assassin used from time to time."

"How do you know?"

"I've supplied him weapons in the past."

"What kind of weapons?"

"He always asks for a nine-millimeter."

"Now, Luka, this is important: Why the hurry to acquire these documents?"

The Russian shook his head. "You Americans, so naive and foolish. You believe the world revolves around you. Can't you figure it out?"

"What do you mean?"

"Something big is on the horizon. Something that's unstoppable."

"An attack? Against the United States?"

"For that you will have to go higher up the chain."

"What chain? Acquaint me with them."

"That, you'll never know."

Reece could tell the Russian was fighting through unimaginable pain. He reached out and felt for radial pulses in the legs and arms.

"No pulses in any of your extremities, Luka. That's a bad sign. How's the pain?"

"*Fuck you!*" Yevgenievich spat out.

Reece thought of his father's letter, his conversations with Poe, Dan-reb, and Vic.

There is one piece that as of this writing remains missing. One link that remains elusive.

"He was convinced he had almost everything he needed, but he was always missing that one final piece."

"Who do you have inside?"

"What? Make sense," the Russian spat.

"Who does Russian intelligence or the Collective have in U.S. intelligence circles?"

"You don't get it. He's everywhere and nowhere."

"I warned you about riddles. I was really hoping to avoid this," Reece said.

He picked up the zip-tie gun and held it in front of the Russian's face.

"Last chance."

"I don't know anything else. *Fuck you!*"

"Luka, I lost my family years ago. I survived. I'm not going to lose those I care about to you, to the Collective, the Bratva, Russian intelligence, or anyone else. Believe me when I tell you, there is nothing I will not do to keep them safe."

"Too late for that, American. You are a walking dead man, as is your friend behind me, his family, your family. You are all *fucked*."

Reece thought of Jonathan and Caroline Hastings; Raife, his wife, Annika, and their son; Katie, Vic, Danreb, Poe.

"When I said last chance, I meant it," Reece said, leaning forward and pulling the Russian's penis and testicles through the loop of the zip-tie gun.

"No! No! No!" the Russian yelled, thrashing his head back and forth while attempting to free his arms and legs, movement that just increased the agonizing sensations in his extremities.

Reece's finger went to the trigger, and he pressed backward.

The thin plastic cable tightened against the soft flesh between Yevgenievich's legs, and the Bratva man let loose an animalistic scream that pierced the night.

The zip-tie gun cut the tie, leaving a thin, tight ring affixed to the Russian's manhood.

"Cyprus," he said.

"What?"

"Cyprus. They meet on Cyprus. *Take it off!*"

"Tell me more."

"They've met on Cyprus in the past. I was there once. Maybe they were going to pull me further in. I don't know. They have rooms, vaults with all their money, gold, silver, diamonds, art. All the oligarchy shit. They can't communicate through emails and texts, so they meet."

"When and where?"

"I told you where, you dumb *fuck*! Cyprus. And I don't know when."

"Where *exactly* on Cyprus?"

"I don't *fucking* know. Take this off!" he screamed, spit flying from his mouth, his eyes in a frenzied rage.

That's not enough. I'm going to need more, Reece thought. *That might be all this guy has to offer.*

Reece looked at his former Teammate, who shook his head.

"How many of them are there?"

"I don't know. No one knows. Thirty? Forty? Fuck, maybe fifty. Get this thing off my dick!"

"And a mole at Langley? Who does the Collective have on the inside?"

The man's head dropped, using what strength he had left to fight—the zip-tie cinched as tight as it could go around his manhood, making resistance futile.

"Please," he sobbed. "The secret to the mole is that he's a part of the Collective. That's all I know. Please."

The man had been reduced to his most vulnerable state. He was broken.

Reece picked up the wire cutters and not-so-carefully snipped the zip-tie from the Russian's genitals.

"You are still a dead man," Yevgenievich said between labored breaths that betrayed the pain in his arms and legs.

Reece placed his hands on either side of the recliner's armrests and leaned forward, bringing his face within inches of the Russian's.

"I want you to know that you failed. Your organization is going down. I'm going to burn it to the ground."

"You are nothing. I'll see you and yours tortured and killed. I'll make you fucking watch," he said, regaining a sliver of strength with the zip-tie removed from between his legs.

"I don't think so," Reece replied, reaching up to undo the tourniquets attached to his legs and then his arms, tossing them to the table.

"Why's that, American?"

"Because you'll be dead."

Reece watched as the Russian's smile faded. Releasing all four tourniquets at once flooded his body with built-up lactic acid, sending him into cardiac arrest. With his arms and legs still tied in position with the 550 cord, he couldn't bring his hands to a chest that felt like it was being crushed by a semitruck. Blood continued circulating in his brain well past the time his heart stopped pumping. His last vision was of his executioner standing over him, not a hint of emotion visible in his brown eyes.

• • •

"Reece?"

Reece remained standing, frozen in place.

"Reece," Raife said again softly. "You okay?"

Reece looked up from the dead Russian.

"I just don't know if it's enough."

"Maybe combined with what Danreb can get from Morgan's files?" Raife offered.

"Maybe."

"He wouldn't have stopped coming for us, Reece. *You* know that. *I* know that."

Reece's eyes connected with those of his blood brother.

"I know. Now, let's clean up and make this fucker disappear."

CHAPTER 65

The Kremlin
Moscow, Russia

LOCATED IN THE CENTER of Moscow along the banks of the Moskva River, surrounded by a defensive perimeter wall bordering Red Square, and within a stone's throw of St. Basil's Cathedral lies the Kremlin. Meaning "fortress inside a city," that is exactly what it is. During the Cold War it had become synonymous with *Moscow, Russia*, and *the Soviets*. Officially it was the residence of the Russian president, though he rarely visited. The de facto presidential residence was in an estate in Novo-Ogaryovo, just west of the capital. He did maintain an office in the Kremlin Senate, with offices off-limits to anyone not on the presidential staff or officially designated by the president himself.

The three senior members of the Security Council met in an office across from the president's on the third floor and took a hidden stairway down to the basement, where they entered a chamber designed to be impervious to outside listening devices. A pitcher of water was set in the center of a rectangular table, along with three glasses. The floors and walls were made of cement. It was rumored the room could withstand a first-strike nuclear detonation, though no one really knew, nor did anyone want to find out.

Chairman Kozak took his seat at the head of the table. Directors Dashkov and Levitsky sat to his right and left.

"The president has given his approval," Kozak said. "Do you have any objections?"

"Where is the device now?" Dashkov asked.

"That Rosatom facility in Zarechny. It will be transported to Khmeimim Air Base in Syria tomorrow. Then on to Cyprus, where we will await weather conditions to be favorable before launch."

Dashkov longed for the Turkish tobacco of his pipe.

"Chairman, as you are aware, an offensive nuclear weapon has not been detonated, other than in tests, since the Americans hit Japan in 1945," he said. "Our collective was created in part to avert a nuclear war, and now, in a matter of days, we plan to start one."

Levitsky remained silent. This was a conversation between Kozak and Dashkov.

"But it won't be us starting it, comrade," Kozak said. "It will be the Iranians."

"And if we are discovered?"

"In that case, we have a crazy colonel running Wagner Group in an unsanctioned operation."

"The Americans will know, Chairman. At the very least they will have their suspicions."

"Even if they do, it will not matter, Director Dashkov. The United States recently designated Wagner as a significant transnational criminal organization in an attempt to restrict travel and freeze assets. The Americans will say Wagner was acting at the behest of the president, but it won't stick. We will bombard them with disinformation and misinformation campaigns. The world media already thinks Wagner is a mercenary organization. Those campaigns will play right into that narrative. In just a matter of days, we give the Americans exactly what they want—another war in the Middle East. Their defense industry lobbyists will guide the political rhetoric, it will boost ratings for cable news networks struggling to find audiences, and the admirals and generals will fall in line, as they always do. We are actually giving them a war they can win—a war they've trained for. They are eager to forget their failures in Iraq and Afghanistan. With added pressure from the Zionist lobby, the Americans will not be able to resist. They won't want to know the truth. All they want is a war."

"I concur," Levitsky said. "All is in place. We stand at the cusp of a new era in our history. We might not get this chance again."

"There is another issue," Kozak said.

"Oh?" Levitsky asked.

"The American, James Reece."

"He is being disposed of as we speak, Chairman," Levitsky said with confidence.

"No, he is not. Seven bodies were recently discovered in the 1917 Spa in New York. None of them was James Reece."

"How do you know this?"

"I too have my sources, Director Levitsky."

"Was Luka Yevgenievich among them?"

"He was not, but he is currently unaccounted for."

Levitsky sat back in his chair.

How did Kozak know so much?

"Those documents unearthed by the son, if they are what our source indicates, expose the Collective's ties to U.S. intelligence," Kozak stated. "We don't know how extensive they are, but we will soon."

"Chairman?" Levitsky asked.

"Our asset on the inside will make them disappear, even at risk of exposure. In the meantime, the mission must go forward. It is time."

Kozak looked at the two men whose consent he needed to commence the operation.

"It is time," Levitsky repeated.

"And you, Director Dashkov?"

The FSB director nodded.

"*Da.* But take caution. 'Be not deceived, God is not mocked: for whatsoever a man soweth, that shall he also reap.'"

"Not very Marxist of you, comrade, so close to Lenin's Tomb."

"That very tomb sits in the shadows of the great cathedrals, Chairman. There is wisdom in those words. You are looking for my support—you have it, and the full resources of the SVR. Just grant me one courtesy."

"Which is?"

"Wait until the wind is blowing south."

PART FOUR

ATONEMENT

What's done cannot be undone.

—WILLIAM SHAKESPEARE, *MACBETH*, ACT 5, SCENE 1

CHAPTER 66

White House Situation Room
Washington, D.C.

PRESIDENT GALE OLSEN WAS already seated at the head of the long rectangular table when Reece entered the room. Reece had contacted Vic on the drive south after burying Luka Yevgenievich on a remote section of the Jäger Club grounds and taking a lukewarm shower in Thorn's cabin to clean up once they figured out how to get the generator running. Reece assumed their destination would be Danreb's house in Westport to compare notes, but he had been told to divert. Someone else wanted to talk with him—the president of the United States.

They had stopped at the entrance to an alley off the 1500 block of H Street, just two blocks from 1600 Pennsylvania Avenue, per Vic's instructions. They made eye contact with a Secret Service officer stationed in a drive-through bank teller–type glass enclosure built into the side of a red English-bond brick building. He hit a button, lowering the red anti-ram wedge barrier into the ground and raising the white-and-red-striped drop-arm gate. Raife was driving and slowly pulled past the barriers and a yellow traffic light that looked at least thirty years out of date. They were waved to the end of the narrow alley, where they were met by four new uniformed Secret Service officers and two agents in suits and sunglasses. Three of the uniformed officers carried Heckler & Koch MP5s. The fourth had a Belgian Malinois that circled the vehicle on a leash, sniffing for explosives.

As Reece and Raife opened their doors and stepped from the vehicle, one of the agents held up a hand.

"Just him," he said, pointing at Reece. "You can wait here."

Reece glanced at his blood brother, glad they had hidden their weapons in the backseat, since they were breaking numerous laws just having handguns in the District of Columbia.

"I'll be back."

"I'll be waiting," Raife responded.

"ID," the agent said to Reece.

Reece handed him his Montana driver's license. The agent examined it and inserted it into a card reader that scanned its information and transmitted it to the Secret Service JOC in their nearby headquarters building.

"Okay," the agent said, handing Reece back his ID.

Reece was impressed with the rapid confirmation he could tell the agent received back through his earpiece.

"They need to wand you."

"No problem," Reece said, holding out his arms as one of the uniformed officers slung his submachine gun and stepped forward with a handheld metal detector.

Reece was still dressed in the Carhartt boots, pants, and sweatshirt they had picked up at Home Depot. The wand beeped over the metal grommets of his boots and at the zipper and front button of his pants. The officer did a quick pat-down of those areas and then nodded to the lead agent.

"Follow me, Mr. Reece," he said, opening a nondescript door at the end of the alley.

Reece fell into step behind the lead agent. The second agent took up a trail position.

"What is this place?" Reece asked as they stepped into a hallway and then through another door to a ramp leading down into a dimly lit tunnel.

"One of the worst-kept secrets in Washington," the lead agent said. "You just stepped through a back door to Freedman's Bank. It used to be the Treasury Department Annex."

The downward-sloping passageway opened into a tunnel where two additional agents joined them.

"This how they used to get Marilyn in?" Reece asked.

"That's classified," the lead agent responded without missing a beat.

Reece couldn't tell if he was joking.

"You've been asked that before, haven't you?" Reece asked.

"Every time we do this."

The tunnel ended at another door that opened into the White House's underground parking garage. From there, Reece was escorted to the "WHIZZER"—the White House Situation Room. The agent opened the door for Reece and then posted up outside, along with the other agents.

Reece wasn't quite sure of the protocol for meeting the leader of the free world in the building that had been home to every president since John Adams. He had first met with Alec Christensen at Camp David in a much less formal setting. This was the opposite.

Reece paused momentarily as he entered the room. It was much smaller than he'd expected. The Presidential Seal, affixed to the wall behind Gale Olsen, left no question as to where one stood. There was one decision maker in the White House Situation Room, and she had been on the job for only three months.

Six black leather swivel chairs lined the table. Four of them were occupied. Reece recognized the new interim director of the CIA, General Marcus Howe, sitting to the president's left. Dressed in a gray suit and without a military regulation haircut, he looked more like a college professor. To her right was Vic Rodriguez. Reece was not surprised to see Vic or Howe, but he was surprised to see Danreb and Poe.

They stopped talking and looked up at their visitor. Sensing the tension, President Olsen stood and walked to greet the former SEAL, extending her hand.

"Commander Reece, I'm Gale Olsen. Thank you for joining us."

"Madam President," Reece said.

She was dressed in a conservative black pantsuit and white blouse with a United States flag pin on her left lapel. Reece remembered that she hailed from Florida's 9th Congressional District, was of Danish-Cuban descent, and had retained her rank of major in the Army National Guard JAG Corps even while serving in Congress. Reece guessed she was probably a lieutenant colonel by now. She leaned heavily left, which had helped balance Christensen's more libertarian views and strong capitalist tendencies. She had delivered Florida and then largely been relegated to the sidelines following the inauguration. She was now the commander in chief of the most powerful military on earth.

"I understand you knew President Christensen quite well."

"I did," Reece said, remembering the former president pouring them bourbons in Aspen Cabin at Camp David.

"Please accept my sincere condolences," she said with a candor Reece found himself thinking would be impossible to contrive, even for a politician.

"And you mine," Reece responded.

"Please," the president said, gesturing to a chair next to Andy Danreb.

The president and Reece took their seats.

"I think you know everyone here except Director Howe," she said.

"Commander Reece," he said. "We knew a few of the same people at SOCOM and JSOC. They all speak very highly of you."

"Thank you, General. I know you by reputation. I was a little further down the food chain during our time in Iraq and Afghanistan. I did watch your congressional testimony. You were the only officer who told them the truth in twenty years."

"And look where it got me," he said, turning to look at the president.

"I apologize for the cloak-and-dagger entrance," the president said, once again taking control of the conversation. "That first tunnel dates back to 1919 as a way for the Treasury to move cash without having to venture outside and risk getting robbed. The other tunnel was built for FDR shortly after Pearl Harbor to get him to a bomb shelter. They tell me he only went down there once and hated it so much he swore off ever going back, even if Germany or Japan bombed the city."

"It's good to have options," Reece said.

"I agree," the president responded. "Now to the business at hand. You are probably wondering what you are doing here."

"It had crossed my mind."

"Director Howe," she said, nodding at the senior ranking intelligence official.

"Commander Reece," he began.

"'Reece' is fine, sir."

"Reece, as you can discern, we are living in unusual and unprecedented times. This here," he said, pushing a stack of papers in front of him closer to the center of the table, "this is an unredacted copy of the President's Commission on the Assassination of President Christensen."

"Are you going to release it?"

"We are."

"Unredacted?"

"We are still debating."

"Why?"

Howe looked at the president, who nodded.

"This report was compiled with the assistance of what I'll call our most advanced quantum computer."

Alice.

"It is quite clear that the assassination was planned by an outside entity. The shooter was just a patsy. He was radicalized online by a virtual network connected to the Spetssviaz—Russia's NSA. He was set up and manipulated into firing shots at President Christensen—all ineffective."

"They weren't meant to be effective," Reece said.

"That's right. The point of those shots was not to kill the president but to trigger a Secret Service contingency plan that would put the president's vehicle on a route lined with EFPs. Unfortunately, it worked."

"Who put them in place?"

"Iraqis that the CIA trained in-country as part of our covert action program."

Reece lowered his head. "I worked with that unit."

"We know, and we think that played into this plan as well. It was another connection between you and the assassination."

"So, the Russians turned them early, let us recruit them, train them, and fight with them. And when we withdrew, we gave them the option to come back to the United States in exchange for their service."

"This report makes that clear," Howe said. "One was still in the employ of Langley as an interpreter at headquarters."

"Where are they now?" Reece asked, though he already knew the answer.

"They died before we could bring them in for questioning: fentanyl overdose, a robbery-homicide, and a suicide. From what we know so far, all three had contact with a former GRU lieutenant colonel named Andrei Sokoloff, who is now the CEO of the Wagner Group."

"Why frame me?"

"We have been discussing that with Mr. Rodriguez, Mr. Danreb, and Mr. Poe," Howe continued.

"It is also why this group is so small," the president interjected. "My national security advisor, DNI, and White House counsel are all noticeably absent, at the request of Director Howe. They all about had coronaries when I told them, but that is one of the perks of being the president. Your staff has to do what you say. Please continue, Director."

"We think it has to do with this 'Collective' mentioned in the documents Mr. Danreb just briefed. If the highest levels of American and Russian intelligence services are compromised by a group with an agenda of their own, we have an entirely new issue with which to contend."

"My mission is first and foremost the safety and security of the American people," President Olsen said. "If we are compromised, until we are certain whom we can trust, our working group is going to remain confined to those at this table. If Mr. Danreb is correct and this Collective is planning a Black Swan event to manipulate markets with the goal of causing a shift in power on a geopolitical scale, then it's something an order of magnitude more devastating than anything we have seen in our lifetimes."

"Reece, what did you and Raife find out from Sidney Morgan?" Vic asked.

"We confirmed he runs finances for this Collective group. We sent the client list to Andy," Reece said, nodding at Danreb.

"It's going to take some time to unravel," the Russia analyst said. "The owners of the accounts are all hidden behind multiple shell corporations. If I had some help from the quantum computer you mentioned, it would speed up the process."

Howe looked at the president.

"Unfortunately, that computer is offline," he said. "But come back to Langley and we can set you up with the tools you need."

"There is something else," Reece said.

"What is it?" Vic asked.

"We had a conversation with one of Morgan's clients, a Luka Yevgenievich."

"A conversation?" Howe asked.

"Yes," Reece responded. "He was not overly forthcoming, but did confirm the existence of this Collective and that they have someone on the inside at the Agency."

"Damn it!" Howe said. "Is Yevgenievich part of the Collective?"

"He said some of the affiliations are more tangential. He's not part of the core group, but he's connected to them for business and intelligence-gathering purposes. He confirmed that some sort of event, possibly a Black Swan, is on the horizon, though he didn't know specifics."

"Sounds talkative," Vic said.

"It's amazing what a little vodka will do. He also mentioned Cyprus."

At the mention of Cyprus, all heads shot up.

"What did I say?" Reece asked as the group exchanged glances.

"That, lad, is what I am doing here," Poe said, speaking for the first time.

"I don't understand."

"Reece," Vic began, "our officers posted around the globe continue to check legacy dead-drop sites, even after an asset, a spy, has gone cold. Frequency depends on freedom of movement and access. Our station in Moscow checks dead-drop locations dating back to the 1970s. One used from 1986 to 2001 recently went active."

"And?"

"Here is where it gets interesting. The original asset who used that location passed away in 2010. It was a good spot and Moscow Station surmised that it wasn't burned, so they added it to a list of locations for future use. Another asset was recruited in 2017 who didn't provide anything of substance and went dark only a few months into the relationship. That same dead drop was utilized, so it was checked from 2017 through last week."

"And?"

"And the person using it isn't the asset from 2017."

"How do we know?"

"The system set up to initiate a meet was a blue-colored tack pushed into the underside of a bench. In this case, our officer removed the tack and later examined it back at the embassy. It was silver, so he went into old records and found that a silver tack was used by an agent recruited back in 1986."

"Who?" Reece asked.

"Natalia Borisova," Poe interjected. "A secretary for various senior-level executives at the KGB, FSK, and the FSB. She came to us after Chernobyl. She exposed much of the cover-up surrounding the incident. She was one of my assets."

"But she passed away over a decade ago. So who made contact?" Reece asked.

"Her name is Kira Borisova. Natalia's daughter. She used the same dead drop I taught her mother to use."

"But her daughter isn't on the payroll."

"No. She's Pavel Dashkov's secretary. He's the director of the FSB. Her mother must have set her on the path."

"Do we know why she's reaching out?"

"Only in part. We set up a meeting as per the established protocols. That led to the next meeting in a location of her choosing—a loud nightclub. She says she has information that is of vital importance to the future of both our nations."

"But she didn't pass it along?"

"No. She wants something in return."

"What?"

"An extraction. She wants to defect."

"Well, let's get her out," Reece said.

"It's not as easy as it sounds, Reece. Pulling an asset out of Moscow right now, with the additional security and tensions over Ukraine, has sensitivities attached that need to be considered. The officer who met with her said that she is spooked. She's also leaving the country on official travel with Dashkov, and she trusts only one person to get her out."

"Who?" Reece asked.

Vic nodded across the table.

"William Poe."

"I'm getting a little old for the crash-and-bang stuff," Poe said. "How about giving an old man a hand, Reece?"

Reece took a moment to consider the events since his release from prison: his father's letter, the files, the Collective that wanted him dead.

"Our only options are sitting at this table," Poe added.

"Let's find out what she has for us," Reece said. "Where are we going?"

"Cyprus."

CHAPTER 67

St. Raphael Marina
Republic of Cyprus

ANDREI SOKOLOFF AND SLAVIK Deynekin stood below deck on the twenty-four-meter custom trawler in a compartment just off the engine room housing twin Cummins 610-horsepower diesel engines.

It was docked at the St. Raphael Marina on the southern coast of Cyprus, on the eastern edge of Limassol. The marina was located between the "new port," used primarily for cargo ships and cruise liners, and the "old port," populated by fishing vessels. St. Raphael catered to the Mediterranean yachting class. It was no stranger to private yachts and sailing vessels, from solo sailors to megayacht jet-setters and everything in between. *Open Passages* fell somewhere in the middle, not so ostentatious as to draw undue attention and not an eyesore that would encourage questions about how its owners could afford to dock in Cyprus's hottest marina. In essence, it was the perfect camouflage.

Built by Magnolia Yachts primarily from laminated acajou mahogany from plans from Taka Yacht Design in Istanbul, *Open Passages* sported a dark green hull that looked almost black from certain angles.

It was designed to berth six guests and three crew members, but the vessel could easily be handled by two, as it was now. The size and design allowed Deynekin and four of his men, along with the former Russian naval captain and first mate, plenty of room to live aboard and guard their cargo.

That the modern trawler would soon be vaporized in a nuclear explosion that would change the course of world history gave Deynekin pause. The plan bordered on genius. The detonation would kill very few people in the short term. In the long term, depending on weather conditions, it would send a number of Israeli citizens to early graves from the aftereffects of radioactive fallout.

Open Passages would anchor five kilometers, just over two nautical miles, off the coast of Israel in the waters between Haifa and Tel Aviv, approximately two nautical miles south of the Leviathan gas field and oil platforms. Several of them would go up in flames and in all likelihood cause one of the world's biggest ecological disasters. That damage would pale in comparison to the war that would follow: Total war between Israel and Iran was inevitable. Deynekin was just speeding up the process and at the same time drawing the Americans out of Ukraine and back into the Middle East. Sokoloff had told him there was more to the plan. He wondered if that second plan was the expected Chinese invasion of Taiwan. That did not concern him. What did concern him was his extraction. This would be his first time rendezvousing at sea with a submarine in the dark.

"Do you have any questions?" Sokoloff asked, turning from the device to his subordinate, his one blue eye piercing. He was dressed in a dark blue polo shirt that accented his physique, beige cargo pants, and deck shoes in an attempt to blend in.

"I am concerned with the lack of a secondary method of extraction. If that sub is a no-show, my men and I are dead."

"We want you off this boat and on the submarine as soon as you drop anchor off Israel. We can't risk an Israeli patrol boat finding seven

Russians on a ship with a nuclear device and transmitting that message back to the mainland. The detonation will occur regardless. They can find a deserted boat, but they can't find you. Trust me, comrade. This is the most important mission of the century. Russia honors its heroes."

Deynekin could hear his men on the spacious flybridge working out with kettlebells while letting the sun tan their pale bodies. Their voices floated through the main salon, past the galley, and down the stairs to the space by the engine room occupied by Sokoloff, Deynekin, and a low-yield ten-megaton nuclear device. The Wagner men were anticipating an at-sea transfer of the package and then a return trip to Cyprus to enjoy a day or two drinking wine and cognac made from grapes grown on the southern slopes of the Troodos Mountains.

"When do we leave?"

"Weather conditions indicate a shift in the prevailing winds later tonight. If that trend persists, you will depart at four a.m. the day after tomorrow. That puts you in position the following midnight."

Deynekin was in sandals, loose-fitting tan pants, and a thin black button-up shirt that was unbuttoned at his sternum. He scratched an itch below his collarbone and turned his attention back to the rectangular polished aluminum case they had removed from the Louis Vuitton trunk a few minutes earlier. A four-inch-by-ten-inch digital timer with a keypad was affixed to the outside.

"We will initiate the countdown just prior to your departure," Sokoloff said. "I'll be here to give you confidence that it won't immediately detonate."

"And so you can report back to Moscow that you personally witnessed the countdown sequence begin. That way, if anything goes wrong, it was either the scientists and engineers in Zarechny, or me somewhere on the high seas."

"Perceptive as usual, Comrade Deynekin. I would expect nothing less. And to be clear—there are no abort codes. Antitampering countermeasures are built into the device. It will detonate on the third attempt to input additional codes."

"How long do we have?"

"The voyage is twenty hours at eleven to twelve knots, depending on sea state. The countdown timer will be set for twenty-two hours. You will arrive at the set lat-long, drop anchor, and await the *Severodvinsk.* They will identify your vessel and surface fifty meters north of your position. Use the tender to approach and board the sub."

"And then?"

"You will be sixty nautical miles away at a depth of five hundred meters when the bomb detonates. The captain will confirm a blast occurred as per the timeline. If it does not, he has orders to return to your anchor point and sink this trawler."

Deynekin nodded.

"Are you having misgivings?" Sokoloff asked.

"No, Colonel. Quite the opposite."

"Good. We do have an unforeseen issue that has arisen."

"Oh?"

"You are going to have two additional passengers on this mission."

Deynekin's brow furrowed. *Already a change to the plan.*

"I take it that one of them is not you."

"There is a traitor in our midst," Sokoloff said.

"Who is he?"

"He is a she, comrade. Pavel Dashkov's secretary. She made contact with the Americans last week."

"What does she know?"

"She seems to have picked up or pieced together aspects of our plan and is going to pass that information to the Americans in exchange for an extraction from Cyprus."

"She's here?"

"*Da,* as are Directors Dashkov and Levitsky. One of the men assigned to extract her is James Reece. His father worked for the CIA and left his son certain documents that are problematic for our employer."

"That makes them a big problem for all of us."

"But not for much longer."

"Why is that?"

"Because you are going to kill them both."

CHAPTER 68

St. Raphael Resort & Marina
Limassol, Republic of Cyprus

THEY TOOK SEPARATE FLIGHTS into Cyprus under aliases, with legends built by the CIA. Both Reece and Poe had names and backstories associated with those names from previous engagements with the Agency, which sped up the process considerably. Poe flew first-class to London out of Dulles on British Airways and then caught his flight into Larnaca, Cyprus. Reece departed from Baltimore on a United Airlines flight with a long layover in Chicago. Due to the late notice and his backstory as a copy editor at the *Baltimore Sun*, all of Reece's flights were economy-class. His Austrian Airlines flight out of O'Hare to Vienna was delayed by an hour, and when he finally did board, he was ticketed in a middle seat. To his left was a rather large man by the window who couldn't stop coughing and who used the restroom rather frequently. On his right was a woman holding a baby. The baby was sleeping soundly until the plane began to taxi, at which point it began to cry and didn't stop until the flight touched down nine hours later. He arrived less than refreshed, but his flight to Larnaca miraculously departed and arrived without incident.

Robbed of sleep, he thought about the mission. Poe should already be at the hotel. The plan was for Poe to check in, get the lay of the land, and purchase local mobile phones, one of which he would set under a towel at the pool later that afternoon to pass to Reece. That would be the closest they would come to one another during their stay. After establishing contact with Kira, they would be extracted by a CIA Maritime Branch asset that had been alerted before they left the States.

The CIA's Maritime Branch operated "covered" vessels the world over. The crew on standby for this extraction operated a yacht brokerage company out of Varkiza, Greece, as commercial cover for their espionage activities. Their location on the southern Greek coast allowed them legitimate access to Southern Europe and North Africa. They were on their way to Cyprus but did not yet have the specifics of the mission; all they were told was that they were to pick up three passengers in Limassol. They would loiter at a mooring outside the marina and get their official tasking after Poe made contact with Kira.

The plan called for Poe to meet Kira at a hotel restaurant. There he would direct her to the marina. He would depart via a slightly different route while Reece followed her to the dock, where she would link back up with Poe. Reece was the primary communicator with the Maritime Branch craft. All three would be extracted from the dock. Heading immediately west, they would rendezvous with a helicopter from the USS *Harry S. Truman* for transport to the aircraft carrier, where they would board a Grumman C-2 Greyhound bound for Naval Air Station Sigonella in Italy. From there a waiting CIA Gulfstream would return them to the United States. Reece and Poe would have the entire flight to debrief Kira, with the goal of identifying and preventing the Black Swan.

Reece felt naked without a pistol, but this operation was about situational awareness and tradecraft. If things got loud, it was almost certainly the Russians who would have the upper hand.

Cyprus had maintained close relations with Russia even after the invasion of Ukraine. Russia currently had a contingent of officials attending a week of conferences with their counterparts in Cyprus. These meetings were a follow-up to the "Russia-Cyprus Business Forum," an annual event organized by the Russian and Cypriot Chambers of Commerce and Industry with the support of the Cyprus-Russia Business Association and the Russian embassy in Nicosia. With most of the Western world making travel difficult for Russian citizens by suspending visas and restricting travel, Cyprus was still an active trading partner with close military and financial ties, which made it an attractive destination for those from the pariah state. There were few places outside the Russian Federation that Kira Borisova could have arranged for an extract. Cyprus was at the top of the list.

Kira had reported that Dashkov and most of the intelligence professionals attached to the talks would be staying in a group of private villas called Aphrodite Hills, in Paphos, about an hour west of the St. Raphael Resort & Marina in Limassol. Many of the expansive villas just so happened to be owned by the Russian oligarchy. Kira had an official schedule, but Dashkov would often deviate, as much for operational security as to enjoy pleasures of the flesh. During his sexual and drinking forays, Kira would have time to shop or run errands for her boss in town. Reece and Poe were to take lunch at the hotel's Octagon Restaurant and dinners at the Palladium Restaurant. They had been shown a photo of Kira before departing the United States. She would know Poe by a Panama-style straw hat, cane, and newspaper. She would initiate contact with Poe to set the extraction in motion.

Reece was snapped back into the present by the voice of his taxi driver, who was intent on using his passenger to practice his English. For most of the forty-five-minute ride down the exquisitely scenic coastal road from the airport to Limassol in the black Mercedes, he regaled Reece with stories of the island in a smattering of Turkish, Greek, and strained English. He recommended that Reece visit Limassol Castle during his stay. Now a museum, it was the site of Richard the Lionheart's wedding on his voyage to the Holy Land during the Third Crusade. It was converted into a prison in the late 1700s and operated in that capacity up until World War II.

"Prison, huh? I'll have to check that out," Reece said.

When they arrived, Reece left a solid tip and entered the large foyer of the five-star resort.

Security appeared to be nonexistent as he approached the front desk to check in. He looked up to admire the high ceilings and modern white bubble chandeliers, noting the locations and angles of cameras. He wondered if they were working or just for show. Plush taupe couches and ornate Qum rugs offset by stunning orchid arrangements struck Reece as an interesting combination of styles. In the lobby, he stepped aside to avoid two kids sprinting for the dining area with a harried mother close behind and an exhausted father a few paces back, returning texts on his phone.

The Agency had provided Reece with new clothes, bags, passport, a Maryland driver's license, and even pocket litter to match his legend. His 5.11 Tactical rolling luggage and Gatorz sunglasses had been replaced with a Sterling Pacific aluminum cabin travel case and Clubmaster Classic Ray-Bans. He had also traded his Carhartt ensemble for a beige cotton twill suit with a lightweight white linen button-up shirt and brown leather Allen Edmonds courtside sneakers. He almost felt like he was on vacation. Almost.

Reece's room on the fourth floor wasn't huge, but it was impeccably clean. It was decorated in modern whites and grays with windows and a small balcony that overlooked a pool, large lawn, beach, and the marina.

I'll have to come back here with Katie.

The bed looked inviting, but there was work to do. A Black Swan was on the horizon, and Kira Borisova might be the only person who could help avert it. While Poe and Reece set up the extraction, Andy Danreb was back at CIA headquarters with the contents of the safe-deposit box.

He was unraveling the shell company structure designed to protect Morgan Holdings' collective clients. That list gave them the potential to uncover the identities of Collective members around the globe. Once Reece had those names, he planned on having another talk with the president. There were options when it came to dealing with enemies of the state. If the extrajudicial route would provide the most protection for those closest to Reece, he was going to be busy.

Reece changed into shorts. He kept his light button-up shirt on and traded his shoes for the flimsy slippers provided by the hotel from his room's closet before heading for the pool. It didn't take long to locate Poe. He was in a lounge chair in the shade of a large umbrella. Dressed in a short-sleeve button-up, shorts, and a straw fedora hat, he looked like he belonged there. A classic derby walking cane leaned against a square white side table that also held a drink with an umbrella, along with a folded edition of the *Times* of London by its side.

"Anyone sitting here?" Reece asked.

"Be my guest. I was just leaving," Poe responded, swinging his legs to the side and gathering up his belongings.

"Thank you," Reece said, moving a towel to the side and settling into his chair.

Even to the most attentive, it would have been difficult to see Reece slip the cell phone into the pocket of his shorts.

As tempting as it was to relax poolside, Reece needed to prepare. Without weapons, this extraction was all about timing. After ten minutes observing tourists and employees around the pool, Reece returned to the hotel and bought a pair of sandals in one of the hotel shops for a little more protection than what was offered by the slippers from his room. He then explored the grounds, noting entry and exit points and service entrances. He made his way past the main pool, along a pathway across the lawn, and paralleled the beach on a path to the marina. He relegated areas of cover and concealment to memory and was careful to pick out a few different boats in berths at the marina that he could steal and crew on his own in case their primary extraction platform fell through.

Confident that he had memorized the resort layout, he returned to his room and placed a call on his newly acquired mobile phone.

"Hello, is this the water taxi?"

"Yes."

"Wonderful. Just wanted to make sure you were still in business."

"We are. We can pick you up anytime."

"Great. I'll be in touch."

Maritime Branch was standing by.

It was now a matter of adhering to what was essentially the loss-of-comms portion of an escape-and-evasion plan. Kira had been passed a time and place by the case officer in Moscow. She knew nothing more than to look for an older man with a cane, newspaper, and straw fedora in one of two restaurants in the St. Raphael Resort hotel. Once she established contact, it was up to Poe and Reece.

In his past life, Reece would have hit the Aphrodite Hills villa complex with a squadron of SEALs, eliminated the threats, and extracted the package. He acknowledged that, in this case, their current plan had a high likelihood of success and didn't involve leaving craters in their wake. Still, he would have preferred to feel the familiar weight of a pistol behind his right hip.

Reece changed into light slacks and his white linen shirt. He arranged a few "tells" in his room to inspect upon his return that would indicate if it had been searched. He then took the stairs to the Palladium Restaurant.

The hostess gave Reece the option of sitting at a table or at the bar. Reece figured a single guy would blend in better at the bar instead of sitting alone among tables filled with families, friends, couples, and business associates. It would also allow him to observe the entire restaurant from a slightly elevated position.

"Bar's fine," he said.

"Follow me, please," she replied, leading him toward the bar and then gesturing with her hand that he could sit anywhere.

"Thank you," Reece said, sliding onto a bar chair.

The bartender gave Reece a moment to get situated and study the bottles against the mirrored wall. But Reece wasn't interested in liquor tonight. He was using the reflection to study the dining room behind him.

No sign of Poe yet. No one who looks like Kira.

The bartender approached and said something in Greek.

"English?" Reece asked.

"Beer? Wine? Cocktail?"

"Do you have a Coke back there? And a menu?"

The bartender frowned but lifted a glass, shoveled in a scoop of ice cubes, and hit a button on the soda gun behind the bar. He placed the drink and a menu in front of his customer before moving on to take his next order.

Kira had been given two-hour windows at lunch and dinner to make contact over the course of the next four days. If she didn't, that meant she could not break free of her responsibilities, and she would return to Russia with the official party. At that point the CIA case officer from Moscow Station would have to convince her to pass him what information she had in exchange for an extraction at the next opportunity, an opportunity that might never come. It might also be too late.

Where was Poe? He should be here by now.

Reece ordered dinner and another Coke, continuing to study the restaurant through the mirror behind the bar. It was beginning to fill up with people waiting for tables or enjoying pre-dinner drinks, which made it more difficult to view the dining area. The clientele looked to be mostly tourists, with a smattering of crew from boats in the marina who appeared to be there solely for the alcohol.

As additional patrons entered the bar and the noise levels rose, Reece became increasingly concerned with Poe's absence.

He should have been here an hour ago.

He failed to notice an older gentleman with a barrel chest and thick arms who was wearing a dark Polo shirt and an English flat cap making his way through the crowd past the bar and toward the restrooms. Even if Reece had seen him, there was nothing that would have made him stand out as a threat. As he approached, he bumped into someone trying to get the bartender's attention and stumbled to the side. He caught himself on the bar, his other hand landing hard against Reece's thigh.

What the hell?

"*Me synchoreís*," he said. *Excuse me* in Greek.

His head still down, he continued toward the restroom.

Reece brought his attention back to the mirror in an attempt to locate Poe at one of the tables in the crowded restaurant.

Something was wrong.

The liquor bottles were blurry.

Reece squinted his eyes and shook his head, trying to clear his vision.

Dizziness and nausea followed.

Reece struggled to remain upright.

Need to get to my room, he thought.

He hardly registered the four men dressed in an assortment of slacks, boat shoes, and various collared shirts moving into position around him.

"What have you been serving our friend?" he heard one of them say in heavily accented Russian, his hand slapping down a stack of euros. "This should cover him. We'll get him back to his boat."

As the combination fentanyl and muscle relaxant micro-pellet continued to incapacitate him, Reece struggled to lift his head. His final vision before he blacked out was of the man in the English cap at the far end of the bar. His thick arms were folded across his chest. Opposite his black eye patch he was watching Reece through one piercing blue eye.

CHAPTER 69

Mediterranean Sea

THE SOUND AND SMELL of diesel engines woke Reece from his drug-induced coma.

He opened his eyes, but there was still only darkness. He struggled to breathe. Something was covering his mouth. *Cloth?*

He tried to move his hands to rip the obstruction from his face but felt the cold steel of handcuffs restraining his wrists and anchoring him to a fixed point that he couldn't see.

The heavy smell of diesel fuel and oil in a confined space overwhelmed him and he retched, the vomit catching in the bag that was duct-taped around his neck.

Don't panic, Reece.

He turned his head to the side, letting gravity pull the bile away from his mouth, spitting out chunks of partially digested food and enzymes as he fought for breath. The sharp acidic taste and smell of his own vomit trapped in the bag, combined with dizziness and vertigo from the lack of spatial awareness, felt like the dark hand of death upon his soul. The sensation brought on a claustrophobia and hopelessness Reece had not even experienced in the depths of solitary confinement.

Was he back in his cell? No, this was worse than his cell.

Reece had spent enough time on the ocean to know he was on a boat. The diesel noise and smells indicated he was in an engine room.

Even with the heat emanating from the engines, he could feel cold sweat emerging from his pores.

How did I get here?

Poe?

Kira?

He remembered being in the bar on Cyprus, using the mirror to scan the room behind him.

Then what?

The man in the cap. The one who had fallen into him. The one with the eye patch who was staring at him from across the bar. That blue eye.

The taste and smell of his vomit hit him again, bringing on another bout of nausea, now combined with a migraine.

Fight it, Reece.

What is happening?

How long have I been in here?

Reece was on his right side on the floor. He used his fingers to feel around the handcuffs. They were attached by a second set of cuffs to a grommet in the deck. He used his feet to explore the area around him. They had taken his shoes, so he was barefoot in pants and a shirt, head bagged, and secured to the floor of the engine room of a moving vessel.

Stay alive. Stay alive and get back to Katie.

Reece concentrated on his breathing and focused on keeping his airway clear of the vomit.

If you can breathe, you can fight. Just wait. Be patient.

Reece went to Montana in his mind, picturing Katie in a sundress picking wildflowers by the lake on a bright summer day.

Stay there, Katie. I'm coming.

Was this a dream, or was he really in Montana? And who was approaching Katie?

He called out to warn her but she just smiled and waved.

The man was getting closer. Who was he?

Reece screamed for Katie to turn around again, pleading with her to run, but his feet were anchored in place, frozen as if secured by cement blocks.

Finally, her radiant smile faded, and she slowly turned.

When she looked at the man, his face became clear to Reece as well. He had an eye patch and one piercing blue eye.

No!

Reece was back in darkness. He heard a door open and footsteps approach. A knee pressed into the side of his head, causing the dried bile to break apart into a gooey paste from the pressure against his skull. He felt another set of hands on his ankles as someone else unlocked the handcuffs that fastened him to the deck. He attempted to lash out, but the three men knew what they were doing.

They pulled him to his feet.

Reece could feel that he had at least one man on each arm and another behind him with his hand around the back of his neck to guide him.

With the bag over his head, it was slow moving, but he could hear the noise of the engine room dissipate behind him. He was pushed up a staircase, across a room, and then into what felt like fresh air, though the sensation came from the colder air against his hands and forearms, with the bag still around his head. He realized that he no longer had the sensation of moving. Had the boat stopped? He was shoved forward and could hear the lapping of waves against the boat's hull. He was then roughly moved into position against what felt like a railing or gunwale. The right-side handcuff was unlocked. His left, still in the cuffs, was yanked over and secured to something else.

He heard a man bark an order in Russian and then felt hands hold his head in place and something cut at the side of his neck. He heard and then felt the tape holding the bag to his head pull free. It was pulled off, and Reece sucked in the cool ocean air.

As his lungs rejoiced at the influx of oxygen, he looked to his left. His hand was not handcuffed to *something*; it was handcuffed to *someone*: Kira Borisova.

Her shoes were gone but she was still dressed in a black skirt and white blouse. There were no outward signs of physical abuse, but the psychological abuse was evident. She was trembling. If there had once been fight in her eyes, it was gone.

Reece looked back to his right. He was on a yacht of some sort. In the dark it was difficult to gauge, but it appeared to be seventy or eighty feet long. In the distance he could see the lights of GOPLATs—gas and oil platforms. He glanced over his right shoulder and saw the glow of a city on the coast. He was on the forecastle—the deck at the front of the vessel—facing five hard-looking men. Four of them held what Reece recognized as Brügger & Thomet MP9 PDWs—personal defense weapons—small 9mm submachine guns on single-point slings fitted with folding stocks, suppressors, SureFire lights, thirty-round magazines, and Aimpoint ARCO red-dot optics. Their ages, body types, and short haircuts gave the impression that they were military. Their clothing, weaponry, and the fact that they were on a yacht somewhere in the Mediterranean told him they were not. SVR? GRU? No, these were Wagner Group mercenaries.

"Mr. James Reece," a man said, stepping forward.

Reece spit a chunk of vomit onto the deck at the man's feet.

"They don't trust you with a B-and-T?" Reece said, nodding at the weaponry in the other men's hands.

He shook his head and looked past Reece at the city in the distance.

"We were not sure if we were going to keep either of you alive," he continued. "We have special holding facilities in Russia for people like you and traitors like her. Places where we can take our time to make sure we have every drop of information before we kill you or work you to death."

"I'll pass," Reece said. "I spent some time in the dark recently. Not a fan."

"How are you feeling from the fentanyl? They told me that concoction we injected you with had about a seventy-five percent chance of killing you. You're a lucky man."

"That's what I keep telling myself. Where are we?"

"The more important question is, why are you still alive?"

"I was beginning to wonder."

"I read a very extensive file on you, Mr. Reece. That man with the eye patch—yes, the one who poisoned you—gave it to me. Nowhere in it did it mention that you had a sense of humor."

"It was obviously incomplete."

"Still with the jokes."

"I find it breaks the tension."

"You are still alive because my boss needed to double-check that some files our employer has been concerned about—files left to you by your father, if I understand correctly—have been located and recovered."

What? That's not possible.

"Nothing clever to say now? Come now, Mr. Reece. Perhaps your file was right after all."

Reece remained silent, his mind running through the possibilities. None of them were particularly appealing.

"Those files mean nothing to me," the man said. "They mean a lot to others. Now that they have been recovered, we do not need you. You will die shortly."

"Why not get it over with?"

"Why the rush? Nothing to live for?"

"I don't like waiting."

The man shook his head. "It is almost a shame we have to kill you. You seem entertaining."

"I try."

"And you, Ms. Borisova," he said, turning to the woman handcuffed to Reece. "You betrayed the country that gave you everything. Why?"

Kira lifted her head and spoke for the first time.

"If you are on this vessel, you know why."

"What we do tonight saves Mother Russia, Ms. Borisova. And you came close to stopping it. What were you going to tell the Americans? Go on. Tell him."

The woman turned her head to Reece, her long brown hair falling to either side of her face.

"They are going to detonate a nuclear device."

"What?" Reece said, unable to hide his astonishment even as his mind put the pieces together.

"Behind us is Israel. Tel Aviv," she continued. "A bomb on this boat was made with Iranian plutonium."

Iranian plutonium?

"They want to make it look like Iran attacked—or was trying to attack Israel—to start a war that pulls the United States back into the Middle East."

"Why?" Reece asked.

"To divert their support for Ukraine. So Russia can take Ukraine and China can take Taiwan."

At the mention of China and Taiwan, Deynekin's head snapped up.

"Ah, even I did not know that," he said. That was the additional part of the plan that Colonel Sokoloff had hinted at. "Thank you for enlightening me, though we would all have found out soon enough."

Reece turned back to the lead Russian.

"Yes, Mr. Reece, you heard that correctly. Nothing is stopping this bomb now. The timer is set. It's counting down. Any minute now our extraction platform will arrive. And I am sad to inform you that we can't leave you on this yacht, as nice as it is, to be vaporized in the explosion."

"Oh, come on, have a heart."

"You can't actually defuse it. It's tamperproof. But who knows, an hour is a long time. You might somehow get free and signal one of the gas and oil platforms or use the radio to transmit a message. That won't do. So, you will have to die. But before you do, someone wants to speak to you both."

Deynekin pulled out the encrypted phone Sokoloff had given him on Cyprus and hit a preprogrammed contact. He set it to speaker mode.

"*Da*," a voice said.

"They are here. They can hear you."

"Good. Mr. Reece, you were not nearly as formidable as I was led to believe. Or maybe I am just that good."

"Speak," Deynekin ordered, moving the phone closer to Reece's head.

"Everybody gets lucky, even one-eyed retirees."

Deynekin's left hand slapped Reece across the face.

"That sounded like a corrective measure," Sokoloff said.

"Hits like that confirm why we won the Cold War," Reece said.

"Before you hit him again or kill him, let me say my piece," the voice said. "Mr. Reece, the contents of that safe-deposit box no longer exist. Without those files, everything in them becomes conspiracy theory nonsense."

But Andy and Vic took the files to CIA headquarters, Reece thought. *Maybe he's bluffing. But why would he bluff?*

"The list from Morgan Holdings is nothing but shell corporations moving money around the way people and institutions do every day to protect their wealth," the voice continued. "Before you die, I wanted you to know that you failed. Though I am almost sorry I won't have the pleasure of interrogating you."

Reece leaned closer to the phone.

"Get used to disappointment."

The men holding the B&T submachine guns laughed as another voice broke over the line.

"Kira."

"Director Dashkov," she replied weakly.

"You. You, of all people. I cared for you. I never hurt you. I took care of your mother. I treated her well. And this is what I get in return?"

"You have all gone mad," Kira said bravely into the phone.

"You *fucking* bitch! And you, James Reece. This has been a long time coming. It warms my old heart to know that you will die at the hands of a Russian."

"In an hour the world changes forever," Sokoloff said. "Fortunately for you, you will not be here to see it."

Reece leaned toward the phone.

"I'm going to *fucking* kill the both of you."

"That's very funny, Mr. Reece," Sokoloff responded.

Think, Reece, think.

"Have you told them that no one is coming for them?" Reece asked suddenly.

"Schoolboy tricks," Sokoloff said.

Reece caught two of the mercenaries looking at each other.

"They are not coming to get you. You are all as dead as I am," Reece said.

"Kill them," Sokoloff ordered. "We have a war to start."

"Shoot the bitch first," Dashkov said, his voice straining with emotion. "Let Mr. Reece go to the grave with another death on his conscience."

A Glock 19 emerged from Deynekin's waistband. It passed in front of Reece's face and went to Kira's face. With the barrel to her right eye, he pulled the trigger. Her head snapped back, showering the water below with brain matter from the exit wound.

The explosion of a pistol firing so close to Reece's head was deafening. It also gave Reece the split second he needed to launch a strike at the inside wrist of Deynekin's right hand, knocking the pistol off line while at the same time throwing himself backward over the railing, pulling the dead woman with him, into the dark waters of the Mediterranean.

CHAPTER 70

REECE CRASHED INTO THE sea still attached to Kira's lifeless body.

Get deep!

As bullets rained down from above, Reece kicked with his legs and clawed his way through the water, frantically pulling himself downward. He knew the bullets would be largely ineffective once they hit the water, but he wanted to get deep as fast as he could. Depending on the angle of the shots, it was still possible for them to do damage if he was close to the surface.

They had gone over the side near the starboard bower anchor, and as Reece continued to kick, he reached out in a desperate attempt to find the chain.

How deep was it this far from shore? Was there a shoal that extended into the Med off of Israel? Did they have grenades? Would they drop them? Would that attract too much attention?

Kick, Reece.

He felt the water getting colder and continued to dive, equalizing the pressure in his ringing ears the deeper he went, the dead body trailing behind.

He was depleting his oxygen reserves quickly.

How much time do you have?

On land you would have minutes.

Here, dragging a dead body with mercenaries shooting at you from above? Probably seconds.

Reece's hand brushed against something hard. Instinctually he pulled it back, the body's intrinsic DNA warning of another creature in the depths. Realizing it was the anchor chain, he grabbed it with his right hand and gave two strong pulls, guiding them deeper down the links.

Reece knew he was deep enough to be safe from bullets. In the darkness he pulled himself up against the chain and gripped the links with his feet. He pulled Kira's body against his, trapping her between his body and the anchor chain.

You can stay in here forever.

No, you can't.

The voices from his cell had returned.

You can do it.

Dad?

You can do it, son.

Reece was back in his cell, then in a tidal pool with his father in Hawaii, then free diving with his father and Raife off the coast of Northern California.

You got this, James. I'm timing you. You are almost up to a full minute.

Reece held fast to the anchor, just has he had to the rocks of the small tidal pool in Kauai as a child. How deep was he? Twenty feet? Thirty? Forty? Fifty? With his free right hand, he found Kira's face, gripping it by the jaw. It was pitch-black at night at this depth, but his mind saw Lauren, blond hair floating in the water, her eyes upturned, her soul already in the next life. *No!* He shook his head and looked back, the salt water stinging his eyes, the tinnitus in his ears echoing like the last ring of the BUD/S bell.

Never ring the bell.

He pulled his face closer to Kira's, though now instead of the Russian intelligence secretary, it was Katie.

Katie!

She was lifeless.

If you stay with Katie, she will die.

No!

Remember what I told you. You are granite, Reece. Those who love you will be battered to death against you. Save them now.

Reece pulled himself to Kira's head, held her nose, and pressed his lips to hers, using his last breath to clear her mouth as he would a scuba regulator. The bullet had severed her brain stem, the portion of the brain that commands the body to breathe. Without those signals she had ceased breathing immediately. She still had oxygen in her lungs.

With his lips still covering her mouth, her dead air gave him life, or at least a few more seconds of it.

Good, son. Now it's time to push past uncomfortable. It's time to transcend your line of control.

Reece felt the handcuffs, attached at the wrist to Kira. If he surfaced with her, he was dead.

Do it, Reece.

Reece exchanged another breath with the dead woman and pulled himself around the chain so that it was between him and Kira. Then he positioned her wrist against the chain and reached around to the other side with his free hand.

I'm sorry.

He extended both his arms and then ripped them back.

Nothing.

He did it again, imagining Katie smiling by the side of the lake, the man with the eye patch approaching. This time he felt the break. He continued to pull back against the chain, running the skin at her wrist up and down against the friction of the shackles. He felt the bones loosen as he wore through more layers of skin, sawing through the wrist between the radius and carpals until he severed her hand from her body.

He was free. He felt her body drift away.

Reece grabbed the chain.

You know what you need to do, son.

I do.

Good. Three, two, one . . . fight!

CHAPTER 71

REECE PULLED HIMSELF UP the chain. Kira's oxygen was now almost depleted. He needed air.

Transcend your line of control.

He stopped short of the surface, holding himself beneath the waves. He could see the lights of the boat above and remembered that beneath the surface he was all but invisible. Back in his enlisted SEAL days he had been tasked with a red-cell operation to test the security of a ship against surface swimmers in Yokosuka, Japan. Reece and his swim buddy had worn black wet suits and camouflaged their faces. They strapped Soviet-era limpet mines to their backs and began the two-nautical-mile swim to their target. The ship's crew knew that the SEALs would attack between 10:00 p.m. and 2:00 a.m. They had watchstanders with lights searching the water of the harbor. Even swimming on the surface, with the ship knowing the four-hour window for the attack, Reece and his swim buddy had successfully planted their limpet mines and evaded detection. That gave Reece a lot of confidence when it came to approaching vessels from the waterline in the dark of night.

Sensing he was close to the surface, he pushed himself off the anchor chain and in two powerful strokes found the keel of the yacht below the waterline. Then he slowly let himself surface next to the dark hull, doing his best to suck in the lifesaving air as quietly as he could.

The noise of the wind and the waves hitting the hull masked what little sound he made.

He treaded water silently next to the side of the vessel, giving the oxygen time to clear his head.

I saw five men, four of them had B&Ts, one had at least a pistol. There could be more. There must be a crew of two or three.

Seven or eight armed mercenaries against an unarmed, partially drowned man on a boat with a nuclear device counting down to a detonation that was less than an hour away.

Those were not great odds.

Fuck the odds.

Reece got rid of his white shirt to give himself a little better freedom of movement and made his way aft, keeping a hand against the hull. He could hear voices above him in Russian. It sounded like they were arguing.

He stopped just shy of the aft swimming platform. One of the mercenaries was standing on it, gazing out to sea, looking for an extraction asset that would never come.

Reece inched his way along the edge of the platform, his nose, mouth, and eyes the only parts of him visible to someone from above.

Do it now, Reece. Before he turns.

If you can breathe, you can fight.

Reece exploded from the depths, sweeping the left heel of his target, which sent him to crashing to the platform.

Did the others hear? Or are you far enough away? You will know soon enough.

Now at eye level with the Russian merc, he yanked him into the water.

There are few things more terrifying than a creature that attacks out of the darkness. When that creature steals your oxygen and takes your sense of sight, it is even more so. Pulling the man beneath the surface, Reece jerked his arm between his own leg and locked him into a triangle choke. He grabbed on to the ledge of the aft swimmer's platform, keeping his face out of the water, taking deep breaths to remain calm and steady as he felt the panic and struggle in his victim beneath the surface. Reece was going to need whatever strength he had left.

Reece felt the man go limp but continued squeezing to be certain. He held the dead man under the water, listening for any indications that their brief struggle had alerted those aboard. He could hear Russian voices from the foredeck and possibly the flybridge above, but nothing to suggest they were moving aft.

Probably searching for their extract.

Good.

The more distracted they are, the better.

How the hell do you disarm a nuclear bomb?

Don't think about that now.

Prioritize and execute.

With his right hand still holding on to the swimmer's platform, Reece reached underwater with his left, sliding it to the single-point sling attached to the small 9mm subgun. Loosening his choke, he pulled the sling over the man's head and set it on the swimmer's platform. His left hand continued to search, eventually finding what he was looking for. Reece took the handcuff key from the man's pocket and inserted it into the steel bracelet on his left wrist, removing the handcuff and setting it and the key on the platform.

That will have to do.

Reece braced himself against the platform and kicked the dead man into the darkness of the sea.

It's time to go to work.

The former naval commando pulled himself aboard and knelt on the aft platform. He slid his neck and left arm through the single-point sling and performed a press check on the compact, purpose-built sub gun. He then ejected the long magazine. It felt heavy, which told Reece that it was loaded to its thirty-round capacity or close to it, meaning the man had most likely exchanged magazines after shooting at him from the deck. Reece quickly examined the three-position select-fire lever and moved it to the semiautomatic position and then to fully automatic. That configuration was where this weapon did its best work, and tonight that was where it would stay. Reece knew that the MP9 was designed for situations where concealability was paramount: close-protection details, vehicle work, and tight environments—like a boat. Its compact size made it an ideal weapon for maneuvering around corners in a game of angles. It was perfect for what needed to be done.

With the B&T ready to rock, Reece put the handcuffs in his back left pocket and the key in his front.

On an opposed ship-boarding operation in the SEAL Teams, Reece would assault the target vessel with a HAF and BAF—a helicopter assault force and a boat assault force. They would come from the ocean in high-speed boats designed for just such a mission while at the same time coming from the air, fast-roping onto the top decks. They would send an element to aft steering to control the ship from below and another element to the bridge, eliminating threats as they moved throughout the ship.

Tonight, though, Reece was alone. But now he was armed with a weapon and already on board. One enemy combatant was down. That left six or seven to go. The suppressor attached to the barrel might give him a moment or two, but he doubted the 9mm ammunition was subsonic. Surprise would not be on his side for long.

Kill them all.

Reece moved to the transom in a crouch and slowly peered over the edge into the aft deck. Under a Bimini roof was a spacious outside dining area with a large table and bar. It was empty.

Reece paused to listen. He could hear voices above and the gears of a crane turning to deploy what was probably a small tender.

The lights were low. A boat with no lights would arouse suspicion and increase the chances of interdiction by coastal patrols. Reece moved to the starboard side, seeing movement in the shadows on the forecastle—the area where Kira had taken the bullet to her head.

Ideally Reece would move to the pilothouse on the bridge to gain control of the vessel and use the communications equipment to transmit a distress call. But he was not there to merely gain control of the vessel. He was there to kill everyone on board.

You have to start somewhere, Reece. Go!

Reece pushed down the starboard side deck, the B&T MP9's foldable stock in his shoulder, his left hand on the foregrip, his finger making light contact with the trigger. There were no friendlies aboard tonight, no blue-on-blue considerations, no hostages, no innocents. Everyone was going to die.

As the man on the foredeck came into view, it was clear he had been posted up to monitor the water around the anchor chain where Reece and Kira had gone overboard. His sub gun was at the low ready and pointed at the water below, where he had seen Reece and Kira disappear less than ten minutes earlier. Sensing someone moving toward him, he looked up and turned, his shock evident as a man he thought was dead stitched him up with four rounds of 9mm.

Two more rounds caught him in his face, and he dropped to the deck.

Reece continued to advance, speeding up, knowing that if anyone had heard or seen the man collapse, he was in for a fight.

Reece took the corner at the front of the pilothouse.

Two down.

A third target had been posted on the port side of the yacht across from the man Reece had just put in the grave. He turned and was bringing up his B&T as the former SEAL took an angle on the pilothouse. Reece pressed the trigger to the rear, sending nine rounds into his enemy's stomach, chest, and neck. Reece crossed the forecastle, putting two more bullets into the man's head as he approached.

A shadow in the pilothouse diverted his attention, and as he turned the front windows exploded from the impact of bullets fired from inside the bridge. Glass being an impediment to bullet trajectory, the first shots missed. Whoever was firing was not firing suppressed. The sound of gunfire echoed through the night, the muzzle flashes lighting up the pilothouse like a strobe. Reece pivoted, swinging the sub gun on his new threat, pinning his trigger to the rear. He sent his last fifteen rounds through the shattered windows, then knelt by the dead merc at his feet. He ripped his empty magazine from his weapon and removed the fresh mag from the corpse's B&T by his side. It was heavy. Good. It took him precious seconds to insert the magazine without a flared magwell in the dark, but he seated the magazine and hit the bolt release to chamber another round. Reece was back in the fight.

He placed his left hand on a combination storage bin and sun lounge just forward of the pilothouse windows and vaulted onto the soft white platform, putting him even with the windows. Reece stood to get an angle on what he now saw were two wounded men. The dim lights from inside allowed Reece to see that there was a Kalashnikov with a folding stock on the bloody floor. Both men had been hit but were still moving in an attempt to crawl from the bridge. Reece finished them with four suppressed rounds apiece. Then he raked the remaining glass from the front windows with the suppressor and swung inside to put another round into each man's head. He noted that the two men he had just killed were dressed differently than the Wagner Group mercenaries.

These men were crew. Were there more? He knew there were at least two more mercenaries aboard, including the leader who had shot Kira in the head. With all the noise from the forecastle and bridge, it was time to reappear elsewhere. Reece opened the door to the bridge and entered the yacht's interior.

CHAPTER 72

WHAT THE FUCK WAS happening?

Slavik Deynekin was beginning to panic.

Their extract was late, and now there was a gunfight aboard their vessel.

At first he thought it was his own men, their tempers and anger getting the best of them as they argued about the extraction, after what James Reece had said before he went over the side.

The Wagner Group commander remained on the spacious flybridge sundeck with his lieutenant, Adrik, working the davit crane to launch the small RIB—rigid inflatable boat—tender.

Then he heard the blasts of the AK from the bridge. With his Glock in hand, he called to his rear security, posted on the aft swimming platform. When there was no answer, he ran to the edge of the sundeck and looked down. The platform was empty.

Maybe he went forward?

Then he heard a more subdued sound coming from one of his men's MP9s.

Then there was silence.

Were his men killing each other?

There could be no other explanation.

Unless James Reece had risen from the dead.

That was impossible.

I'm going to fucking kill the both of you. Deynekin felt a chill that didn't come from the crisp night air, as he remembered the certainty in the American's voice even when restrained, outgunned, and moments from death.

"Adrik! Go below and deal with this."

Adrik looked at the RIB that now floated in the water on the yacht's port side.

"I'll wait for you. Now go!" Deynekin ordered.

Adrik pulled the B&T into position against his shoulder and moved his support hand to the foregrip.

"Go!" Deynekin ordered again.

Adrik marched toward the starboard-side stairs across from the crane that led to the lower outside deck and disappeared from view.

Deynekin scanned the dark seas in search of the submarine. *Was Reece right?*

They had disabled their onboard comms system, but his calls to Sokoloff had been answered. He had assured Deynekin that the submarine was inbound and that there was still plenty of time to clear the blast area. The Russian subs were much faster than their publicly available specifications would indicate. Deynekin holstered his Glock and began to climb down on the flexible boarding ladder now hanging from the gunwale.

As he downclimbed past the port-side windows he saw a man enter the main salon. It was not one of his men, though he carried an MP9 in the way of someone quite familiar and comfortable with weapons, nor was it one of the two SVR crew members. He was barefoot and shirtless—the devil incarnate. It was James Reece.

Deynekin froze against the ladder, slowly moving his hand to his pistol.

He hasn't seen me yet.

Reece had paused at the entrance to the salon, scanning with his eyes and muzzle across the table, chairs, cabinets, and bookcases.

As Deynekin's hand reached his Glock, he saw Reece's attention and the barrel of his weapon swing to the left.

Adrik had reached the bottom of the stairs, cleared the external aft deck, and turned to enter the main salon.

Deynekin watched as both men saw each other's movement at the same time. As his palm made contact with the backstrap of his pistol, he stopped.

Thick glass. A pistol in a one-handed grip. Hanging by one hand from a ladder off the side of a trawler-class vessel at night on the open water.

As he saw both men on board let loose with bursts from their submachine guns, Deynekin released the grip on his Glock and continued to downclimb into the tender.

CHAPTER 73

REECE SAW MOVEMENT, BUT it was only a hand and part of a weapon and arm. Complicating matters was that it was through a glass door, but it was all he had.

He also knew that there was at least one more threat to contend with, a threat that at this very moment might be flanking or approaching from the rear.

Fight!

Their weapons discharged at the same moment. Their bullets punctured the glass aft salon doors, sending spiderweb fissures shooting out from the holes and making it difficult to discern what the other man was doing.

The rule of shooting through glass, as Delta Force operator Kyle Lamb had taught him years ago, was *P* for *Plenty*. Meaning, shoot! Regardless of what the experts said, you never really knew what was going to happen to your bullet when you sent it through glass. Thickness of the material, angles of the glass and of the weapon, shape of the bullet, along with the environmentals associated with any gunfight, made predicting exactly where your bullet would impact a guess at best. That was why you fired until the threat ceased being a threat.

Reece kept the trigger pinned, moving at an angle across the salon toward the adjacent corner, continuing to shoot through the glass door that led to the aft deck.

He saw his adversary mirroring his movement across the aft deck as the bullets continued to fly in both directions.

How many rounds was that?

A shadow from outside moved toward the splintering glass. Reece continued to fire even as the shadow fell forward, his body contorting around wounds to his abdomen, chest, and neck. He crashed through the shattered glass, his body coming to rest half inside and half outside the compartment, his lower section impaled on the clear shards that rose from the frames to form deadly stalagmites.

Reece felt the bolt of his weapon lock to the rear, his last bullet having found the man's head, sending brain matter across the inside of the dark mahogany varnished floor. He immediately moved to grab the magazine from the dead man's weapon when he heard the engine of an outboard motor come to life.

Realizing that the last merc was escaping, Reece pulled the sling of the empty sub gun over his head and grabbed a chair from the nearby table, sending it crashing through what was left of the glass doors. The frogman followed right behind it, bursting onto the aft deck. He heard the engine RPMs increase and the sound began to move up the port side of the yacht.

No way you live.

Reece bolted for the port-side deck, turned the corner, increased speed, and with a guttural roar launched himself over the side directly at the sound of the engine.

CHAPTER 74

REECE WAS AIRBORNE FOR less than a second before impacting the deck of the small RIB between the outboard engine and a seatback in front of a console manned by the Wagner Group leader.

Reece was instantly on his feet, his left hand grabbing the right wrist of his enemy, who had twisted at the controls and whose hand now held a Glock 19. The SEAL's right fist connected with the side of his opponent's head and then continued downward, smashing the pistol from his grip. Reece then threw his elbow back, catching the Wagner man high on the cheekbone.

Reece saw the bow of the ship out of his peripheral vision.

I come from the water.

With his right hand now close to his antagonist's face, he closed it around his throat, pivoted left, and launched them both into the sea.

Reece sensed the panic in his enemy as they hit the water. The man's arms flailed, lashing out at Reece and clawing for the surface. Reece remembered Pool Comp at BUD/S, the portion of Second Phase that tested how comfortable one was in the water. A lot of good men washed out in Pool Comp simply because they could not get comfortable in stressful situations underwater. It was dreaded by most. It was Reece's favorite part of BUD/S.

He grabbed the mercenary by his shirt and ripped him back underwater. The movement pushed Reece to the surface, where he took a massive breath of air, held it, threw his body into a pike position, and dove, still gripping the man's clothes.

In a desperate attempt to escape, the Russian twisted, throwing punch after punch at the man propelling him downward. The resistance of the water slowed the blows down so that their impact was negligible. Realizing he was outmatched in the water, he began to scratch and claw but Reece remained unfazed, staying calm and continuing to kick downward.

What little light there was grew dimmer and dimmer.

A cornered wild animal could summon an incredible reserve of strength just before death. Man was no different. Deynekin thrashed and grabbed Reece's face, trying to push a finger into his eye, which Reece countered by clearing the man's hands. He lost contact with his prey for a moment and the Russian broke for the surface. Reece could see the bioluminescent trail in the dark. Just as the man was about to crest, Reece's hand wrapped around his left ankle like a vise, pulling him back into the depths.

Reece could feel the man struggling to fight his way up while the frogman pulled him down. In the darkness Reece ran into the portside anchor chain from the yacht. With his left hand he held fast to a link. With his right he yanked down, pulling the man to him, taking his back. Reece inserted his legs in front of his opponent and sank them in—getting his "hooks in," in jiu-jitsu terminology. He brought his left leg up, horizontal across his opponent's midsection, his ankles flexed upward. He then brought his right leg up and over his left foot, bending at the knee and throwing his right foot behind the Russian's upper thigh, wedging his left leg in place like a seat belt. Reece squeezed his legs, forcing the air from the Russian's body. The body triangle allowed Reece to hold on to the anchor chain with his right hand while his left went to his back pocket and removed the handcuffs.

With Deynekin's hands pushing at Reece's legs in a desperate attempt to free himself, Reece cuffed the Russian's left hand, yanked it back, and then attached the other end to an anchor chain link, locking in place the man who had killed Kira Borisova.

Reece released his legs from the body triangle and separated himself from the mercenary. He paused and then kicked upward, feeling the vibrations of the man's final underwater screams dissipate as he made his way back to the surface.

CHAPTER 75

REECE BROKE THE SURFACE and sucked in some much-needed oxygen.

No time to waste.

Opting for speed over stealth, he propelled himself in a freestyle stroke to the aft swimming platform and heaved himself aboard.

There was still a possibility that there were more mercenaries or crew aboard. He needed to clear the rest of the vessel.

How much longer did he have until the nuke detonated?

Forty-five minutes? Thirty minutes?

First, he needed another weapon.

Reece ran down the deck to the body of the merc he had taken out by the starboard anchor. Reece's body was so cold that he didn't even notice the bloody footprints he left in his wake. First the adrenaline and now the cold masked the pain generated by the shards of glass that had sliced his feet to shreds.

He knelt and removed the MP9 from the dead man, ensuring it was ready to go to work. He then returned to the aft ladder well, climbed to the top deck, and began a methodical top-down clearance of the vessel.

He moved as fast as he could, looking for threats while also searching for a nuclear bomb.

What does a hand-carried nuke even look like?

He had seen pictures of the American SADM—Special Atomic Demolition Munition—being jumped back in the 1980s by Navy SEALs and Army Special Forces soldiers. He remembered it looking like a beer keg wrapped in a nylon bag. He had talked about it to some of the older SEALs over beers when he was a "new guy." They all thought any operation involving an SADM was a suicide mission and that it would blow as soon as they armed it, regardless of what senior ranking officers or the manual told them.

Satisfied the vessel was clear, Reece sprinted to the bridge. Stepping over the two dead bodies he had dispatched earlier, he looked at the navigation and communications suite. Neither seemed to be working. Did they pull a fuse? No time to troubleshoot. Reece looked to the oil rigs in the distance. Maybe the workers heard the gunfire? He did not see any lights moving in his direction. He turned to his right and saw the lights of Tel Aviv.

Okay, Reece. Stay calm. Find that nuke. Maybe the Russian was lying and there is a switch to just turn it off?

Reece ran down a stairwell and began to toss the rooms, dumping out bags and opening closet doors.

They wouldn't keep it in someone's room, would they?

Wait. He remembered a Louis Vuitton trunk on a bench seat just outside the engine room from his clearance. Sprinting to the engine room, he threw open the trunk. On top was an assortment of clothing. Reece reached in and tossed the clothes to the floor to uncover a stainless aluminum case. Affixed to the outside was a keypad attached to a red LED timer. It was counting down.

"Twenty-two minutes and thirty-seven seconds," Reece whispered.

He reached inside to see if it had some sort of an on/off switch but the confines of the case made that difficult, so he pulled it from the trunk.

Damn, it was heavy.

Reece needed room. And he needed to think.

There is no time to think, Reece.

Yes there is. There is always time to think. Just be calm.

He took the case to the main salon area just in front of the shattered glass doors and windows where the dead Wagner merc lay on the floor. Reece set it on the table. He unslung the B&T battlefield pickup and put it down next to the device.

Now what? It doesn't look like there is an off switch. What did the Russian say? It was tamperproof?

What would he attempt to punch in, anyway?

Reece looked at the dead man behind him.

A phone?

Reece stepped through the glass, noticing his bleeding feet for the first time and also realizing that was the least of his problems.

He knelt and went through the man's pockets.

Everyone has a phone.

Reece grabbed the man's hair and lifted his face, putting the phone in front of it to unlock it. He then stood. He had a signal in Israel.

The characters and apps were in Russian, but the visuals made it decipherable. Reece tapped in a memorized number and hit send.

"Yes," a voice said.

"Vic, it's me."

"Where the fuck are you?"

"I'm on a boat off Israel. Kira is dead. So are the Russians who abducted us."

"Reece, what's going on?"

"Listen closely. I am on a boat with a nuclear device. If it goes off, you have to understand that it wasn't Iran. The plutonium will have an Iranian signature, but it wasn't Iran. It was Russia—well, not exactly Russia. It was the Collective, Vic. Israel and the United States have to know that it wasn't Iran. Vic, tell me you understand. We have to avert a full-scale nuclear war between Iran and Israel."

Silence.

"Vic?"

"Vic!"

Reece pulled the phone from his ear. It was dead.

CHAPTER 76

REECE LOOKED AROUND. ONE of these guys had to have another phone. He ran to the bridge and patted down the two men he assumed were the captain and first officer. He found cigarettes and a folding blade, but no phone. He exited onto the forecastle and went through the pockets of the men by the port and starboard anchors. No phones.

Maybe that guy in the main salon was part of the leadership team and only the leaders had phones?

The man Reece thought was their commander was now handcuffed to the anchor chain forty feet down. If he had a phone, it was useless now.

There have got to be at least two chargers in here, Reece thought as he ran back to the bridge and started throwing open drawers and cabinets.

There. Reece recognized a Pelican case with an Iridium sticker on the outside.

Yes.

He ran back to the salon and flipped open the case. An Iridium Extreme satellite phone stared back at him.

Must be an emergency phone that came with the boat.

He grabbed it and hit the power button.

Dead.

The case also contained the charger.

Reece quickly plugged it into an outlet on the wall behind the table.

"Come on!" he yelled, as it slowly went through its power-up sequence.

There. It was "searching for satellites."

Reece extended the antenna and adjusted it so that it was up against a window, the power cord stretched to the maximum.

Why don't they make these cords longer?

Reece was familiar with Iridium satellite phones, having used them his entire time in uniform.

He typed in the USA code and then Vic's number.

The CIA man picked up on the first ring.

"Reece?" Vic's voice was garbled in that strange, otherworldly tone associated with satellite phones.

"It's me. Okay, did you hear me last time?"

"I caught a part. Tell me again."

"No time. Just know if a nuke goes off near Israel, it wasn't Iran. It wasn't even Russia. It was the Collective."

"Reece, what are you saying?"

"I'm saying I need you to patch me through to Andy Danreb, *right now*!"

The line went silent for a moment, and then Reece heard a third voice. Even via sat phone he could distinguish Danreb's Chicago accent.

"Andy, it's Reece."

"Reece, did you hear?"

"What? No, listen to me. I am on a boat with a nuclear suitcase bomb counting down. I've got twelve minutes to disarm it. If I toss it over the side, it still explodes and has the same political impact as if it went off in downtown Tel Aviv. Israel will take that as an attack and launch against Iran."

"What? Reece, I'm not qualified. We need to get you in touch with an EOD tech at Dam Neck or Delta."

"No time, Andy. Come on. I need you to do some of that Marine EOD shit for me."

"Andy," Vic broke in. "I'll fill you in with what Reece told me after this is over."

"Okay, okay, describe it to me," Danreb said.

"It's in an aluminum case—like a large, heavy suitcase. There's a keypad on the outside. It's part of an LED-type timer. The numbers are red. It's counting down. Ten minutes and fifty-six seconds. They said it was made with Iranian plutonium. No pressure, Andy, but if we fuck this up, we just might plunge the world into World War Three."

"Iranian plutonium? Never mind. Describe what you have around you."

"I don't know," Reece said. "It's a fucking boat. Like a trawler but supermodern and nice. About seventy feet long. Diesel engines, so I have fuel and oil. I also have a bunch of dead Russians."

"Okay, there's not enough time to figure out how to disarm it."

"Terrific."

"Is there a barbecue?"

"What? Yeah, I saw one on the top deck."

"Good. Reece, I want you to listen to me very carefully."

"I have all the time in the world. Precisely nine minutes and forty-one seconds."

"That's just enough time."

"Time for what?"

"Time for you to build a bomb of your own."

CHAPTER 77

REECE SPRINTED TO THE top deck and threw open the cabinet under the barbecue.

Connected to the grill's gas line was a white propane tank. A backup was next to it.

Thank God.

Reece unhooked the line and carried both tanks to the yacht's galley. One felt full and the other felt about half-full.

Danreb had told Reece that for a nuclear device to function properly, the internal detonation sequence must happen precisely as designed. Any deviation would mean no splitting of atoms and no release of atomic energy. Instead, if Reece could pull it off, they would have a conventional explosion with the possible dispersion of radioactive material depending on the condition and shape of the plutonium, which was a far cry from an actual nuclear explosion.

To do that, Reece had to disrupt the internal detonation sequence by creating his own explosion.

A BLEVE is a boiling liquid expanding vapor explosion. It is caused when a container with a pressurized liquid reaches a temperature above its boiling point. If Reece could increase the pressure inside the tank at a faster rate than the container's safety valve could off-gas that pressure, the tank would rupture. Upon contact with open flames the propane would ignite, causing an explosion.

Easy day.

Reece set the propane tanks on the gas stove and fired up all four burners. He then ran to the salon and carried the suitcase bomb into the galley, setting it on the stove to the side of the two tanks.

Five minutes and seven seconds.

Not done yet.

Reece ran to the engine room and rummaged through a tool kit until he found a hammer. On his way back to the main deck he pulled sheets, blankets, and comforters from the beds, dragging them up behind him. Reece smashed the hammer against the pressure release valves, hoping to cause them to malfunction. He arranged the bedding on top of the stove's gas burners, making sure they caught fire as he laid more bedding materials on top of the flames. He then dragged two dead Russians into the cabin and heaved them onto the stove to the side of the tanks in an attempt to tamp the explosion and direct its energy into the aluminum case.

Smoke filled the cabin, causing fire alarms to pierce the night air. Reece felt the blaze licking at his exposed skin. When the inhalation threatened to burn his lungs, he stumbled from the galley into the main salon, gasping for breath.

Two minutes left.

There was about to be a big bang. Would that explosion be nuclear or dirty? If it was nuclear, Reece would never know. If it was dirty, he wanted to be as far away from the detonation as possible. Reece threw open the hinged bench seats on the aft deck, expecting to find life jackets. They were empty.

No time to look anywhere else. Get off this boat!

Reece sprinted across the aft deck and dove off the back swim platform, returning to the water for the third time that night. His body sliced through the dark sea, arms stretched in front of him, legs propelling him away from the burning yacht. When he needed a breath, he ascended, rolled slightly to the side and turned his head, his arms now adding their power to the freestyle stroke.

Keep swimming. Don't look back.

Reece estimated the time until nuclear detonation.

About a minute left.

Sixty, fifty-nine, fifty-eight, fifty-seven . . .

Reece counted in concert with the rhythmic motion of his stroke.

I failed.

He saw Lauren and Lucy, dressed in white, standing in a meadow under a beautiful rainbow. Only it wasn't the picture Lucy had drawn for him all those years ago. It was real. Reece was between them, holding their hands. They smiled up at him, full of life. They were happy. *He* was happy.

I'm sorry, Katie. I've got to go now. Live your life. Be happy. I love y—

The concussive blast from the explosion penetrated Reece's body beneath the wave tops. At the same moment he felt a hot wave of pressure roll over his head, jolting his senses and robbing him of oxygen as he went to take a final breath.

I love you.

CHAPTER 78

REECE TREADED WATER. ALONE.

In the distance he watched the yacht burning. Smaller pieces of debris burned in a good two-hundred-yard radius around the main wreckage but were already being extinguished by the whitecaps.

Was he alive?

It seemed so.

The ringing in his ears and the pain in his lungs from the smoke inhalation indicated he was alive and breathing.

If you can breathe, you can fight.

He almost couldn't believe it. It had worked.

How much radiation did I absorb?

He continued to tread water as the trawler tipped forward and sank beneath the surface.

Reece craned his neck and took in the stars. It was a beautiful night. Were Lauren and Lucy looking down on him?

I'm sorry, baby girl. I really wanted to see you. I miss you.

Did someone see the explosion? Was search and rescue inbound? Would they see him treading water? He could hope, or he could act.

Hope is not a course of action, Reece recalled from his SEAL days.

He looked at the oil rigs against the horizon to the north and at the lights of Tel Aviv to the southeast. It was difficult to judge distance over the open water. It was even more difficult at night. He estimated he was between one and three nautical miles off the coast of Israel. The distance to the GOPLATs was harder to figure. What he did know was that they were a smaller target and he could easily miss them, depending on currents. His decision was made.

He had put in a lot of mileage on the ocean in his time. Weekly timed two-nautical-mile swims were part of the BUD/S curriculum, and a five-nautical-mile swim was required to graduate. Some of those swims took place in the frigid waters off San Clemente Island, off the coast of Southern California, where the third and final phase of SEAL training took place. It also happened to be a great white shark breeding ground, a fact the instructors took extreme pleasure in relaying to students just prior to ordering them into the ocean for a timed swim. Everyone's swim times got exponentially better off San Clemente. The sooner you were out of the water, the less chance you had of being eaten by the man in the gray suit.

Reece turned his back to the oil rigs and looked at the glow from Tel Aviv. He had friends in Israel.

Reece started to swim.

With the explosion a thing of the past and fragments of Iranian plutonium rods now on the floor of the Mediterranean, Reece concentrated on his stroke, doing all he could to forget about his feet leaving a bloody trail behind him.

CHAPTER 79

Chaim Sheba Medical Center
Ramat Gan, Tel Aviv District
Israel

REECE SLOWLY OPENED HIS eyes. His vision was blurry.

Above him the sun beat down, causing him to shield his eyes with an arm, an arm that felt restrained.

"What the hell?"

"Not hell, Reece. Israel."

Reece blinked to bring the glowing ball above him into focus. It wasn't the sun; rather, it was a light fixture in the ceiling. And his arm wasn't restrained by straps or handcuffs but by an intravenous fluid line. He turned his head to the side. The man who had spoken was seated in a bright green faux-leather chair next to Reece's hospital bed.

"So, I made it?" Reece asked.

The man looked at him and offered a rare smile. "You did."

"You do smile after all," Reece said. "Don't worry. Your secret's safe with me."

Though short, Ronen Katz was powerful both physically and within the world of Israeli intelligence. He held a paper coffee cup with an unlit Noblesse cigarette between his nicotine-stained fingers. His buzz cut made it hard to tell where his receding hairline stopped. He was dressed the same way Reece remembered him, in scuffed leather shoes, tan slacks, and a tucked-in white short-sleeved button-up shirt. He never wore a tie. He was known simply as "K" on the grounds of Mossad Headquarters, where he ran the branch responsible for what the Israelis termed "negative treatments." He and Reece had history.

Ronen Katz was Kidon, an assassin, or he had once been one. Now he was the director of what was known as Caesarea and had a direct line to the prime minister. His mandate, in addition to removing Hamas and Hezbollah terrorists from the battlefield, was to prevent Iran from building or acquiring a nuclear bomb.

He had also been responsible for recruiting an operative to whom Reece had grown quite close in Iraq, a dual U.S.-Israeli citizen named Aliya Galin. She had been killed when a Strela-2 missile took her Air France flight out of the sky over Burkina Faso last year in an attempt to draw James Reece out of hiding.

"I must admit, I did not expect to see you again so quickly, Reece. I certainly didn't expect to find you washed up on one of our beaches. Next time you plan a trip to Israel, please let me know ahead of time. I'll arrange transport and a nice hotel."

"A smile *and* a sense of humor?"

"It seems appropriate, considering your current state."

"I'm fine."

"You arrived unconscious, dehydrated, hypothermic, with burns on much of your body, and with feet cut to ribbons by glass. The surgeons believe they removed all the shards, but some of the smaller splinters may fester and work their way out over time."

"Something to look forward to," the SEAL replied, turning his head back to look at the light above.

"I'm surprised the sharks didn't get you out there."

"Me too. Is that coffee?"

"Yes, but it's cold, and it's not for you. You are on an IV drip with antibiotics of some kind."

"Lovely."

"They also ran a slew of tests. They found fentanyl and muscle relaxants in your system, as well as higher-than-normal levels of radiation, though I am told it is not life-threatening and that your levels should return to normal. All that would indicate you had quite a night."

"Where am I, anyway?"

"Chaim Sheba Medical Center—the best hospital in the country. In Ramat Gan. It's in a district of Tel Aviv."

"How did I get here?"

"An old man combing the beach with a metal detector found you at daybreak. He called the police, who notified the closest military checkpoint. A United Hatzalah EMS ambucycle was there ninety seconds after notification and started working on you. You looked dead but you had a pulse and were breathing, so they called an ambulance, which took you to the closest trauma center, where they rewarmed you. When you regained some semblance of consciousness, you started to mumble a name."

"Yours?"

"Yes. I was notified and had you moved here. Security is posted outside."

"To keep others out or me in?"

"Both, of course."

"Is the room bugged?"

"This is Israel, Reece. Assume everything is bugged."

"Okay," Reece said, pushing himself up on his elbows, wincing at the exertion of the movement. His body ached everywhere. "After this, do you think you can send someone to get me a McKebab? I had one last time I was here, and it was delicious. I'm starving."

Katz barked a name at the door, which was opened immediately by a plainclothed security agent. Katz spat out something in Hebrew. The man closed the door.

"Your McKebab will be here shortly. Now, let's get to the part that led up to you illegally crossing into Israeli territory."

"Before I lay this out," Reece said, "I'm going to ask you something, and I want you to answer me honestly."

Katz's face remained emotionless.

"Was Aliya trying to recruit me in Iraq?" Reece asked the spymaster.

Katz studied the man in the hospital bed. He was beat up but not beaten, and he had a story to tell, a story that Katz needed to hear. He answered honesty.

"Yes, James. She was. That's what we do."

Reece nodded.

"Okay," Reece said, switching back to the current dilemma. "The main thing I want you to take away from this is that Iran did *not* attack Israel."

"I don't understand."

"You will."

Reece filled Katz in on everything that had led up to last night's events in Israeli waters.

Katz listened intently. He did not take notes, which confirmed to Reece that he was recording the conversation.

"I am probably breaking all kinds of nondisclosures and confidentiality agreements," Reece said. "But without you knowing the whole story, when you recover what's left of that device, whether intact or leaking plutonium, it will have an Iranian signature. And when the bodies start to surface, they will be Russian Wagner Group mercenaries, which should help confirm what I told you. Vic Rodriguez can verify as well."

Katz leaned back in the visitor's chair and removed a Zippo from his pocket. It was engraved with the Sayeret Matkal symbol, and, despite being in a hospital, he lit the cigarette. He took a long drag and blew the smoke up toward the ceiling.

"This is a delicate situation. Politics will come into play, depending on how it is handled."

"I can see it spinning out of control very easily," Reece said. "I am sure we have people and industries in the United States that would love nothing more than for Israel to launch against Iran in retaliation for an attempted nuclear attack in Israeli territory."

"Here as well," Katz said, contemplating his next move.

"If this had gone down in international waters, I would probably not be telling you this. I'd probably also be dead, but if I somehow got picked up by a passing ship, I'd have recommended that the U.S. Navy recover the rods and conduct a classified cleanup operation to prevent an Israeli retaliation, nuclear or otherwise."

"We have never confirmed that we are a nuclear nation."

"You have never denied it, either."

"You did all this for Israel?" Katz asked.

"Well, and world peace and all that. Plus, Aliya's kids live here. How are they?" Reece suspected that Katz would keep tabs on the family members of former agents, especially those who were killed in the line of duty.

"They are doing as well as can be expected. After the attack on the kibbutz they moved to Herzliya, on the coast. It was better for the kids, and the grandparents, that way."

"I understand," Reece said, thinking of his own family gunned down in Coronado.

"Reece," Katz continued, "I am going to call for an immediate emergency meeting with the prime minister. It will just be the two of us, so I will be able to speak freely. I am going to recommend the highest levels of classification. If the public and other politicians believed that Iran attempted to hit us with a nuclear device, even the story you just told me would not be enough to stop a retaliation. The prime minister might still need to take some sort of action even if we manage to keep a lid on it."

"I just might be able to help."

"Oh?"

"How long have I been in here?"

Katz looked at the old Eterna KonTiki Super on his wrist.

"About twelve hours."

"Then there is still time."

"Time?"

"Pavel Dashkov and Andrei Sokoloff are still on Cyprus."

"They would now know that their plan failed. They are probably back in Russia," Katz said.

"Or maybe they stayed because they are unsure of what went wrong and don't want to arouse suspicion. They are scheduled to be there for two more full days, which gives us three cycles of darkness to make a move."

"What are you suggesting? A hit on Cyprus?"

"That's exactly what I'm suggesting. I know their location—a villa complex in Paphos. We keep it quiet, but if things are exposed in the press, the prime minister can take credit for uncovering the plot, foiling the attack, and holding 'rogue elements' responsible. It's bold. It's decisive, and, if I daresay, it's very Israeli."

"It could also start a war with Cyprus or Russia."

"I am not a politician or a diplomat, but the world is opposed to Wagner Group almost across the board, much more so than they are aligned against Russia."

"But only one of the targets is Wagner."

"In today's day and age, label them Wagner and a Wagner associate, if it comes to that. I think Russia will want to save themselves the embarrassment."

"I will propose it. How long do we have?"

“Three more nights. Then they will be back in Russia and much harder to take down.”

“At the very least, the prime minister is going to want to award you the Medal of Valor or the Presidential Medal of Freedom, probably both—classified, of course.”

“Tell him to keep them.”

“How very American.”

“Not that I wouldn’t appreciate them, but I’d rather ask for a favor.”

“Oh?”

“You guys are pretty secretive about your submarines, aren’t you?”

“We are.”

“I’m going to need to borrow one.”

CHAPTER 80

Paphos
Republic of Cyprus

IT HAD BEEN A few years since Reece had been on a rebreather. This one, unlike the Dräger LAR V he had used in the SEAL Teams, was back mounted. The French-designed TBO Multi-Mission Military Rebreather was not the only new piece of kit that Reece was loaned for tonight's mission. He had whispered a quiet prayer when his liaison at Shayetet 13, known in the West as Flotilla 13, had shown him the Patriot3 Jetboots. Regardless of what he told Katz, he was still recovering from the events of the past week. Not exactly boots, as the name would suggest, they consisted of small propellers, called thrusters, and motor mechanisms encased in hard black anodized aluminum housings. They strapped high to the outside of an operator's legs and were attached to a belt harness on which was mounted the control box and battery pack.

Reece had experimented with them briefly in the SEAL Teams, but these new versions were the fifth-generation models. They were streamlined and efficient.

It had taken two days, but Ronen Katz had gotten it done. The mission was a go, and Reece was authorized to "advise and assist," against the protests of the Shayetet 13 commander.

S-13 is the elite naval commando unit of the Israel Defense Forces. They trace their lineage back to the 1940 creation of an all-Jewish British Special Operations Executive commando unit in Palestine before Israel's founding in 1948. The training required to earn the vaunted silver and black metal *Knafei A'taleif*—"bat wings"—insignia is some of the toughest ever designed by a modern military. Known as the "people of silence" in Israeli special operations circles, most of their missions remain cloaked in secrecy. And while some special operations units had taken a knee at the behest of senior officers concerned with promotion by way of incorporating social experimentation into the ranks as a substitute for preparing for war, Shayetet 13 retained their motto: "As the bat emerges from the darkness, As the blade cuts through with silence, As the grenade smashes in rage." Reece felt right at home.

Headquartered on the coast at Atlit, less than thirty minutes south of Haifa, their base was located on the grounds of Château Pèlerin, a Crusader fortress dating back to the Middle Ages. Everything about the unit suggested you did not want to fuck with them.

Israel had required that Reece sign more papers than he remembered ever signing for his security clearances in the United States. They were serious about maintaining the secrecy surrounding their undersea capabilities. Tonight he was operating with S-13's Haposhtim unit. Unlike the U.S. military, which always framed its missions as "capture/kill," Israel's naval commandos were not required to add the "capture" qualifier. They would emerge from the surf zone, hit their target hard, and disappear back into the darkness of the sea.

Following the prime minister's explicit order, Reece signed his paperwork, was issued gear, and boarded the *Dolphin II*–class submarine in a secure facility at Haifa. His E&E kit consisted of gold coins and a civilian cell phone from Europe. On an island nation like Cyprus, there were plenty of watercraft to buy, rent, or steal, if need be.

The special operations–capable *Dolphin II*–class INS *Rahav* sub was fitted with an Italian-built Deep Guardian shelter, manufactured by CABI Cattaneo. Reece was relieved to learn that they would not be using SDVs—SEAL Delivery Vehicles, wet mini-submersibles that could launch and recover from submarines. Riding in the back of one was not high on Reece's list of things to do. With Cyprus so close to Israel, it was tempting to use surface vessels, but the submarine option was selected to avoid Russian satellites that might be monitoring the area. This was a mission that would never be publicly acknowledged. Pavel Dashkov and Andrei Sokoloff had been approved for "negative treatment"—assassination—by the state of Israel.

With the assistance of Vic Rodriguez at the Central Intelligence Agency, IMINT—imagery intelligence—confirmed that the Russian Federation planes that had flown the delegation to Cyprus were still on the deck at Larnaca International Airport. SIGINT—Signals Intelligence—put Dashkov and Sokoloff in a villa owned by a Russian oligarch and friend of the president just southeast of Paphos, overlooking the Mediterranean between Ranti Forest Beach and Aphrodite Hills Park.

The Israeli submarine force was on standby to launch at very short notice. Reece assumed this was so they could retaliate against an attack by Tehran with submarine-launched nuclear cruise missiles. Had the Collective's plot succeeded, the submarine INS *Rahav*, tasked with tonight's mission, would have put to sea and launched against Iran as part of a broader, full-scale war. Instead, tonight she would conduct a smaller war.

The captain of the *Rahav* received orders at 0724 on Saturday. By 0930 the dry deck shelter was installed and secured. Katz had sent two Mossad officers to check Reece out of the hospital and escort him to Atlit Naval Base, where he was turned over to his S-13 shadow. There he met the mission commander and was issued his gear before loading passenger vans with the assault force for the drive to Haifa Naval Base. They were on board the sub and under way by 1300.

At midnight, Reece and the S-13 operators conducted a Mass Swimmer Lock-Out of the dry deck shelter to put their twenty operators into the waters off Cyprus. Unlike some of the more complex dives navigating underwater into harbors to disable or board ships, this dive plan was as straightforward as they come. The coast of Cyprus was a straight shot. Just like in the SEAL Teams, each diver was paired up with a "buddy" and attached to him with a cord. In addition to the dive buddy system, two black PVC pipes were added to the mix. Ten divers were assigned to each pole, and each pole had a primary and secondary navigator using Patriot3 Micro Navigation Boards with compasses, depth gauges, and timers. That meant that most of the combat swimmers were along for the ride on this portion of the op. And with ten sets of Jetboots per pole, they navigated to the beach landing site and arrived at their rally point at the base of the cliffs without having to overexert themselves. Surf had been light, and the absence of a moon only aided their mission.

If only it were raining, we would have perfect operation weather, Reece thought.

They transitioned out of their dry suits at 0130, adopting 50/50 security. They removed weapons from shoot-through dry bags and donned helmets with L3Harris GPNVG-18 four-tubed night-vision goggles. Weapons consisted of 5.56 Mk 12s for the four snipers and Heckler & Koch MP7 A2s for the assaulters. Reece would have liked to put a few more M4s in the mix to have more guns with the ability to reach out and touch someone at distance if they were contacted on their way to or from the target house, but tonight's mission was all about stealth, and the 4.6x30mm H&K MP7 fitted with a B&T Rotex-II suppressor and using subsonic ammunition was about as quiet as it got. While they were originally designed as personal defense for use by second-line troops, with ATPIAL laser aiming devices, EOTech holographic sights, and SureFire lights, the operators of Flotilla 13 had converted them for offensive use. Reece's SEAL Teammate Freddy Strain had once told him to make sure to dump a mag into someone with the MP7's little bullet to make sure they went down. Reece had heeded that advice in the past, and he would remember it tonight.

With the assault force kitted out for direct action, they cached their waterborne gear and left five operators behind to guard it. They would also act as a base element in case the assault force needed cover as they exfiltrated the target area.

Reece's feet were wrapped in multiple layers of gauze to absorb the blood he could already feel oozing into his boots. With a mile to patrol to the target, he used the pain as fuel and as a reminder of why he had just inserted over the beach with an Israeli naval commando unit. He had made a promise when he was handcuffed to Kira Borisova on the yacht just before she was shot in the head. It was time to keep it.

CHAPTER 81

PAVEL DASHKOV COULDN'T SLEEP, even with the help of more vodka than usual.

The girl they had sent up had not helped much. Even as her hands worked their magic over his oiled body, he couldn't stop wondering about the fate of *Open Passages*. He could hardly contain his anger with Sokoloff. That psychopath acted as if nothing were wrong. A nuclear device was missing, as were the Wagner Group mercenaries and both SVR crew members. Even worse, the money that had been transferred through shell companies around the world was now gone. The value of their financial contracts was contingent on the second- and third-order effects of a nuclear detonation off the coast of Israel and the total war between Israel and Iran that would follow. This was a disaster of epic proportions. He could only imagine the thoughts and conversations between the president, Kozak, and the Chinese. This colossal failure would set them all back years, if not decades.

Dashkov threw his feet to the side of the bed and looked at the clock. It was almost 3:00 a.m. It would be good to get out of Cyprus. He had only stayed to confer with Sokoloff and head off any questions in the event the boat, bomb, or mercenaries surfaced. He had to keep his schedule, as much as he desired a return to Moscow.

Soon enough.

He grabbed his robe from the bedpost and tightened the sash around his waist.

If sleep wouldn't come, he would continue trying to distract himself from the catastrophe at hand. Another vodka was a necessity. Perhaps he would have the girl sent back up, or better yet, a different girl? Maybe a more experienced set of hands would do the trick?

Dashkov felt a slight difference in the room. What was it? A change in pressure? Temperature? A ghost? It had been a long time since Dashkov had believed in ghosts.

In the dark it was hard to tell, but had the door to his room opened?

Had he not been looking at it, he wouldn't have believed it.

It was a ghost, or at the very least a ghoulish entity. Was it the manifestation of death?

Dashkov stood transfixed as a black-clad specter slid quietly into the room. In the dark it was seemingly just a shadow. The FSB director felt a cold sweat at his temples as another one entered, moving along the wall in the opposite direction of the first one. They were followed by two more, who floated to the sides of the door. They seemed to be suspended in the darkness, almost disappearing. Then he felt, rather than saw, them move. They were coming for him.

As the apparitions closed in, he thought for a moment that they would float right through him. Instead, he felt the very real sensation of a metal cylindrical object make contact with his face, shattering his front teeth. His mouth filled with blood, and he was thrown to the floor. His arms were violently twisted behind his back as knees and hands held his head and legs in place.

With his face pinned to the floor and a mouth full of blood and broken teeth, he attempted to cry out for help, but it ended up coming out as a stifled grunt, which earned him a smack to the side of his head.

Where was his security detail? You couldn't throw a rock at the villa without hitting a Wagner Group thug with a gun.

He was forced into a tuck position and then rolled up on his knees.

He thought he heard a whisper in heavily accented English.

Was that Hebrew?

Then it became clear. *Israelis.* They knew.

Someone took a knee in front of him.

Then he heard a voice he recognized from the deck of *Open Passages.* It was a voice he had scoffed at. It now came to him not over a phone but inches from his face. It wasn't so much a whisper—there was emotion in whispers. This was different.

"Do you know who I am?"

"No," Dashkov managed.

"For an intelligence professional, you're a shitty liar."

"I don't know who you are."

"In case you are wondering, your security detail is dead."

Shit.

"As you know, your stunt with Sokoloff didn't work."

Dashkov felt the man stand and move away. He heard hushed voices but couldn't make out what they were saying. Then the man he knew was James Reece returned.

"I'm only going to ask you this once. Where is Andrei Sokoloff?"

What? He should be here.

"I have his phone but no Sokoloff," Reece said.

That fucking Sokoloff. He was staying in the villa next door, but he left his phone here in mine? Dashkov felt the anger rising. If he was going to die for Sokoloff's incompetence, he was not going to be the bait that let the Wagner man escape with his life.

"He's staying in the villa next door," Dashkov said, spitting blood and tooth fragments onto the floor.

Headlights flashed across the front of the villa and, through the windows, the whine of an accelerating engine was audible in the still night air. Reece sprang from his position and went to the window. That brief moment of light once again gave way to the darkness, but it was enough time for Dashkov to see who had come for him. Men in black. Commandos with night vision and suppressed weapons. Assassins. *Americans and Israelis?*

Dashkov's breathing grew heavy as the American assassin returned and knelt once again.

"You missed him," Dashkov said between breaths. "He's a snake, that one."

"He won't make it far. Before we go, what do you want to tell me about the Collective?"

Dashkov coughed up blood.

"Just because you know a name doesn't mean you know anything about it."

"I know enough," Reece said.

"Enough to what?"

"Enough to burn it to the ground."

Dashkov felt the man stand.

"You are an enemy of the United States and a traitor to your own people. You had no problem ordering your Wagner underling to shoot your secretary. She was right next to me."

"My mistake was not killing you first," Dashkov said.

"It was. And it's one you will not have a chance to make again."

Reece depressed the trigger on the MP7 and sent eight rounds of 4.6x30mm into Dashkov's chest. He stepped forward and finished the Russian spymaster with two shots to the head. The loudest sound in the room was the brass casings cascading to the floor.

CHAPTER 82

"WE DO NOT HAVE authorization to push further inland," the Shayetet 13 commander said. "We need to extract immediately."

He had already made the call. The Israeli commandos were collapsing into a prearranged room on the ground floor.

Reece had made it to the window in time to see a lime-green Lamborghini speed off into the night. A man with an eye patch was at the wheel. The oligarchs loved their flashy planes, boats, cars, and women—all that money bought a lot of obnoxious toys.

At the base of a massive staircase, Reece stopped. The ground-force commander turned.

"Come on," he said.

"I'm sorry," Reece said, unslinging his MP7 and handing it to the commander. "Sokoloff almost wiped Israel off the map three days ago. You can't pursue him past this target, but I can."

"Don't be crazy. It's time to move to extract. We will have to get him another time."

"There might not be another time. Thank you for all you risked tonight, sir. Sokoloff is not leaving Cyprus."

Reece bent down and took an AR from the body of a dead Wagner man.

The Israeli commander looked at Reece in disbelief.

"It's okay. I do this sort of thing all the time."

"Fucking American."

"Oh, I need to keep the NODs," Reece said before turning and taking off at a sprint for the garage.

• • •

Reece ran through the villa and out a side door toward the detached garage that he remembered from the brief. He stopped briefly to press-check the rifle and ensure a round was in the chamber—just in case.

He stepped over a dead Russian and opened the door to the outbuilding. Even under night vision the sight that met his eyes was a surprise.

Reece flipped up his NODs and hit the lights.

It looked like a Ferrari museum. He counted two rows of eight. Some looked like they dated back to the 1940s, while others looked brand-new. Right now, all he needed was one that worked. There was an old Grand Prix car, a Formula 1 racer, a few that looked extremely new, and a couple he recognized from 1980s television shows. Reece hit the garage door openers above the light switches and both doors began to rise.

As Reece descended the steps, he noticed that all the older Ferraris were parked in front of the newer ones. They seemed to be arranged by year. His eyes fell on the car closest to him in the front row. It was the newest unblocked vehicle. There was no time to waste. Reece ran to the vehicle, opened the door, and slid inside, placing the M4 barrel down against the seat next to him. Keys were in the ignition.

Reece pressed in the clutch and turned the key.

The engine sputtered.

Come on!

He tried again and the vehicle came alive.

Reece turned on the lights, let off the parking brake, and tore out of the garage in a red 1978 Ferrari 308 GTS.

CHAPTER 83

FROM THE BRIEFING, REECE knew that the road out of the villa complex led down to the Limassol–Paphos Highway. That road paralleled the coast to Limassol and then continued on to the airport in Larnaca. Sokoloff had a head start, but Reece had an advantage as well. When he got to the base of the hill, he turned off his headlights, pulled down his NODs, and sped onto the highway.

Reece's first impression of the car that looked so fast was that it wasn't, at least not as fast as he thought it would be. He worked through its five-speed manual gearbox as he raced east, the cliffs of the Mediterranean on his right.

The Ferrari was a left-hand drive, so there was nothing new to adapt to there. What did take adaptation was the fact that Cyprus was a left-hand-traffic country, but with no vehicles on the road at 3:30 a.m., staying on the left-hand side of the road was not Reece's main concern. He was focused on catching up to Sokoloff.

The classic sports car passed 80 mph, then 90 mph, then 100 mph. Reece shifted down to fourth and third gears in some of the turns and back into fifth on the straightaways.

He didn't see any lights on the road ahead through his NODs, which was concerning. The Lamborghini that Sokoloff took off in looked a lot newer than what Reece was driving. He started to second-guess his decision.

What if they moved the plane to a different airport? What if he wasn't even going to the airport? Drive, Reece. He's going to the airport. He thinks he's home free.

Reece downshifted again into a corner and accelerated out.

Where is he?

Then Reece saw taillights in the distance. Under NODs it was unmistakably a car. But was it the Lamborghini?

He pushed the vehicle faster. Reece knew he was on the edge of being out of control. He also knew that he could not allow Sokoloff to get to the airport. He thought of the smug look on the colonel's face across the bar after he had injected Reece with fentanyl. He thought of the dead Iraqis who had fought for their country and for the United States, men whom Sokoloff had turned years before. He had inserted them into the heart of the West to use the skills taught to them by the CIA to assassinate President Christensen. It was a plan meant to end in Reece's death or imprisonment.

Reece pinned the accelerator to the floor, gaining ground.

He could now clearly identify the Lamborghini. It was moving quickly, but not so fast that Reece couldn't catch it. He was sure the Russian was looking in his rearview mirror for cars in pursuit. On this open road along the coast, one could see for miles. There was urgency in the Wagner man's speed but not a life-or-death urgency. Reece's urgency was fueled by atonement. Reece was coming out of the darkness.

The SEAL saw taillights as he came out of another turn. They were larger and brighter now. It was almost time.

The high-performance evasive driving training Reece had received over the years in the SEAL Teams left him confident behind the wheel: hotwiring vehicles, mobile surveillance, attack recognition, J-turns, driver-down drills, close-proximity driving, evasive maneuvers, barricade breaching, and something called a Precision Intervention Technique, more commonly referred to as a PIT maneuver. Reece was going to turn his Ferrari into a weapon.

He was going to get only one shot. Once Sokoloff was aware that Reece was behind him, he would leave the old V-8 in the dust.

You are a sniper. You need only one shot.

Reece floored the Ferrari, watching the Russian disappear into a turn. He downshifted, took the turn, and exploded out of it, pulling to the Lamborghini's back right quarter panel and placing the nose of his Ferrari just behind Sokoloff's right rear tire. Reece turned his vehicle to the left, made contact, and turned more sharply into his prey.

Even at lower speeds a PIT maneuver can be exciting. On a coastal road at night at high speed, it can be deadly.

The Lamborghini started spinning to the right as Reece completed the technique in what was essentially an aggressive lane change. That lane change saved Reece's life. The road turned sharply to the left, and with no control, the Russian's car shot from the highway halfway through its spin. Reece turned his head as he sped past, watching it go over the side and disappear from view.

Reece locked up the brakes, scarcely avoiding plunging over the cliff on the sharp curve as well. He quickly shifted into reverse and pulled the car off the road and onto the shoulder on the side across from the drop-off. He put the vehicle in neutral and pulled up the parking brake. Grabbing the M4 from the seat beside him, he exited the Ferrari and sprinted across the road.

Where is he?

Reece never would have found him without the NODs.

The lime-green Lamborghini Huracán Sterrato had cartwheeled down the jagged cliffs and impacted the rocks below.

Did he survive? Was that movement or steam? No way he survived that crash.

Knowing the resiliency of the human body, Reece examined the M4 in his hands.

What kind of Russian or Chinese knockoff sight is this? No IR aiming device. Might have to walk these rounds in.

Reece saw movement from the driver's-side window of the upside-down vehicle. He went prone on the edge of the cliff.

Just get close with your first shot. Identify the impact through these NODs and then walk the rounds into him.

Reece pushed the rifle's selector to "fire" and began taking up slack in the trigger.

The shot wasn't necessary.

Just before the shot broke, the Italian sports car went up in a ball of flame.

• • •

As Reece drove toward Limassol, now with his Ferrari's lights on and traveling at normal highway speeds, he fished a Ziploc bag from a cargo pocket of his pants. The Wagner M4 was in the passenger seat, along with his helmet and NODs.

He powered up the E&E mobile phone he had been given in Israel. Before they left, he had entered a number into the contacts. He called it now.

A male voice answered in Greek.

"Water taxi?" Reece asked.

"That's us," the Maritime Branch operator said, switching to English.

"You guys still in business?"

"We are."

"Great, I'd love a ride."

"Sure thing. When?"

"Right now."

CHAPTER 84

The White House
Washington, D.C.

THE PRESIDENT ROSE FROM the *Resolute* Desk and greeted her visitor halfway across the Oval Office.

"Welcome home, Commander Reece."

"Madam President."

"Please," she said, motioning toward the sitting area by the fireplace.

"After you."

"Have you been in the Oval Office before?"

"No, this is my first visit."

"I like this area by the fireplace," she said. "I do find it odd that the colors and patterns of the couches match the wallpaper. Makes me feel like I'm visiting a Florida retirement community. You might notice that the two sofas are pretty far apart, but for some of the people who come in here, they aren't far apart enough."

She laughed, and Reece recognized that she had the politician's gift of making everyone feel as if they were her best friend.

A portrait of Franklin Roosevelt hung above the fireplace, flanked by portraits of George Washington, Alexander Hamilton, Thomas Jefferson, and Abraham Lincoln.

"So much history in this room," Reece commented.

A door opened and a Navy steward approached with a tray.

"Coffee?" President Olsen asked.

"Always," Reece said.

The president took her coffee black, while Reece quickly doctored his up with the honey and cream provided on the side.

"How do they know?" he asked as the steward left the office.

"One of the great mysteries," she said, taking a sip and setting her cup on a coaster with the Presidential Seal on the table at the far end of the sofa.

"Some things are best left that way," he said.

"Some," the president acknowledged. "Commander, I received a briefing from Director Howe and took a call from the Israeli prime minister on the events of the past few days. He offered his sincere thanks and appreciation. I believe medals are forthcoming."

"It's been an interesting couple of weeks," Reece admitted.

"This country owes you, Commander. Without your efforts, the world would be a different place today."

"It was a team effort. Without Vic Rodriguez, Andy Danreb, William Poe, Raife Hastings, and Katie Buranek, we never would have put together what we did. I'm more of the blunt instrument."

"Modesty becomes you."

"It's also true."

"I understand that Mr. Danreb is back at the CIA, now as a contractor, at least until he has deciphered the Morgan Holdings clientele list. And I believe we have Ms. Buranek on the calendar for an exclusive interview."

"Thank you for that," Reece said.

"It's the least I can do. What are your plans, Commander?"

"I think I'm going to get off the grid for a while. Go back to Montana. I have some personal items to attend to."

"A wedding, perhaps?"

Reece raised an eyebrow.

"This is the most powerful office in the land," she said.

"I'll remember that," Reece replied.

"Commander, according to my classified briefing, if that suitcase nuke had detonated, Israel would have hit back quickly and decisively, probably with land-based and sub-based nuclear weapons. We evaluated this scenario using CAE's Single Synthetic Environment, the most advanced simulation platform in the world. It allows us to predict and demonstrate the outcomes of attacks like this. The impact on Tel Aviv would have been devastating. We would have supported Israel and played right into the Collective's hands. As it stands, Russia and the Collective lost billions, possibly trillions, from what Director Howe briefed. Russia remains bogged down in Ukraine, and China has not invaded Taiwan. Israel has recovered most of the debris through an undersea salvage operation that has given them insights into Iran's nuclear program they would not have had otherwise. The Israeli prime minister has managed to keep the number of those who know what really happened to an absolute minimum. They don't mess around with security violations over there."

"No, they don't," Reece agreed.

"That is something I wanted to discuss with you."

"What's that?"

"You have heard by now that there was an inexcusable breach of security at the CIA. The documents you recovered have gone missing."

"Vic told me."

"You don't seem overly concerned, Commander. That surprises me."

"We still have the list from Morgan Holdings and can sanction individuals and corporations that are either a part of the Collective or act on their behalf."

"I wish it were that easy," the president said.

"It's not easy, but it's something."

"It is something."

She paused, thinking through how to proceed.

"Commander, I am not going to accept my party's nomination to run in the next election."

"Oh?" Reece asked, curious about where she was taking the conversation.

"I hear what they say—that I am only the first female president because the man in front of me was assassinated, and that the only reason I was even on the ticket was to deliver Florida. But now I am here. I am the president, and I plan to do what I can to improve our standing in the world and here at home for all Americans. Then I'll step away."

"I think that is wise and admirable, Madam President."

"My party will hate me for it, but it means all the decisions I make are to advance the prosperity and security of the American people. That makes me almost as dangerous as President Christensen. The other side—see, 'the other side'—that divisive rhetoric has become the norm. They are going to do what they can to undermine executive initiatives simply for political gain. The days of statesmanship are behind us, I'm afraid. They died with President Reagan and Speaker O'Neill."

"It's a brutal game, Madam President. I'm not built for it."

"Commander, there will be more about me that will hit the news when I announce I am stepping aside. I am guessing you do not follow the tabloids."

"I tend to think most of what I see these days is a manipulation. That's part of why I want to get back to my cabin."

"The short backstory is that soon after the next inauguration, my husband and I will separate. A few news organizations have already speculated that to be the case. Even as a politician, which also means you need to be an actor of sorts, I have a hard time faking it."

"Faking what?"

"I got married young. I was a bit naive in the beginning. I saw what my future husband wanted me to see—that he was a high-powered attorney on the rise. He was an attorney, but certainly not high-powered, and definitely not on the rise. He was a lobbyist."

"What kind of lobbyist?"

"First it was tobacco. Then it was opioids. Then a vape company. And then he worked for a few different firms focused on influencing the USDA—there is big money in their dietary guidelines. I've seen it firsthand. Makes me sick, but that's how Washington works. My political climb has helped him."

"I'm sorry to hear that."

She waved her hand. "I was about to leave him when President Christensen asked me to be his running mate. A divorce at that time would have torpedoed the offer. It was a true honor to be asked, even if I knew the ticket only needed me to bring in Florida on election night."

"I guess that's how politics works."

"I'll serve him papers the day after the inauguration. He will be there with me on the steps of the Capitol. That's the last I plan to see of him."

"You're not asking me to pay him a visit, are you?"

The president almost spit out her sip of coffee.

"Goodness, no."

"Sorry. In my line of work, that sort of request is not too unusual."

"I'm glad we turned off the recording devices in here," she joked. "My husband," she continued, "got to know a lot of members of the armed forces through my service and from events we attended in my role as a representative and then as vice president. He's enamored with special operations, particularly SEALs. He falls in the fanboy category, as there is no way in hell he could have made it through any sort of selection. He's more the paintball, airsoft type."

Reece laughed.

"As you know, Florida is home to SOCOM and the UDT/SEAL Museum," she continued.

"I've been. It's impressive."

"It is. At a SEAL Foundation event a few years back, he swindled two veterans out of their stories. He lied by saying he was a writer. What a joke; he wrote a couple of articles for a regional Florida magazine that were dreadful. They never asked him back. He got these operators to sign contracts that essentially gave him control over their stories, thinking my political standing would open doors in the publishing world. He's a charmer, but he's also a scam artist. He didn't serve, yet he is trying to profit from their sacrifice. Plus, he's a horrible writer. There were warning signs, but I ignored them. Even with my progressive tendencies I am still old-fashioned in some respects—don't tell my constituency."

Reece liked her more the longer they talked.

"Then there is the cheating part of it. I have records, and my attorneys are on it. We are just waiting until I leave office. The Secret Service has been extremely helpful. He's been influence-peddling with foreign nationals, promising to sway or guide my decisions. Countries like China and Ukraine fall for it hook, line, and sinker. Little do they know I only communicate with him through my personal attorneys. Oh, my memoirs will be spicy."

"I'll be sure and stock it in my bookstore. You asked me my plans earlier. I have a vison of owning and running a small bookstore in Montana. Of course, mine would also have coffee and whiskey and be attached to an archery shop."

"That's unique. I would not have guessed that. When I'm out of office and on a book tour, we'll do a signing."

"Deal."

"Commander, I believe we share a belief that the country is at a crossroads."

"You sound more optimistic than I am."

"That's the political way of saying 'I don't know if we can save it.' The lobbyists, big tech, the defense industry, pharmaceutical companies—they have real power, real control. The people, as you correctly noted, get manipulated and taxed, with no recourse other than to vote, but that vote means less and less the more power and control these corporations accumulate."

"It's a machine," Reece said. "I don't want any part of it."

"There is no New World, Commander. No faraway lands in which to plant a flag and start over."

"That's why I'm going to the mountains and tossing my phone in the dumpster before I leave D.C."

"I thought you would say that. I believed I could do something about the country's trajectory from this office. Now that I'm in this seat, I know how monumental a task that is. I will do what I can through executive order to deal with the Collective as Mr. Danreb compiles his report, but another oligarchy here at home continues to gain power. I fear the republic as we know it is dead."

"Why are you telling me this, Madam President?"

"Because, before I leave office, I have a proposal for you."

"What's that?"

"I think it's better if she tells you."

"'She'?"

"Please don't get up," the president said. Gale Olsen stood and walked to the *Resolute* Desk. She opened a drawer and returned with a KryptAll phone. She handed it to Reece.

Reece accepted it uneasily, looking at the president with skepticism as she took her seat on the couch across from him.

"It's okay, Commander."

Reece slowly raised the phone to his ear.

"Hello, James." The female voice on the other end of the line was eerily familiar. It sounded a bit like Lauren. "I've missed you," she said.

Reece placed the phone on his lap and looked at the president in disbelief.

She nodded. "Alice is back."

• • •

After Reece left, the president walked past her desk and stood in the window of ballistic glass that overlooked the rose garden.

James Reece.

The national flag was to her left and the flag of the president of the United States was to her right.

I will faithfully execute the Office of President of the United States, and will to the best of my ability, preserve, protect and defend the Constitution of the United States.

President Olsen turned and sat at the desk used by every president since 1880 other than Johnson, Nixon, and Ford. She opened a drawer and returned the KryptAll phone they had used to contact Alice. She picked up a second phone and closed the drawer, staring at it for a few long moments before bringing it to life.

She swiveled her high-back black leather chair to the left and gazed upon the dark blue flag embroidered with the presidential coat of arms. Fifty stars encircled an eagle holding arrows in its left talon and an olive branch in its right: war and peace. In its beak above a shield of red, white, and blue was a banner inscribed with "E Pluribus Unum"—"Out of Many, One."

As the encrypted phone powered on, the president made her decision.

She tapped a six-digit KryptAll number into her device and hit the green phone icon under the numeric keypad.

Her report would be brief and disguised in layers of code.

An associate was awaiting the disposition of and status of the CIA's top assassin.

CHAPTER 85

Constitution Gardens
National Mall and Memorial Parks
Washington, D.C.

REECE SAT ON A bench to the side of the Constitution Gardens pond on the National Mall in Washington, D.C. He knew the small island in the pond contained a rock memorial to the fifty-six signers of the Declaration of Independence. He wondered what they would think of the generations that had inherited the gift of freedom for which they had sacrificed so much. Reece had been here many times. Located to the north of the Lincoln Memorial Reflecting Pool, it is a quiet area that is often neglected in favor of the grander Washington Monument to the east, Lincoln Memorial to the west, and World War II Memorial in between. Vietnam and Korea are offset from one another across the reflecting pool.

It was overcast, and Reece was back in his normal attire of Salomon shoes, Origin jeans, a dark green Triple Aught Design sweater, brown Kühl jacket, Gatorz sunglasses, and Hoyt ball cap. He watched Vic Rodriguez approach from the east. He was dressed in a dark blue suit and overcoat. He took a seat next to Reece on the bench and set his black briefcase next to him.

"You don't really blend in around here, Reece."

"Good. I was just leaving. You blend in perfectly. Almost didn't see you coming."

Vic smiled. "Yeah, I don't think you want to adapt to this place."

"I think you're right, though I do like it here on the Mall. My dad used to bring me, you know."

"Every kid should spend time here," Vic said.

"Right down there," Reece said, pointing west. "That's the Vietnam Veterans Memorial, and just across from it is the Korean War Veterans Memorial. Did you know that those are the only two memorials to the Cold War on the Mall?"

"I hadn't thought of it that way, Reece, but you are right."

"We abandoned our POWs in both those wars."

"Your father's investigation seems to confirm it."

"There are a lot of lessons here, Vic."

"There are."

"And there," Reece said, pointing at the World War II Memorial. "Some of us learned that war is big business in that one. We've been fighting and losing them ever since. Patriots stand up to fight and die in them while businessmen sign contracts worth billions to support them."

"I think that's always been the way, Reece. What you did in Israel averted a war that would have seen a lot of people die. Maybe there is a memorial that's not going up on this Mall in the future because of what you did."

Reece shook his head. "There will just be another one. We can't help ourselves."

"Reece, what are you going to do? The president wants an answer."

"Katie and I are packing up what's left of her condo and heading to Montana. I'm going to take a breath."

"Technically, you still work for the Agency."

"Then I quit."

"Damn it, Reece."

"My father gave me some advice in that letter. I'm going to take it."

"Andy is still working his way through that client list," Vic said. "We are going to get the names attached to the shell companies, and we will present that report to the president."

"And then what?"

"We will have to see," Vic said.

"Yeah, we'll have to see. Did you find what I asked for?"

"I did," Vic said, moving the briefcase to his lap.

"Well?"

Vic opened the case and handed Reece a manila folder.

"It's in there."

Reece took the folder and tapped the spine against the palm of his left hand.

"Thanks, Vic."

"I do have a bit of bad news."

"What is it?"

"Martha Stowe is dying."

Reece looked toward the pond.

"I know."

"Reece, we are not all bad guys. That evil you've been fighting, it can be closer than you think. Sometimes you don't see it because it's right next to you."

Reece looked at Vic as he closed and locked his briefcase.

"You didn't answer my question about the president."

"I'll catch her next time."

Vic nodded and stood.

"Take care of yourself, Reece."

"You, too."

The CIA man turned and walked in the direction of the Washington Monument, leaving his top operative alone with his memories of the dead.

CHAPTER 86

Cologne, Germany

MAX GENRICH TOOK THE lift to the twelfth floor of his flat overlooking the Rhine. It was a large flat for this part of the city. He was pleased with his interior decorator. At night the views could be spectacular. Tonight it was cloudy, so Max dropped his gym bag with his sweaty jiu-jitsu gi by the small washer-dryer and went to the kitchen, where he poured himself a glass of water. He then walked to his home office, which enjoyed the same expansive view as the main living area.

He had made it home much faster than he expected. First to Mexico, then to South Africa, then Frankfurt, and then to Bonn. He had spent most of the flight deciding what to do about James Reece. He had been home for a week and was now back in his routine. By the time he realized that the desk chair was missing, it was too late.

"Hands," a man said from the missing chair. He was in the far left corner of the room, his face in shadow. His right leg was crossed over his left, his right hand resting on his right thigh, a hand that held a SIG P365 pistol with a suppressor.

"No sudden movements, eh?"

Was that a South African accent? It sounded close.

"Raise your hands."

"Do you want my pistol?"

"No. I want to see your hands."

Genrich slowly raised his hands to either side of his head.

"Put them on the desk so I can see them. Palms up."

Genrich did as he was told.

"You should really look into a building with better security. I expected more from an SVR assassin."

"Who are you?"

"Someone you almost crossed paths with recently. Unfortunately for you, I did spend some time with a Russian mob boss in New York who pointed me in the right direction."

Fucking Bratva.

"What do you want?"

"I'm just here to tie up a loose end. In case there is any confusion, you are the loose end."

"If I am not already dead, that means you want something."

"I do."

"What is it?"

"I want to hire you."

CHAPTER 87

Martha's Vineyard
Dukes County
Massachusetts

THE STAIRS CREAKED JUST like Reece remembered as he took them to the second floor.

He stopped at the top. A light beckoned at the end of the hallway.

He walked down the quiet passage and knocked on the side of the open door.

"Mrs. Stowe? Martha?" he asked softly.

There was no response, so he said it again louder.

"Speak up. Is that you, James? They told me you'd be by tonight."

Reece stepped into the room.

The floral wallpaper was the same, as were the dresser and armoire.

The difference was that Martha Stowe no longer occupied the rocker near the glass doors to her balcony. She was in her four-poster bed, propped up with pillows. She wore a pink flannel nightgown, and her arms were on the outside of the baby-blue comforter. Her left hand held her reading glasses, and a small stack of books was on her nightstand. She looked frail.

"What are you reading these days?" Reece asked as he approached.

He pulled a chair from a desk against the wall and sat down. In her bed she had him by a couple of inches.

"After you left, I decided to stop reading trash and go back to some of my old favorites. I've been revisiting the classics and have been thoroughly enjoying them."

"I'm glad," Reece said. "Can I get you anything?"

"No, dear, I've had my dinner and my tea. I don't have long. I tire easily, I'm afraid. Even more so than when you were here, which was not all that long ago, though I do stumble a bit on my dates and times."

"What's this?" Reece asked, reaching for a thick book with which he was familiar.

"That! Now, that's exciting. After you left, I had the woman who helps me dig it out. It was in a box in the attic. She said it was in the last one she searched, but I can't be sure. Do you recognize it? Your father gave it to Walter a long time ago."

"He did?" Reece asked, turning the book over in his hand. "*Once an Eagle*, by Anton Myrer."

"After Walter read it, he tried to get me to read it, but I was being stubborn, you see. I told him I didn't want to read a war book about Vietnam."

"It's not really about Vietnam. Well, it is, but not directly."

"So, you've read it?"

"My dad gave it to me, too. It's one of my all-time favorites. I passed copies of it to SEALs I worked with as they started their time in the profession of arms. In fact, I'd put a letter in the front for them to read before they dove in, and then another at the end for them to read after they were done."

"Why the two letters?"

"The first one framed why I was giving them the book, and the second one was my take on what they had just read. I didn't want to influence their reading experience with my personal interpretation beforehand, so they had to read it first to get to my second letter."

"That is very thoughtful, James. Your dad inscribed it for Walter."

Reece opened the front cover to see his father's familiar handwriting.

> Walter,
>
> It was an honor to serve a tour in-country with you.
>
> "You've never lived until you've almost died. For those who have fought for it, life has a flavor the protected shall never know."—MACV SOG
>
> The lesson in the pages ahead of you, just as in life, is to see to your character, and your reputation will take care of itself.
>
> Remember those left behind.
>
> Strength and Honor.
>
> Thomas Reece

When Reece looked back up, Martha's eyes were on him.

"You keep that, James. I can order another."

"Thank you, Martha."

"I'm tired. Would you be a dear and turn out my lights?"

"I can do that," Reece said. "Do you want the curtains open or closed?"

"Open, please. One never knows how many sunrises they have left."

Reece filled her water glass and set it next to her bed. Then he helped move one pillow aside so she could lie flat, and he ensured the comforter was pulled up tight. Then he moved the chair back to the desk and turned out two of the bedside lamps.

"Thank you, dear." Her voice was soft. "Did you find him?"

Reece knelt by the bed.

"I did. He was closer than we thought."

She kept her eyes closed.

"Who?"

Reece leaned down and whispered something in her ear.

She nodded. It was time for her to rest.

"What are you going to do, James?" Her voice trailed off.

Reece stood.

"I'm going to finish the job."

Then he bent down, kissed her forehead, and walked to the bedroom door. He paused and looked back before turning out the final light.

"Good night, Martha," Reece whispered. But she was already asleep.

EPILOGUE

There are no secrets that time does not reveal.

—JEAN RACINE, *BRITANNICUS*

Almont, Colorado

REECE CAME IN FROM the north. He used to know these mountains like only a boy can. No map, compass, or GPS. Just tennis shoes, jeans, T-shirt, a flannel, and a small backpack with a lunch. Maybe a fly rod or BB gun. Running, exploring, climbing trees, building forts. True freedom. The mountains and freedom were still familiar to him.

He watched the old man for a few days from his hide site on the hill.

The man went to town once for groceries in the Lexus. No one visited, not even the caretaker.

He fished every morning but didn't venture far from the house.

There were no signs of security, no new cameras, no drones, no guards, and no new dogs, just the two black Labs that ran and played in the grass in the front of house, stopping every now and then to drink from the river and watch their master cast before tearing back up the bank to chase one another through the woods.

He would catch and then release the hearty Brown trout beneath the surface to catch them again another day.

In the afternoons he would take a short walk to the nearby bridge with the dogs, a walking stick in hand and his Browning 12-gauge over his shoulder.

He grilled on the Weber in the evenings, with a cocktail or glass of wine in hand.

The light in the upstairs room went out at 9:00 p.m. sharp and turned on again at 6:00 a.m.

William Poe had become a creature of habit.

On the morning of the fifth day, Reece stuffed his gear into his pack and set it by a nearby rock formation. Then he hiked down the hillside and worked his way around the open field across from the house.

Poe came out with his rod and his dogs at 9:15 a.m., picked his way down the bank in his waders, and made a beautiful cast.

It was only minutes before he caught his first Brown. He placed his rod under his right arm, using his left on the leader to guide the fish closer and then remove the barbless hook with forceps. He then stretched, examined his equipment, and made another cast.

"How long are you going to sit there, lad?"

Reece stood and approached from the opposite side of the river and descended the bank until his boots were in the water he had loved so much as a boy.

"I've been waiting on you," Poe said, making another cast. "Beautiful morning, isn't it?"

"It is," Reece replied. The Vietnam-era Mk 22 "Hush Puppy" pistol with its distinctive suppressor and skeletonized stock was in his right hand, pointing at the ground.

"When did you figure it out?"

"That you were part of the Collective?"

"Yes."

"It took me longer than it should have. Did my dad ever get close?"

"Oh, he was close the entire time. I knew you would get it as soon as

Danreb decrypted the clientele list from Morgan Holdings. My father set it up. I should have changed the name, but that's more steps in a modern world where transactions and changes like that are documented electronically."

"Taylor River Ventures," Reece said, shaking his head. "So, it's always been about the money for you?"

"Look around, James. This place is nice, but it's not extravagant. It was never about money for me."

"Then what?"

"Loyalty."

"Loyalty?"

"The country is on life support, James. That has nothing to do with the Collective. It has everything to do with apathy. The World War Two generation knew it. That's why they formed the Collective—to ensure that East and West didn't destroy the world in their race for nuclear dominance."

"It has also made you, and them, extremely wealthy."

"Out of necessity. The dumbing down of the citizenry, whether intentional or not, is happening. There will be a shift in the world order; it's inevitable."

"And you and the Collective want to control it?"

"Why not? The republic is lost. Even you know this current system is not worth fighting for."

"I'm not ready to give up on it yet."

"You already have. You just don't know it. Your father and I did good work together for a long time."

"So it wasn't all a lie?"

"Oh no. We both lost men in Vietnam. I brought him into the Agency, and we tracked down all the GRU advisors who had worked in Southeast Asia that we could find."

"You turned him into an assassin?"

"He was already a killer. He just needed targets. Just like you, James."

"And the POWs?"

"At first I was on board. Neutralizing GRU advisors was in line with U.S. interests in the Cold War. But then Tom started extracting information from them."

"About POWs?"

"Yes. We found out that some had been transferred to the Soviet Union. That was a problem. Back then people still cared. Today, I'm not so sure."

"So as the mission expands and you and my dad start investigating the MIA-POW issue, you have to undermine it because of the interests of the Collective."

"A nuclear war was not outside the realm of possibility in those days."

"But my dad keeps pushing. He suspects there is a group of Russians and Americans who are coordinating efforts to advance an agenda not in alignment with either country's national security or economic goals. A group with an entirely different set of loyalties."

"He was on the right track."

"So, you had him killed."

"Eventually, but that was much later."

"I had Vic go back in the records. I was curious where my dad was before he went to Argentina. Turns out he was here, on official business."

"I slowed him down with Walter Stowe and the aborted POW mission. That kept him busy for twenty years."

"And Kennedy?"

"That was a surprise. How Tom got so close on that one I don't know. He shared bits and pieces with me over the years. Little did he know he was talking to one of those who set the plan in motion."

"You had a hand in killing your own president?"

“Now two presidents. I was working in Vietnam in 1963 when Kennedy and the CIA betrayed Diem and his brother. They knew a coup was coming. At first it was just insurance. I didn't think Kennedy would turn on Diem. But when he did, the plan was already in place. What was interesting is that I didn't see anything about it in Tom's files.”

“How did you get the files out of CIA headquarters? You weren't even in there.”

“We have people everywhere, James.”

“I want you to tell me more about them.”

“I'm afraid it wouldn't be helpful. By its very nature it's an ambiguous connection at many levels. That's why Danreb's client list will be helpful to you, but it's certainly not all-encompassing. There isn't a membership roster. It's not organized that way. Even I don't know everyone who is associated. That's its strength, and why your father could never put it all together, try as he might.”

“You were the missing link. You were the connective tissue between all of it: Walter Stowe, my dad, the CIA. You were in front of him the whole time.”

“Yes. He was blinded by the wrong kind of loyalty—to God and country. We were hiding in plain sight. That's how I got the files. Like I said, we have people everywhere.”

“Where are the files?”

“I burned them a week ago. They are gone, James. There was enough information in that box to take down the Collective. I was able to get it out of the Agency before they even made copies. Everything that you may have seen is now just a wild conspiracy theory.”

“What if I were to tell you there was a copy?”

Reece's statement interrupted Poe mid-cast.

“What if I were to tell you there were multiple copies?”

"Bullshit."

"Shouldn't have left me alone in that bank for so long."

"What have you done, James?"

"They had a copy machine, and I had wads of cash."

"Jesus Christ. Where are they?"

Reece looked down at the Rolex Submariner on his wrist, the same watch his dad was wearing when Poe had him killed.

"James, what did you do?"

"I mailed them."

"What?"

"I mailed them," Reece repeated.

"Where?"

"I mailed a copy to every major news organization in the country. I set it up with the bank before I walked back outside."

Poe hung his head.

"It's over, Poe."

"You just think it's over, Reece. There will always be the few who rule over the many. You stopped nothing."

"I stopped you."

"What do you believe in, James? God? Country? Freedom? Or do you believe in the lofty ideal of some nonsense like truth? Let me tell you. There is no truth. There is only power. That power crosses borders and ideologies. It's not about an allegiance to dying countries. It is an allegiance to broader governance, control, and safety. You made the world less stable today. Is that what you believe in?"

Reece paused.

"I believe in accountability. And I believe in consequences."

Reece lifted his father's Hush Puppy to his shoulder.

The dogs played on the lawn. The river rushed by as it had for millennia.

"Come with me," Reece said. "It's over."

Poe looked up at the clear blue sky and then back at the house that he loved.

"Take care of my dogs for me," he said as he undid the fastener on his wading belt designed to keep rushing water from dragging an angler down. Poe pulled it from his waist and dropped it into the river.

"Good-bye, James."

The old man took two steps forward into the deeper, swifter-running water. The current pulled his legs from underneath him and swept him into the Taylor. Reece watched him disappear, surface again, and then vanish forever.

Reece lowered the Hush Puppy. His feet were getting numb in the cold runoff.

He stepped out of the river and worked his way up the rocky embankment to begin his journey home. The sun was getting higher in the sky and spring was in the air. It smelled the same way it had at this time of year when he was young. When he got to the top of the bank at the edge of the clearing, he closed his eyes, putting himself into darkness and heightening his other senses: leaves in the trees, a light breeze, birds, insects, the river running over and around rocks below.

He turned to look at the cabin and guesthouse, remembering a time when multiple generations had gathered there to fish, break bread, share stories, and pass on lessons. There was no going back.

Use the time you have, James. When you put down the gun, walk away. Don't live in the past. Love your wife. Raise your kids. And don't look back. Treasure each moment, because once it's gone, it's gone forever.

"I will, Dad."

Reece made his way back up the mountain and found his pack where he had left it. He watched the cabin for a few more hours, spending precious moments with his dad. Then, as the sun started to drop in the sky, he stood and hoisted his pack to his shoulders. It was time to get home. Katie was waiting.

He turned and walked into the setting sun, toward the light of salvation.

• • •

Kumba Ranch
Flathead Valley, Montana

Reece heard footsteps behind him on the gravel. Instead of turning, he continued to stare into the flames. A glass of red wine appeared over his right shoulder.

"This is the last of the Semper," Katie said.

"Thank you. I think I know where Jonathan is hiding another case. I'll see what I can do about liberating it. Security has improved up here, but I still have a few tricks up my sleeve."

Katie stepped forward and then rocked back onto his lap, sliding an arm around his neck and pulling a wool blanket over them both.

They had built a fire by the lake after dinner, as had become their custom. As the days grew longer, they would have dinner on the back deck and then enjoy a glass of wine together by the fire, watching the light dancing on the lake as the sky turned magnificent hues of orange and red before the sun dropped below the horizon. Mule deer and elk were common sightings.

They still had a lot to work out, but Reece was no longer sleeping on the floor or shoving towels under the door to keep the light out, so they were making progress. Every now and then she would find him by the window that overlooked the front deck, the window through which he had watched the FBI vehicles descend upon them and throw their lives into turmoil.

His feet had healed, and he was working out with Raife twice a day, putting muscle back on a frame that had leaned out in prison. They ate a lot of wild game with vegetables that Katie would pick up in town or that

Caroline Hastings would bring down from her garden. The Wagoneer was still inoperable, and Raife was threatening to put it out of its misery. Fixing it was on Reece's list of things to do. He shot a lot of arrows using his new Hoyt, and he had one built up for Katie at the local archery shop that he and Raife were still thinking of buying. He rarely went to town. When he did, it was usually to take delivery of a new firearm at the local FFL; the Hastingses' lawyers were still working with the FBI and ATF on getting back what had been confiscated in the raid. Reece was slowly building back his arsenal.

His fly fishing had improved drastically, even though there was really nowhere for him to go but up. Katie had been raised with a fly rod in her hand. They would go out together for an hour or two in the mornings, and she would work with him on his cast.

Then Katie would spend a few hours writing in the peace and serenity of the cabin. She would use the Internet at local coffee shops and do her news hits from a studio in town. Life was much more pleasant and calm without the constant connection to the rest of the world.

Reece paid little attention to the national news though he was aware of the firestorm sweeping the nation. He had tossed his cell phone into a trash can before leaving D.C. earlier in the month, and the cabin was not equipped with Internet, but they did still have cable, so Katie could stay on top of developments, which also forced Reece to not completely disconnect from the events he had played a role in shaping.

Leading the news was the joint report issued by the Commission on the Assassination of President Alec Christensen. The Senate committee disclosed that a Russian private military company was behind the president's assassination. The group responsible had been eliminated in a joint interagency special operations mission earlier in the month off the coast of Israel, though specifics remain classified. The Russian president had been placed under house arrest in his palace on the Black Sea, along with the deputy chairman of the Security Council of the Russian

Federation. Tanks surrounded the Kremlin, and several senior Russian generals were calling on the legislature to impeach the president and install the vice president as acting president. That news had followed reports that Russian Federal Security Service Director Pavel Dashkov had been assassinated on Cyprus the same day that a vehicle accident had claimed the life of Wagner Group CEO Andrei Sokoloff. Receiving less coverage were reports that Russian Foreign Intelligence Service Director Rostya Levitsky had been found dead in a Moscow park. He had been shot at close range with a nine-millimeter pistol.

Stocks had taken a dive as the Securities and Exchange Commission and Commodity Futures Trading Commission filed charges against Sidney Morgan and Morgan Holdings. In a highly publicized arrest, Morgan had been taken into custody by federal agents at his Darien, Connecticut, home. The criminal indictment charged him with wire fraud, conspiracy to commit wire fraud on consumers and lenders, conspiracy to commit commodities fraud, securities fraud, securities fraud conspiracy, conspiracy to commit money laundering, and conspiracy to defraud the Federal Election Commission and violate campaign finance laws. His attorneys quickly released a statement that Morgan Holdings was applying for Chapter 11 protection. Reporters had linked Morgan Holdings to several prominent government officials, including Congressman Douglas Linden. In what they termed "unrelated news," the congressman announced he would finish his term and step away from politics, citing unspecified health issues.

Reece did turn up the volume on their television earlier in the day when news began to break concerning former CIA officer and financier William Poe. He had been reported missing weeks earlier. His body had turned up downriver from his Colorado home. The death was reported as an accidental drowning. In a related story, multiple news outlets had recently received identical packages from an anonymous source containing information on his involvement in illegal CIA programs dating back to the 1960s. Some of those documents confirmed that American POWs from the Vietnam War were transferred to Soviet prison camps in Siberia in the 1960s and 1970s, something both the United States and former Soviet Union had vehemently denied in the past. Journalists were also investigating a nexus of Russian and American elites allegedly conspiring to control the world economy in a plan dating back to the Bretton Woods Conference of 1944. The news anchor reported that the CIA was scrambling to suppress the documents as classified, but they had already been posted to multiple websites and downloaded more than fifteen million times and counting.

Reece reached down to scratch Castor behind the ears. Then, as per their SOP, Pollux stretched to insert his block head into the mix for a little love as well.

"It's getting chilly," Katie said. "What can I do to entice you inside?"

"I can think of a few things," Reece said mischievously.

"Another glass?" she asked.

"That would be great."

Katie leaned in close and brought her lips to his.

"I love you, James."

"I love you, too, Katie."

The dogs stood. The sun had set and the temperature had dropped, which meant it was time to go in.

"The dogs are with me," Katie said.

"I'll be right behind you," Reece said.

"I'll be waiting. Castor! Pollux! Come on, boys!"

Katie took off for the house, the dogs dancing around her feet in their version of hot pursuit.

Reece took a moment and then set his wineglass to the side. He picked up a long stick and stoked the fire, watching the sparks rise into the night sky.

He looked back at the house. He could see Katie through the windows, and as she turned on the news, Reece heard the anchor begin to give the nation an update on the week's developing stories. He turned to the fire and pulled the letter left to him by his father in the safe-deposit box from his jacket pocket. Katie was the only other person who had read it. By the light of the flames, though he had already committed it to memory, Reece read it one last time. When he was done, he fed each page into the glowing embers of the fire.

He watched them go up in smoke and then went to join Katie in the cabin.

AUTHOR'S NOTE

IF YOU HAVE READ David Morrell's novelizations of *Rambo: First Blood Part II* and *Rambo III*, you will most certainly have noticed the tribute to him and his work at the beginning and end of this novel. David Morrell created and introduced the world to Rambo in his 1972 debut thriller, *First Blood*, a novel that has not been out of print since publication. David again broke the mold in 1984 with *The Brotherhood of the Rose*, combining the most engaging elements of American and British spy fiction to create something entirely new that moved the genre forward. I discovered David's work when I was eleven, and it cemented me on my path into the SEAL Teams and into publishing. To find out exactly how, check out my conversation with David Morrell celebrating the fiftieth anniversary of *First Blood* on my *Danger Close* podcast. I also highly recommend you spend some time on his website, davidmorrell.net, and in the pages of his novels.

"One breath behind the truth" is a line from the prepublication publicity package for Charles McCarry's classic 1974 espionage tale, *The Tears of Autumn*, which inspired the Kennedy assassination tie-in to this novel. Rarely have I heard a catchphrase that so succinctly and eloquently captures the essence of a novel. His protagonist even whispers, "I believe in consequences," as does James Reece, though I didn't make the connection until I had already written that chapter and was going back through McCarry's book in December 2022, after the executive branch once again refused to release the remaining documents related to the Kennedy assassination. Close to sixty years after the assassination, the Central Intelligence Agency convinced two different presidents from two different parties that it is in the best interest of the country to defy congressional mandate and keep the unreleased files a secret. If they bear no culpability, they have sure spent a lot of time going out of their way to make themselves look guilty. I first read *The Tears of Autumn* in high school. The theory explored in its pages has stayed with me. Before Charles McCarry devoted himself to writing full-time, he served in the United States Army and then in the CIA. He sets the tone of *The Tears of Autumn* with a quote from the Pentagon Papers: "The Pentagon's secret study of the Vietnam war discloses that President Kennedy knew and approved of plans for the military coup d'état that overthrew President Ngo Dinh Diem in 1963. . . . Our complicity in his overthrow heightened our responsibilities and our commitments in Vietnam, the study finds." Would I have come up with McCarry's theory on my own? Not in a million years. But McCarry did. He worked for the Agency from 1958 to 1967. I would have loved to have talked with him and asked him about his, or I should say his character's, theory. He passed away in 2019 at the age of eighty-eight. "To the living, one owes consideration; to the dead, only the truth," writes Voltaire in *Lettres sur Œdipe*.

What of Able Archer and the events of 1983 that brought the world to the brink of a nuclear exchange? Those events are as described to include the recent successful efforts of the CIA to reclassify the Perroots memo. Why would they "reclassify" something that had already gone through a four-year declassification review process? The Perroots memo was in the public domain long enough for anyone with a printer to preserve it. I may know a guy with a copy. It contains insights that could help us better understand Russian strategic thinking, and lessons that we would be wise to apply to the decisions of today regarding Russia and

Ukraine. Why would the CIA not want you to read it? I can think of a couple of reasons. For more information on Able Archer and the events of 1983, read *The Brink* by Marc Ambinder, *1983* by Taylor Downing, and *The Able Archers* by Brian J. Morra. You can also watch or listen to my conversation with Brian J. Morra on my *Danger Close* podcast.

The United States Penitentiary Florence Administrative Maximum Facility Range 13 Special Housing Unit, exists in Fremont County, Colorado. Other than putting James Reece in the dark, as far as I know, the rooms are as described.

If you happen to be on the Black Sea in the vicinity of Krasnodar Krai, Russia, be sure to steer clear of the Residence at Cape Idokopas, more commonly known as "Putin's Palace." Some liberties were taken in its description, but not many.

The Soviet "closed" or "secret" cities were, and are, real. They were built and operated as described in the novel.

If you are looking for the Jäger Club two hours north of New York City, just west of the Hudson and north of the Ashokan Reservoir on the edge of the Indian Head Wilderness, you will not find it. It goes by another name, in another location.

Were U.S. POWs abandoned in Vietnam? Were U.S. POWs sent to the Soviet Union? There is little I have observed of government either from the inside or the outside that would persuade me to believe that they would not act as depicted in the pages of this novel concerning the POW-MIA issue. In reading *Inside Delta Force* by Eric L. Haney upon its publication in 2002, I was stunned to read that Delta had been put on alert for a mission to rescue American POWs in Laos. The year was 1981. It is one of the most heartbreaking and disturbing episodes in modern American military history. For additional information, read *Survivors: Vietnam POWs Tell Their Stories* by Zalin Grant, *Why Didn't You Get Me Out* by Frank Anton, *The Men We Left Behind* by Mark Sauter and Jim Sanders, and *Soldiers of Misfortune: The Cold War Betrayal and Sacrifice of American POWs* by James D. Sanders, Mark A. Sauter, and R. Cort Kirkwood. If you were involved in intelligence collection focused on American POWs held in Laos, Cambodia, or Vietnam, or if you were a planner or policy maker or connected with plans to rescue Americans left behind in Southeast Asia, look me up. I'm working on a list.

"The Collective," as far as I know, is fiction. But if you take Colorado Road 742 northeast out of Almont toward the Taylor Park Reservoir, you will pass a nondescript entrance to a ranch along the Taylor River. If you were to explore further, you might find a house and guest lodge that fit the description in this novel. Whether it was ever used as a safe house or way station for rogue elements of the Central Intelligence Agency with ties to the Collective is unknown.

GLOSSARY

160th Special Operations Aviation Regiment: The Army's premier helicopter unit that provides aviation support to special forces. Known as the "Night Stalkers," they are widely regarded as the best helicopter pilots and crews in the world.

.260: .260 Remington; .264"/6.5mm rifle cartridge that is essentially a .308 Winchester necked down to accept a smaller-diameter bullet. The .260 provides superior external ballistics to the .308 with less felt recoil and can often be fired from the same magazines.

.300 Norma: .300 Norma Magnum; a cartridge designed for long-range precision shooting that has been adopted by USSOCOM for sniper use.

.375 CheyTac: Long-range cartridge, adapted from the .408 CheyTac, that can fire a 350-grain bullet at 2,970 feet per second. A favorite of extreme long-range match competitors who use it on targets beyond 3,000 yards.

.375 H&H Magnum: An extremely common and versatile big-game rifle cartridge, found throughout Africa. The cartridge was developed by Holland & Holland in 1912 and traditionally fires a 300-grain bullet.

.404 Jeffery: A rifle cartridge designed for large game animals, developed by W. J. Jeffery & Company in 1905.

.408 CheyTac: Long-range cartridge adapted from the .505 Gibbs, capable of firing a 419-grain bullet at 2,850 feet per second.

.500 Nitro: A .510-caliber cartridge designed for use against heavy, dangerous game, often chambered in double rifles. The cartridge fires a 570-grain bullet at 2,150 feet per second.

75th Ranger Regiment: A large-scale Army special operations unit that conducts direct-action missions, including raids and airfield seizures. These elite troops often work in conjunction with other special operations units.

AC-130 Spectre: A ground-support aircraft used by the U.S. military, based on the ubiquitous C-130 cargo plane. AC-130s are armed with a 105mm howitzer, 40mm cannons, and 7.62mm miniguns, and are considered the premier close-air-support weapon of the U.S. arsenal.

Accuracy International: A British company producing high-quality precision rifles, often used for military sniper applications.

ACOG: Advanced Combat Optical Gunsight. A magnified optical sight designed for use on rifles and carbines, made by Trijicon. The ACOG is popular among U.S. forces as it provides both magnification and an illuminated reticle that provides aiming points for various target ranges.

AFIS: Automated Fingerprint Identification System; electronic fingerprint database maintained by the FBI.

Aimpoint Micro: Aimpoint Micro T-2; high-quality unmagnified red-dot combat optic produced in Sweden that can be used on a variety of weapons platforms. This durable sight weighs only three ounces and has a five-year battery life.

AISI: The latest name for Italy's domestic intelligence agency. Their motto, *scientia rerum republicae salus*, means "knowledge of issues is the salvation of the Republic."

AK-9: Russian 9x39mm assault rifle favored by Spetsnaz (special purpose) forces.

Al-Jaleel: Iraqi-made 82mm mortar that is a clone of the Yugoslavian-made M69A. This indirect-fire weapon has a maximum range of 6,000 meters.

Alpha Group: More accurately called Spetsgruppa "A," Alpha Group is the FSB's counterterrorist unit. You don't want them to "rescue" you. See Moscow Theater Hostage Crisis and the Beslan School Massacre.

AMAN: Israeli military intelligence.

Amphib: Shorthand for Amphibious Assault Ship. A gray ship holding helicopters, Harriers, and hovercraft. Usually home to a large number of pissed-off Marines.

AN/PAS-13G(v)L3/LWTS: Weapon-mounted thermal optic that can be used to identify warm-blooded targets day or night. Can be mounted in front of and used in conjunction with a traditional "day" scope mounted on a sniper weapons system.

AN/PRC-163: Falcon III communications system made by Harris Corporation that integrates voice, text, and video capabilities.

AQ: al-Qaeda. Meaning "the Base" in Arabic. A radical Islamic terrorist organization once led by the late Osama bin Laden.

AQI: al-Qaeda in Iraq. An al-Qaeda–affiliated Sunni insurgent group that was active against U.S. forces. Elements of AQI eventually evolved into ISIS.

AR-10: The 7.62x51mm brainchild of Eugene Stoner that was later adapted to create the M16/M4/AR-15.

Asherman Chest Seal: A specialized emergency medical device used to treat open chest wounds. If you're wearing one, you are having a bad day.

AT-4: Tube-launched 84mm anti-armor rocket produced in Sweden and used by U.S. forces since the 1980s. The AT-4 is a throwaway weapon: after it is fired, the tube is discarded.

ATF/BATFE: Bureau of Alcohol, Tobacco, Firearms, and Explosives. A federal law enforcement agency formerly part of the U.S. Department of the Treasury, which doesn't seem overly concerned with alcohol or tobacco.

ATPIAL/PEQ-15: Advanced Target Pointer/Illuminator Aiming Laser. A weapon-mounted device that emits both visible and infrared target designators for use with or without night observation devices. Essentially an advanced military-grade version of the "laser sights" seen in popular culture.

Avtoritet: The highest caste of the incarcerated criminal hierarchy. Today used in association with a new generation of crime bosses.

Azores: Atlantic archipelago consisting of nine major islands that is an independent, autonomous region of the European nation of Portugal.

Barrett 250 Lightweight: A lightweight variant of the M240 7.62mm light machine gun, developed by Barrett Firearms.

Barrett M107: .50 BMG caliber semiautomatic rifle designed by Ronnie Barrett in the early 1980s. This thirty-pound rifle can be carried by a single individual and can be used to engage human or vehicular targets at extreme ranges.

BATS: Biometrics Automated Toolset System; a fingerprint database often used to identify insurgent forces.

Bay of Pigs: Site of a failed invasion of Cuba by paramilitary exiles trained and equipped by the CIA.

BDU: Battle-dress uniform; an oxymoron if there ever was one.

Benelli M1 Super 90: An auto-loading shotgun.

Beneteau Oceanis: A forty-eight-foot cruising sailboat, designed and built in France. An ideal craft for eluding international manhunts.

Black Hills Ammunition: High-quality ammunition made for military and civilian use by a family-owned and South Dakota–based company. Their MK 262 MOD 1 5.56mm load saw significant operational use in the GWOT.

Blue-badger: Often used to denote a "staff" CIA paramilitary operations officer. Why? Because their badges are blue.

Bratok: Member of the Bratva.

Bratva: The Brotherhood. An umbrella term for Russian organized crime, more technically referring to members of the Russian mafia who have served time in prison.

Brigadir: Lieutenant of a Bratva gang boss.

Browning Hi-Power: A single-action 9mm semiautomatic handgun that feeds from a thirteen-round box magazine. Also known as the P-35, this Belgian-designed handgun was the most widely issued military sidearm in the world for much of the twentieth century and was used by both Axis and Allied forces during World War II.

BUD/S: Basic Underwater Demolition/SEAL training. The six-month selection and training course required for entry into the SEAL Teams, held in Coronado, California. Widely considered one of the most brutal military selection courses in the world, with an average 80 percent attrition rate.

C-17: Large military cargo aircraft used to transport troops and supplies. Also used by the Secret Service to transport the president's motorcade vehicles.

C-4: Composition 4. A plastic-explosive compound known for its stability and malleability.

Caesarea: A department of the Mossad. It is wise to stay off their list.

CAG: Combat Applications Group. See redacted portion of glossary in the "D" section.

CAT: Counter-Assault Team; heavily armed ground element of the Secret Service trained to respond to threats such as ambushes.

CCA: According to *Seapower* magazine, the Combatant Craft, Assault, is a forty-one-foot high-speed boat used by Naval Special Warfare units. Essentially, an armed "Cigarette" boat.

CDC: Centers for Disease Control and Prevention. An agency of the Department of Health and Human Services, its mission is to protect the United States from health threats, including natural and weaponized infectious diseases.

Cessna 208 Caravan: Single-engine turboprop aircraft that can ferry passengers and cargo, often to remote locations. These workhorses are staples in remote wilderness areas throughout the world.

CIA: Central Intelligence Agency.

CIF/CRF: Commanders In-Extremis Force/Crisis Response Force; a United States Army special forces team specifically tasked with conducting direct-action missions. These are the guys who should have been sent to Benghazi.

CISA: Cybersecurity and Infrastructure Security Agency. Its official Web page states: "CISA is the Nation's risk advisor, working with partners to defend against today's threats and collaborating to build more secure and resilient infrastructure for the future." For an agency with such an innocuous Dunder Mifflin–esque mission statement, in times of crisis they assume an inordinate amount of control.

CJSOTF: Combined Joint Special Operations Task Force. A regional command that controls special operations forces from various services and friendly nations.

CMC: Command Master Chief, a senior enlisted rating in the United States Navy.

CQC: Close-quarter combat.

CrossFit: A fitness-centric worldwide cult that provides a steady stream of cases to orthopedic surgery clinics. No need to identify their members; they will tell you who they are.

CRRC: Combat Rubber Raiding Craft. Inflatable Zodiac-style boats used by SEALs and other maritime troops.

CTC: The CIA's Counterterrorism Center. Established during the rise of international terrorism in the 1980s, it became the nucleus of the U.S. counterterrorism mission.

CZ-75: 9mm handgun designed in 1975 and produced in the Czech Republic.

DA: District attorney; local prosecutor in many jurisdictions.

Dam Neck: An annex to Naval Air Station Oceana near Virginia Beach, Virginia, where nothing interesting whatsoever happens.

DCIS: Defense Criminal Investigation Service.

DEA: Drug Enforcement Administration.

***Delta Force*:** A classic 1986 action film starring Chuck Norris, title of the 1983 autobiography by the unit's first commanding officer, and, according to thousands of print and online articles, books, and video interviews across new and legacy media, the popular name for the Army's 1st Special Forces Operational Detachment–Delta. I wouldn't know.

Democratic Federation of Northern Syria: Aka Rojava, an autonomous, polyethnic, and secular region of northern Syria.

Det Cord: Flexible detonation cord used to initiate charges of high explosive. The cord's interior is filled with PETN explosive; you don't want it wrapped around your neck.

DIA: Defense Intelligence Agency.

Directorate I: The division of the SVR responsible for electronic information and disinformation.

Directorate S: The division of the SVR responsible for their illegals program. When you read about a Russian dissident or former spy poisoned by Novichok nerve agent or a political rival of the Russian president murdered in a random act of violence, Directorate S is probably responsible.

DO: The CIA's Directorate of Operations, formerly known by a much more appropriate name: the Clandestine Service.

DOD: Department of Defense.

DOJ: Department of Justice.

DShkM: Russian-made 12.7x108mm heavy machine gun that has been used in virtually every armed conflict since and including World War II.

DST: General Directorate for Territorial Surveillance. Morocco's domestic intelligence and security agency. Probably not afraid to use "enhanced interrogation techniques." DST was originally redacted by government censors for the hardcover edition of *True Believer*. After a five-month appeal process, that decision was withdrawn.

EFP: Explosively Formed Penetrator/Projectile. A shaped explosive charge that forms a molten projectile used to penetrate armor. Such munitions were widely used by insurgents against coalition forces in Iraq.

EKIA: Enemy Killed In Action.

Eland: Africa's largest antelope. A mature male can weigh more than a ton.

EMS: Emergency medical services. Fire, paramedic, and other emergency personnel.

ENDEX: End Exercise. Those outside "the know" will say "INDEX" and have no idea what it means.

EOD: Explosive Ordnance Disposal. The military's explosives experts who are trained to, among other things, disarm or destroy improvised explosive devices or other munitions.

EOTECH: An unmagnified holographic gun sight for use on rifles and carbines, including the M4. The sight is designed for rapid target acquisition, which makes it an excellent choice for close-quarters battle. Can be fitted with a detachable 3x magnifier for use at extended ranges.

FAL: Fusil Automatique Léger: gas-operated, select-fire 7.62x51mm battle rifle developed by FN Herstal in the late 1940s and used by the militaries of more than ninety nations. Sometimes referred to as "the right arm of the free world" due to its use against communist forces in various Cold War–era insurgencies.

FBI: Federal Bureau of Investigation; a federal law enforcement agency that is not known for its sense of humor.

FDA: Food and Drug Administration.

FLIR: Forward-Looking InfraRed. An observation device that uses thermographic radiation—that is, heat—to develop an image.

Floppies: Derogatory term used to describe communist insurgents during the Rhodesian Bush War.

FOB: Forward Operating Base. A secured forward military position used to support tactical operations. Can vary from small and remote outposts to sprawling complexes.

Fobbit: A service member serving in a noncombat role who rarely, if ever, leaves the safety of the Forward Operating Base.

FSB: Russia's federal security service, responsible for internal state security and headquartered in the same building in Lubyanka Square that once housed the KGB. Its convenient in-house prison is not a place one wants to spend an extended period.

FSO: Federal Protective Service. Russia's version of the Secret Service.

FTX: Field Training Exercise.

G550: A business jet manufactured by Gulfstream Aerospace. Prices for a new example start above $40 million, but, as they say, it's better to rent.

Galil: An iconic Israeli-made rifle incorporating elements of the Kalashnikov and Finnish RK 62.

Game Scout: A wildlife enforcement officer in Africa. These individuals are often paired with hunting outfitters to ensure that regulations are adhered to.

Glock: An Austrian-designed, polymer-framed handgun popular with police forces, militaries, and civilians throughout the world. Glocks are made in various sizes and chambered in several different cartridges.

GPNVG-18: Ground Panoramic Night Vision Goggles. Forty-three-thousand-dollar NODs are used by the most highly funded special operations units due to their superior image quality and peripheral vision. See Rich Kid Shit.

GPS: Global Positioning System. Satellite-based navigation systems that provide a precise location anywhere on earth.

Great Patriotic War: The Soviets' name for World War II; communists love propaganda.

Green-badger: Central Intelligence Agency contractor.

Ground Branch: Land-focused element of the CIA's Special Activities Center, according to Wikipedia. May now go by Ground Department but that does not sound nearly as cool.

GRS: Global Response Staff. Protective agents employed by the Central Intelligence Agency to provide security to overseas personnel. See 13 Hours. GRS was originally redacted by government censors for the hardcover edition of *True Believer*. After a five-month appeal process, that decision was withdrawn.

GRU: Russia's main intelligence directorate. The foreign military intelligence agency of the Russian armed forces. The guys who do all the real work while the KGB gets all the credit, or so I'm told. Established by Joseph Stalin in 1942, the GRU was tasked with running human intelligence operations outside the Soviet Union. Think of them as the DIA with balls.

GS: General Schedule. Federal jobs that provide good benefits and lots of free time.

Gsh-18L: According to Forgotten Weapons, a rotating-barrel Tula pistol "designed around a 9x19mm AP cartridge."

Gukurahundi Massacres: A series of killings carried out against Ndebele tribe members in Matabeleland, Zimbabwe, by the Mugabe government during the 1980s. As many as twenty thousand civilians were killed by the North Korean–trained Fifth Brigade of the Zimbabwean army.

GWOT: Global War on Terror. The seemingly endless pursuit of bad guys, kicked off by the 9/11 attacks.

Gym Jones: Utah-based fitness company founded by alpine climbing legend Mark Twight. Famous for turning soft Hollywood actors into hard bodies, Gym Jones once enjoyed a close relationship with a certain SEAL Team.

Hell Week: The crucible of BUD/S training. Five days of constant physical and mental stress with little or no sleep.

Hilux: Pickup truck manufactured by Toyota that is a staple in third-world nations due to its reliability.

HK 416: M4 clone engineered by the German firm of Heckler & Koch to operate using a short-stroke gas pistol system instead of the M4's direct-impingement gas system. Used by select special operations units in the U.S. and abroad. May or may not have been the weapon used to kill Osama bin Laden.

HK 417: Select-fire 7.62x51mm rifle built by Heckler & Koch as a big brother to the HK 416. Often used as a Designated Marksman Rifle with a magnified optic.

HK G3: Classic 7.62x51mm battle rifle.

HK MP5: A submachine gun extremely popular with hostage rescue and counterterrorism units, until it became evident that it might be wise to have a rifle, especially if you run into a fight going to or from your target.

HK P7: A favorite of Hans Gruber's.

HRT: Hostage Rescue Team. The FBI's premier continental United States–focused hostage-rescue, counterterrorism, and violent criminal apprehension unit.

HUMINT: Human Intelligence. Information gleaned through traditional human-to-human methods.

HVI/HVT: High-Value Individual/High-Value Target. An individual who is important to the enemy's capabilities and is therefore specifically sought out by a military force.

IDC: Independent Duty Corpsman. Essentially a doctor.

IDF: Israel Defense Forces. One of the most experienced militaries on the planet.

IED: Improvised Explosive Device. Homemade bombs, whether crude or complex, often used by insurgent forces overseas.

Internet Research Agency: Commonly referred to as a "Russian Troll Farm," it is a de facto arm of the Russian political-military-intelligence apparatus conducting online influence operations. Connected via ownership to the Wagner Group.

IR: Infrared. The part of the electromagnetic spectrum with a longer wavelength than visible light but a shorter wavelength than radio waves. Invisible to the naked eye but visible with night observation devices. Example: an IR laser-aiming device.

Iron Curtain: The physical and ideological border that separated the opposing sides of the Cold War.

ISI: The Pakistani Inter-Service Intelligence.

ISIS: Islamic State of Iraq and the Levant. Radical Sunni terrorist group based in parts of Iraq and Afghanistan. Also referred to as ISIL. The bad guys.

ISR: Intelligence, Surveillance, and Reconnaissance.

ITAR: International Traffic in Arms Regulations. Export control regulations designed to restrict the export of certain items, including weapons and optics. These regulations offer ample opportunity to inadvertently violate federal law.

JAG: Judge Advocate General. Decent television series and the military's legal department.

JMAU: Joint Medical Augmentation Unit. High-speed medicine.

JOC: Joint Operations Center. Like a Tactical Operations Center, but more high-speed.

JSOC: Joint Special Operations Command. According to Wikipedia, it is a component command of SOCOM that commands and controls Special Mission Units and Advanced Force Operations.

Katsa: Mossad case officer.

Katyn Massacre: Soviet purge of Polish citizens that took place in 1940 subsequent to the Soviet invasion. Twenty-two thousand Poles were killed by members of the NKVD during this event; many of the bodies were discovered in mass graves in the Katyn Forest. Russia denied responsibility for the massacre until 1990.

KGB: The Soviet "Committee for State Security." Excelled at "suppressing internal dissent" during the Cold War. Most often referred to by kids of the eighties as "the bad guys."

KIA: Killed in Action.

Kidon: "Bayonet." The unit of the Mossad's Caesarea tasked with executing "negative treatments."

Kudu: A spiral-horned antelope, roughly the size and build of an elk, that inhabits much of sub-Saharan Africa.

Langley: The Northern Virginia location where the Central Intelligence Agency is headquartered. Often used as shorthand for CIA.

LaRue OBR: Optimized Battle Rifle. Precision variant of the AR-15/AR-10 designed for use as a Designated Marksman or Sniper Rifle. Available in both 5.56x45mm and 7.62x51mm.

Law of Armed Conflict: A segment of public international law that regulates the conduct of armed hostilities.

LAW Rocket: M-72 Light Anti-armor Weapon. A disposable, tube-launched 66mm unguided rocket used by U.S. forces since before the Vietnam War.

LE: Law Enforcement. A blanket term used to denote police officers, sheriffs, state troopers, highway patrol, federal agents, and other local, state, and federal law enforcement.

Leica M4: Classic 35mm rangefinder camera produced from 1966 to 1975.

Long-Range Desert Group: A specialized British military unit that operated in the North African and Mediterranean theaters during World War II. The unit was made up of soldiers from Great Britain, New Zealand, and Southern Rhodesia.

L-Pill: A "lethal pill" or suicide pill developed during World War II and later issued to high-risk agents and operatives on both sides of the Cold War.

M1911/1911A1: .45-caliber pistol used by U.S. forces since before World War I.

M3: World War II submachine gun chambered in .45 ACP. This simple but reliable weapon became a favorite of the frogmen of that time.

M4: The standard assault rifle of the majority of U.S. military forces, including the U.S. Navy SEALs. The M4 is a shortened carbine variant of the M16 rifle that fires a 5.56x45mm cartridge. The M4 is a modular design that can be adapted to numerous configurations, including different barrel lengths.

MACV-SOG: Military Assistance Command, Vietnam–Studies and Observations Group. Deceiving name for a group of brave warriors who conducted highly classified special operations missions during the Vietnam War. These operations were often conducted behind enemy lines in Laos, Cambodia, and North Vietnam.

Mahdi Militia: An insurgent Shia militia loyal to cleric Muqtada al-Sadr that opposed U.S. forces in Iraq during the height of that conflict.

Makarov: A Soviet-era pistol favored by the bad guys.

MANPADS: Man-Portable Air-Defense System. Small antiaircraft surface-to-air guided rockets such as the U.S. Stinger and the Russian SA-7.

Marine Raiders: U.S. Marine Corps special operations unit; formerly known as MARSOC.

Maritime Branch: It's best to just google it.

Mazrah Tora: A prison in Cairo, Egypt. You do not want to wake up here.

MBITR: AN/PRC-148 Multiband Inter/Intra Team Radio. A handheld multiband, tactical software–defined radio, commonly used by special operations forces to communicate during operations.

McMillan TAC-50: Bolt-action sniper rifle chambered in .50 BMG used for long-range sniping operations, employed by U.S. special operations forces as well as the Canadian army.

MDMA: A psychoactive drug whose clinical name is too long to place here. Known on the street as "ecstasy." Glow sticks not included.

MH-47: Special operations variant of the Army's Chinook helicopter, usually flown by members of the 160th SOAR. This twin-rotor aircraft is used frequently in Afghanistan due to its high service ceiling and large troop- and cargo-carrying capacity. Rumor has it that, if you're careful, you can squeeze a Land Rover Defender 90 inside one.

MH-60: Special operations variant of the Army's Black Hawk helicopter, usually flown by members of the 160th SOAR.

MIA: Missing in Action.

MI5: Military Intelligence, Section 5. Britain's domestic counterintelligence and security agency. Like the FBI but with nicer suits and better accents.

MIL DOT: A reticle-based system used for range estimation and long-range shooting, based on the milliradian unit of measurement.

MIL(s): One-thousandth of a radian; an angular measurement used in rifle scopes. 0.1 MIL equals 1 centimeter at 100 meters or 0.36" at 100 yards. If you find that confusing, don't become a sniper.

MIT: Turkey's national intelligence organization, and a school in Boston for smart kids.

Mk 46 MOD 1: Belt-fed 5.56x45mm light machine gun built by FN Herstal. Often used by special operations forces due to its light weight, the Mk 46 is a scaled-down version of the Mk 48 MOD 1.

Mk 48 MOD 1: Belt-fed 7.62x51mm light machine gun designed for use by special operations forces. Weighing eighteen pounds unloaded, the Mk 48 can fire 730 rounds per minute to an effective range of 800 meters and beyond.

Mosin-Nagant: Legendary Russian bolt-action service rifle found on battlefields across the globe.

Mossad: The Israeli version of the CIA, but even more apt to make their enemies disappear.

MP7: Compact select-fire personal defense weapon built by Heckler & Koch and used by various special operations forces. Its 4.6x30mm cartridge is available in a subsonic load, making the weapon extremely quiet when suppressed. What the MP7 lacks in lethality it makes up for in coolness.

MQ-4C: An advanced unmanned surveillance drone developed by Northrop Grumman for use by the U.S. Navy.

Robert Mugabe: Chairman of ZANU who led the nation of Zimbabwe from 1980 to 2017 as both prime minister and president. Considered responsible for retaliatory attacks against his rival Ndebele tribe as well as a disastrous land redistribution scheme that was ruled illegal by Zimbabwe's High Court.

MultiCam: A proprietary camouflage pattern developed by Crye Precision. Formerly reserved for special operators and air-softers, MultiCam is now standard issue to much of the U.S. and allied militaries.

Nagant M1895: As described in the novel, this pistol was used to execute Czar Nicholas II and his family.

NATO: North Atlantic Treaty Organization. An alliance created in 1949 to counter the Soviet threat to the Western Hemisphere. Headquartered in Brussels, Belgium, the alliance is commanded by a four-star U.S. military officer known as the Supreme Allied Commander Europe (SACEUR).

Naval Special Warfare Development Group (DEVGRU): A command that appears in the biographies of numerous admirals on the Navy's website. Joe Biden publicly referred to it by a different name when he was the vice president.

NBACC: National Biodefense Analysis and Countermeasures Center. A facility on Fort Detrick in Maryland that for sure does not weaponize and test infectious diseases in the Bat Cave.

NCIS: Naval Criminal Investigative Service. A federal law enforcement agency whose jurisdiction includes the U.S. Navy and Marine Corps. Also a popular television program with at least two spin-offs.

Niassa Game Reserve: Sixteen thousand square miles of relatively untouched wilderness in northern Mozambique. The reserve is home to a wide variety of wildlife as well as a fair number of poachers looking to commoditize them.

NKVD: A federal law enforcement arm of the former Soviet Union. Best known as the action arm of Stalin's Great Purge under the guise of protecting "state security" and responsible for mass executions and imprisonments of "enemies of the people."

NODs: Night observation devices. Commonly referred to as "night vision goggles," these devices amplify ambient light, allowing the user to see in low-light environments. Special operations forces often operate at night to take full advantage of such technology.

NSA: National Security Agency. U.S. intelligence agency tasked with gathering and analyzing signals intercepts and other communications data. Also known as No Such Agency. These are the government employees who listen to our phone calls and read our emails and texts for reasons of "national security." See *Permanent Record* by Edward Snowden.

NSC: National Security Council. This body advises and assists the president of the United States on matters of national security.

NSW: Naval Special Warfare. The Navy's special operations force; includes SEAL Teams.

Officer Candidate School (OCS): Twelve-week course where civilians and enlisted sailors are taught to properly fold underwear. Upon completion, they are miraculously qualified to command men and women in combat.

OmniSTAR: Satellite-based augmentation system service provider. A really fancy GPS service that provides very precise location information.

Ops-Core Ballistic Helmet: Lightweight high-cut helmet used by special operations forces worldwide.

Orsis T-5000 Tochnost: Russian bolt-action precision rifle.

OSS: Office of Strategic Services. The U.S. World War II national intelligence agency led by William Joseph "Wild Bill" Donovan. Forerunner of the CIA.

P226: 9mm handgun made by SIG Sauer, the standard-issue sidearm for SEALs.

P229: A compact handgun made by SIG Sauer, often used by federal law enforcement officers, chambered in 9mm as well as other cartridges.

P320: Striker-fired modular 9mm handgun that has recently been adopted by the U.S. armed forces as the M17/M18.

P365: Subcompact handgun made by SIG Sauer, designed for concealed carry. Despite its size, the P365 holds up to thirteen rounds of 9mm.

Pakhan: The highest-ranked blatnoy in prison. Now more synonymous with "senior criminal."

Pakistani Taliban: An Islamic terrorist group composed of various Sunni Islamist militant groups based in the northwestern Federally Administered Tribal Areas along the Afghan border in Pakistan.

Pamwe Chete: "All Together"; the motto of the Rhodesian Selous Scouts.

Panga: A machete-like utility blade common in Africa.

Peshmerga: Military forces of Kurdistan. Meaning "the one who faces death," they are regarded by Allied troops as some of the best fighters in the region.

PETN: PentaErythritol TetraNitrate. An explosive compound used in blasting caps to initiate larger explosive charges.

PG-32V: High-explosive antitank rocket that can be fired from the Russian-designed RPG-32 rocket-propelled grenade launcher. Its tandem charge is effective against various types of armor, including reactive armor.

Phoenix Program: CIA-run covert operation in Vietnam focused on neutralizing Vietcong infrastructure. That's a civilized way of saying the program targeted Vietcong leadership for assassination.

PID: Protective Intelligence and Threat Assessment Division. The division of the Secret Service that monitors potential threats to its protectees.

PKM: Soviet-designed, Russian-made light machine gun chambered in 7.62x54R that can be found in conflicts throughout the globe. This weapon feeds from a non-disintegrating belt and has a rate of fire of 650 rounds per minute. You don't want one shooting at you.

PLF: Parachute Landing Fall. A technique taught to military parachutists to prevent injury when making contact with the earth. Round canopy parachutes used by airborne forces fall at faster velocities than other parachutes and require a specific landing sequence. More often than not, it ends up as feet-ass-head.

PMC: Private Military Company. Though the profession is as old as war itself, the modern term *PMC* was made infamous in the post-9/11 era by Blackwater, aka Xe Services, and now known as Academi.

POTUS: President of the United States; leader of the free world.

POW: Prisoner of War.

PPD: Presidential Protection Detail. The element of the Secret Service tasked with protecting POTUS.

President's Hundred: A badge awarded by the Civilian Marksmanship Program to the one hundred top-scoring military and civilian shooters in the President's Pistol and President's Rifle matches. Enlisted members of the U.S. military are authorized to wear the tab on their uniform.

Professional Hunter: A licensed hunting guide in Africa, often referred to as a "PH." Zimbabwe-licensed PHs are widely considered the most qualified and highly trained in Africa and make up the majority of the PH community operating in Mozambique.

Project Delta: One of the most highly classified and successful special reconnaissance units of the Vietnam War. Basically, their job was to be badasses.

***The Protocols of the Elders of Zion*:** An anti-Semitic conspiracy manifesto first published in the late 1800s by Russian sources. Though quickly established as a fraudulent text, *Protocols* has been widely circulated in numerous languages.

PSO-1: A Russian-made 4x24mm illuminated rifle optic developed for use on the SVD rifle.

PTSD: Post-traumatic stress disorder. A mental condition that develops in association with shocking or traumatic events. Commonly associated with combat veterans.

PVS-15: Binocular-style NODs used by U.S. and allied special operations forces.

QRF: Quick Reaction Force. A contingency ground force on standby to assist operations in progress.

Quantum Computing: A rapidly emerging technology that employs the laws of quantum mechanics and physics to perform computations.

Ranger Panties: Polyester PT shorts favored by members of the 75th Ranger Regiment that leave very little to the imagination, sometimes referred to as "silkies."

REMF: Rear-Echelon Motherfucker. Describes most officers taking credit for what the E-5 mafia and a few senior enlisted do on the ground if the mission goes right. These same "people" will be the first to hang you out to dry if things go south. Now that they are home safe and sound, they will let you believe that when they were "downrange" they actually left the wire.

RFID: Radio Frequency Identification. Technology commonly used to tag objects that can be scanned electronically.

RHIB/RIB: Rigid Hull Inflatable Boat/Rigid Inflatable Boat. A lightweight but high-performance boat constructed with a solid fiberglass or composite hull and flexible tubes at the gunwales (sides).

Rhodesia: A former British colony that declared its independence in 1965. After a long and brutal civil war, the nation became Zimbabwe in 1979.

Rhodesian Bush War: An insurgency battle between the Rhodesian Security Forces and Soviet-, East German–, Cuban-, and Chinese-backed guerrillas that lasted from 1964 to 1979. The war ended when the December 1979 Lancaster House Agreement put an end to white minority rule.

Rhodesian SAS: A special operations unit formed as part of the famed

British Special Air Service in 1951. When Rhodesia sought independence, the unit ceased to exist as part of the British military but fought as part of the Rhodesian Security Forces until 1980. Many members of the Selous Scouts were recruited from the SAS.

Rich Kid Shit: Expensive equipment reserved for use by the most highly funded special operations units. Google JSOC.

RLI: Rhodesian Light Infantry. An airborne and airmobile unit used to conduct "fireforce" operations during the Bush War. These missions were often launched in response to intelligence provided by Selous Scouts on the ground.

ROE: Rules of engagement. Rules or directives that determine what level of force can be applied against an enemy in a particular situation or area.

RPG-32: 105mm rocket-propelled grenade launcher that is made in both Russia and, under license, in Jordan.

SAD: The CIA's Special Activities Division. Though it is now called the Special Activities Center, it's still responsible for covert action, aka the really cool stuff.

SADM: Special Atomic Demolition Munition. A man-portable atomic demolition munition system developed by the U.S. military during the Cold War. Better known as known as "backpack nukes," they even had their own 1965 Army Field Manual—*FM 5-26: Employment of Atomic Demolition Munitions.*

SALUTE: A report used to transmit information on enemy forces. Size / Activity / Location / Unit / Time / Equipment.

SAP: Special Access Program. Security protocols that provide highly classified information with safeguards and access restrictions that exceed those for regular classified information. Really secret stuff.

Sayanim: Usually non-Israeli, though most often Jewish, worldwide network of Mossad facilitators.

Sayeret Matkal: The General Staff Reconnaissance Unit of the IDF responsible for hostage rescue and counterterrorism operations beyond Israel's borders. The Israeli equivalent of the British SAS, U.S. Army's Delta Force, and a certain SEAL Team between the numbers of 5 and 7.

SCAR-17: 7.62x51mm battle rifle produced by FN. Its gas mechanism can be traced to that of the FAL.

Schmidt & Bender: Privately held German optics manufacturer known for its precision rifle scopes.

SCI: Special Compartmentalized Information. Classified information concerning or derived from sensitive intelligence sources, methods, or analytical processes. Often found on private basement servers in upstate New York or bathroom closet servers in Denver.

SCIF: Sensitive Compartmented Information Facility. A secure and restricted room or structure where classified information is discussed or viewed.

Scouts and Raiders: World War II forefathers to today's Navy SEALs. The original Naval Special Warfare Commandos.

SEAL: Acronym of SEa, Air, and Land. The three mediums in which SEALs operate. The U.S. Navy's special operations force.

Secret Service: The federal law enforcement agency responsible for protecting the POTUS.

Selous Scouts: An elite, if scantily clad, mixed-race unit of the Rhodesian army responsible for counterinsurgency operations. These "pseudo-terrorists" led some of the most successful special operations missions in modern history.

SERE: Survival, Evasion, Resistance, Escape. A military training program that includes realistic role-playing as a prisoner of war. SERE students are subjected to highly stressful procedures, sometimes including waterboarding, as part of the course curriculum. More commonly referred to as "Camp Slappy."

Shin Bet / Shabak: Israel's equivalent of the FBI or MI5.

Shishani: Arabic term for Chechen fighters in Syria, probably due to "Shishani" being a common Chechen surname.

SIGINT: Signals Intelligence. Intelligence derived from electronic signals and systems used by foreign targets, such as communications systems, radars, and weapons systems.

SIPR: Secret Internet Protocol Router network. A secure version of the internet used by DOD and the State Department to transmit classified information.

SISDE: Italy's Intelligence and Democratic Security Service. Their suits are probably even nicer than MI5's.

SISMI: Italian version of the CIA. Formerly called the AISE until scandals forced a housecleaning and name change.

SOCOM: United States Special Operations Command. The Unified Combatant Command charged with overseeing the various Special Operations Component Commands of the Army, Marine Corps, Navy, and Air Force of the United States armed forces. Headquartered at MacDill Air Force Base in Tampa, Florida.

Special Boat Team-12: The West Coast unit that provides maritime mobility to SEALs using a variety of vessels. Fast boats with machine guns.

Special Reconnaissance (SR) Team: NSW Teams that conduct special activities, ISR, and provide intelligence support to the SEAL Teams.

Spetsnaz: An umbrella term for Russian special operations units and special operations units in post-Soviet states.

Spetssviaz: Officially the Special Communications and Information Service of the Federal Protective Service of the Russian Federation. The Russian version of the NSA. Yes, they have all your personal electronic data and credit card information.

SR-16: An AR-15 variant developed and manufactured by Knight Armament Corporation.

SRT: Surgical Resuscitation Team. You want these guys close by if you take a bullet.

Strela-2: Cold War–era Soviet-designed shoulder-fired surface-to-air missile.

StrongFirst: Kettle-bell-focused fitness program founded by Russian fitness guru Pavel Tsatsouline that is popular with special operations forces.

SVD: Officially the SVD-63 to denote the year it was accepted for use in the Soviet military, it is known the world over as the Dragunov.

S-Vest: Suicide vest. An explosives-laden garment favored by suicide bombers. Traditionally worn only once.

SVR: The Foreign Intelligence Service of the Russian Federation, or as John le Carré describes them, "the KGB in drag."

Taliban: An Islamic fundamentalist political movement and terrorist group in Afghanistan. U.S. and coalition forces had been at war with members of the Taliban since late 2001.

Targeting Officer: The CIA's website reads that as a targeting officer you will "identify new opportunities for DO operational activity and enhance ongoing operations." Translation: They tell us whom to kill.

TATP: Triacetone triperoxide. An explosive compound nicknamed "Mother of Satan." Its chemical precursors can be found in commonly available products the world over.

TDFD: Time-delay firing device. An explosive initiator that allows for detonation after a determined period of time. A fancy version of a really long fuse.

TIC: Troops in contact. A firefight involving U.S. or friendly forces.

TOC: Tactical Operations Center. A command post for military operations. A TOC usually includes a small group of personnel who guide members of an active tactical element during a mission from the safety of a secured area.

TOR Network: A computer network designed to conceal a user's identity and location. TOR allows for anonymous communication.

TQ: Politically correct term for the timely questioning of individuals on-site once a target is secure. May involve the raising of voices.

Troop Chief: Senior enlisted SEAL on a forty-man troop, usually a master chief petty officer. The guy who makes shit happen.

TS: Top Secret. Information whose unauthorized disclosure reasonably could be expected to cause exceptionally grave damage to national security and that the original classification authority is able to identify or describe. Can also describe an individual's level of security clearance.

TST: Time-sensitive target. A target requiring immediate response because it is highly lucrative, is a fleeting target of opportunity, or poses (or will soon pose) a danger to friendly forces.

UAV: Unmanned Aerial Vehicle. A drone.

UCMJ: Uniform Code of Military Justice. Disciplinary and criminal code that applies to members of the U.S. military.

UDI: Unilateral Declaration of Independence. The 1965 document that established Rhodesia as an independent sovereign state. The UDI resulted in an international embargo and made Rhodesia a pariah.

V-22: Tilt-rotor aircraft that can fly like a plane and take off and land like a helicopter. Numerous examples were crashed during its extremely expensive development.

VBIED: Vehicle-Borne Improvised Explosive Device. A rolling car bomb driven by a suicidal terrorist.

VC: National Liberation Front of South Vietnam, better known as the Viet Cong. A communist insurgent group that fought against the government of South Vietnam and its allies during the Vietnam War. In the movies, these are the guys wearing the black pajamas carrying AKs.

VI: Vehicle Interdiction. Good fun, unless you are on the receiving end.

***Vor v Zakone*:** An individual at the top of the incarcerated criminal underground. Think godfather. Top authority for the Bratva. Today, each region of Russia has a *Vor v Zakone*.

***Vory*:** A hierarchy within the Bratva. Career criminals. More directly translated as "thief."

VPN: Virtual Private Network. A private network that enables users to send and receive data across shared or public networks as if their computing devices were directly connected to the private network. Considered more secure than a traditional internet network.

VSK-94: Russian-made Sniper/Designated Marksman rifle chambered in the subsonic 9x39mm cartridge. This suppressed weapon is popular with Russian special operations and law enforcement units due to its minimal sound signature and muzzle flash.

VSS Vintorez: Integrally suppressed Soviet rifle chambered in 9x39mm.

Wagner Group: A Russian private military company with close ties to the Russian government.

War Vets: Loosely organized groups of Zimbabweans who carried out many of the land seizures during the 1990s. Often armed, these individuals used threats and intimidation to remove white farmers from their homes. Despite the name, most of these individuals were too young to have participated in the Bush War. Not to be confused with ZNLWVA, a group that represents ZANU-affiliated veterans of the Bush War.

WARCOM/NAVSPECWARCOM: United States Naval Special Warfare Command. The Navy's special operations force and the maritime component of United States Special Operations Command. Headquartered in Coronado, California, WARCOM is the administrative command for subordinate NSW Groups composed of eight SEAL Teams, one SEAL Delivery Vehicle (SDV) Team, three Special Boat Teams, and two Special Reconnaissance Teams.

Westley Richards Droplock: A rifle or shotgun built by the famed Birmingham, England, gunmakers that allows the user to remove the locking mechanisms for repair or replacement in the field. Widely considered one of the finest and most iconic actions of all time.

Whiskey Tango: Military speak for "white trash."

WIA: Wounded In Action.

Yamam: An elite unit of Israeli border police that conducts high-risk hostage rescue and counterterrorism operations in Israel.

Yazidis: An insular Kurdish-speaking ethnic and religious group that primarily resides in Iraq. Effectively a subminority among the Kurds, Yazidis were heavily persecuted by ISIS.

YPG: Kurdish militia forces operating in the Democratic Federation of Northern Syria. The Turks are not fans.

ZANLA: Zimbabwe African National Liberation Army. The armed wing of the Maoist Zimbabwe African National Union and one of the major combatants of the Rhodesian Bush War. ZANLA forces often staged out of training camps located in Mozambique and were led by Robert Mugabe.

Zimbabwe: Sub-Saharan African nation that formerly existed as Southern Rhodesia and later Rhodesia. Led for three decades by Robert Mugabe, Zimbabwe ranks as one of the world's most corrupt nations on Transparency International's Corruption Perceptions Index.

ZIPRA: Zimbabwe People's Revolutionary Army. The Soviet-equipped armed wing of ZAPU and one of the two major insurgency forces that fought in the Rhodesian Bush War. ZIPRA forces fell under the leadership of Josh Nkomo, who spent much of the war in Zambia. ZIPRA members were responsible for shooting down two civilian airliners using Soviet SA-7 surface-to-air missiles in the late 1970s.

Zodiac Mk 2 GR: A 4.2-meter inflatable rubber boat capable of carrying up to six individuals. These craft are often used as dinghies for larger vessels.

ACKNOWLEDGMENTS

THIS NOVEL IS DEDICATED to the memory of **Thomas M. Rice**. Tom was the first man in his stick to exit his C-47 over Normandy, France, on June 6, 1944, as a paratrooper with the 101st Airborne Division 501st Parachute Infantry Regiment. Tom Rice passed away on November 17, 2022. At his memorial service in Coronado, California, **Rev. Dr. David H. McElrath** reminded us that "death is not a destination—it's a doorway." Those words found their way from that service into the letter from Tom Reece to his son, James, in the pages of this book.

This book, as with those that preceded it, would not exist without **Brad Thor** and my SEAL Teammate **Johnny Sanchez**. As with anything in life, you have to be prepared to kick in the door when that crack appears. Thank you both for cracking the door.

Nor would this book exist without those authors whose work lined the shelves of my bedroom growing up and inspired me to pick up the pen in those formative years: **Richard Connell, Geoffrey Household, Ian Fleming, John le Carré, Ken Follett, Frederick Forsyth, Robert Ludlum, John Edmund Gardner, David Morrell, Nelson DeMille, Stephen Hunter, Tom Clancy, Clive Cussler, J. C. Pollock, Marc Olden, Louis L'Amour, Eric Van Lustbader, and A. J. Quinnell**. As I continued my journey into the SEAL Teams I would discover **Vince Flynn, Daniel Silva, Kyle Mills, Lee Child, Brad Thor, Michael Connelly, Steven**

Pressfield, and Mark Greaney. Their books kept me company on many a deployment.

I want to thank all those whose names will not be found in these acknowledgments because they are still living and working in the secret world. Thank you for all you do.

To **Dr. Robert Bray** for your dedicated service to this nation, for patching me and so many of my Teammates up, and what you continue to do for special operations veterans. These books and this postmilitary chapter of life for me and my family would not be possible without you. My deepest heartfelt thanks to you and **Tracey** for all your love and support.

To **Dylan Murphy** for once again going above and beyond in developing the fight sequences in these pages. If readers could only see the fight choreography videos. One day we might have to post them. And to **Elyse** for always being the best sport and playing the thankless part of terrorist or assassin.

To **Jeff Rotherham** for your friendship and for taking a look at the parts that explode. I sincerely appreciate all your assistance.

To **Larry Vickers** and **James Rupley** for the **Vickers Guide** series. These beautifully photographed and painstakingly researched books are always my first stop as I write the weapons-centric portions of my novels. You can find them at vickersguide.com.

To **C. E. Albanese** for taking time to read the federal law enforcement–specific sections. Don't worry, your secrets are safe.

To **James R. Jarrett**, soldier, horseman, professor, writer, gunman, patriot, and U.S. Army Special Forces Project Delta Vietnam veteran—the Last of the Breed. Thank you for passing on your lessons learned in blood. The advice in Tom Reece's letter to James—"JDLR—if something 'Just Doesn't Look Right,' it's probably not"—originated with James R. Jarrett. I recommend that anyone reading this heed it.

To **Walter McLallen** and **George Kollitides** for the master's-level course in finance, a battlespace that is completely foreign to me. Thank you for coming to the rescue. Any mistakes on that front are mine and mine alone.

To **James Rupley, Dan Gelston, Kevin O'Malley,** and **David Lehman** for the time you took to put first eyes on the manuscript. It would be impossible to express just how helpful it was and how much I appreciate it. Thank you.

To the **Garand Thumb YouTube** channel—always a fun and informative stop as I research the weapons used in my novels.

To **Ben Nicholson**, who scoured Washington, D.C., for answers on the differences between the president's and vice president's oaths of office. *Against all enemies, foreign and domestic . . .*

To **Alec Pascua** for your service to the nation, being a top-notch hunting guide at **Pineapple Brothers Lanai**, and for answering my questions on all things Hawaii.

To **Stephanie Doyle** for your assistance in all things equestrian.

To **Ray Porter** for narrating the audiobooks and giving these stories a voice. Nobody does it better.

To World War II veterans **Walter Stowe** and **Jack Stowe**, we are forever indebted to you for our freedom.

To the cast and crew of the **Amazon Prime Video** series adaptation of *The Terminal List.* What an incredible experience! The book could not have been in better hands. Thank you to **Jennifer Salke** at **Amazon Studios** and **Elise Henderson** at **MRC** for seeing the potential and supporting us every step of the way. And to be able to not just continue with a second season based on *True Believer* but to also get the Team back together for a Ben Edwards origin-story prequel series FIRES ME UP! Thank you to **Chris Pratt, Antoine Fuqua, David DiGilio, Jared Shaw, Max Adams, Kat Samick, Ray Mendoza,** and all the producers and writers who gave us a tremendous season one and are working to expand this universe of stories and characters. Thank you to the executive teams of **Vernon Sanders, Laura Lancaster, Odetta Watkins, Brian Harvey,**

Liz Mackintosh, and the **Amazon** team that helped nurture our stories. And the same goes to their counterparts at **MRC**, including **MaryClaire Manley, Stacy Fung, Neil Thomas, Jennifer Watson, Sarah Karas, Tim Mickso, James Sterling, Kristen Kuroski**, and so many more. Thank you to those who worked so hard on marketing and publicity to help introduce James Reece and our shows to the world: **Heather McClure, Jared Goldsmith, Evan Otis, Arpi Ketendjian, Michael Samonte, Irving Lopez, and their teams at Amazon**, and **Jonathan Golfman** and **Kristin Robinson** at MRC. Thank you for all you do! And a huge thank-you to everyone who stepped in front of the camera to bring these characters to life: **Chris Pratt, Constance Wu, Taylor Kitsch, Jeanne Tripplehorn, Riley Keough, JD Pardo, Tyner Rushing, LaMonica Garrett, Arlo Mertz, Jared Shaw, Christina Vidal, Nick Chinlund, Matthew Rauch, Sean Gunn, Paul McCrane, Stephen Bishop, Arturo Castro, Patrick Schwarzenegger, Marco Rodríguez, Michael Broderick, Warren Kole, Alexis Louder, Carsten Norgaard, Tom Amandes, Remi Adeleke, Nate Boyer, Catherine Dyer, Ryan Sangster, Erin Switzer, Jason Westley, Cowboy Cerrone, Ajay James, Derek Phillips, Kenny Sheard, Justin Garza**, and **Jai Courtney**. Thank you!

To **Brian J. Morra**, author of *The Able Archers*, for your time in uniform and for sharing your story.

To **Ron Cohen, Tom Taylor, Jason Wright, Samantha Piatt**, and **Morgan Baker** at **SIG Sauer** for your continued friendship and support and for all you do for freedom.

To **Daniel Winkler** and **Karen Shook** of **Winkler Knives** for your years of friendship and for all you have done for the special operations community.

To **Rafael Kayanan** for designing the most savage tomahawk in existence.

To the **Park City Gun Club** for always taking such good care of me.

If you are passing through Park City, Utah, be sure to stop in and give one of their fully automatic rifles a run.

To **Joe Rogan** for fun, honest, engaging conversations and for being such a strong voice for freedom.

To **Evan Hafer, Tom Davin**, and the entire crew at **Black Rifle Coffee Company**. Looking forward to checking out the new coffee shop in Kalispell, Montana, operated by my SEAL Teammate **Andy Stumpf**.

To **Mike Glover** at **Fieldcraft Survival** for all you did for this nation in special operations and for all you continue to do in the private sector.

To **Jen Caro** at **Fieldcraft Survival** for always going the extra mile and exceeding expectations with all you do.

To **Mike and Laura Bill** for giving me the key to your beautiful Park City home when I needed some quiet time to write this novel. You are the best!

To **Frank Lecrone**, I will never be able to thank you enough for all you have done for my family. Thank you, my friend.

To **Mike Stoner** of **Mike Stoner Photography**—let's get on the bikes as soon as the snow melts.

To **Katie Pavlich** for being incredible in each and every way and for your cameo in *The Terminal List*! If you have not read Katie's book, *Fast and Furious*, pick it up today!

To **Gavy Friedson**—looking forward to meeting the rest of the family in Israel!

To **Clint** and **Heidi Smith** at **Thunder Ranch**. If you have not made the pilgrimage to train at Thunder Ranch, make this your year! Maybe I'll see you on the range!

To **Rick** and **Esther Rosenfield** for your love and support.

To **Larry Ellison** for your kindness, generosity, and keen insights.

To **Jimmy** and **Pam Linn** for making our day every time we see you!

To **Danny Wolff** for great conversation, cigars, and that incredibly special rifle.

To **Andrew Kline** for always being there for my family. Thank you!

To **Kyle Lamb** for your friendship and your time at the tip of the spear.

To **Kevin Holland**, the real "Skinner," for all you have done for our nation, most of which will never see the light of day.

To **Jim Shockey** for your leadership and inspiration. I can't wait for your book to hit the shelves!

To **Donnie Edwards** and **Kathryn Edwards** for all you do for our nation's veterans through the **Best Defense Foundation.** You have created something truly special.

To **Ben Harper** at the **Best Defense Foundation** for all you put into the Battlefield Return Programs for our World War II veterans. It is an honor to know you.

To **Austin** and **Sarah Bishop** for all you do for the **Best Defense Foundation** and our nation's veterans.

To **Andrew Arrabito** and **Kelsie Bieser** at **Half Face Blades** for crafting such devastatingly effective works of art.

To **Taran Butler** of **Taran Tactical Innovations** for your support and for always having a spot for me on the range.

To the **Real Book Spy, Ryan Steck**, for all you do for thriller authors and readers.

To *The Crew Reviews* podcast for always doing a fun and informative show. If you are a writer or author and are not listening to every *Crew Reviews* podcast, start today!

To **Jon Dubin** for your friendship, your time at the FBI, and for **Pineapple Brothers, Lanai**. Let's get afield again soon!

To **Chris Cox at Capitol 6 Advisors**—get out here to visit soon!

To **Eric** and **Sarah Cylvic** for always coming to the rescue, rain or shine. River trip soon!

To **Stacey Wenger** for the incredible book launch cakes. They are remarkable! And delicious! Thank you!

To **Taylor Matkins** and **Katie Manhart** at **Lucky Ones Coffee** in the **Park City Public Library** for building such an amazing community around Lucky Ones!

To **Trig** and **Annette French** for always having a spot for me and the crew in your guesthouse. And thank you for inspiring a few locations in this novel.

To **Caleb Daniels** at **@CommandoBond** on Instagram for always having an answer for my James Bond questions.

To **@WatchesOfEspionage** on Instagram for being my go-to feed for military and intelligence timepiece information.

To **Peter Zeihan**, whose books and insights continue to inspire plot lines for my novels.

To **Jocko Willink** for setting the standard.

To **Paul** and **Cori Russell at Fortitude Coffee Company** for your time in uniform, all you do for the **Best Defense Foundation**, and for the amazing roasts!

To **Cadan Flynn**—stay strong, stay true, and do your best not to blow up your dad's barn.

To **Dom Raso** of **Dynamis Alliance**, who embodies "The Will To Fight!"

To **Nick Seifert** at **Athlon Outdoors** for three *Ballistic* magazine covers and such incredible content. Thank you, my friend.

To **Dana Didriksen** for inspiring the fight sequences in "Spa 1917."

To **Bob Warden** for being a part of that spa conversation and for letting me steal your boat.

To **Fred Burton**, author of *Beirut Rules*, for your friendship and support.

To **David Bolls** for setting so much of this in motion.

To **John Stryker Meyer**, Vietnam MACV-SOG Special Forces veteran and author of *Across the Fence: The Secret War in Vietnam*, *On the Ground*, and *SOG Chronicles*. Thank you for preserving the history and passing on the lessons. Find *SOGCast: Untold Stories of MACV-SOG* wherever you get your podcasts.

To **James Stejskal** for your service and your book, *Special Forces Berlin*.

To **Jason M. Hardy** for your stunning series of books on MACV-SOG. Find them at thedogtag.com.

To **Christian Craighead**. Always come back.

To **Barbara Peters** at the **Poisoned Pen Bookstore** in Scottsdale, Arizona, **Michaela Smith** at **Dolly's Bookstore** in Park City, Utah, and to all the independent bookstores across the country that do so much for authors and readers.

To **James Scott**, author of *Black Snow*, *Rampage*, *Target Tokyo*, *The War Below*, and *The Attack on the Liberty*—I am looking forward to launching our new project! *Targeted: The 1983 Beirut Barracks Bombing* hits shelves in the fall of 2024.

To my wonderful publisher and editor, **Emily Bestler** of **Emily Bestler Books**, for making all this happen. I think about it every single day. Thank you. Your friendship and support mean the world.

To **Lara Jones** for being so kind and patient . . . even when I'm a day or two late.

To **David Brown** for making all this so much fun! Thank you, my friend. I don't know what I'd do without you.

To **Libby McGuire**, senior vice president and publisher of **Atria Books**, for your support of this entire series!

To **Jon Karp**, president and publisher of **Simon & Schuster**, for your leadership and for all you do for authors and, most important, for readers!

To everyone working behind the scenes at **Simon & Schuster**, **Atria Books**, and **Emily Bestler Books** who make it all possible! **Al Madocs**,

James Iacobelli, Tom Pitoniak, Dana Trocker, Suzanne Donahue, Paige Lytle, Shelby Pumphrey, Karlyn Hixson, Nicole Bond, Liz Perl, Sue Fleming, Sienna Farris, Gary Urda, Colin Shields, Chrissy Festa, Janice Fryer, Leslie Collins, Gregory Hruska, and **Lexi Dumas**. Thank you all!

To **Sarah Lieberman, Gabrielle Audet, Chris Lynch,** and **Tom Spain** at **Simon & Schuster Audio** for making the audiobooks such a hit!

To **Jen Long** and the team at **Pocket Books** for transforming the hardcover editions into beautiful paperbacks. I am looking forward to unveiling the new look for the paperback edition of *Only the Dead*.

A special thank-you to the entire team at **CAA**. To my literary agent, **Alexandra Machinist** in New York, for being amazing. To **Josie Freedman** in Los Angeles, for your expertise on all things TV and film. To **Howie Tannenbaum** on the scripted TV ventures. To **Courtney Catzel** on the documentary filmmaking side of the house. And to **Jennifer Simpson** for navigating the world of podcasts. More projects to come!

To **Ironclad** for producing the *Danger Close* podcast and the award-winning book trailer videos, and all you do behind the scenes. You are a **Tier One** operation, and your partnership from the very beginning means more than I can express. Thank you to **Jeremy Carey, Jesse Carey, Catey Carey, Kevin Kelleher, Noah Kight, Danny McCusker, Ryan Berry, Ashley Morrison, Nico Johnston, Daniel Peebles, Hannah Puder, Liz Schultz-Swainston, Jason Chalk, Matt Turley, Bruna Vilela, Paul Glover, Jess Harn, Austin Balls,** and **Kasey Brabham**. Thank you to all the *Danger Close* podcast guests. I have enjoyed every single minute!

To **Navy Federal Credit Union**, where I have been a member for over twenty years. Thank you for all your support and for being such an amazing partner on the *Danger Close* podcast.

Thank you to the people and companies that collaborated on such cool projects this year: **Matt Graham** at **ARES Watch Company, Mark Bollman** at **Ball & Buck, Pete Roberts** and **Jocko Willink** at **Origin**

USA, the team at **KC Cattle Company**, and **Norm Hooten, Tim Young,** and **Mark Taylor** at **Hooten & Young Whiskey**.

To **Karl Austen** and **Marissa Linden** at **Jackoway Austen Tyerman Wertheimer Mandelbaum Morris Bernstein Trattner & Klein** on the entertainment legal front. You CRUSH IT! Thank you!

To **Norm Brownstein** and **Steve Demby** at **Brownstein Hyatt Farber Schreck** for all your advice and counsel.

To **Mitch Langberg** at **Brownstein Hyatt Farber Schreck** for your ideas, for your friendship, and for continuing to have my back.

To **Brock Bosson, Ted Lacey, Tina Davis, Alexander Haberman,** and the legal team at **Cahill Gorden & Reindell** and to **Steven Lieberman** and **Leo Loughlin,** and **Lisa Locke** at **Rothwell Figg** on the wild world of trademarks.

To **Taylor Matkins** for taking charge of organization and scheduling. It was much needed!

To **Garrett Bray** for your friendship, strategic advice, and design work, and for your support from day one!

A very special thank-you to everyone who reads or listens to the novels, leaves reviews, subscribes to the ***Danger Close*** podcast, is signed up for the newsletter on my website at officialjackcarr.com, and engages on the social channels @JackCarrUSA—it is sincerely appreciated. That you have trusted me with your time is a responsibility I take extremely seriously, which is why so much thought goes into all I do. Thank you for sharing your time with me.

To **Mom** and **Dad**, who instilled a love of reading and adventure in me from my earliest days. And thank you for continuing to correct my papers. I love you both.

And to my beautiful wife, **Faith**, and our **three amazing children**. I love you with every fiber of my being.

Turn the page for an exclusive look at Jack Carr's next James Reece thriller,

RED SKY MOURNING

CHAPTER 1

Kumba Ranch, Flathead Valley, Montana

"YOU SURE YOU STILL want to do this?" Liz Riley asked the man in the left seat of the small vintage 1976 Lake Buccaneer amphibious aircraft.

The plane floated comfortably on its hull at the western end of the lake, its fuel-injected 200 horsepower Lycoming IO-360 engine mounted atop the pylon behind the cockpit at idle.

The big man next to her did not answer immediately. His eyes were focused ahead on the light ripples visible on the dark water. He tilted his head to the right, looking to the skies above. Blue with scattered clouds. Perfect flying weather.

"You got this, Reece," Liz said. Her voice was strong and confident, the southern accent a proud reminder of days lying in the grass in the backyard of her family's house on the outskirts of Fort Rucker in Alabama, looking skyward, dreaming. The near constant echoes of turning rotors from Blackhawk and Apache helicopters overhead had instilled in her a love for aviation. She would follow that passion into the Army's Warrant Officer Flight Program and into the cockpit of an OH-58D Kiowa Warrior helicopter. Injuries sustained in combat cut short her Army career, but did nothing to diminish her love of flying.

James Reece turned to his passenger, a passenger who in this case was also his flight instructor and dear friend, Elizabeth Riley. She looked perfectly at home in the confines of the aircraft, almost as if it had been built around her. It did help that she was a full seven inches shorter than Reece's six-foot frame. Her dark hair was pulled back in a ponytail under a crimson University of Alabama ball cap. Ray-Ban aviator sunglasses shielded her eyes from the glare. She was a professional in her element.

"What?" she asked, prompting him to explain the look on his face.

"You know, I intensely dislike flying."

"You tell me that every time," Liz replied. "What you mean to say is, you 'used to intensely dislike flying.'"

"Ah, that's it," Reece confirmed.

"And, as I recall, it wasn't necessarily the flying; it was the taking off and landing."

"Once again: true," Reece said. "Just like jumping."

"Out of planes?" Liz asked.

"Yeah. I always loved the actual jump. Not a big fan of the pull."

"Why?"

"That was the moment of truth. Either that chute was going to open, or you were going to have a malfunction, in which case you would need to go through your EPs—your emergency procedures. After that you would have a clean canopy overhead or you were fucked and would have to cut away. Once you did that you were stuck to that last option. I'd pack my main, but our riggers would pack our reserves."

"I can see how that could be disconcerting," Liz said.

"That was one of the reasons we kept our parachute riggers happy with cases of beer on jump trips."

"Wise."

"I also didn't like the fact that you had a bunch of other jumpers in the air you needed to account for and who needed to account for you."

"And the landing?" Liz asked.

"Well, with a static-line jump your landing is a hot mess regardless. You do what they call a PLF—a parachute landing fall. It realistically requires about two days of training. The Army manages to cram those two days into three weeks at Fort Benning. The PLF does help reduce injuries, but most of the time it turns into feet, ass, head."

Liz laughed.

"Didn't they rename Fort Benning like they did Rucker?" she asked.

"Fuck if I know," Reece replied.

"How about freefall landings? Those look fairly graceful," Liz said.

"With freefall it's different, but you can still hit hard, especially when you are loaded down with gear."

"Well, in this case, no jumping," she said.

"That's good, considering we don't have chutes," Reece observed.

Liz ignored his comment.

"We are going to take off, spend some time exploring northern Montana and then land right back at the lake. I'll be here if you need me," Liz said, motioning to the controls in front of her.

"That's reassuring," Reece responded sincerely. He turned back to the instruments.

"Might want to close the door," Liz remined him.

"Good tip," Reece said. He reached up, pulled the gull wing door shut, and twisted the latch.

"What are our procedures if we have an engine failure?" Liz queried.

Scouting the channel ahead for debris, Reece replied: "if we are on the lake I'll power forward. If we are in transition, I'll make a judgment call—but please feel free to take over. If we are airborne over six hundred AGL I'll turn back. Turn will be to the right to avoid the mountains."

"Correct."

Reece scanned the lake and the skies to his right and left.

"Skies and lake look clear," he said.

"Clear," Liz confirmed, doing the same checks from her seat.

Reece's left hand went to the yoke. Liz's eyes hesitated over his left ring finger, a finger that would soon be adorned with a wedding band. A stainless-steel watch she knew had been purchased by his father, Tom, in Saigon during Vietnam was on his wrist below a powerful forearm. Reece's arms had once hoisted her to safety in violation of orders in the war-torn streets of Najaf, Iraq. To Liz, it felt like yesterday. She suspected it always would.

She would never be sure if it was the RPG or the resulting crash that had killed her copilot. Liz had struggled in an attempt to release his harness, the metal slick with blood, screaming at him to wake up even though his head was partially crushed, and a large section of his upper-body cavity had been torn away. The unmistakable crack of AK fire from Muqtada al-Sadr's Mahdi Militia penetrating the aircraft's mangled frame forced her onto the streets of Old Town Najaf with her M4. She remembered thinking that being killed in the crash would have been preferable to what would befall her should she be captured by the Mahdi Militia. She also knew that she would not be alive today had it not been for James Reece.

Reece and his four-man sniper team had been in position just blocks away when they witnessed the helo go down. She found out later that he had radioed his command-and-control element back at the forward operating base and requested permission to move to the crash site. That request had been denied. A risk-averse higher command authority, concerned with the political fallout of losing five more SEALs in combat, had ordered Reece to stay in position to provide overwatch while an Army Quick Reaction Force was dispatched to the scene. As soon as Reece heard Liz's M4 start to mix with the sounds of AK fire he moved to assist in a clear violation of orders.

Liz's helmet had been torn off in the crash, and she had ditched her body armor so she could move unencumbered as quickly as possible toward friendly lines. By the time Reece arrived the adrenaline that had allowed her to escape the Kiowa had worn off. The back injury, the effects of which she still kept at bay with a vigorous MTNTOUGH daily functional fitness training routine, had all but immobilized her. She was also on her last round, a round she was saving for herself.

Reece had stripped off his own body armor and secured it around the injured pilot. He then secured his helmet to her head, hoisted her over his shoulder and ran to a stolen vehicle that his Teammate Boozer had maneuvered into a nearby alley. He didn't stuff the hole caused by a bullet that passed through his calf until they had survived the harrowing drive back to base.

For Liz it was an airlift to Balad for emergency surgery; then a flight to Landstuhl Regional Medical Center in Germany; and then another to Walter Reed Army Medical Center in Washington, D.C.

For Reece it was an ass-chewing for insubordination and threats of Trident Review Boards, Captain's Masts, and court-martials. Those threats quickly turned to accolades when Liz Riley's commanding officer called the commander of Naval Special Warfare to express his gratitude to the entire SEAL chain of command for their quick thinking and audacity. He followed up by awarding Army Commendation Medals with Valor to Reece and his sniper team.

The battle in Najaf had bonded Liz and Reece for life. Reece's wife, Lauren, and daughter, Lucy, had become Liz's family as well. After they were ripped from the earth she had been by Reece's side as he brought those responsible to justice. In her mind, the debt she owed Reece would never be fully repaid.

He deserved to finally be happy, Liz thought.

Reece's strength had returned after his recent ordeal in solitary confinement and the events that followed. She knew that he and Raife Hastings trained every day, pushing each other on steep trail runs, swims in the frigid lake, and in the Sorinex gym they had set up in the barn. They had also improved the range on Kumba Ranch, the Hastings sprawling property in the Flathead Valley, with barricades and TA Targets. Daily competitions with pistols, rifles, and shotguns kept the two men sharp. He looked stronger than Liz had ever seen him. She didn't need to ask why he trained so hard. She knew.

Though he didn't talk with her about his time in the darkness, Liz knew it had left an impact. How could it not? His own government had locked him in a small cell with no light and no visitors for three months, an action tantamount to torture. She didn't know if he talked about it with his fiancée. Men like Reece tended to keep some things locked away, though if she were being honest, there really weren't "men like Reece."

She must have asked him a thousand times over the years to let her take him up and work with him on getting his pilot's license. He had never shown any interest until recently. And, as with everything he did, Reece was all in.

"It won't happen today in these conditions," Liz said, "but tell me what causes it and what you do if we start to porpoise."

"Just like a boat with too much weight up front, in the Buccaneer it's caused by choppy conditions and too much power, which causes a nose-low attitude. Excess weight in the cockpit can also be a factor, but I've been working out so that won't be an issue," he said, tapping his trim stomach in jest.

"And if it is?"

"I use more up-elevator until it stops."

"If it doesn't?"

"Then I reduce power and come off step, and, discretion being the better part of valor, we try this again another day."

"Pretty close; remember to *slowly* reduce power," Liz reminded him.

"Right. Slowly."

"There are ripples today, so we have perfect training conditions for your first water takeoff. If it was glass, we wouldn't be doing this. Glassy water is the enemy. Well, not really, but it's dangerous, especially on landings. You lose your depth perception. We'll do it, but not until you have more experience reading the water."

"I trust your judgment," Reece said.

"What's the airframe's no-go criteria for water takeoffs?"

"Any waves over twelve inches," Reece replied.

"Your time sailing will help you when maneuvering on the water," Liz continued.

"Yeah, I'm noting a few similarities."

"Think of the Lake Buccaneer as a boat on the water and a plane in the air. As soon as we are airborne, things will change. What's happening on the lake is different than what is happening up there," she said, looking skyward.

"Understood."

"Take me through it," Liz said.

"All right," Reece began. "Seat belts—check. Briefings complete. Doors secure. Magnetos—both. Circuit breakers on. Flap handle down. Hydraulic pressure gauge up. Water rudder up. Trim set." Reece checked the indicator and twisted his head to visually confirm the tabs on the tail were in the correct position. "Fuel selector on. Mixture rich. Prop full forward."

Liz pulled her headset down around her neck.

"This is a loud aircraft, but on the water I like to have auditory cues. You did great by the numbers, now it's time to get a 'feel' for the plane. We can put the headsets back on once we are in the air."

"Just like our Peltors back in the day," he said, following Liz's lead with his headset. "Some guys liked them, and others couldn't stand them. They protected your hearing but made it tough to identify the direction of incoming once the bullets started flying."

The distinct growl of the engine coupled with the propeller behind the exhaust filled the cockpit.

"This thing sounds like my old Harley," Reece observed.

"Greg O'Neal and Harry Shannon down in Florida refer to them as 'Sky Harleys,'" Liz responded. "The sales pitch for these birds back in the seventies and eighties was 'the most fun you can have with your clothes on.'"

"I'll keep that in mind," Reece said.

Jonathan Hastings had sent Liz to Kissimmee, Florida, for the Lake Amphibian 25-hour owner's course under the tutelage of instructors who lived and breathed these classic airframes. Already a Certified Flight Instructor, Liz received her specialized Lake Amphibian qualification at the O'Neal's Seaplane Base managed by Greg's son, Ben, on nearby Live Oak Lake, close to where Armand Rivard set up shop after buying the Lake Amphibian company in 1979. Greg O'Neal had put her through the paces during the certification process, and Liz had fallen in love with a plane that traced its roots back to the iconic Grumman Goose, Widgeon, Mallard, and Albatross aircraft of the 1930s and 1940s. The legendary aviation mechanic and Lake Amphibian guru, Harry Shannon of Amphibians Plus, had passed along his intimate knowledge of the unique aircraft as well.

Liz glanced from the former SEAL to the instruments, double-checking her student before turning to look in the two seats behind them. A small Eberlestock go bag pack was on its side partially obscuring a new coyote tan SIG Sauer MCX-SPEAR LT with Tango6T 1–6 x 24mm optic. From the size of the magazine, she could tell it was the 7.62 x 39 version. Liz was more familiar with weapons than she was with earrings or purses. It had a Dead Air suppressor, VTAC sling, folding iron sights, a Surefire Scout light, and an ATPIAL laser aiming device. All of Reece's weapons had been confiscated in an FBI raid almost two years earlier so the SPEAR was a new addition to the arsenal. Because they had been seized in an investigation into the assassination of the president of the United States and Reece had been taken to the Federal Penitentiary in Florence, Colorado, and locked in solitary confinement in violation of the Fifth, Sixth, Eighth, and Fourteenth Amendments, getting them back had proven to be a bureaucratic nightmare.

Reece noticed Liz staring at the rifle behind them.

"Just in case, Liz."

"Just in case," she repeated.

Reece nodded and his right hand went to the overhead throttle.

• • •

Katie Buranek sat in a chair on the small beach, her feet propped up on the stone fire ring, gazing out across the lake through binoculars at the single-engine aircraft that appeared to be more of a boat with wings. It had a unique, almost odd, configuration with the engine and propeller mounted above and behind the pilots. She tucked a strand of blond hair behind her ear and rested the Swarovski 10 x 42 binos in her lap. The fingers of her right hand found the diamond engagement ring on her left ring finger, the dazzling gemstone fixed in a simple but elegant and timeless platinum setting.

They had made Montana home, and though they had not set a date, a wedding was on the horizon. Reece had been intentionally vague on the how and why behind the injuries he had returned with a few months back; he seemed different. She didn't know whether it was the investigative journalist in her or her instincts as his lover and fiancée, but there were changes; some stark, others subtle. Though he was never far from a gun, his eyes no longer had the look of a hunted animal, cornered and tensed, ready to explode in a sudden fight to the death at any moment. His eyes still shifted from brown to green to hazel depending on the environment; it wasn't that. It was a sadness.

Katie reached down to pet Pollux behind his right ear, and her hand was soon nudged by Castor. The two black Labrador retrievers had been in the back of the old FJ40 Toyota Land Cruiser that Reece had borrowed from Caroline Hastings when he returned from a trip a few months back. He had told Katie the dogs used to belong to an old friend who could no longer care for them; he didn't specify why. Healthy and strong, they had taken to her and loved when Zulu, the Hastingses' Rhodesian Ridgeback, came down to play.

Katie had started a vegetable garden in a small greenhouse that Reece and Raife had built by the barn where Reece's old 1985 Jeep Waggoneer still sat inoperable. They shared her 4Runner, but she knew his friend Kurt Williams of Cruiser Outfitters in Utah was on the lookout for a 1988 FJ62, Reece's preferred mode of transportation.

Caroline Hastings, the matriarch of the Hastings family, would drive down from the main house with Zulu a few times a week. The three dogs would chase each other and swim while the two women worked in the garden and Caroline passed along what she had learned of gardening and life to someone she already considered a daughter-in-law.

Though Reece had never been what one would call a "morning person," some days before dawn, Katie would feel him swing his legs from the bed and slip from the room still cloaked in darkness. After he was gone, she would slide her naked body into one of his T-shirts and move to the bedroom window, watching in the early nautical twilight as Reece walked barefoot down to the lake with coffee in hand to watch the sun rise over the mountains. In the dim light of a new dawn, Reece would disappear as he walked down the well-worn path. As the sun crept closer to the horizon, Katie would begin to make out familiar shapes: the deck, the sloping lawn, the beach, the fire pit, the dock, and finally the man she loved, a silhouette against the rising sun, the sky changing brilliant hues of red, yellow, and orange. He would come into focus at the end of the dock, leaning casually against a pylon, sipping what she knew was a light blend coffee mixed with cream and local honey.

What was he thinking about?

Her?

Their future?

His future?

His wife, Lauren, and daughter, Lucy? Was he asking them for forgiveness or was he communing with their memories as the world came to life?

Their lives had been violently extinguished, their final moments filled with horror. Reece blamed himself. But instead of waiting for what he thought was a terminal brain tumor to reunite them in the afterlife, he had done what he did best. Reece had visited a violence and terror unlike anything his enemies could have ever imagined upon them. And Katie had helped him. She had become part of the story.

Was he thinking of his SEAL Teammate Ben Edwards, standing behind Katie, her neck wrapped in det cord, a detonator in his friend's hand?

Or was he thinking about Boozer and the 9mm pistol used to take his life in an attempt to make it look like suicide, a mistake that had exposed the conspiracy?

Katie knew now that Boozer had been the key. Boozer was a .45 guy and would never have taken his own life with a 9mm. That realization had started Reece down the warpath toward a reckoning.

Or was he thinking of Freddy Strain? His former sniper partner had tracked Reece down in Africa and presented him with a choice, one that had ultimately led to Freddy's death on a rooftop in Odessa.

Was he thinking of Raife's sister, Hanna, hunted for sport on an island in the Bering Sea? Or was it something more recent? The assassinated president? His father? Or something else? Something of which she was not aware. A classified mission?

Reece had known pain. Was it possible for him to move on? Had he forgiven himself? Had a new chapter finally begun for them both?

Katie would never intrude on Reece's memories of the dead. Those were his. She suspected these quiet mornings were his time with ghosts. They would always be with him.

Once the sun had broken the horizon, she would watch him turn and walk back to the cabin, where he would make her a cup of coffee in the kitchen. Before he cracked the door, she would strip off her shirt and settle back into bed for a reawakening from the man she loved.

She would hear him set her coffee on the nightstand to the side of the bed, and then feel him slip back under the covers, his cool body quickly warming next to hers before making love with a passion and intensity that left them drained and breathless. They were free.

Reece and Raife had started construction on their archery–bookstore–coffee shop–whiskey bar concept in Whitefish. The owner of Glacier Archery had retired and sold it to the two former frogmen. The shop was now undergoing an extensive remodeling along with the building to which it was attached. Glacier Archery was on one side and Abelard's Bookstore, Coffeehouse, and Whiskey Bar was on the other. The Hastings Family was bankrolling the project, not because they expected or even cared about a return, but because Jonathan and Caroline wanted their boys close. Reece was family.

Katie did most of her writing on her laptop at the lake and would send her op-eds from a coffee shop in town that offered WiFi. A studio in Whitefish made it possible to do her weekly news spots. Reece would check on progress with the renovation and pick up supplies while she worked. They had installed a fly rod holder to the Gobi rack on her 4Runner and on their way home would stop and hike to an alpine lake or stream. His cast was improving; she enjoyed watching him progress at something she had been doing since she could walk.

Katie heard the whine of the plane's engine increase and watched as it surged forward. The white aircraft with green pinstriped markings gained speed as it moved across the lake into a light headwind, finally lifting off and arching toward the heavens.

Maybe the flying was a replacement for the mission? Could Reece survive without a mission?

And what of Reece's concerns? Was he still worried that violence would find them? She knew better than to push. Reece would tell her in good time. And right now, it felt like they had all the time in the world. In the interim, she had a wedding to plan.

Katie was so lost in thought that she never heard the sound of the approaching vehicle.

• • •

Reece found it therapeutic and meditative up among the clouds with the familiar feel of the noise canceling headset against his ears. Now, instead of muffling the deafening sounds of gunfire and explosions, they reduced the monotonous hum of the piston-driven engine to a more tolerable level. The peace would be broken only by the voice of his instructor or that of Air Traffic Control at the airport in Kalispell if they were using the retractable tricycle landing gear to practice runway landings. Using equipment like the headset in pursuit of a new goal, something challenging, felt right. And useful. He imagined a day when he would fly Katie and their kids from their lake house on the Hastings' property to former senator Tim Thornton's hunting cabin in northern Idaho close to the Canadian border or to one of the numerous secluded lakes in the high country. Anything farther than that, he would enlist the services of Elizabeth Riley.

Reece had never cared much for orders coming from the top. Those removed from the blood, dirt, and grime of the battlefield oftent had different priorities. The consequences of violating orders did not weigh on him in the slightest or cause even a moment's hesitation. The decision to rescue Liz in Najaf had been a natural one. While Reece's leadership had built trust with his men and was dangerous to a constantly adapting enemy, it often caused strain between him and those above him in the chain of command. Making rank and climbing to the next rung of the military advancement ladder never entered into his calculus. As Reece saw it, his job was to crush the enemy and bring his men home.

Reece also knew the importance of maintaining the moral high ground, something that was one of the few, and perhaps only, differentiators between U.S. forces and the enemy. That he had abandoned his principles when his troop and family had been murdered was not lost on him. The conspiracy permeated his own SEAL command and included a nexus of governmental, financial, and pharmaceutical entities; all their power allied against him. Reece had become the terrorist. He had become the insurgent. And he was good at it. Maybe even better than he was as a SEAL. It didn't matter now. He was done. He had left that life behind. It was time to move on.

The urge to fly had taken even Reece by surprise. He had never been a huge fan of flying; it was more of a convenience and necessity. That was until he began sifting through his father's old documents; some had been left behind in boxes and a few had been passed along by contacts at the CIA. Reece had been shocked to discover that Tom Reece had been a pilot. The files indicated that he had earned his private pilot license and instrument rating while at the Agency in preparation for an assignment in Central America.

Why had he never talked about it? He had never once mentioned it that Reece could remember. Why had he never taken Reece or his mother flying? Reece imagined the three of them around a campfire on the shore of a remote lake grilling freshly caught trout over the coals, a plane like the one he was currently flying beached nearby. Had he told his wife? Had he ever taken her flying? Reece would never know. Another mystery left behind by Tom Reece.

And he thought of his father's letter.

Use the time you have, James. When you put down the gun, walk away. Don't live in the past. Love your wife. Raise your kids. And don't look back. Treasure each moment, because once it's gone, it's gone forever.

Since his return from Cyprus, he and Raife had been spending more and more time with Raife's father, Jonathan. The old Selous Scout was getting on in age and they all knew the rough living would eventually catch up with him. In one of their conversations Reece had asked if he knew that Tom had his pilot's license. Jonathan shook his head.

"Some men compartmentalize certain parts of their life for the benefit of their families," he had said, the ghosts of Rhodesia still strong in his voice.

Reece knew, even better than Raife, what part of Jonathan's life he had locked away. Caroline had once told him the story. A story of Sunday, September 3, 1978. The day Jonathan's sister had died in a terrorist attack that had taken Air Rhodesia Flight 825 out of the sky. And she had told him of the events that followed. Caroline had confided in Reece and sworn him to secrecy, passing along a lesson of forgiveness.

"He may not have shared flying with you, lad, but that doesn't mean you can't share it with Katie and perhaps one day your kids, eh?" Jonathan had said, taking a drag on a freshly rolled cigarette. "Liz will get you settled. I've got an old Lake Buccaneer I think you might like. I've been storing her for years. It's time she flew again."

"What's a Lake Buccaneer?" Reece had asked.

"It's better if I show you."

Jonathan had taken Reece to one of his hangars at Glacier Park International Airport and unveiled the unusual flying boat.

"I don't fly much anymore. Years ago, Caroline told me to pick between the cigarettes and the flying, thinking I'd choose flying."

"You sure showed her," Reece joked.

"My flying days were behind me, as it was," he said, taking a drag of his cigarette. "Smarter to have Liz behind the controls."

"What is this thing?"

"A Lake Buccaneer. Made by Lake Aircraft. I found her in 1985. The original owner made a rough water landing with the landing gear down and wanted nothing more to do with her. This one was built at their factory in Sanford, Maine, in '76. It was $26,000 new back then. In '85 I got a hell of a deal."

"How did you find her?"

"I wound up in hunting camp with Armand Rivard, a former Lake

Amphibian dealer who had purchased the company a few years earlier. Made the deal over the campfire, fueled by a few too many whiskies."

Jonathan laughed at the memory.

"After the hunt we linked up in Kissimmee, Florida, where he had moved the company headquarters. He wouldn't let me have it until I went through his course. It's been back to Florida a few times over the years. Flew her down in '88 when they realized the alligator population was getting out of control. Caught a gator with Armand from her nose there," Jonathan said, pointing to the front of the plane. "Damn dinosaur had a deer in its mouth. Gator got away but we ate venison that night. Anyway, this Buccaneer became my first plane in America."

"I didn't realize you learned to fly in Africa," Reece said.

"Ah, in the Rhodesia of my youth one had to be skilled and resourceful out of necessity."

Reece nodded.

"You like her?" the old man asked.

"Like her? I love her," Reece said, running his hand along the wing.

"What do you say we give her a second life, eh?"

Reece had looked at the aging patriarch of the Hastings clan.

"I'll ask Harry Shannon to make sure she's air- and seaworthy and then Liz can go to work."

"What do you mean?" Reece asked.

"I mean, it's time for you to fly. In fact, you are looking at your wedding present."

"Reece. *Reece.*"

The familiar voice in his headset broke him from his memories.

"Yeah."

"Thought I lost you, buddy," Liz said.

"Just thinking," Reece replied.

"Well, it's time to think about this landing."

"Got it."

"Complete the turn. What are we looking for?"

Reece had banked the plane to the left with flaps down. He came out of the turn at 800 feet above the lake.

"Debris. Wires. Boats. Paddlers. Surface conditions. Depth. Area clear," Reece said.

"Clear," Liz confirmed. "What else are you looking for?"

"Enemy submarines?"

"How about wind direction?"

"Oh yeah, wind direction. Moving east to west across the lake. We will come in from the west, into the wind," Reece said.

"Correct."

Reece banked the plane again, the forest of northern Montana like a dense green carpet below.

"Stay on this base heading," she advised. "What do we want to avoid?"

"A crash?" Reece responded.

"Be more specific."

"We want to avoid a water loop," he said.

"That's right, no high speed turns on landing. Before that, what's the first thing we want to check?" she nudged.

Reece looked across the instrument panel, going over the procedures in his head.

"Landing gear," he said. "Hydraulic pressure is up."

He turned his head to visually confirm that the landing gear was up. "Visually confirmed."

Liz double-checked her student.

"Alternator switch on," Reece said, deep in concentration as he went through his checklist. "Fuel boost pump on. Hydraulic pump on. Wheels up. Flaps down. Water rudder up. Trim set. Propeller set. Mixture set."

"Good," Liz said. "Now, remember to control the rate of descent. Small throttle adjustments."

"Small throttle adjustments," Reece repeated.

"Speed?" Liz asked.

"Between eighty and eighty-five miles per hour," Reece responded, remembering that speed in a Lake Amphibian was relayed in miles rather than knots.

"And?" she coaxed.

"And . . ."

"What else?"

Reece's eyes scanned the instrument panel as the plane continued to descend.

"You told me it was something you did constantly on mission."

"Oh yeah—an out. If we need to abort or touch and go, egress will be to the south to avoid the mountains."

As a leader, Reece had constantly played the "what if" game on patrol, anticipating his actions and calls if his SEAL element was hit at that precise moment. Flying was no different. Well, it was different in that no one was shooting at them.

"Reducing power to eighteen inches MP," Reece said, referring to the manifold pressure gauge which indicated the engine's current operating power.

"Good. You've got this, Reece."

"Nose down. Reducing power to twelve inches MP. Wings level."

"Great work. Don't rush it. This plane knows what to do. Hold attitude and wait."

As Reece continued to descend, he briefly turned his attention to the house and dock, expecting to see Katie watching his first water landing. He didn't expect to see another figure standing next to her.

Reece shifted focus from the water, his mind switching gears.

"Reece!" Liz said, the urgency apparent in her tone.

Instead of looking at his instructor, Reece turned to the rifle in the backseat.

"Reece, your rate of descent is too fast. *Reece!*"

Katie, I've got to protect Katie.

"Reece, slow your rate of descent!" Liz ordered.

But Reece wasn't there.

"Take it," he said, looking back out the window at the two people on the dock.

"I've got the controls," Liz said.

"You've got it," Reece whispered, remembering the procedure for triple confirmation of positive control when turning over control of an aircraft but forgetting the visual check to ensure the person next to him was actually flying the plane.

"It's my airplane," Liz said, completing the third step in the process and expertly bringing the amphibious aircraft into a picture-perfect water landing.

Ever the professional, Liz slowly put the throttle into idle while easing forward on the yoke, relaxing backpressure, and bringing the plane off step.

"Well, that was *fucking* western," Liz said, turning to face her student. "What the hell happened?"

"Just get me to the dock," Reece said, looking back at the rifle. Thinking better of it, his hand went to the grip of the Grayguns Bruiser Sig Sauer P210 in the leather Alessi holster behind his right hip.

"Reece, what are you doing?"

"Just be ready," Reece said, his eyes scanning the shoreline.

Liz maneuvered the plane toward the dock, approaching from the west to ensure that the wind was directly on the nose. She shut the engine down and told Reece to put out bumpers.

Reece pushed the left gull wing door open and unfastened his seat belt.

He recognized the man standing with Katie.

It was a man from the CIA.

A man Reece knew well.

Reece stood, stepped onto the nose of what was now essentially a boat, and then leapt to the dock, a line attached to a cleat on the nose of the plane in his hand.

"Make yourself useful, Vic," Reece said, handing the man the line and stepping between him and Katie to attach a separate line to the left wing float. He then secured it to another cleat on the dock, head on a swivel in search of threats.

"It's good to see you too, Reece," Vic said, pulling the line taut and kneeling to attach it to a cleat at his feet.

Victor Rodriguez was the director of the Agency's Special Activities Center and was responsible for the darkest of CIA operations around the globe. He stood back up and nodded at Liz, who now leaned against the open cockpit.

"Ms. Riley," he said.

"Mr. Rodriquez," she acknowledged.

"You are a hard man to get ahold of," Vic said, directing his attention back to Reece.

"That's obviously by design," Reece responded, his eyes piercing past the Agency man to the hillside behind the house, noting that Raife and Jonathan Hastings stood watch on the back deck.

"I didn't give them much warning," Vic acknowledged. "I'm alone."

"Maybe call next time," Reece offered.

"It would help if you got a phone."

"What do you want, Vic?" Reece asked, putting his arm protectively around Katie.

"We need to talk."

"About what?"

"We need to talk about Alice."

Praise for *Only the Dead*

"He's the real deal. I'm a fan."

—David Morrell, *New York Times* bestselling author of *First Blood*

"Carr presses emotional buttons that other writers wouldn't dare explore."

—*The Real Book Spy*

"Carr delivers a graduate level course in geopolitical politics while delivering the raucous good time that thriller fans have come to expect from the apex warlocks of combat storytelling. Don't miss the finest thriller of the summer."

—John Nantz, *Townhall*

"Superb action, Ludlum-like intrigue, and le Carré–like duplicity make this a seminal thriller and a brilliant entry in a great series."

—Jon Land

Praise for *In the Blood*

"Gripping . . . fast-paced . . . fans will get their money's worth."

—*Publishers Weekly*

"Quality plot, well-developed characters, and not too over-the-top. Add James Reece to your list that includes Harvath (Brad Thor), Reacher (Lee Child), Bob Lee Swagger (Stephen Hunter)."

—*Men Reading Books*

"Hands down, IN THE BLOOD is the best book I've read this year. I've said from the beginning that covering Carr is what I'd imagine it would have been like to discover Vince Flynn at the beginning of his career. . . . Carr deserves to be mentioned alongside all-time greats like Flynn, Thor, Clancy, and Silva . . ."

—*The Real Book Spy*

"IN THE BLOOD is Carr's best book to date and demonstrates a mastery of the genre—it rightly belongs in the constellation of Clancy, Thor, Morrell, and Flynn."

—*Townhall.com*

Praise for *The Devil's Hand*

"Take my word for it, James Reece is one rowdy motherf***er. Get ready!"

—Chris Pratt, all-around great guy and star of the #1 Amazon Prime series *The Terminal List*

"Carr delivers engrossing back story, incorporates current events seamlessly, and never flinches from breathless depictions of violence."

—*Publishers Weekly*

"Carr continues to draw on his own experiences as a SEAL to give the story a level of realism that writers who've not actually served sometimes have a hard time achieving."

—*Booklist*

"THE TERMINAL LIST is widely regarded as one of the best debut thrillers of all-time, and rightfully so, but THE DEVIL'S HAND is even better, and should go down as one of the best books in the genre, period."

—*The Real Book Spy*

"An action thriller extraordinaire that is not to be missed."

—*Providence Journal*

Praise for *Savage Son*

"A great book . . . its f*cking riveting!"

—Joe Rogan

"A rare gut-punch writer, full of grit and insight, who we will be happily reading for years to come."

—Gregg Hurwitz, *New York Times* bestselling author of the Orphan X series

"Absolutely fantastic! SAVAGE SON is savagely good, and puts Jack Carr at the very top of the thriller genre."

—Marc Cameron, *New York Times* bestselling author of RED WINTER

"A badass, high-velocity round of reading! The three parts of this masterfully crafted experience says it all—THE TRAP, THE STALK, THE KILL."

—Clint Emerson, *New York Times* bestselling author of 100 DEADLY SKILL and ESCAPE THE WOLF

"Carr writes both from the gut and a seemingly infinite reservoir of knowledge in the methods of human combat. Loved it!"

—Chris Hauty, *LA Times* bestselling author of *New York Times* Editors' Choice DEEP STATE

"Jack Carr triples down with SAVAGE SON. From the book's gut-wrenching opening to its sleep-stealing conclusion, Jack's homage to THE MOST DANGEROUS GAME delivers the goods and then some."

—Don Bentley, *New York Times* bestselling author of HOSTILE INTENT

"A masterfully told, heart thumping tale of modern conflict."

—LtCol Oliver North, USMC (Ret.), *New York Times* bestselling author of THE RIFLEMAN and UNDER FIRE

"SAVAGE SON is amazing! This is the kind of book every author wished he could write . . . mind-blowingly good!"

—Simon Gervais, former RCMP counterterrorism officer and bestselling author of HUNT THEM DOWN

"Accurate, intense and raw, SAVAGE SON taps into our most primal of instincts. Jack Carr draws you into this predatory pursuit like no other because he's lived it!"

—John Barklow, Hunter, Navy Diver, Special Operations Cold Weather Survival Instructor, and Sitka Gear Big Game Product Manager

"Jack Carr is back and at the top of his game in SAVAGE SON, a heart-pounding, sleep-robbing, edge-of-your-seat thriller."

—Joshua Hood, 82nd Airborne veteran and author of Robert Ludlum's THE TREADSTONE RESURRECTION

"Whether you are a hunter of four-legged game or of man, SAVAGE SON will stoke the inner fire of your soul. Jack Carr's attention to detail and experience from the battlefield to the backcountry draw the reader into the field to experience the art of war through the eyes of a man who has lived it."

—Cole Kramer, Kodiak Island Brown Bear Guide and Outfitter

Praise for *True Believer*

"This is seriously good. I mean—seriously."

—Lee Child, #1 *New York Times* bestselling author of THE SENTINEL

"A powerful, thoughtful, realistic, at times terrifying thriller that I could not put down. A terrific addition to the genre, Jack Carr and his alter-ego protagonist, James Reece, continue to blow me away."

—Mark Greaney, #1 *New York Times* bestselling author of SIERRA SIX

"Jack Carr creates an incredibly vivid, emotional, action-packed tapestry of carnage and death."

—Justen Charters, Black Rifle Coffee Company, *Coffee or Die Magazine*

"Packs a punch. Carr's second effort is a well-crafted thriller with timely reflections on the increasingly complicated world of international terrorism."

—*Kirkus Reviews*

Praise for *The Terminal List*

"Double the trouble, twice the action, and quadruple the enjoyment. Careful while reading this one, it could leave a mark."

—Steve Berry, #1 *New York Times* bestselling author of THE OMEGA FACTORY

"Absolutely awesome! So powerful, so pulse-pounding, so well-written—rarely do you read a debut novel this damn good."

—Brad Thor, #1 *New York Times* bestselling author of DEAD FALL

"Told with a deft hand and a keen eye for detail, THE TERMINAL LIST . . . is explosive and riveting."

—Kevin Maurer, co-author of the #1 Bestselling NO EASY DAY and DAMN LUCKY

"Like a bullet from Jack Carr's custom built sniper rifle, the story arrives on target with devastating impact. Trust me, you won't be able to put this one down!"

—Mark Owen, *New York Times* bestselling author of NO EASY DAY and NO HERO

"Crackerjack plotting, vivid characters both in and out of uniform, and a relentless pace to a worthy finish. It's a great start!"

—Stephen Hunter, #1 *New York Times* bestselling author of THE BULLET GARDEN

"An extremely unique thriller! Absolutely intense!"

—Chuck Norris

"Bravo! Jack Carr is the real deal!"

—Sean Parnell, *New York Times* Bestselling author of ONE TRUE PATRIOT

"Not since Stephen Hunter have we seen an author who so accurately captures the essence of the gun—Jack Carr is a shooter."

—Clint Smith, Founder of Thunder Ranch Shooting School

"Jack Carr's THE TERMINAL LIST is a page turning thriller you won't be able to put down. The detail focused writing, personal characters and heart pounding plot line will keep you coming back for more. An absolute must read!"

—Katie Pavlich, *New York Times* Bestselling Author, Fox News Contributor

"Any fan of the novels by Brad Thor and the late Vince Flynn will realize that Jack Carr will soon be joining their ranks."

—*The Washington Times*

"The best debut thriller of 2018."

—*The Washington Times*

ALSO BY JACK CARR

Fiction

Red Sky Mourning

In the Blood

The Devil's Hand

Savage Son

True Believer

The Terminal List

Non-Fiction

Targeted: Beirut

ONLY THE DEAD

A THRILLER

JACK CARR

EMILY BESTLER BOOKS

ATRIA

NEW YORK LONDON TORONTO SYDNEY NEW DELHI

EMILY BESTLER BOOKS

ATRIA

An Imprint of Simon & Schuster, LLC
1230 Avenue of the Americas
New York, NY 10020

First Emily Bestler Books/Atria Paperback edition September 2024

EMILY BESTLER BOOKS/ATRIA PAPERBACK and colophon are trademarks of Simon & Schuster, LLC

Simon & Schuster: Celebrating 100 Years of Publishing in 2024

For information about special discounts for bulk purchases, please contact Simon & Schuster Special Sales at 1-866-506-1949 or business@simonandschuster.com.

The Simon & Schuster Speakers Bureau can bring authors to your live event. For more information or to book an event, contact the Simon & Schuster Speakers Bureau at 1-866-248-3049 or visit our website at www.simonspeakers.com.

Interior design by Dana Sloan

Manufactured in the United States of America

7 9 10 8

Library of Congress Cataloging-in-Publication Data is available.

ISBN 978-1-9821-8169-7
ISBN 978-1-9821-8171-0 (pbk)
ISBN 978-1-9821-8172-7 (ebook)

For Thomas M. Rice

14 August 1921–17 November 2022

101st Airborne Division

501st Parachute Infantry Regiment

First in his stick out of his C-47 over Normandy, France,

June 6, 1944

We have the watch,

and

For all those who stand vigilant in the shadows.

Only the dead have seen the end of war.

—GEORGE SANTAYANA, COMMONLY MISATTRIBUTED TO PLATO

I do solemnly swear that I will support and defend
the Constitution of the United States . . .
Against all enemies . . .
Foreign . . .
And domestic . . .

—OATH TAKEN BY MEMBERS OF THE UNITED STATES ARMED FORCES,
THE VICE PRESIDENT, AND EVERY MEMBER OF CONGRESS

"Against all enemies, foreign and domestic" is not included in the president's oath of office as specified by Article II, Section 1, Clause 8, of the Constitution of the United States.

PREFACE

"WE MAKE OUR DECISIONS. And then our decisions turn around and make us." Those wise words from F. W. Boreham are as true for each and every one of us as they are for James Reece, the protagonist in these pages.

Perhaps that is why Reece has resonated with readers of the series and with the audience that tuned in to watch Chris Pratt stack bodies as former Navy SEAL Sniper James Reece in the Amazon Prime Video series adaptation of *The Terminal List*.

Reece is on a journey, as are we all. That is something that brings us all together; it is something we all have in common—we are all on a journey. But our journeys are finite. Tomorrow is not guaranteed for James Reece, just as tomorrow is not guaranteed for any of us. If you have read my previous novels, you have noticed that time plays a central role. The essence of time is physically manifested through Reece's watch and theoretically manifested through lessons from Reece's father—*You are fast, James. I've seen you run, but even you can't outrun time.* None of us can outrun time.

James Reece is also evolving over the course of his journey. In this novel, he is not the same Reece as he was in *In the Blood*, just as that James Reece was not exactly the same as he was in *The Devil's Hand*. He is learning, evolving, becoming wiser, and he is applying the lessons of the past to his decisions in the present. Those decisions are "making him."

But we don't make decisions out of the blue. James Reece makes decisions based on a foundation that guides him. Decisions that come from solid foundations allow us to survive more experiences and hence gain additional wisdom. But Reece's goal is not just to survive. It is to prevail. He is a warrior, hunter, protector, and student. Always a student, he is constantly learning along his journey, arming himself with the tools he needs to prevail when the chips are down.

He is also human. The protagonist in these pages is not a superhero. If you are looking for highly sanitized depictions of combat, I suggest you look elsewhere. Through the medium of popular fiction, I explore the mind and heart of a warrior. I don't interview snipers who worked in Ramadi, Mosul, or Najaf, ask them what it was like to press the trigger in combat, and then try to describe it on the page. Nor do I talk with operators who were once trapped in an ambush in Baghdad in an attempt to pull from them how they felt and reacted in the moment. Rather, I remember. I remember what it was like to be a sniper in Ramadi, and I remember what I did on the receiving end of a night ambush in Baghdad. I then apply those feelings and emotions to a fictional narrative. The feelings and emotions in these pages are real. They come from my heart and soul and flow directly onto the page. If you are looking for a little more fiction and a little less emotion and truth, I recommend you put this book down now and pick up another. James Reece is not for everyone.

Each of my novels has a theme that guides the writing process. *The Terminal List* was a story of revenge without constraint. For my second novel, *True Believer*, I thought it would be disingenuous to just drop Reece right into his next adventure after the traumatic events of